D1432197

ANTAGONIST

GORDON R. DICKSON

ANTAGONIST

and DAVID W. WIXON

TOR®

A TOM DOHERTY ASSOCIATES BOOK

NEW YORK

This is a work of fiction. All the characters and events portrayed in this novel
are either fictitious or are used fictitiously.

ANTAGONIST

Copyright © 2007 by Gordon R. Dickson and David W. Wixon

All rights reserved, including the right to reproduce this book, or portions thereof,
in any form.

This book is printed on acid-free paper.

A Tor Book
Published by Tom Doherty Associates, LLC
175 Fifth Avenue
New York, NY 10010

www.tor.com

Tor® is a registered trademark of Tom Doherty Associates, LLC.

Library of Congress Cataloging-in-Publication Data

Dickson, Gordon R.
    Antagonist / Gordon R. Dickson and David W. Wixon.—1st ed.
        p. cm.
    "A Tom Doherty Associates book."
    ISBN-13: 978-0-312-85388-4 (alk. paper)
    ISBN-10: 0-312-85388-2 (alk. paper)
    I. Wixon, David W. II. Title.

    PS3554.I328A8 2007
    813'.54—dc22   2006050929

First Edition: March 2007

Printed in the United States of America

0 9 8 7 6 5 4 3 2 1

FOR MIKE AMUNDSON,
WITCH DOCTOR:

There for Gordy's computers,
Here for mine.
Thanks, Mike!

ANTAGONIST

CHAPTER 1

From where he knelt on the dirt floor, Bleys could see the soldier's body up against the far wall of the roughly dug, timber-framed bunker. Its uniformed back was to Bleys, but he felt that the body was that of a tall, thin young man—and he found himself thinking about a raccoon that, as a boy on a brief visit with his mother to Old Earth, he had seen lying dead along a rural road in a part of the mother planet where wheeled vehicles could still be found. This body before him had that same curled-inward shape that spoke of a being that, able to accomplish some slight movement before death came, huddled into itself to seek what comfort it could find in the face of its fear and pain. . . .

Abruptly, Bleys was torn out of his near-trance as something pulled at his right hand, and he realized he had been holding some-one else's hand—a hand that had just jerked slightly in his.

I must have had another blackout.

He still got them periodically, as his medician, Kaj Menowsky, had warned him would happen. They were one of the by-products of the damage caused by the genetic invader the rulers of Newton had injected into him, in their attempt to get him under their con-trol, back when they still opposed him, a few months ago. The black-outs were becoming less frequent since his body began to recover from both the invader itself and the medician's countermeasures that had killed it; but he had apparently just gone through one.

This experience was alarmingly different, however; he usually came out of his blackouts in his sleep.

The medician had warned him that stress would make a black-out, or any of his other symptoms, more likely; but Kaj had also said that every human body was slightly different, and reacted to a given stimulus in a slightly different way than any other human body. So perhaps it was also true that the same human body would react differently to different levels of stress.

Bleys could immediately pinpoint one apparent difference between this blackout and his previous blackouts: he seemed to be experiencing some form of amnesia . . . at least, he thought so, since he had the feeling that he was missing a period of time longer than his normal blackouts. In fact, he could not seem to pin down exactly when this particular sequence had started. Always before there had been a clear point prior to which he could, later, remember everything—and after which he could never remember anything, up until his awakening.

Looking about guardedly, to try to learn what had been happening, he saw that the bunker was occupied by a small group of soldiers—and it came back to him that he was on Ceta, that large planet where he had been on a tour of areas where units of Friendly troops were leased out to one or another of the many Cetan states. As First Elder of the government of the two Friendly planets, Harmony and Association, Bleys could find good cover for his visit to this planet, in a junket to visit those troops—a visit the most cynical of observers would believe sufficiently explained by the political need of a Friendly politician to assure the fervently religious folks back home that their leaders cared about their sons in uniform.

The visit might have been less congenially received had his hosts realized that Bleys' interests extended far beyond the Friendly worlds, all the way to their own governments.

The soldiers in this bunker, he saw, were not wearing the black uniforms of the Friendly troops; so he guessed they must be native Cetans. Several were lying about wounded, in addition to the one whose hand he was holding. Toni was nearby tending to one of them. But all of the unhurt soldiers—seven, he counted—were in two groups on either side of the bunker's only entrance.

From where he knelt he could not actually see that entrance, since it had apparently been built on the other side of a barrier wall intended to prevent direct access into the bunker from outside; anyone trying to attack into the room would be slowed by the need to turn either left or right as soon as they came through the doorway.

The soldiers were up against the sandbag-reinforced bunker wall in which the actual entrance was cut, and thus a little farther from him than was the barrier wall.

Those soldiers were silent, but they appeared tense as they crouched low against the wall beside the entrance, their eyes flickering between the interior of the bunker, their comrades and the entrance—but always returning to a leathery-looking, brown-skinned man, perhaps in his mid-thirties, whose short, roughly cropped dark hair protruded a little from beneath his fiberglass helmet. The man wore the insignia of some kind of noncommissioned officer—a sergeant of some grade unknown to Bleys—and he was noticeably less nervous than his men. At least, he showed it less.

Looking again at the man whose hand he was holding, Bleys saw that he was somewhat better dressed than the other soldiers, and that his collar bore the tabs of a junior officer. Also, Bleys saw, he was now dead. The blood-soaked bandages across his chest and stomach showed that his wounds had been severe—Bleys' eye caught movement, and he shifted his focus to catch Toni looking up and across at him.

"He's dead," Bleys reported. "Just now."

He saw the noncom look across at him bleakly.

"There was no way to stop it," Toni said. "Not with those wounds." She paused, and her tone changed.

"How are *you* doing?" she asked; and he felt the hidden meaning in her words. Antonia Lu was one of the few who knew of the attack on his DNA, and of the occasional relapses he experienced as his body slowly recovered; and although he seemed, when in a blackout state, generally not to show many signs of that state to others, he was not at all surprised to guess she was sufficiently attuned to him, after all these years together, to know when he might be in such a condition.

"I'm all right," he said. "Do you need any help?"

"No," she replied. "There's nothing more we can do until we can call for help." She paused a brief moment, before continuing, almost cheerily.

"Of course, we're cut off, and surrounded, and our communications are totally jammed. I'm pretty sure this isn't the local war

heating back up. I think it's an assassination attempt aimed at you."
Her blue eyes were looking into his calmly.

The noncom looked at her curiously, as if wondering why she was rehearsing what they all already knew. But Bleys knew she was using the apparent babble as a way to fill him in on events he might have lost while in his blackout.

She never lost her nerve, he thought.

CHAPTER 2

Dahno Ahrens, Bleys' older half-brother and the nominal head of the Others, the organization of crossbreeds from the major Splinter Cultures that the two of them had led into positions of leadership on five of the Younger Worlds, had objected more than a little when Bleys decided to travel to Ceta—a world not yet under the control of their organization—and check on the situation there. Bleys, Dahno objected strongly, had had them traveling almost nonstop for months now, orchestrating the political alliances that had opened the doors to their control of the latest three of those five and cemented their position on the two Friendly worlds. Moreover, Dahno pointed out, Bleys was still recovering from the effects of the Newtonian Council's attack on his DNA, and was only recently recovered from wounds received during their escape from that planet.

"Why?" Dahno asked again. "Why do you need to do this now? I'll admit you've taken us farther and faster than I ever had dreams of, but don't we have our hands full with consolidating our control of Newton, Cassida and New Earth? And for that matter, there's always work to be done here on Association, and on Harmony as well. You've got this Hal Mayne fellow on the brain!"

Dahno was being as open about his feelings as was possible to him, Bleys thought, which could be a bad sign. Bleys was glad Toni had left before Dahno arrived, because his brother was usually a good deal more circumspect when Toni—or, for that matter, anyone else—was around, and Bleys preferred it when his brother was more open. Still, Bleys wondered if Toni might be listening, somehow . . . he would have been.

"Perhaps," Bleys replied to his older, larger sibling. "But he's a dangerous man, I've told you that before."

"Yes, you have," Dahno said, "but how much of a danger could he really be? He's only one man, and a young one—he's not even in his mid-twenties yet!"

"True," said Bleys. "But you were around that age when you started to take over the Others social group here on Association, and change it into a tool you could use for your own purposes."

Dahno had raised his left arm from the elbow in a short, dismissive wave. "You know perfectly well, brother, that I was a special case—as, for that matter, are you."

"True enough," said Bleys, "but I think *he's* what you call a 'special case,' too."

Dahno took a moment before answering, more quietly.

"I'll admit it was quite an accomplishment for a sixteen-year-old to elude us after our people took over his estate on Old Earth and killed his tutors," he said. "And he's managed to dodge your efforts to find him ever since. But he's been in hiding and on the run for most of the six years since, and he's still a lone wolf at best."

"I don't think so," Bleys answered. "It was no small feat for him to escape from that prison cell on Harmony after Barbage caught him, and get to the Exotic embassy—he was apparently ill at the time, too. But it ought to be a matter of major concern for us that the Exotics not only took him in, but then smuggled him off the planet before we could take any action—"

"Before your creature Barbage could take any action, you mean," Dahno interjected.

"Yes, again," Bleys said. "Come on, sit down."

He moved across the room, in this lounge that doubled as his unofficial office, to the two oversize chairs reserved specifically for their large bodies, and sat in the dark gray one. His brother took the other, blue chair and leaned back, crossing one leg over the other.

"I know," Dahno said, before Bleys could speak again. "Barbage had no power to stop the Exotics even if he'd known where Mayne was."

"Don't forget," Bleys said, "we were away at the time, wrapping up New Earth."

Dahno nodded.

"That's so," he said. "Barbage's fanatic nature rubs on me even more than most of the Fanatics I've met." It was half of an apology, Bleys realized, and the most he would ever get. But Dahno was continuing.

"I suppose it's useful to have an able and ruthless resource like that Militia captain on tap. But you have to realize that the fanaticism must eventually detract from the usefulness. Fanatics never work *for* you, you know; they're always working for themselves. The best you can hope for is that their goals will match yours—and in the end, there'll always be a point where their interests diverge from yours."

"Fanatics don't seem to be any more susceptible to our abilities to persuade people than are their direct opposites, the True Faith-Holders," Bleys said, thoughtfully. He had spent a lot of time pondering why that should be so, since those days when he had realized his own power to make people want to follow his lead. The ability to resist the powers of persuasion he, along with many of his fellow Others, possessed, was a trait those two sorts of ultra-religious Friendlies apparently shared with both the Exotics and the Dorsai, and he was at a loss to explain what those groups had in common.

Hal Mayne had not fallen under his spell, either, on that single occasion when they had met, in Hal's cell on Harmony. Mayne was an Earthman, rather than a member of one of those apparently immune groups . . . and in that moment, Bleys had the feeling he was on the verge of something important.

But Dahno was not the person to explore the matter with, he knew.

"We always use what we have to hand, as you know very well," he said now, putting speculation aside for more pressing matters.

Not to be diverted, Dahno backtracked to his main point. "Over the years, you've spent a lot of time and resources trying to track Mayne down; and now you're running a little economic extortion on the Exotics, to try to force them to give him up—they won't, you know—but you've never convinced me it was all justified."

"I know they won't," Bleys said, referring to the Exotics, still safe on their two worlds under the star Procyon. "I'm just hoping to slow the progress of whatever connection Hal Mayne and the Exotics are building."

"*Is* there some justification?"

"Maybe it could be called a hunch," Bleys said. "But I've been feeling a sense of—call it caution—ever since I learned about his history, even before we got to his estate. I knew from the start there was something unusual about him, even beyond the way he was found as a two-year-old alone on an interstellar ship floating in space near Old Earth."

"However strange his history," Dahno said, "what about that past indicates any danger to us?"

"I can't answer that," Bleys said. "I just feel it, if you want me to admit that. It's a mystery no one has explained, topped by the enigma of the substantial abilities he's shown just by getting away from us—and all that now in an alliance with the Exotics."

"Mysteries from twenty years ago cut no ice with me," Dahno said. "I said it earlier—we've got our hands full. Your ability to deduce what really motivates people, and then to convince them that going along with you will give them whatever that is, has made your plans work out for us—better than I ever expected; and our people are showing more ability to do that same kind of convincing than I ever realized they had, in their work on the planets I—we—sent them to. But the number of our people is tiny compared with the populations of those worlds, and all of us are up to our ears in work to do, just to consolidate our control and keep things moving."

"That's exactly why I need to go to Ceta again," Bleys said.

"Because of Hal Mayne and the Exotics?" Dahno chuckled, but there was no humor in his eyes.

"Yes," Bleys said, ignoring the skepticism. Dahno seemed to be baiting him, but he never played his brother's games. "I learned something from Hal Mayne's escape."

"So the Exotics have been helping him," Dahno said. "So what? They've never even tried to bother us before."

"Well, that's true," Bleys said. "But haven't you ever wondered *why?* I mean, why they never tried to stop us, in those years when we were just getting set up on the other Younger Worlds? Even though we were barely beginning to gain positions of influence on those planets, starting as lobbyists and information brokers, you know as well as I do that the Exotics, with all those tools of their social sciences, had to have recognized us as a new power that could only be a danger to their own position."

"Why should they—try to stop us, I mean?" Dahno answered. "What's it to them, anyway? They could never've guessed we'd manage to take over those worlds, until we'd gone too far to be stopped." He laughed. "At that point, even *we* weren't thinking about really taking over any of the Younger Worlds!"

"That's not what you were telling the classes of Others you ran through your training program and sent out to the Worlds to work for you," Bleys said. Dahno gestured, as if waving his brother's words away from his face.

"You know perfectly well I only told them that to motivate them," he said. "Greed and ambition make people work harder. I never really intended any such thing, and I figured they'd forget about it, over time . . . until you came along, with your talk about making it happen."

"There's not much in your secret files about it," Bleys said, ignoring Dahno's last jab, "but I know that when you started sending your newly trained Others to begin infiltrating the various worlds, you never sent any to Mara and Kultis, the Exotic planets—and not to the Dorsai, either. I think you knew from the start that our abilities to influence and convince people wouldn't work on those worlds."

"That's so," Dahno said. "The Dorsai doesn't even have much of a government, and not much by way of a corporate environment, either—so there was just no place for one of our people to get into Dorsai society, even leaving out their notorious clannishness." He paused; and then uncrossed his legs and leaned forward, putting the points of his elbows on his massive thighs.

"You and I both know," he went on—his voice was lower and quieter now, his eyes earnest, as his hands moved as if to cup the open air between their two faces—"if only out of our mother's Exotic background, that the Exotics tend to have personalities that are largely immune to our abilities. I certainly wouldn't try to crack a way into either of those societies, and I wouldn't waste my trainees trying it, either. It's a culture-based characteristic that makes them immune to our persuasive talents, I think."

The mention of their mother, Bleys thought, was intended to emphasize the seriousness of Dahno's words; the subject had always been a flash point for Dahno's temper, and for him to voluntarily bring her up was either a sign of great concern or a calculated arguing tactic.

"I'm sure you're right about that," Bleys said, controlling an impulse to lean back in his chair, away from his brother, and cross his own legs. "But as I said, why didn't the Exotics ever try to stop our efforts to take control of other worlds? They have a centuries-old position as the major mercantile power among the Younger Worlds, second only to Old Earth itself—and for all their image as philosophers, they didn't get there by philosophy alone. They've always shown themselves to be pragmatic enough to quash potential threats to their position—they were a frequent employer of the Dorsai, remember."

"What could they do?" Dahno said, leaning back again. "Ours was an attack they couldn't use military force against. And anyway, we weren't acting directly against them, and in fact we were going about it very quietly."

"I'll tell you why they didn't act," Bleys went on, once more ignoring his brother's last words. "It's because they *couldn't* do anything!"

"Isn't that what I said?"

"It's not what you think," Bleys answered. "They couldn't respond because they were under attack themselves."

"Attack? By who?"

"That's just it, I don't know," Bleys said. "The *attack*, as I called it, hasn't been so major as to make the Exotics totally helpless. I think it's been strong enough, and going on long enough, to at least distract them, or confuse them—but let me tell my story in a proper order." This time he did lean farther back in his chair, but it was for the purpose of looking up at the great interstellar map mounted on the wall above them, on which he had tried to chart Hal Mayne's movements.

"When I got the news that Hal Mayne had been taken in by the Exotics," Bleys began, "and then taken to Mara, it suggested to me that maybe the Exotics were going to try to get involved in his campaign against us—"

"'His campaign against us'?" Dahno echoed. "What campaign is that? I haven't seen him doing much more than just trying to get away from you."

"He's campaigning," Bleys said. "Trust me on that."

Dahno put on his most skeptical expression and re-crossed his legs. Bleys continued.

"You yourself said it," he went on. "We've got our hands full with those Younger Worlds we've gained controlling positions in. That means we're walking a knife edge in trying to balance the disparate groups we've manipulated, who are still at odds with each other. It's a system of control that might be tipped over with a nudge or two in the right places."

"All the more reason to stay at home and consolidate our positions as fast as possible," Dahno said.

"But don't you see," Bleys said, "that if the reason the Exotics haven't taken a hand against us before is because they're too weak and distracted to do much—and I'll concede that there're more reasons than one for that weakness, and some of it is based in the inevitable changes that come to any civilization in the course of its historic development, but if one of the reasons for that weakness is because they've been under a covert economic attack for more than thirty years—don't you think we should know who's been attacking them?"

Dahno's face had sobered, but he said nothing.

"I didn't realize it, either," Bleys nodded. "It's been a very quiet operation, and it's stayed that way for decades, at least. That alone suggests a group so disciplined it can keep its very existence secret for a long time—"

"How could that be possible?" Dahno interrupted. "We've had the best intelligence-collecting organization on the Younger Worlds for the last ten years—well, maybe except for the Exotics themselves—and we've never even picked up a sniff of anyone out there!"

"That's right," Bleys said, pointing an index finger at his brother for emphasis. "But the author behind that fictional Old Earth detective Sherlock Holmes once put his finger on it, when he spoke of how strange it was that a dog *didn't* bark. . . ." As Dahno rolled his eyes, Bleys nodded and raised his hands, palm out, to forestall the acid comment he saw coming. Mercifully, Dahno kept his silence, although there was something very near a sneer on his face.

"More technically put," Bleys went on, "the absence of something that ought to be there is itself a piece of data. . . . At any rate, once I realized that the Exotics might be taking an active role against us, I started to research what the combination of Hal Mayne and the Exotics could do to our plans—which meant I had to understand the bases of the Exotics' power. And *that's* how I learned more than I expected about what's been happening behind the scenes."

He paused for a brief moment to marshal his presentation.

"I mentioned the historical forces, a moment ago," he went on. "And as I said, some of the weakening of the Exotics' position is traceable to those very normal historical forces—the same ones I've told you about in the past. But I've also told you before that I believe our civilization—the whole human race—made a big mistake by going out into space too fast; and that I believe that mistake has accelerated the normal decline that comes to all civilizations over time."

He could see Dahno's face beginning to take on the bored expression it generally wore when Bleys was giving one of the speeches he had become famous for, around the Younger Worlds, and which had earned him the honorary title of *Great Teacher*.

"Look at it this way," Bleys said. "We Others in particular have been helped tremendously by that decay I'm speaking about."

That got his brother's interest back.

"Decaying societies are more corrupt than their earlier forms," Bleys went on. "And corruption in the leadership, in particular—in whatever form it may take—exacerbates frictions within the society. And *that*, in the case of every planet we've taken over, gave us entry and provided a way for us to leverage our relatively weak position into one of control."

"Does that go for the Exotics, too?" Dahno asked. "I mean, are *they* decaying, too?"

"In several ways, yes," Bleys said. "But their decline is not of a form that gives us any power over them. However, it *has* weakened their ability to oppose us—perhaps even their will—which is to our advantage. Decay at the tops of societies usually means that the richest elements of the society have found a way to take, and keep, control—which in turn means that their planets spend more on keeping the rulers secure, as well as on importing luxury goods, and less on what's needed by the masses. The less well-off get less chance to rise in the society, a comparatively lower standard of living, fewer social services . . . and the gap between rich and poor increases—that's where we got a hook into New Earth, remember."

"But that hasn't happened to the Exotics," Dahno said.

"That's right," Bleys said. "And maybe that's because of those culture-based characteristics you mentioned a few minutes ago. At any rate, the consensual bases of their culture—the things they all live by, deep down inside, whether you mean beliefs or feelings or even instincts—seem to be very different from those of peoples on the other planets. For instance, they've been rich for centuries; but that doesn't seem to have induced any desire for more money or things."

"And yet you say they've decayed, too?" Dahno asked. "In what fashion? And if they haven't spent their money on luxuries, where has it gone?"

"To answer the last question first," Bleys said, "they've remained consistent to their purpose of advancing what they regard as the evolution of the human race. Remember, as just one example, that the Exotics provided the funds for the construction of the Final Encyclopedia, possibly the single most expensive project in the history of the race . . . it was almost an act of faith for them, made out of a belief that somehow the Encyclopedia would be important to human evolution."

"But once set up and running in its orbit around Old Earth," Dahno said, "I know the Encyclopedia makes enough money on its own, out of its research facilities and so on, that it supports itself . . . but we've gone off the subject: you suggested that the Exotics, too, have been decaying. What form does that take, that we can't make use of it?"

"You know," Bleys said, "if you stop to think about it." He looked squarely into his brother's eyes, knowing he was risking an explosion.

CHAPTER 3

"Our mother," Dahno said after a moment. He was calmer than Bleys was used to seeing him, on those rare occasions when the subject of their Exotic parent came up.

"Yes," Bleys nodded. "A highly intelligent woman from a rich society designed to help people rise to the limits of their talents—and yet somehow she came to feel she wasn't getting the recognition and status she deserved."

"All societies produce people who just don't seem to fit in," Dahno said. "But that's probably been true all through history. So how do you come to see that as a sign of the Exotics' societal decay?"

"I don't know of any way to prove it," Bleys said, "but I suspect that the proportion of people in similar situations has been increasing over the last century."

"That I can believe," said Dahno, "if only because the very existence of crossbreeds like us can probably be largely traced to that fact."

"If you mean that the dissatisfied tend to leave their worlds and move elsewhere, yes," Bleys said. "But don't make the mistake of thinking that our abilities arise out of a simple mixing of bloodlines from different worlds—we're the result of the mixing of cultures, not genes."

"I'm not entirely convinced of that," Dahno said. "You and I are something special physically, too."

"We may be," Bleys said. "But size doesn't mean all that much; remember that there are people on other worlds who can match us physically—some of the more legendary Dorsai, for example. But it's our power to persuade people to follow us that sets us apart, and that isn't based in any physiological part of us, as far as I can see.

Remember, many of our Others have been showing great persuasive powers, too, even though none of them match us physically."

Dahno, clearly reluctant, only nodded.

"Your point was well taken," Bleys went on. "Our very existence, and that of the Others we've been recruiting, is a strong indicator that such decay must have been going on."

"Well, it's a strong indicator that people have been moving about between the Younger Worlds," Dahno said. "I'll give you that. But there might be plenty of reasons for that, and some of them directly opposite to the idea of decay."

"That's certainly true," Bleys said. "But we were talking specifically about the Exotics, and what form the decay of their society might take; and I repeat that our mother's life might illustrate that decay."

"She was probably the single most self-centered person either of us has ever known," Dahno mused. "It must have frustrated the Exotics to have that result from one of their most celebrated and nurtured bloodlines—but are you saying that selfishness is the form decay has taken among the Exotics?"

"She may well be an extreme example," Bleys said, making a note in his head to follow up on that remark about their mother's genetic heritage. No one had ever mentioned anything about that before, and he had never thought to look into it; Dahno's tendency to react strongly when their mother came up in conversation had generally led Bleys to avoid the subject. But Dahno seemed to be handling it well, for the moment.

"After all," Bleys went on, "most of the Exotics haven't rejected their entire culture to go chase dreams of personal status among the wealthy of other planets. But it only takes a little extra concern for oneself to weaken a society's faith in what was once its ultimate goal—when that small amount of self-concern is exhibited by each one of millions of people."

"How can you possibly prove something like that?" Dahno said. "You can't compare how the individual Exotic of today measures up to those of, say, two centuries ago. Even if you had Exotics of each time side by side, you couldn't measure something like selfishness."

"You're absolutely right," Bleys said. "And I never claimed to be able to prove that the Exotics, taken as individuals, are decayed versions of their ancestors. But what I *do* claim to be able to prove is that the Exotic culture is no longer as strong and vibrant as it once was. The simple drop in their wealth as a society is an indirect proof of that. The rest is extrapolation—theory, if you want—that I use to try to explain what I've found.

"All I'm telling you is this: whatever flame once burned inside the average Exotic, that caused them to work together for a common goal—that flame is weakened today." He raised a hand to forestall the interruption he saw coming from his brother.

"It's not out. It's still there—strong yet, probably, in some. But it's weaker."

"Even if you're right, we can't make use of anything like that," Dahno said. "We work by offering people something they want and convincing them, in a way that bypasses their usual rational abilities, that they can get it by working with us—which in turn works because of our ability to override their normal skepticism for at least long enough for them to fall into line—and then inertia, in the form of the normal human inclination to avoid painful self-examination, tends to keep them in line. And the Exotics, taught from birth to question everything, are just too skeptical to fall for our usual line."

"That's one way to put it," Bleys said.

"Well, as you say," Dahno said, "we may not be able to bring the Exotics under our control, but it must be to our advantage to have them become less rich, and so less powerful. But how did that come about?"

"Except for the occasional expensive bit of advanced medical equipment and that kind of thing," Bleys said, "the Exotics have never been about manufacturing goods that other planets need to import. It's always been knowledge that they exported—the experts they sent out to the other worlds. The expense of interstellar freight has always meant that the biggest credit producer for any planet is the people it can send out to do things for other planets, things those planets couldn't manage to do for themselves. And the various Younger Worlds have, more and more, been producing their own experts, shrinking the market for the Exotic experts."

"I understand that," Dahno said. "I know that the Friendlies, for instance, who used to discourage their people from going off-planet, changed that policy some time ago. And that was only because of their desperate need for the hard currency of interstellar credits."

"Exactly," said Bleys. "If you think about it, that by itself is an example of the kind of decay that's infected all the societies on all the planets. And it's only one illustration of my reasons for believing the race will die out unless it's made to grow up." He looked at his brother keenly, wondering if he might get through to him this time.

"In the case of the Friendlies," he went on, "the change you mentioned was just one of many small ways they relaxed an old principle because of the pain of living up to it."

"Or they finally started to become a little more human," Dahno said, almost to himself.

"It was just that kind of decay," Bleys said, ignoring that remark, "that allowed you, followed by myself, to rise into a position of power here among the Friendlies. In past centuries we'd have been denounced as godless, and made virtual outcasts." He shrugged. "Some think that way about us even today, and many of them are willing to say so, and oppose us. But enough of the population finds reasons to go along with us that we're not only safe, but in control."

"There are places on these worlds where I wouldn't go without a well-armed escort," Dahno said, scowling.

"Yes," Bleys said. "That's true. But because Friendly society is divided, those parts cancel each other out, and we can keep control even though there are still many, possibly close to a majority, who would have rejected all those little things—and us—if they had realized what was going on. In their weakness they listen when we tell them, couched in the comforting words of their faiths, what they want to hear; and never notice, until it's far too late, that we've done something else entirely."

"We're off the subject again," Dahno said.

"Only a little," Bleys said, "but I'm getting there. You see, I expected, when I started researching the Exotics' power base, that I'd find just what I said: that the Exotics had suffered—undergone—a number of changes of the sort that could be expected to arise simply out of the workings of normal historical forces over a couple of centuries. I found, instead, evidence that the Exotics—and the

Dorsai, too—have been under covert economic attack for decades; an attack apparently aimed at cutting them off from access to interstellar credits."

Overriding the start of a comment from his brother, Bleys pressed on: "The first thing I looked for was a way to estimate Exotic wealth; and I found that in whatever terms you might want to measure it, it's been decreasing steadily for some time. That led me to a long-term pattern of Exotic-owned shipping being outbid for freight contracts and passenger carriage. I started to analyze traffic patterns, and found that shipping outbound from every one of the Younger Worlds for the Dorsai and the Exotics has been decreasing steadily over several decades at least—"

"*Where* do you find that kind of information?" Dahno exclaimed.

"The government, of course," Bleys said. "I'm First Elder, remember? Those gray bureaucrats over at the Commerce Cabinet were happy to winnow through several decades' worth of the raw data that all governments accumulate—and then largely bury."

"Why would the Friendly government have raw data on Exotic shipping?" Dahno asked, a puzzled look on his face.

"You, more than anyone, know the value of accumulating raw intelligence," Bleys said. "Governments always accumulate lots of raw data, simply because it's out there and some functionary can justify his position by grabbing it."

"But raw data is useless if no one is looking at it and thinking about it," Dahno nodded. "You're right. But—"

"Stop right there!" Bleys said. "Let me get back to the Exotics."

"You're right, you're right," Dahno said. "It's just that I've spent so much of my life trying to find information. . . . Anyway, back to the Exotics—didn't you also mention the Dorsai? Where do *they* come in?"

"Well, that's another thing I wasn't expecting," Bleys said. "The changes in traffic patterns involving the Exotics were virtually echoed by the changes involving the Dorsai."

Dahno leaned back in his large chair, looking vaguely in the direction of the ceiling while holding one hand up to stop Bleys from continuing.

"I think I can see a pattern of sorts," he said. "Both of those are societies that lived principally on exporting knowledge—in the case of the Dorsai, military expertise that made them better at soldiering than anyone else around." Now he looked back down at Bleys, challengingly. "So both societies would be hurt when the other planets just stopped needing their experts, right? For instance, when the other planets either began producing more of their own experts, or got caught up in fewer wars."

"That's just what I expected to find," Bleys said. "And I did find it. You're right as far as that goes."

"What did I miss?"

"The balance of trade reports every government produces for its own use," Bleys said. "Academics and economists have been watching and charting that kind of number for centuries, trying to see patterns. And usually they produce pretty accurate data on the trends in all the major economic categories—including expert leases."

"I was never able to keep up an interest in that kind of thing," Dahno said.

"Dry as dust, I know." Bleys nodded. "But it's like any mathematical formula—somewhere under the dryness is an underlying reality that might be important, even exciting. . . . At any rate, it's true the other planets have been steadily increasing the numbers of experts—in a wide variety of fields—they produce. But what's exciting is that the increase hasn't been enough to account for the size of the disparity."

"Is that disparity in expert leases enough to cause the decrease in Exotic wealth you found?" Dahno asked.

"No," Bleys said. "There's another, even more measurable, disparity to be found in the commerce records. Specifically, in the shipping records."

"You mean, cargoes?" Dahno asked. "You said yourself that the Exotics were never about exporting goods—"

"That's right," Bleys said. "But I don't mean the cargoes. I mean the ships."

"Oh, of course!" Dahno said. "It's been pretty much a stereotype that the Exotics' merchant fleet carries most of the cargoes between the worlds—but I haven't seen anything to suggest there's been a change in that perception."

"Yes," Bleys said. "In fact, Exotic ships have been carrying a progressively smaller portion of interstellar trade. And the fact you didn't realize it shows the genius of the attack. It's been going on for a long time, and yet no one has really noticed—well, I'm sure the Exotics have noticed, but they're not likely to advertise the fact someone is trying to take, and succeeding in taking, their leading position away from them. It's been a remarkable fall for two worlds that once were the richest, and thus the most powerful, of the societies on the Younger Worlds."

"So maybe they've lost some market share," Dahno said. "That kind of thing is to be expected. It's in the nature of history, you just said that; things like that change over time, as conditions change and motivations change."

"True enough," Bleys said, "but this goes beyond that. What I found convinces me of the existence of a quiet campaign over a long period of time that apparently sought to undercut the Exotics' wealth and position, by means that can only be described as a covert conspiracy."

"All right," Dahno said, "so someone has targeted the Exotics in order to get a share—even a big share—of their money. That's understandable; and since it seems to have been working, I'd say it was a pretty good tactic. But whoever those people are, if they're in it for the money and the power, they'll likely be susceptible to our ability to influence them, in the end."

"They may be vulnerable to us," Bleys said, "but I'm not sure money and power are the reasons they targeted the Exotics."

"Oh?" Dahno said. "Can you think of some other motive?"

"Yes," Bleys said. "Revenge, for one."

"Well . . . ," Dahno started slowly before warming to his thought, "I suppose the Exotics might have made enemies with their trade practices over the centuries, but I can't imagine anyone creating a secret society of some sort to oppose them. Have you been reading more of those Old Earth novels again?"

"Not revenge against the Exotics, necessarily," Bleys went on, ignoring the gibe. "Revenge against the Dorsai, perhaps."

"The Dorsai?" Dahno said, after a moment of silence.

"Yes," Bleys said. "I think I mentioned that the traffic patterns indicating a downturn in the Exotics' fortunes were being echoed by the patterns involving the Dorsai. At first I thought the Dorsai were being crippled simply as a by-product of the attack on the Exotics—but then it occurred to me it might be deliberately intended, as a way to deprive the Exotics of a weapon."

He paused, thinking.

"Even then, I was too focused on the Exotics," he went on after a moment. "But now I'm coming around to the notion that it's possible the Dorsai were the original intended targets of this action I've called a conspiracy."

"I don't understand—" Dahno started; but Bleys continued.

"It's the only way it makes sense," he said. "Someone started, decades ago at least, to try to cut the Dorsai off from any sources of interstellar credits. You know as well as I do that none of the Younger Worlds is totally self-sufficient. The standards of living on all of them are far lower than that on Old Earth; but they all, each and every one, need to import a lot of things just to survive; and to do that they need interstellar credits. And no one more so than the Dorsai, a planet so poor it's always had to export its people to be mercenary soldiers, just to earn enough to stay alive."

"And you're saying someone has been trying to starve the Dorsai by cutting them off from credits?" Dahno said.

Bleys nodded.

"Where do the Exotics come into this, then?" Dahno said. "Are there two such plots going on? That's a little much to swallow."

"No," Bleys said. "One plot. If you remember your history, it follows naturally. The Exotics have always been a major customer for the Dorsai's services as the leading military professionals on all the worlds. To weaken the Exotics is to weaken the Dorsai's single largest market—and their single friend among the other worlds."

"Is it that the Exotics are being crippled to prevent them from helping the Dorsai, or that the Dorsai are being crippled to prevent them from helping the Exotics if they come under attack?" Dahno said. "Couldn't it go either way?"

"That's true, it could," Bleys said. "The records I've found hint that the campaign against the Dorsai came first, but I'm far from certain about that. . . . In any event, it doesn't really matter, does it?"

"No," Dahno said, thoughtfully. "I suppose not." He raised an eyebrow as he looked closely at his brother. "So you have some reason for going to Ceta to try to unravel this?" he said.

"Yes, of course," Bleys said. "Ceta seems to be where these attacks originated."

"You can tell that somehow?"

"Yes. Remember, among the Younger Worlds, Ceta was always the Exotics' main competition in commerce, after Old Earth."

"So they had the greatest motive to try to undermine the Exotics," Dahno said. "Doesn't that come down to money and power, as I said earlier?"

"True," Bleys said, "but I think there's something extra involved."

"Why do you think that?"

"Because there's been a strain of vindictiveness involved in all this," Bleys said. "Some of the things I've found in the records have no other good explanation."

"Such as?"

"Such as the Dorsai being charged more for some products than other worlds have been paying," Bleys said. "Such as collusion between companies—usually Cetan companies—competing against the Exotics, to undercut Exotic bids, even when it means the competitors must have been losing money."

"A certain amount of that could simply be good—well, maybe sharp—business practice," Dahno said.

"Now and again, yes," Bleys said. "But not when it's a pattern repeated frequently over decades."

"So you're going to Ceta to try to uncover this," Dahno said. "Then what?"

"Well, think about the other ramifications of this," Bleys answered. "If I'm right, why don't our Others, who've been working on Ceta for years, know about it?"

"I see," Dahno said, his eyes narrowing slightly. "If our people don't know about whoever's doing all this—then we're being played."

"Which means our own plans are being undermined," Bleys said.

"Yes, I see that," Dahno said. He was suddenly tight-lipped, and Bleys knew his brother was concealing the effect of a severe blow.

Dahno had always been almost obsessive about maintaining his personal independence—it was a reaction to the way he had been treated by their mother, as a kind of personal accessory—and Bleys could think of little that would shock his brother more than to find out he had been manipulated.

CHAPTER 4

"Uncle Henry, are you busy?"

"Nothing that can't keep, Bleys."

"I'd like to speak with you about preparations for another trip," Bleys said into his wristpad. "Off-planet, I mean; and soon. Continue with what you're doing, but I'd appreciate it if you'd come to see me when you're finished."

"God has willed that it would be appropriate to do so," Henry MacLean said. "Carl and I have been comparing opinions on the new Soldiers we've brought in since Newton, and I wanted to speak with you about that when we are finished." Henry's voice and words often became more formal when the God he believed in was mentioned, but he had never used the antique-sounding speech affected by many of those who thought themselves unusually devout.

"Good," said Bleys. "Come up when you're ready, then."

"I will."

When faced with a problem, Bleys often worked it out in his head while pacing relentlessly up and down the length of his private lounge, in the tall building that now housed the headquarters of the Others, in Ecumeny, the capital of Association. But not this time. This time, he felt scattered and unable to focus.

That, he thought, as he tried to impose his usual discipline on his mind, was because there wasn't really a problem to focus on. The task he faced was simple; unfortunately, it was going to be difficult.

His uncle Henry was going to be coming up to see him soon. Henry MacLean was the organizer and leader of Bleys' Soldiers, the picked bodyguards Bleys had to surround himself with, these days.

Henry had to be told, right away, to make the preparations necessary for the trip to Ceta.

Faced with mentioning Ceta to his uncle, Bleys had found that, at some deep level, he was afraid. Because it was on Ceta that Henry's younger son, Will, had been killed, some years ago, while serving with a unit of Friendly Militia leased to a principality on that planet.

Bleys had never seen Henry display any deep emotional reaction with regard to Will's death. But Bleys knew, on a level so detached that it might have happened to someone else, that he himself had reacted strongly to the news. He could no longer recall—he avoided trying to recapture—the explosion of emotion he had felt at the time.

He was afraid to see what Henry's reaction might be.

He stopped short in his pacing, remembering, suddenly, that he had lied to Henry, the first time he saw his uncle after Will's death.

Bleys had been on Cassida, one stop on his first tour of the Others' organizations on the various Younger Worlds, when he received the news. He had finished his tour, including a stop on Ceta, before returning to Association—and almost his first stop upon arrival was a visit to Henry's farm, where Henry, almost casually, had asked Bleys whether his trip off-planet had taken him to Ceta.

Bleys had immediately told Henry he had not gone there.

Bleys could no longer recall, if he had ever known, why he had lied to his uncle. For the first time now it occurred to him he might have been trying to avoid reminding himself of the uncomfortable emotional reaction he had himself experienced.

At any rate, he had lied, and it was a good thing he had recalled that fact now, before dealing with Henry face-to-face. He would have to watch how he spoke in front of his uncle, from here on—either avoiding any reference to that previous trip, or giving a vague impression it had occurred at some other time.

For a moment he felt a touch of irritation, that he had let himself be so paralyzed; but the feeling was quickly forgotten as he turned to the screen that accessed his information stores. This trip was going to require a lot of preparation.

By the time Toni was due back from whatever errand she had

been on, Bleys was deep in his study of the Cetan situation, taking his researches down byways he had not had time to pursue before. His staff had prepared digests of all the materials relating to Cetan society available in the Chamber Library, here in Ecumeny, as well as of information gleaned from a number of government departments. He reserved for himself, however, the task of integrating that material with the data sent back, over the last decade and more, by the Others who had been sent to work on Ceta . . . the staff here never saw that kind of report.

This was a time he could regret that the computers on each world were not fully connected to each other, as they had once been on Old Earth; it would have made his researches much easier. But humanity had taken to heart the lesson it learned when the Super-Complex, the great supercomputer, had rebelled and wreaked havoc on the mother planet: no one would ever again link computers in any quantity sufficient to risk that kind of incident.

Instead, Bleys had to send out for information, including dispatching messages to the Others' groups on all the Younger Worlds—except, specifically, for Ceta—instructing them to send him as much data on that planet as they could locate on their worlds, and to do so quickly, sending it in installments, if need be. The information was unlikely to arrive on Association in any quantity before he himself left for Ceta, though; and in any case it would be so voluminous as to require it be winnowed by his staff . . . he would have to be sure to leave instructions on that.

He realized he was becoming irritated again. He hated it when that happened; emotion hampered the mind's cool functioning.

After a few moments of self-examination, he concluded that the irritation, this time, arose out of his deeply buried discomfort at having to leave it to his staff to digest the information for him. He had tried to select for intelligent people, and had worked to train them; but it bothered him nonetheless . . . it was just so likely they would miss something important that he would have found, if only . . .

Pulling himself out of that train of thought, he checked the time, wondering where Toni was. Explaining the need for this trip to her would be considerably easier that it had been with Dahno. He could depend on her for that, he knew; whatever the motivation might be behind Toni's voluntary attachment of herself to him, she brought to her position much more of a judicious wait-and-see attitude than did his half-brother.

"What are you planning?" Toni said, immediately after her arrival.

"Am I that obvious now?"

"You know you aren't," she said, smiling at him, the blue of her eyes seeming to stand out in the room, as if strengthened by the turquoise scarf she wore at her neck. "But I have more experience with reading you than almost anyone."

"That's true," he said.

The only other people who had much experience with him at all were Dahno and Henry, he reminded himself. Were they able to get information just from watching his face?

Once Toni had been filled in on the need to go to Ceta, and while they were waiting for Henry to arrive, the two of them laid out a rough plan for the trip.

For public consumption, it would be portrayed as a semi-official trip by Bleys, as First Elder among the Friendlies, and his brother, Dahno, an elected member of the Chamber on Association, to visit the various units of Friendly Militia that had been leased out to several states scattered about Ceta. It was a good enough excuse for the trip, that on the two Friendly worlds of Harmony and Association, images of the brothers apparently lending support to the young soldiers would be politically useful; within a few days the population at home—and, indeed, people on other worlds—would be seeing images of Bleys the philosopher listening to the concerns of young enlisted troops as they shared a meal, or imparting quiet words that obviously inspired the young soldiers.

This kind of trip, Toni pointed out, would provide great fodder for political commentary by anyone who was opposed to Bleys personally, or to the Others—or even to the McKae administration. But Bleys dismissed that worry: with the Others' steadily increasing control of both the government and the media, on both Friendly worlds as well as on several other planets, such jaundiced views could be effectively marginalized in a number of ways.

And even the more sophisticated among the viewing audience would find themselves somewhat disarmed when it became obvious that the elected politician on the trip, Dahno, although alongside his brother and lending support, was obviously not pushing himself in front of the lenses.

"Is Dahno in agreement with all this?" Toni asked. "He doesn't usually want to be in the public eye, and I'm pretty sure he's not really interested in being reelected to the Chamber."

She had learned a lot about his brother, Bleys reflected.

"Not in detail," he responded now. "But he'll go along with this—I've already convinced him of the need for the trip, and he'll see the usefulness of concealing the real purpose of our trip behind this façade."

"Layers within layers," she said. "That would appeal to Dahno, all right."

"You're right about another thing, too," Bleys said. "Dahno only took the Chamber seat when I vacated it because at the time we needed someone there who could control the place—and that's no longer a worry."

"Has this trip been cleared with McKae?"

That question was, in a way, a test for Bleys, himself. Darrel McKae was the Eldest, the highest officer of the two Friendly planets, elected by the populace of both worlds—and the man who had appointed Bleys to his position. But Bleys had made it clear to McKae some time ago that he would not be bound to the dictates of his nominal superior. And McKae, who had achieved his own position only with Bleys' aid, lacked any real desire to fight him.

Toni had reacted with strong approval, Bleys remembered, the first time he had refused an order from McKae. She seemed somehow to see that as an indication of a kind of moral ascendancy on Bleys' part. Since that time, McKae had largely been acquiescent in whatever Bleys had planned.

Darrel McKae, Bleys reminded himself now, had not gotten to his position by being a weakling. And for all that he might have become

overly fond, of late, of both wine and his office—and even been repelled, or frightened, by something he had been able to see in
Bleys—the fact was that in large part he had not opposed Bleys because he was smart enough to know he had very little to gain by
getting into a public spat with the First Elder he himself had appointed . . . but that implied truce would work only so long as nothing happened to upset the Eldest.

"Not yet," Bleys told Toni now. "But we'll clear it with his office
anyway. He won't object. Could you have the Office of the First Elder draft an official communication to the Eldest's Office?"

"I will," she said. "And may I suggest we ask both Offices for
suggestions for one or two diplomatic missions you could undertake
while on Ceta? It would add weight to the official purpose of the
trip—"

"You're right," he said, interrupting her. "Having a second level
of reasons for doing something always tends to deflect observers."

"—and also provides justification if you find you have to move
about Ceta, to places where there are no Friendly troops to visit; or
if you're noticed to have been moving about in secret."

"Thank you," he said. "I hadn't thought of that."

"You're not yet used to thinking of yourself as a public officer," she
said.

"I know," he said, a little ruefully. "To tell the truth, I'm uncomfortable with having the extra position. It's a drag on me, holding
me down from being free to go when and where I want."

"It's one of the prices you have to pay to carry out your own mission," she said. He knew she was thinking of the plan he had made
his life's task, which only she—and to a much more limited extent,
Dahno—knew: to gather the worthwhile elements of the human
race back together on Old Earth, shutting the Mother World away
from space travel and forcing the race to give up its reckless adven-
turing until it grew up . . . a plan he knew would result in the slow
deaths of all of the Younger Worlds, and likely the faster deaths of a
lot of their people.

The alternative was to let the undisciplined, immature people
who made up the human race continue to be distracted from the

need to grow up by shiny dreams of future adventures—to let them continue to feel no concern for the hurts they did to others, or for the dangers that surely lay out there among the stars.

After a brief pause, she continued in a much lighter tone: "You'd have thought of it yourself. You just haven't had time to get down to the details yet."

She smiled at him.

"Shall I begin?" She uncrossed her black-trousered legs in anticipation of his response.

"Yes," he said. "No, wait—we also need to arrange transportation. Can you find out the status of both *Favored of God* and *Burning Bush?*"

"I can, of course," she said, looking slightly puzzled. "It's standing orders that one of them's always available to go on eight hours' notice—are you concerned it won't be ready? Or is it that you want a particular ship?"

"I want both ships," he said.

"Both?"

"Yes," he said. "I want to travel, officially and openly, in one of them. But I want whichever one is able to get off first to precede us under a false name and papers, to be in place already on the ground, and in no way associated with us, before we ourselves get to Ceta."

"Are you expecting that much trouble? You have diplomatic immunity now, you know."

"I had immunity when we went to Newton," he pointed out, "and it didn't stop the Council from attacking me. While I'm certainly a much more important figure now, politically, the fact is I simply don't know what to expect. I don't know who those people we'll be looking for are, or what their reactions might be when they notice us sniffing around on their trail. We only managed to get off Newton because the authorities there didn't know which ship we were trying to reach when we crossed the spaceport pad, remember."

"Perhaps some of the Soldiers should go on the ship that travels— well, incognito," she suggested. "They won't be part of our official party, which could make them more useful in some situations."

"True," he said. "We'll have to get Henry's input on which ones would be best suited for that kind of job—it'll demand initiative and experience . . . in fact, I can think of several things they can be doing on the planet before we get there."

"That sounds as if you want to send some of the technical teams," she said. "Carl Carlson might be a good choice to lead that group." She was referring to Henry's second-in-command.

"No," Bleys said. "He's been with us too long."

At her questioning look, he explained: "We have to assume someone might know about the people who work most closely with us," he said. "Carl might be recognized."

"All right," she said. "I see that. But I was about to remind you that some of the Soldiers are originally from Ceta. They might be particularly useful on the first ship, since they'll blend better into the population."

"Unless they have some reason for not wanting to go back," he said. "We generally don't ask if our people have legal problems elsewhere, but those on the first ship won't be covered by my diplomatic immunity."

"Henry will be able to judge that." She nodded.

"Having Soldiers already in place undercover," Bleys went on, "will allow my 'official party,' as you put it, to be smaller. I know I need the bodyguards, but I worked hard to craft my image as a peace-loving philosopher who travels about the Younger Worlds giving common-sense talks, and I've been uncomfortable with the conflict between that image and my apparent need for guards."

"I don't think you really mean you, personally, are uncomfortable with that apparent contradiction," she said, after taking a moment to think. "I think you mean you don't like it because the need for bodyguards detracts from the message your image is crafted to present."

"Well, that's true, too," he replied. "But I did mean what I said, literally."

"What do you mean?"

"I mean that appearing to be a philosopher is not exactly a lie," he said. "At least, whether I am one, or not—I'd like to be one."

"You are," she said. "You couldn't have seen the way to your mission if you weren't."

"I guess that's so," he said. "But there seems to be a little bit of the idealist left in me—enough to regret that I need bodyguards at all. It seems . . . unphilosophical."

"Oh, there's a *lot* of the idealist left in you," she said—and for a brief moment a smile lit her face; but quickly vanished. "There's no reason for your mission that isn't based on ideals—and selfless ones, too."

He didn't want to go any further with the conversation, so he let the silence stretch on; until at last the subject could be considered dropped, and she left to begin her assignments.

When the spare, late-middle-aged figure of Henry MacLean stepped off the disk of the private elevator, Bleys was standing in front of the Mayne-map, waiting for him.

"Thank you for coming, Uncle," Bleys said. He felt ready to handle mentioning Ceta to Henry, now. He had lost his balance for a few moments, he told himself, but now he had recovered, just as he would after making a mistake during a martial-arts workout.

Henry wasted no time on preliminaries.

"How quickly do we leave for Ceta?" he said.

"I can't answer that so simply," Bleys said. He was determined not to let himself be thrown off balance again so quickly.

"You make it sound complicated," Henry said. "I need details on what will be required."

"Come and sit with me," Bleys said. "Toni and I have laid out a tentative plan, and I'd like to run through it with you, as well as discuss some special arrangements—we can work out what's needed together."

Henry nodded, and moved to a chair.

"How did you know this trip was to Ceta, Uncle?" Bleys asked, settling into the dark gray, oversize chair that was always his.

"Dahno told me," Henry said.

Bleys nodded. It had to be so, of course. But Dahno had not known of Bleys' later decision to take two ships.

Bleys went on to explain to Henry that between having to get the second ship ready, and having to make diplomatic, political and administrative preparations, it would be five days or more before his own party could get off; but that he wanted whichever ship could take off first to take some of Henry's people. Going over the requirements took the rest of the afternoon.

Neither of them brought up Will's name.

"For all that's happened," Toni said late that evening, after *Favored of God* had been sent off with its instructions, "it's only a few weeks since you told me you thought it would be best to leave Ceta to the last, because it would be, well, messy to try to take over that splintered world—do you remember?"

"Of course I do," Bleys said. "But I'm not really figuring on trying to take control of Ceta, just now. It's still uncontrollable. I'll be talking differently, when we're there, but don't let that distract you— we're going on what might be called an intelligence mission, and some of the talk will be a ruse aimed at smoking out whoever's hiding from us."

"I know that," she said. "And I applaud the flexibility it shows. But I wonder—I've been assuming that was only what might be called a 'tactical' shift, and that your long-range plan has not changed—"

"No," he said, interrupting her. "My goal hasn't changed." He paused, watching her face for reaction.

"I haven't changed," he said. "I never change."

"Your plan is so—" She groped for a word. "—so *large!* Isn't that daunting, even to someone with *your* abilities?"

"Is it daunting for you?" he asked. "To be in on this, I mean."

"No," she said. "I'm committed to you. You know that."

"I know," he said. "And you know you're the only one who really knows what I'm after, in the very long term. Even Dahno has no real idea of the full scope of my purpose."

"I don't know the details of your plan—"

"Most details have to await the moment," he said.

"I understand that. But what you told me when you were ill— what you spoke, perhaps for the first time out loud, tells me you expect to be strongly opposed."

He nodded.

"And that you don't intend to shrink from doing whatever might be required to quench that opposition." She looked into his eyes.

"I know you recognize the implications of that," she went on, "because it was clear, in some of the things you said. You foresaw a lot of suffering and death."

"Yes," he said. His voice seemed flat and curt, even to himself.

"I know you care about me," she said. "And about Dahno, Henry—others, too, I think, and even the whole human race. You're not some kind of conscienceless mass murderer. So aren't you bothered by the deaths you foresee?"

"Yes," he said. "Of course I am."

He looked down into her face, feeling a heaviness in the pit of his stomach. He recognized it; he felt it every time he imagined talking about the future he planned.

"You know I never told you my plans of my own volition," he said. "It was forced out of me by that—that *thing* the Newtonian Council attacked me with."

She nodded, simply waiting.

"I didn't tell you," he went on, feeling the words forcing their way out past his instincts, "for the same reason I haven't told anyone else: I thought you—just as I've always thought of everyone else—would be repelled, and—and leave me."

"You know better now," she said, her voice low, almost throaty.

"You have to know, too," he went on, remorseless even for himself, "that if you *had* decided to leave me, it wouldn't have altered my plans."

She nodded, lifting an arm to his shoulder and beginning to gently knead the hard muscles there.

"That goes for Dahno, too," he said. "And for Henry. Because no matter how much I might love them—or you—my duty to the race has to come first."

"No matter what the cost," she said. It was not a question.

"No."

"Are you prepared for the fact you could go down in history as the greatest butcher in the history of the race?"

"Yes," he said.

"Does it bother you?"

He took a short moment to think that over.

"Yes and no," he said; and paused again.

"Do you know," he went on, "that question never even occurred to me before . . . because, I think, it's irrelevant."

"Irrelevant?"

"Yes," he said. "If my plans succeed, I will have saved the race, and that's worth any cost; and while the price will become obvious in the near term, that result will only be seen far in the future, and I'll be dead anyway.

"And if I fail, the race will die."

"I told you once," she said softly, "about what my father said, about the need to be true to yourself, even if it costs you your life."

"*Inochi o oshimuna—na koso oshime!*" Bleys said. His memory seldom failed him. "That Japanese saying you quoted to me—I remember. What about it?"

"How much greater is the power of your honor," she said, "when the cost you're willing to pay is so much more than merely your own life?"

Both of them were silent for a long moment.

"Don't start seeing more in me than there is," he said, finally. "I weaken, sometimes."

"There is none who does not," she replied.

CHAPTER 5

Henry MacLean had been lying in the dark for some time, wondering if he was committing a larger sin than he knew.

When he went to his bed, after seeing his quickly picked contingent of Soldiers off to the pad where *Favored of God* lay waiting, he had known his night would be full of memories—memories of Will, who lay buried somewhere on that planet that Bleys would soon take Henry to. Still, the self-discipline he had schooled himself in, over a lifetime of either fighting or farming, had gotten him some sleep—eventually.

And when he awoke in the darkness of his tiny room, it had been Bleys who was at the top of Henry's mind—it never occurred to Henry to think, as some might, that possibly he had somehow betrayed his real son, Will, by thinking of Bleys at this time.

Henry MacLean had come here, to the Others' headquarters in Ecumeny, for the purpose of trying to keep Bleys alive until the boy—Henry still thought of Bleys as a boy, which was unfair, since Bleys was deeply involved in a man's sins—until the man who had grown out of the boy could shake off the hand of Satan that clutched at his heart.

Henry was convinced that Satan did not yet own that heart—that inside himself, Bleys was still the boy Henry knew, who wanted desperately to do good. And so Henry had deliberately placed his own soul in jeopardy.

Because Henry MacLean was now aiding and abetting doings he was highly suspicious of. Even though he did not know what Bleys' ultimate purpose was, Henry had heard things in Bleys' words, and seen things in Bleys' manipulations of other people, that made him sure he would not like that purpose.

Yet there remained a chance that Bleys would see his danger, and turn back. And it was Henry's self-appointed task to keep Bleys alive until that time came.

Another task, too, remained in the back of Henry's mind, one he feared he might have to undertake: he might have to kill Bleys himself, if it began to appear that the boy's soul was about to pass beyond redemption.

Henry had left the farm on which he grew up, on which he raised his children and buried his wife, precisely for the purpose of protecting Bleys—Bleys, who might still be reachable. Bleys, who might be damned now but perhaps not irredeemably so.

There were those in some of the more radical churches, Henry knew, who preached the doctrine of the blood atonement: the belief that one who had sinned grievously could be saved only by the shedding of his own blood—by those who cared enough to want to save him. Henry did not believe in that doctrine. He thought it smacked of blasphemy for men to claim to have the power to redeem lost souls.

Henry had observed that doctrines such as the blood atonement always seemed to enslave their followers to the voice of their patriarch, and that those patriarchs were themselves usually corrupted by the power they wielded. Henry would have none of that; like most on the Friendly planets, he believed firmly in his right, and duty, to decide, for himself alone, what his path to his God must be.

What he feared he might have to do did not fall within that blood-atonement doctrine, because he had no hope that by killing Bleys he could save the boy's damned soul. Rather, Henry's hope was that he might have a chance, at the point where Bleys was about to commit himself to damnation, to kill him before he took that last step over some invisible line in front of his soul. . . . Better to kill him when he was still, deep inside, that lost, vulnerable boy— if Henry waited too long, to the point where Bleys had crossed that line and become one with Satan's purposes, it would be too late for killing him to do any good.

But Henry could not avoid wondering whether he was taking too much upon himself . . . perhaps, deep down, he was hoping for a miracle of some kind, that would take the burden from him—and now he shied away from that thought, recognizing the blasphemy of comparing himself, even if only implicitly, to the suffering Christ in the Garden the night before the crucifixion.

He turned restlessly onto his side, to look out the window beside his small bed. He had awakened long before Association's star would begin to gray the eastern sky, but the lights of the city made all of its nighttime hours luminous, in an evil-seeming orange tone—a thing which still seemed strange to him, born and raised in the country-side, where they knew what black night was.

He had lived his entire life as either a farmer or a killer, and he had found that both vocations required early risings. These hours were habit with him, and he was not comfortable with other ways, even though he now lived kilometers away from the old farm.

He had left the window open, as he did every night, having found a way around the builders' intention to keep this building, the Others' main headquarters, sealed; he liked the feel of the air moving across his face, even if it stank of city. His view was domi-nated by the side of an office building across the wide street, since he had chosen a room on a low floor.

Joshua was probably awake by now, too, he thought. His eldest son now worked the old farm, living there with his wife and sons. Henry smiled: there was another child on the way. He hoped it would be a little girl, this time. He had always regretted not having a daughter of his own, for all that he loved his two boys deeply; and at times he wondered how his life would have been altered with a girl in the house, in those years after Miriam died. Would Joshua and Will have come out differently?

Not that he had anything to complain about. Joshua had become a fine, sturdy man, more levelheaded and calm than his years would suggest. And Will—Will had done his duty despite his fears; and for all Henry regretted he would never see the type of citizen and fa-ther Will would have become, he was proud of his boy.

No, his *man*. Will had by his death earned recognition as an adult, and as one of God's own.

As for Dahno and Bleys: how would they have been affected, if they had come to live with him in a house that had a girl, or even a young woman, in it?

Henry remembered how it had been in those days when Miriam and he lived alone together, working on the shared dream of farm and home and family. His life had seemed warm and blessed, and he worked on the stony land with joy in his heart, knowing he would see her soon, bringing him out a lunch at noon or greeting him in the farmyard as he walked back in, driving the goats to be milked— Miriam would help with that, too; she was a far better milker than he was.

Dahno had come to them when Miriam was still alive, but she had died a year after his arrival, shortly after Will was born. Henry wondered what effect her death might have had on the eleven-year-old newcomer. What did he make of it all?

Henry had tried to make time for Dahno, too, as well as for Joshua, trying to fill part of the hole left by Miriam. He didn't know if he had managed it rightly.

Joshua had turned out very well, though. And the report of the psychomedician who had analyzed the young Dahno on Cassida, where his mother was living at the time she sent the boy to Henry, had suggested that the boy's character was already set as in concrete long before Henry ever saw him.

Henry could accept that as a fact; he had seen for himself the unbreakable shell the boy Dahno had developed.

When Bleys had been sent to the farm, almost ten years after Dahno, his older half-brother had already left, to move into Ecumeny and set up on his own.

Bleys had been a very different kind of boy.

Dahno had already been beyond Henry's ability to reach, but Henry had never felt that way about Bleys. There had always been a kind of vulnerability to the boy; not the kind of weakness most people had—in some ways, Bleys was stronger than anyone Henry had ever met—but a kind of yearning quality, as if he were someone who had been deprived of something important in life, and ached for it. . . .

Dahno, Henry thought, might well be damned already—it was hard to tell, through the wonderful façade of cheer and charm he maintained for all comers. But Henry, for all that he felt that charm himself, knew it was in truth just a kind of armor, through which no one had ever penetrated.

That woman has much to answer for, he thought, thinking of the two boys' mother. He had heard, with no surprise, that she had committed suicide, at about the time Bleys left the farm. He had never passed that information to the brothers; it was at best a secondhand report, of whose truth he could not be confident.

The news had come in a note from Ezekiel, Henry's younger brother, reporting a story he said he had only heard . . . warm, cheerful, irreligious Ezekiel, who had found the Friendly worlds too harsh, and fled—only to find himself somehow emotionally bound to the cold, hard renegade Exotic who had birthed first Dahno, then Bleys. Birthed them, only to warp them and throw them away.

Henry had not heard from Ezekiel again.

He blinked a couple of times now, and tried to turn his thoughts; until after a moment his eyes focused on the building across the street. At this hour that building was sidelit by the orange city lights, which seemed their most evil when the night got very late and few were on the street . . . the lights of the building in which he lay gave off a whiter glow, but they seemed to be overwhelmed by the sickly orange . . . who was in there?

It struck him that, for all this building was armored against even the charges from power pistols, the distance across the street was short, and there were other weapons. . . .

There were roving bands of rebels on both Friendly worlds, he knew. To some extent, that had always been so—a society built on religious discord was certain to produce those whose dissent would reach the stage of armed rebellion. But it seemed there were more of those bands—*Commands,* some called them—than ever in his lifetime.

He had not, himself, ever joined such a Command—his time of war had been fulfilled in other ways. There had always been plenty of warfare to go around.

Henry knew that the Commands, which had always been bitterly, violently opposed to the organized religious groups that wielded governmental power on the Friendly worlds, had seen clearly, some time ago, that the Others, that strange group organized by Dahno and now led by Bleys, were now the true controlling force on Association and on Harmony.

Would that not make Bleys a target for the Commands?

Henry was not certain assassination was in the Commands' book of tactics, but he did not want to make any assumptions.

Those Commands were made up of hard, experienced warriors—it was not long since some of them had managed to sabotage the new Core Tap under construction on Harmony, blowing up a goodly part of its infrastructure . . . what would such a quantity of explosives do to this building?

This needed consideration.

Henry rolled away from the window, not bothering with a light— the street lighting provided illumination, and in any case he was used to moving about in the darkness of early mornings. Many technological tricks had come into his life since he moved here to be with Bleys, but he was most comfortable making use of only those that were absolutely necessary.

Now his hand moved unerringly to the controls for the in-house communications system, and punched the number for Carl Carlson, his second-in-command.

"Carl," he said, "we're doing a drill. Wake section B of the new class and get them up—no breakfast—and ready to go to Siloam Park. Exercise Twenty-seven. Wake all the trainers and get the vans organized—we leave in fifteen minutes."

The new recruits were joking and laughing, even engaging in a little horseplay, as they headed back to the parking lot after their training session. It was a normal reaction, Henry thought, for any group of healthy men and women just released from hard work, and not yet completely over the hormonal spikes that came with hard, and somewhat dangerous, training—which still showed in their flushed faces and perspiration-soaked hair.

In the last few hours, without benefit of breakfast, these recruits had been run through a strenuous series of exercises designed to test both their fighting skills and their abilities to analyze situations; they all felt they had performed well today.

None were raw youngsters; in fact, they were all blooded veterans out of a variety of conflicts. Most had fought in inter-Church skirmishes here on Association, or on Harmony, and all of them, including the few offworlders among them, had graduated to larger conflicts, often as mercenaries.

These were people, Henry knew, who had discovered they liked fighting—that ordinary life was too tame for senses honed on the emotional and hormonal rushes ignited by the proximity of immediate, violent death. Henry knew that because he, himself, had been one of those people—and still was, to his shame.

Like most of the Friendlies among his recruits, he had entered the ranks of the killers innocently, believing he was doing God's will by defending his own Church, and his neighbors, against occasional raiding parties from rival Churches. But as he matured, and found himself involved in more and larger inter-Church wars, he had come to realize that somehow he had shifted over from fighting in defense to fighting because he found it exciting, even thrilling.

He had known it was sinful; and yet each time he entered some new war—now as one of those called, in the Friendly culture, a *Soldier of God*—there had been some justification, some reason that could be argued made the killing necessary and pardonable, even righteous.

However, the same intellectual abilities and temperamental self-control that had made of the young, uneducated Henry MacLean one of the best at his profession also made him able at times to look at himself with a critical eye, and by the time he neared his late twenties, a ten-year veteran of the wars, he was no longer able to let himself be overwhelmed by the unthinking enthusiasms of youth.

So he had quit, returning to the farm that had been untended since his mother's death, during the sixth year of his time of war—and to the religion of his childhood. He had taken a wife and raised their two sons, as well as the two boys his younger brother, Ezekiel— whose sin took a completely different form—had asked him to take in . . . that memory brought Henry's mind back to the problem he had been struggling with, earlier this morning.

Ezekiel had never actually said that first Dahno and later Bleys were his own children, but Henry had raised the boys as if they *were* his own sons—as much, at any rate, as they would let him; for they had come to him nearly in their teen years, and much of what they were was already formed, beyond Henry's power to reshape.

Henry suspected, though, that he had failed both boys.

Dahno, almost ten years older than Bleys, and older than both of Henry's own sons, had come to the farm almost as a wild animal. The psychomedician's reports Ezekiel had sent indicated that the boy, molded by the way his mother had treated him, lived without regard for anyone else, driven by a need to find the freedom and independence he had been denied.

Even those reports had only hinted at the boy's ability to make himself likable, even beloved, by anyone on whom he turned his attention. Henry himself had felt that charm, despite his familiarity with the reports, but it had not prevented him from trying to teach the boy, and to mold a conscience into him. However, Henry suspected—he could not know, for Dahno never let anyone inside— that he had failed in that task.

Dahno, however, had been a vast help around the farm, with his extraordinary size and strength; and if he had not cared for Miriam, Henry's wife, and for Henry's firstborn son, Joshua—and then for Will—Henry had not been able to tell it.

Bleys, when he arrived some years later, was a completely different kind of boy. He had lacked Dahno's ability to charm, but had been a serious, even humorless, boy, intent on finding his correct place in the world, in the universe. He had the ability to love, Henry thought; and Henry believed Bleys loved him and his two sons, as well as Dahno—and now, Toni. But Henry grieved for the boy, and now for the man.

Because it had come to seem to Henry that Bleys, for all his desire to love, and to be right with the universe, was more lonely than anyone Henry had ever known. It was as if he observed the entire world, and all of humankind, from behind a translucent wall in his own head.

Bleys had tried desperately to belong to Henry's world, but when his ultimate effort failed, he had gone off to Ecumeny to join his older brother's enterprise. He had gone on to become a philosopher and speaker known throughout the Younger Worlds.

Bleys was now richer, and more powerful, than anyone Henry MacLean had ever known; but he was, deep inside—or so Henry believed—still alone, and still wanting to find his right place in the world—to find his God, or some substitute for the God he could not believe in.

In all his time on the farm, Henry had been acutely aware of the pistol that lay buried in a field, a presence that silently accused him of the imperfection of his own faith. Yet he had preserved it against a day of need, and that day came when he saw clearly the direction of Bleys' life; and so Henry had dug up that pistol, cleaned it, and taken it into Bleys' service—but on his own mission.

In his mission of protecting Bleys until he could save himself, Henry had created a team of warriors, to be bodyguards; for he knew that Bleys walked dangerous paths. Assassination was not uncommon on the Friendly worlds, and Henry had no reason to believe other worlds were any different.

Those bodyguards, however, could never handle the alternative mission Henry had taken on himself.

Henry firmly believed that inside the large, strikingly handsome man, known around the Worlds for his vast intellect and golden tongue, the earnest boy still lived—the boy who had come to Henry's farm wanting nothing more than to be loved and wanted. But the man, Henry feared, might be pursuing a course even the Exotics, that people the Friendlies called the Deniers of God, would find themselves appalled to contemplate.

Henry remembered his thoughts of early morning—it was not hard; the thoughts came to him in many dark moments . . . and yet, the boy was still in there.

More than two dozen of the Soldiers Henry first recruited for Bleys had been lost in their escape from Newton. That planet, which deified scientific accomplishment, had proven to be ruled by people willing to inject Bleys with a substance that, Henry thought, could as easily be called a poison as anything else.

Henry knew little about such things as genetics; Harmony and Association, the poorest of the Younger Worlds, were not able to provide more than a few of their people with much formal education. But Henry came to work for Bleys knowing his own limitations, and his new life had given him facilities and time never before available to him—facilities and time he had tried to use wisely. And he was adept at picking up information just by being around people like Bleys and those he associated with.

They had succeeded in escaping from Newton, although at great cost; and in the time since, while Bleys was recovering from both his poisoning and a wound received during the fight to reach the ship, Henry, although wounded himself, had been trying to find replacements for the men and women he had lost.

Lost was too innocent a word for what he had done, he reproached himself now. His actions had led directly to their deaths.

Now Henry dropped back behind his latest batch of recruits, as, moving in a straggling group, they neared the edge of the trees and began to cross the grassy apron, beyond which waited the three vans that had brought them here. No one was in sight.

Henry watched keenly as Steve Foster, who had been on one edge of the group ahead of him, slowed his pace for a fraction of a second—before picking that pace back up again while making a casual, angling turn that put him, within seconds, on the other side of a public sanitary facility. He paused there, as if thinking about answering a call of nature.

Ahead of him, four more of the recruits had stopped, raising their heads to look about—and in that moment, seven armed figures rose from behind various vehicles parked in the area, while two more came around from behind the waiting vans. Their weapons were still being raised when the recruits began to scatter, some leaping for the nearest bit of available cover, two reversing their course to dash back toward where Henry stood at the edge of the trees—and those who felt themselves to be too far from concealment dropping to the pavement while reaching into their carrybags—

"All right, all right!" Henry yelled. "It's just another test!" The armed figures who had been waiting in ambush prudently ducked out of sight, in case someone failed to hear Henry's words; and

Henry himself refrained from striding into the midst of his recruits, until he could be sure their brains had all had a chance to override their instincts.

A few of the recruits actually managed to get in a few trigger-pulls, only to find that their weapons had been rendered inoperable; but no experienced Soldier was going to let himself be killed by some sort of mistake in the carrying-out of that particular bit of sabotage. So, in the end, no one was hurt.

Except, perhaps, for some feelings, Henry told himself. Being ambushed generally caused warriors to feel foolish, and no one liked that, even if the ambush had been totally unavoidable.

Henry wanted people he could depend on, and he knew that picking the right people required more than simply getting those whose alertness might have tipped them to the possibility of an ambush; he also wanted his people to be able to handle sudden floods of the hormones and emotional reactions engendered by alarms and humiliations, without losing their judgment.

Henry, along with all of his senior Soldiers, had been watching the reactions of these recruits—and of the other two sections of recruits, who were elsewhere at the moment—since they arrived; that evaluation process would continue as long as any of them were Soldiers.

It would take more than simply being caught flat-footed by this test ambush to get a recruit dropped from the class; just as it would take more than having done well here—or on any other test—to be accepted.

Henry had the recruits loaded into the vans, and on their way back to headquarters, within moments. He wanted them to be still in the reaction stage as they went back, so that they could be monitored and studied while they thought themselves free to relax.

Henry loved this job.

God help him, he knew that some of these young people would die as a result of his choosing them . . . but then, they were all in God's hands at all times, in any case.

CHAPTER 6

Pallas Salvador, head of the Others' organization on Ceta, was awakened by the shocking shrillness of her bedside communicator's *EMERGENCY* tone. Groggily peering at the time display, she fumbled hurriedly for the control pad, driven by that gut-level, unthinking fear that accompanies any sudden alarm in the night. But the fear gave way to irritation as she saw the call was from her own office.

Before answering she glanced reflexively behind her to be sure her companion from earlier in the evening had indeed left. Then she punched at the *ANSWER* button with a stiff, forceful index finger.

"Pallas Salvador, here," she said. "What is it?"

Professional. Be professional.

She tried to begin some breath-control exercises, recognizing that her irritation was showing.

"My apologies for disturbing you at this hour, Pallas Salvador," a calm, contralto voice said in her ear. There was no reproach in that voice; perversely, that irritated Pallas Salvador even more.

"Gelica? Is that you?" Pallas had recognized the voice as that of her assistant, who was normally in the office during conventional daytime working hours. "What are you doing in the office at this hour?"

"Yes, Pallas Salvador. The night communications officer called me first when a message arrived, in accordance with our procedures."

"A message? Why didn't you—yes, yes, what is it?"

"A communication has arrived, sent ahead from an incoming starship. It is from Antonia Lu."

Her irritation instantly wiped away by apprehension—along with her breathing exercises—Pallas took a short moment to think.

A message from Antonia Lu was for all intents and purposes a message from Bleys Ahrens, the de facto head of the Others.

"I'll be right in," Pallas said. Communications from the home office were not to be casually discussed over open comm circuits.

Starships were still the fastest way to send messages at interstellar distances, the now fully awake Other was thinking as she climbed into an automated cab twelve minutes later, but light-speed radio beat a starship that was on its approach to a planet. For that reason, the fastest—and most expensive—way to get a message to a planet under another star was to give it into the care of a ship's communications officer, paying extra to have it radioed ahead when the ship came out of its last phase-shift.

She wondered what could be so important that Bleys Ahrens would have sent her a message in that manner.

The Others' headquarters for Ceta was located in the city of the same name, comprising two floors of a tall office tower within walking distance of the government center, and nestled near the heart of the cluster of corporate campuses that made this city the commercial hub of the planet, and thus of a lot of interstellar trade. Pallas arrived there twenty-one minutes after being awakened.

She immediately learned she had every right to be apprehensive: the superscript on the message indicated it had been sent from *Burning Bush,* one of a number of starships of which the Others' organization was the majority owner. And Antonia Lu's message confirmed that both Bleys Ahrens himself and Dahno Ahrens were on board the vessel.

Bleys Ahrens, the message said, wanted to meet with all of the Others' top leadership on the planet as soon as he landed. *All* of them. A confirmation was required.

This was unprecedented. And unprecedented was invariably bad.

She grimaced, recognizing there was no choice but to comply.

"Send a confirmation to *Burning Bush*—just that, no more," she told Gelica.

She looked at her assistant challengingly, almost willing the gray-haired, stocky figure to make some gesture of rebellion. Gelica gave her nothing but a crisp nod.

"I want all the headquarters staff here within twenty minutes," Pallas continued, ignoring the fact that she herself had needed more time than that to make the trip, and her staff all lived farther out. "Then wake the top two caterers and get two spreads set up, one—wait: first call the port and get an estimated arrival time for *Burning Bush*—"

"I already have," Gelica said. "They say around ten and a half—and they also say they expect there to be a brief welcoming ceremony."

"Oh, that's right," Pallas said, "Bleys Ahrens is now a political dignitary, isn't he? All right then, the catering: one spread to be fresh at noon and the other at thirteen. Top-level spreads for a minimum of—let's say seventy people, just to be on the safe side."

"Who do you want alerted to attend the meeting?" Gelica asked.

"I guess you can't do it all at once," Pallas said. "When the first staff arrive, start—no, I'll do it. Just forward our complete TO to my screen right now, and then make those calls. While you're doing that I'll draft a list of attendees and send it back to you, and you can get them alerted—some will have to come around the planet, of course, so you'll need to get started."

She strode toward her office, then stopped and turned around.

"While you're waiting for the staff to arrive, start drafting a plan for the layout we'll need in the large conference room."

She closed the office door behind her, but Gelica's intercom beeped almost immediately.

"Yes, Pallas Salvador?" Gelica said.

"You'd better count on spending the day here, too," Pallas said. "I don't know whether Bleys Ahrens has it in mind to see any of our staff as well as the top leadership, but you're senior staff, so you'd better stay close."

"I will," Gelica said.

Alone in the front office, she smiled as she called up from the datafiles the table of organization Pallas Salvador had ordered. There was a great deal of trouble on the way, but it might be worth it. . . .

Having been met at the landing pad and recorded having his hand shaken by a variety of officials, Bleys was finally turned loose to be convoyed into the city; and he and some of his party, after quick greetings to the junior staff in the reception area of the Others' planetary head office, were led into the conference room some minutes after noon, local time. Many of the waiting Others' leadership—even those for whom this was the middle of the night—were visibly pleased to see Dahno, for whom they had all developed a great fondness during their time in the training program he had run them through on Association.

Bleys was quickly introduced to the more senior staff people, including some who had flown in with their particular bosses. Bleys was polite to each of them, but Dahno, he saw, was off to one side working his usual genial magic on all comers.

"And finally, Bleys Ahrens, this is Gelica Costanza, my top administrative assistant," Pallas Salvador said, as they at last reached the head table. Bleys found himself exchanging greetings with a short, blocky female figure with graying dark hair and a reddish complexion. Her gray-blue eyes, he saw, were sharp and alert.

"Are you from Ceta?" he asked her.

"I've spent much of my life here, Great Teacher," she said. "But I'm a crossbreed, too, born and raised on Mara."

Bleys knew she was too old to have gone through Dahno's training course, so she must have been a local hire, one result of Bleys' program to increase the size of the organization by reaching out to untrained Others. Apparently this one had worked out well.

On a sudden impulse, he turned to Pallas Salvador:

"How many of your senior leadership are here?" he asked. "Do we have any empty seats?"

"We called in forty-four," she said. "But only thirty-five have arrived so far."

"Nine are missing? Didn't they have enough time to get here?"

Standing behind Pallas Salvador and engaged in another conversation, Dahno turned his head. He said nothing as his eyes met Bleys'.

"They've all had at least seven hours' notice," Pallas Salvador said, embarrassed. "We've had no word from any of them, and their staff all say they don't know where their bosses are."

"Is it possible they're out on their routes?" Bleys asked. His question showed that he had been studiously reading the reports sent in from the Cetan Others: on this large planet, the small number of senior Others had developed a pattern of spreading their individual attention over a number of states, between which they moved like nomads tending their flocks.

"Their staff people would know where they were, in that case," Pallas pointed out. Then she grimaced, embarrassed at her own temerity, as Dahno moved over to stand beside Bleys, looking down at her.

"That seems strange," Dahno said, ignoring her discomfort. "Has anyone gone looking for them?"

"There's been no time."

"Can you have someone follow up right away?" Bleys said. "Have someone call the various transportation facilities; and if the missing people aren't found, arrange for dependable people to catch the first flights out to each of those offices."

"I'll do it myself," Pallas Salvador said, starting to turn away; Bleys put a hand on her arm.

"Not you," he said.

"I can do that," Gelica said.

"Not you, either," Bleys said, suddenly aware that he had been overlooking something. He turned to Pallas again, as Dahno silently moved off once more, to be greeted by another group of his old trainees.

"I want to start the meeting right away, and I want you both there. Toni—" He turned to look, and found she was right at his side and had been listening. "Can you do this?" he asked her.

"Of course," she said, "if I can borrow some of the local staffers who won't be wanted in the meeting." She was looking at Pallas Salvador as she said that.

"Certainly," Pallas said. "Gelica, find Sandra for us, won't you?"

"Right away," Gelica said; and raised her wristpad to her face, turning away slightly and activating the *HUSH* setting that kept her voice from being overheard as she spoke into the pad.

"Sandra used to hold Gelica's job," Pallas said, in a lower tone, to Bleys and Toni. "She left us when her husband was transferred to Azul, and has been working part-time in Janet Bovovo's office there. I suggest her for that job, Antonia Lu, because she has a lot of experience with our organization and will be obeyed by the junior staff, but is no longer considered senior staff, since she's just been working part-time. . . . Here she is now."

Toni left for the front office immediately, Sandra in tow, and Pallas and Gelica turned their attention back to Bleys. He was watching curiously as Toni and Sandra left.

"If she's only a part-timer in an outlying office, why is she even here?" he said as he turned to look at Pallas again.

"Janet—that's her boss—had to move fast to get here," Pallas said, "and she told me she just grabbed the nearest couple of staff people to accompany her." She leaned toward Bleys and continued in a confidential whisper: "The fact that Sandra's parents live here in Ceta City, and that her mother's been ill for some time, might have entered into the choice."

Bleys nodded. "I assume she's capable of the job?"

"Of course," Pallas said. "I depended on her, until she had to leave." She looked sideways at Gelica Costanza. "I didn't think I'd find someone able to replace her, but Gelica has been very good, too."

"That's good to know," Bleys said. "And since there are some open seats in the meeting, let's have some of the senior staff in there with us, too—but only," he raised one finger in emphasis, "Others, and only if you're sure they're absolutely dependable and committed to us."

A bit shocked, Pallas agreed; and between them, she and Gelica quickly winnowed through the list of senior staff on hand.

While he waited, Bleys rethought his idea of inviting some staff members to sit in. The idea had only just come to him, and he had had no time to think it through. If the notion was a good one, it had to be carried out quickly; and he had learned to trust the ideas that sometimes sprouted full-blown from the back of his mind.

His initial plan had been to use shock tactics on the Others' leaders attending the meeting, suspecting that one or more had been lazy, irresponsible or even corrupt; Pallas Salvador was the most likely candidate, in fact, given her top position here. But Gelica Costanza's presence, and her apparent importance, had suggested that local staff were more important in the Ceta operation than were staff on other worlds; so he decided to widen his range of inquiry to include them.

In less than ten minutes, almost everyone who was not invited to sit in had been shooed out, Toni making her way through them to come back into the room. The remaining chatter died swiftly as Bleys, who had remained standing, silenced Pallas Salvador's welcoming remarks with a gesture. He himself remained silent until one of his own staff signaled that the room was free of listening devices—and then that staffer, too, left. Now only Bleys, Dahno, Toni, the Association-trained Others and some of the senior Cetan staff were present.

"You may have heard," Bleys began, his voice soft enough that they almost—but not quite—had to strain to hear him, "that our people on New Earth, Newton and Cassida are now in strong position to influence the leaderships of those worlds."

Some in the audience nodded, and all their faces were intent. They had heard, in fact, that it was Bleys who had orchestrated a series of negotiations that resulted in those alliances—and they also knew that *influence* was not a strong enough word to describe the position the Others now occupied on those three planets.

"You've known," Bleys continued, "since soon after you joined this organization, that our ultimate goal has always been to become the ruling force on all the worlds." He paused, turning his head to look at Dahno, seated near him at the head table; he knew that the very drama in that pause would convey his message as effectively as any words he could speak.

Some had already caught on, he saw; and he looked about the room, making note of faces showing perception and eagerness.

"You are the ones who may find yourselves in at the very beginning of a new Ceta," he said, finally. Beside him, Dahno, playing his part, smiled broadly.

For the next few minutes Bleys eased his audience into the notion of taking control of the planet. It had to be done that way, he knew, because for all that they had been introduced to the idea of controlling the Worlds long ago, it was a very different thing to suddenly have the prospect looming up before them. Some of the faces in his audience showed fright, he thought; but even those also showed interest.

Which of them, if any, were the ones he was trying to smoke out—the ones who either had been working to conceal the true situation on this planet, or had been stunningly inept?

Does the fear mean they're more intelligent? he asked himself. Or just more timid? I'll have to know them better before I can answer that.

Within himself, he knew he was hardly likely to ever get the time to do that. He thought he understood now, a little better, why Dahno so strongly resisted the need to delegate responsibilities, even to his own, handpicked people.

Be careful, Bleys told himself now. *You can't afford to start believing everything you say. You're not here to take Ceta, and you can't forget this is only a ruse.*

But there was a rising tide of excitement in him, as if the deepest part of his mind sensed something approaching from beyond the horizon.

"The task we face is huge," Bleys continued, "and Dahno and I don't pretend to have a schematic to show you exactly how to do it. Ceta, as a large world comprised of a large number of independent states, presents a very different problem than did the monolithic planetary governments we dealt with on New Earth, Newton, Cassida—yes, and on Harmony and Association, too." He paused to sweep their faces with his eyes, one of his oldest attention-getting techniques.

"We are far too few to have any hope of really controlling the Worlds in detail," he went on. "Even after the recruiting efforts we've all been making for the past five years, our numbers remain minuscule in comparison to the populations of the Younger Worlds. And you know as well as I that many of the newly recruited Others will never receive the training some of you have gotten from Dahno and our organization—yes," he said, "if you haven't noticed, we're joined by some of your senior staff, who of course haven't had that training."

He paused for a moment, looking about the room.

"Our numbers long ago overran our ability to train people," he said. "While we will continue to train suitable candidates, more of the responsibility for training new recruits is going to have to fall on you people in the field—but Dahno will speak of that in more detail later."

Beside him, his brother nodded, now looking serious.

"You must never forget," Bleys went on, "that going through Dahno's training program is not what makes one an Other. You who are here from the staff are Others—you always have been—and neither you nor the trained Others who are your leaders can ever forget that."

There was a small stir in the room.

"There's hope," Bleys said. "I know you're all aware that one of the major keys to the success of our organization has been our unique ability to influence other people, to persuade them to trust us and follow our lead. But I tell you now, if you haven't realized it already: not all who get chosen for training display the persuasive abilities that have allowed us to get this far."

There were troubled frowns among his audience now.

"That doesn't mean those people aren't Others," he said. "Never think that. Just as in the remainder of the human race, some have higher levels of talent than do others."

He paused, trying to refocus them by his brief silence.

"Dahno and I," he continued after a moment, "have been working to develop techniques that may help us multiply the effects of our powers; and before too long we'll all be talking about that. But none of you must ever forget those Others who haven't been able to receive our training—like the members of your senior staff; they've been loyal, and they, too, will share in our future."

Smiles broke out, not only on the faces of the staff people, but on those of some of the top Others.

"Now to the more specific matter of Ceta," Bleys said. Faces sobered.

"Dahno and I have been working among the Worlds," he continued. "We face different challenges out there than you do, here on your target world. But don't ever think we're unaware of your work. Your work is vital to our work; we know that . . . and our work *is* your work, in the long run."

He paused, looking at them seriously; then leaned forward, bending over the table with his extended arms supporting his bowed shoulders while he tilted his head to look into their faces.

"At the same time, you must never forget," he said, his voice lower, more serious, less comradely, "that you were set up here for the purpose of carrying out the organization's mission. And that mission is not limited only to Ceta. The organization—the Others—*we*—" He raised himself from the table as he raised his voice again, sweeping his arms in great circles to include them all in his words. "—we have a larger mission, among all the Younger Worlds."

He could see them reacting positively to that message, smiling, bringing their heads up.

"You all live and work here," he went on softly. "That's your job. But Dahno and I are the ones who've been out among the Worlds. We're the ones who see the bigger picture."

He paused, looking from side to side. His next words were uttered so quietly they almost had to strain to hear him.

"That's how we've learned the things that tell us the time is now ripe for the next step," he said. "But we, Dahno and I, don't have the necessary expertise about Ceta—its situation, its needs and wants, even its idiosyncrasies.

"However—" He nodded, confidentially, at them. "—we know where to come to get that expertise: here!" Two of his audience actually laughed, as if afflicted by some spasm, before silencing themselves abruptly.

"Yes," Bleys said. "You, who have been here on the ground all these years—you're our experts. So we've come to consult with you."

The faces were smiling, the eyes gleaming.

"Of course, officially Dahno and I are here to visit the troops," he said, with an air of one letting them in on a secret. "But we've learned a lot in dealing with five other worlds, and now we think we—all of us—may be in a position to make something happen that will mean your work hasn't been wasted."

They spent the afternoon in collegial fashion, snacking from the extensive sideboards and discussing the prospects. Sometimes they all listened to individual comments following up on particular thoughts; at other times they separated into smaller groups, which formed, broke up, and were replaced by different combinations. There was discussion about whether to continue to work with the multitude of local governments, or whether it might in the long run be more effective to try to encourage the formation of a planetary government. A single planetary government could be more efficiently controlled by their relatively small numbers, they all clearly agreed; but they also agreed that creating such an entity within any reasonable period of time would be virtually impossible.

Bleys was pleased to hear that particular discussion; it set them up nicely for what he had planned for later.

As the afternoon drew to a close, he could see that fatigue was sapping their enthusiasm. He withdrew gracefully from the particular group he had been listening to, and made his way back to the head table, where he used his wrist control pad to play tones that got their attention.

Dahno, involved in another discussion, turned and started to move toward the head table; but after a few steps he stopped, simply listening from the crowd.

"We've had a big day," Bleys told his audience now, "and I'm going to suggest we adjourn, in a few moments, to sleep on it. But before we do, let me mention a lesson we've learned from our experiences on other worlds: the fastest route to being able to wield influence on a planetary scale, is to locate some organization already set up on that scale—and coopt it.

"For the most part, it hardly matters if that organization's ideas and purposes differ radically from ours," he went on. "If only someone has such an organization already in place, we can get them to hand it over to us, already staffed—and even to support us as we bend it to our will."

He stopped to raise both arms up and behind his head, in a lazy, tension-relieving stretch that made them all aware of how long they had been cooped up in the conference room.

"I don't know if that can work on Ceta, though," he said, as if musing to himself. "Your reports have never mentioned that any such organization exists here. In fact, not even the potential for such an organization."

He yawned, and stood up.

"Think about it," he said. "And you'll have time to do so, since Dahno and I have to appear at some minor diplomatic functions for a few days, and then go out to visit the Friendly troops. We'll be all around the planet; but if we're needed, Pallas Salvador—" He turned to look at her. "—will know where to find us at any given time. Keep in mind that we're going to have our hands full.

"For now, get some rest; then take a few days to think about all the things we've discussed. Consult with each other, if you're so inclined—or whatever helps you, individually, think better. If you can come up with suggestions for coordinated action, we'll all want to hear them." He smiled tiredly. "Shall we say, eight days from now, at noon, here?"

CHAPTER 7

On the second day of their visits to leased Friendly troops, Bleys overrode his local driver and had his limousine turn off their scheduled route, separating from the rest of his official party and reaching, in slightly more than an hour, the coordinates he had been given for the place where Will MacLean, along with the rest of his unit, had been buried. They had all spent the previous night in a very good hotel, but Bleys had to wonder how much sleep Henry had gotten.

His uncle, as usual, showed no signs of either fatigue or emotional reaction.

"Was this a good idea?" Dahno whispered, as they stood beside their vehicle on the edge of an unpaved and overgrown roadway, looking out across a featureless field. Their view was poor, because the field sloped slightly downhill from their position; anything that might once have been visible was totally obscured by the brush.

"You know it was," Toni answered for Bleys. "How would Henry feel if we went back to Association without even trying to find his son's grave? Not that he would ever say anything, of course."

"I know, I know . . . you're right." Dahno looked about. "But where exactly is the cemetery? It's been years, and it looks like everything's been overgrown—all I see is a field full of nasty-looking weeds."

Henry, who had been standing several meters in front of the others, up to his knees in drying vegetation and facing a wide gap in the weathered wooden fence, chose that moment to stride down into the field. Toni immediately followed, accompanied by Bleys, and Dahno trailed.

If the field they were crossing had ever been under cultivation,

Bleys could not tell it. The surface, hidden by tussocks of a dried-out grasslike plant, was uneven, and he quickly discovered that a foot incautiously planted on the edge of one of those clumps of vegetation was likely to slide sideways into a hidden narrow patch of bare dirt. Henry turned to warn the others of the danger of a twisted ankle, and they slowed their pace; but Henry himself seemed to move as fast as before over the broken footing.

The going was made even more difficult in those spots where the tussocks were obscured by the longer, still-green blades of a different plant that sprang up around and among them. Three of the party, at least, quickly found that the green blades were sharp-edged and needle-pointed, able to work their way through the light material of trousers meant for urban wear. The three younger ones began to weave so as to avoid the worst-looking patches, but Henry's strides never wavered from the direct line he seemed to be set on. The others only caught up with him when he stopped.

They came up behind Henry as he looked down on a foot-high block of pale gray granite, roughly hewn on the sides but polished on top. For the first moment, the others stood in a row behind him, but as he continued to stand without sound or movement, they moved up beside him.

A simple cross had been incised into the polished top surface of the stone. Beneath it was a legend:

Here lie 27 men of the Militia of Association,
who were blessed with death in the service of our God.

In the silence, a stiff breeze fluted softly among the reedlike weeds. Bleys had prepared himself to deal with some sort of emotional reaction when this moment came, but he found he was numbed, as if his feelings had been removed from his body and deposited on the other side of the planet.

The stone before them seemed to connect to nothing, to be only a neutral and dead object. It had nothing to do with his young cousin—and with that thought, he remembered the day it had been abruptly decided that he, Bleys, must leave Henry's farm and move into Ecumeny.

Will had reached up to hug his tall cousin, and Bleys had returned the hug—so strange a thing for him to do . . . and with that memory the reaction Bleys had feared rose up in him after all. But it was far worse than he had imagined, and he was totally unprepared for the chaos that fell on his mind.

It was as if he had been treacherously abandoned by that rational watcher in the back of his head, who in the past had always guided him, shielded him from the dangers of emotional crises, by keeping him separate from the world. His vision blurred, and his mouth flooded with saliva, so that he had to gulp to keep from choking; the effort made his nose burn inside.

His legs trembled with a wild impulse to turn on his heels and walk away, and he knew if he did so he would have to discipline his steps, to keep that walk from turning into a run. He was vaguely aware that his breathing had become rapid and shallow, and he could not seem to order his eyes to come back into focus . . . and as he hung there, motionless and struggling, some thoughtless level of his mind futilely tried to pick a tune out of the sound of the wind in the weeds.

His memories, out of his control, skipped from that leavetaking through a series of fragments, bits and pieces that he felt rather than saw: Henry holding a gun on the crowd in the churchyard . . . his mother turning from her mirror to look at him with murder in her eyes . . . the sound of a sword searching for him in a darkened corridor . . . They popped into his head and then blew away, without being worked on by his rational mind at all; as if it had all happened to someone else, and he was held immobile, forced to watch someone else's life story.

Looming like a wall behind all those memories lay the searing experience of the night he had received Joshua's letter telling him of Will's death—but that memory, too, was like a story related by a stranger. He could not really remember his emotions of that moment—he remembered the fact of them, and that he had found his fist in the wall of his hotel room; but the emotions themselves were gone, as if consigned to lie here with Will.

He did not want to remember. His mind was a repugnant jumble . . . but his rational watcher still failed to reach out with a comment that could serve as a lifeline to his accustomed control.

Immobilized, afraid to react, he stood there in an agonized eternity . . . and after a while he found his mind was noting the way the breeze tugged at his clothing. The tide of emotion had swept over him and passed on; he had survived it unchanged, and could begin to look outside himself once more.

In his peripheral vision he could see motion that was Toni's hair being ruffled by the breeze; something kept him from looking directly at her face. Henry was beyond her, but Bleys did not try to look at him.

After a few moments, Henry spoke, softly: "Thy will be done—that day, now, and forever."

What remained of the spell broke. Bleys looked at Toni, to see a tear creeping down her cheek. There must have been an earlier one, he thought, because this one was following a moistened track.

Bleys still saw no sign of emotion in Henry's face, or in his body language.

Henry turned without another word, and started back to their vehicle, Dahno beside him. Toni put a hand on Bleys' arm, holding him back.

"Is this all there is?" she asked. She seemed to be trying to whisper, but anger made her words carry farther than she intended, and Henry stopped and looked back at them.

"What do you mean?" Bleys asked.

"Look at this!" she exclaimed, her arm swinging out in a great semicircle that took in the whole of the weed-overgrown field. "They buried these young men and just went away, and no one even bothers to—to *mow* these, these *weeds!*"

She blinked, looking up into his face, her eyes filling with moisture.

"They never even put those boys' names on that stone!" And she sobbed, once, so quietly that it seemed almost a gulp.

As Bleys stood there, at a total loss for words, Henry spoke.

"I know you speak out of your heart, Antonia," he said. "But you are mistaken."

He shook his head, a gentle smile on his face.

"Such things as this monument are mere vanities, placed here as a sop to our weaknesses," he continued. "These young men need them not. They have carried out their duty to the fullest extent of their abilities, and now rest with their God, Who is well-satisfied with them. And His embrace is all they need."

He smiled directly at Toni, raising a hand—almost in blessing, Bleys thought.

"If these young men lay in unmarked graves," Henry said, "unknown to all the human race, it would make no difference. For the Lord knows them, and that is all that will ever be needed."

He started to turn away; but stopped once more, turning to look at Toni again.

"I understand that your concern is for me, Antonia," he said. "And I would not have you think me ungrateful. But there is no need for concern in this matter. God has blessed my human weakness by bringing me to this place, for some purpose of His own. I am grateful, yet it changes nothing."

On their way back to their vehicle, its driver popped out of its door, waving at them.

"Hurry!" she yelled. "Move it! Emergency!"

Seeing them speed up, she turned back to the limousine; and by the time they reached the vehicle its doors were open, the engine was running, and a comm channel was being piped through to the rear compartment's speakers.

"—not return the way you came," a voice was saying. "We're working out the fastest way to get an escort to you, but get moving right now! Go north, and then take the first east you come to. By that time we'll have instructions for you."

"I've got it," their driver said. She looked back at her passengers through the now-open privacy window that usually screened off the rear compartment.

"Secure yourselves," she said; and almost immediately a burst of acceleration blew them up above the roadway and down it in the direction they had been facing, the initial cloud of dust their fans threw up quickly dying down behind them as they rose to greater height.

"Driver, what is it?" Bleys asked. He put into his question all the authority he could muster, not wanting to let her take total control of the situation.

"Your convoy was attacked," the driver said, keeping her attention on the forward windscreen. "A bomb blew up the front of the Hotel Monaco as your convoy drove up. The government's sending an escort to take you to a safe place."

"Is there any word on casualties?" Toni asked.

"No one told me anything about that," the driver said. "Hang on—turn coming up!"

She took the turn at speed and managed to keep control even though they slid far enough off the roadway to bounce off the fence on their left side.

"Carl," Bleys heard Henry's voice say from beyond Toni, "what is your situation?" After a few seconds Henry's second-in-command answered:

"Henry, we're all right," Carl said. "A few bumps and bruises, but the blast occurred before we had fully pulled up, and we were partly shielded by a local delivery van . . . there were a number of casualties among the locals."

"God be with them," Henry said. "We need a rendezvous. I understand—"

"Get off the air *now!*" a new voice interrupted them. "This is Area Command, New Francisco, ordering you to stand down and maintain radio silence!"

Bleys gestured Henry to silence even as he leaned across Toni's front to grasp his uncle's left wrist and lift it before his own face.

"This is Bleys Ahrens," he said, using his authoritative voice, "First Elder of the United Sects of Harmony and Association. We are here—" He was cut off.

"We understand, First Elder," the voice replied. "An armed escort is on its way to you now, and we request that your—" The voice paused for the briefest of moments. "—staff please avoid interfering with military operations."

Henry reached over to silence the comm link.

"They mean it," he said. "They've been embarrassed."

"So what should we do?" Bleys asked.

"Nothing," Henry replied. "Carl can't beat the military to us, so we might as well cooperate."

"Do you need to tell Carl that?"

"No," Henry said. "He'll understand what to do—interactions with the military are always included in our contingency planning."

"So he'll just wait for the military to reunite us?" Bleys asked.

Henry touched the control that closed the window into the driver's compartment, then reached under his seat for the traveling case in which he carried a variety of useful items. He quickly pulled out a monitor and scanned for listening devices, then activated its inhibiting field, just in case; he had scanned the vehicle before they entered it, but they all understood he was determined to take no further chances.

Next to him, Dahno reached into a pocket and pulled out a small silver device. He held it out before the rest of them, looking a question at them.

"No," said Bleys. "Not here and now. It's not really meant for a confined space like this."

Bleys was referring to a device they had obtained on Newton, some time back. Activated, it would generate a force-bubble preventing anyone from overhearing their words.

"Yes and no," Henry said a moment later, responding to Bleys' question. "Carl and a number of the Soldiers will likely stay visible enough to let the locals think they've got them under control; but he'll probably send some of them undercover—perhaps with the aid of some of the people from *Favored of God*, who of course are not known to be with us—and put them to monitoring our situation at a distance. And he'll already have alerted the people we left in Ceta City."

"All right," Bleys said.

"Can we trust these military people?" Dahno asked.

"No," Henry said. "Not in everything. But chances are very good that whoever planted that bomb had no backup attack ready to go. It will have taken them some time just to learn they didn't get you, in any case—and they won't know where you are unless they have ears in the military."

"Which they might," Dahno said.

"Which they might," Henry agreed. "But until we return to an urban area and some independent transportation, we have no better option."

"We need to figure out who would have done this," Dahno said.

"Yes," Bleys added. "And we need to think about changing our plans."

"Security is what we need above all," Henry said. "I have a few ideas. . . ."

They spent the next twenty minutes comparing ideas and making plans, breaking off when the driver signaled for their attention.

"You probably can't hear it because of the soundproofing back there," she said over the intercom, "but we've got two helicopters overhead. Our escort is here."

"Are you sure they're with our escort?" Dahno asked.

"It's confirmed by Area Command," the driver replied. "They tell me the armored cars will be coming into sight in a moment." After a moment's pause she spoke again.

"They're serious," she said. "I mean, there aren't very many helicopters on the whole planet. They're just too expensive and too vulnerable. . . ."

"I know," Bleys said, hoping to forestall a lecture on the shortage of metals on the Younger Worlds. "Are we going to stop here?"

"No," said the driver. "I've been told to just keep going, and they'll fit the escort in around us as we go."

As she spoke, the ground component of their escort came into sight ahead of them; and by activating the video screen that gave them a forward view, those in the passenger compartment were able to watch as the first four armored cars pulled off the roadway, leaving a lane up which their limousine could proceed without slowing. Ahead of them, the last four armored cars in the group could be seen spinning end for end, to take up station preceding them and accelerate.

CHAPTER 8

The escort sent by the New Franciscan government led them to a small town about seventy kilometers from the burial site, where they stopped in a public park that was bordered on two sides by the town's tiny commercial district. As their escort's weapons menaced the nearby buildings, it was strongly suggested they abandon their limousine and proceed, riding inside the armored cars, to the security of a government facility.

Bleys' initial refusal raised enough consternation among the New Franciscans that no one noticed when Henry slipped away; in fact, Bleys, Toni and Dahno went on to make such a production out of agreeing to be split up for the trip, and then of agreeing on a destination, that Henry was not missed when they all loaded up and left town.

As they drove away Bleys could see their limousine being left behind, its driver casually lounging on a small bench nearby. She had removed her dark green tunic, perhaps because of the warmth of the sunlight, and her white shirt gleamed in the brightness, startling above her green livery trousers.

Too casual, he thought.

On their arrival at the border with Andrade, a neighboring state, they were met by officials of the governments of both Cetan states, as well as by people from the nearest Friendly consulate. No one seemed to know who had carried out the bombing, and it was not even considered certain that it had in fact been intended for Bleys and his party. But the assembled officialdom agreed it would be the wisest course for Bleys to withdraw from his itinerary and return to the safety of Ceta City.

Bleys, however, insisted that his visits to the troops would go on; and at last, as a concession, he agreed to alter the originally scheduled order of the visits, and to accept the military escorts that would be provided by the governments of every state they entered.

"The last thing I want is for these people to hover over me," he told Toni. "I still have work to do here."

Bleys' bodyguards could be brought along, they were told, if they agreed to be disarmed. Bleys declined the offer, pointing out that unarmed bodyguards were of little value. However, he requested that at least two of his staff people, along with his personal medician, Kaj Menowsky, be allowed to join them; but that request had been anticipated, and three of the staff arrived even as they prepared to leave.

Kaj Menowsky, the staff reported, had been concussed in the bombing, and had been hospitalized. Such medical care as Bleys and his party might need, the locals informed him, would be immediately provided by their hosts.

Unwilling to explain about his unusual medical condition, Bleys decided not to press the issue.

Early the next morning they were placed aboard a shuttle that took them more than a third of the way around the planet, arriving late in the day at a sizable, and well-guarded, encampment of Friendly Militia. This visit was kept out of the Cetan media, but was recorded for later broadcast; and thereafter they spent the night in the secure, if less than luxurious, midst of the troops.

In the morning they moved on in a couple of civilian vehicles, again surrounded by an escort provided by the local government.

It was only after they had left the Friendly unit some distance behind that trouble arose once again.

The Cetan state they had spent the night in, the Solomon Hills Republic, although an independent entity, had been part of an alliance during the recent war; and since the allied states had acted together in hiring the Friendly troops that had bolstered their own military establishments, units of those Friendly forces were deployed in a number of locations. But the escort the Cetans insisted on providing was made up of local troops; no one, Dahno suggested wryly, wanted armed Friendly troops moving freely about the countryside, for all that they were supposed to be on the same side and there was a truce in place.

They were roughly halfway to the unit they were to visit next when their escort, a full company from the best mechanized infantry division among the Solomoni forces—or so they had been told—came to a halt, pulling off the wide, paved trafficway to park in a lushly green field, one of the few flat spots in a region of low, rolling hills. Bleys, Toni and Dahno climbed out of their limousine, hoping to learn why they had stopped.

In a few moments they were approached by the captain in charge of their escort, an older man who had largely ignored his charges up to this point. Now he seemed pleased to report there had been a flare-up in the fighting nearby; he was, he said, taking his unit off in pursuit of a party of raiders that had just attacked a small outpost behind the line of truce. For the protection of Bleys and his party, he was leaving them two armored cars—and also sending the two civilian limousines back; Bleys and his people were to continue the trip inside two armored troop carriers.

The company had formed itself, and the two limousines were vanishing down the road, when the captain returned to speak to them one last time, a nasty grin on his face.

"I didn't trust those people from the beginning," he said. "And now they're gone I'll tell you your escort is going to change its route, too. You're going off the road and directly cross-country toward your destination. These ducted-fan vehicles don't need the road, so while it'll be a little uncomfortable, you'll be safe."

He turned away, ignoring attempts to engage him in a dialogue, and strode aggressively over to his command vehicle. Ducking inside it, he immediately popped out of the hatch in its topside, giving a hand signal that started the unit in motion.

The company was already disappearing over a thinly treed rise when an apologetic junior lieutenant appeared, to repeat that they were ordered to leave the trafficway. He shepherded them into the two troop carriers; and in moments the vehicles rose on their fans and crossed the paved road, tilting alarmingly for a moment as they slid down the embankment on the other side, before leveling out on the rock-strewn terrain that fell away unevenly from the road.

Inside one of the carriers, Bleys found himself becoming distinctly uneasy. Dahno was clearly thoroughly irritated by these events, as well as by the cramped, dusty conditions, but Toni, Bleys saw, was calm and watchful.

They shared the carrier's center compartment with six young soldiers; and all of them were reduced to perching on the small benches that lined the carrier's interior, their hands clutching straps as the vehicle, for all that its fans kept it above the rough ground, bounced and swayed in crossing the terrain at a relatively high speed.

Bleys was beginning to wish his medician had been able to join them. He could feel a headache coming on, accompanied by a sick, feverish achiness. Apparently it showed enough that Toni was concerned about him.

Bleys tried to make an unobtrusive check of his wristpad, to be sure it was continuing to emit the periodic homing signals Henry had suggested. He noticed that Dahno and Toni did the same thing.

They appeared to be making good time, but the young officer now in charge of this detachment was in one of the armored cars, and would not communicate with them beyond having a subordinate tell them they were less than an hour from the Friendly unit they had intended to visit next.

Bleys' feeling that something was wrong got all the confirmation it needed when the lead armored car exploded ahead of their own vehicle. The blast front caused their own carrier to rear like a frightened animal and then plunge down the side of a narrow gulley; they never learned whether the driver did so in order to avoid further attack, but as they went over the edge a bolt from some sort of power weapon caved in the roof above them, despite its armor.

The carrier hit bottom almost on its side, but Bleys managed to hang on to his strap, to avoid falling across the width of the vehicle's interior, while swinging out an arm to help Toni keep her seat on his left side. Across the vehicle, Dahno had been thrown back against the wall, entangled with soldiers who were thrown at the wall in the same moment.

The gyros whined, righting the carrier enough that the fans could level it out, and the vehicle began to move forward down the length of the gulley. But almost immediately a series of bolts slammed into its front, opening the driver's compartment and shredding its interior, and its crew, back to the firewall that protected the passenger compartment. All power went off, and the vehicle settled to the dirt floor of the gulley even as it nosed into the bank on their right side.

Dahno pushed a body away and lunged for the hatch's manual controls, but Bleys grabbed his shoulder, trying to hold him back.

"I don't think it's a good idea to go out there," Bleys said.

"We have to," his brother shouted. "We're sitting ducks in here!"

"At least in here we have some armor," Bleys said. He was trying to keep his voice low so as to defuse the emotions they were all feeling now.

"That won't last long," Dahno said, more quietly. "There's only one exit left here, and if it's not already covered it soon will be. Outside, we might be able to make it to some cover."

Before Bleys could respond there was a sudden burst of firing from above them. "That's coming from where we fell over the side," Toni said.

"Yes," Bleys said. "And it doesn't seem to be directed at us."

"It's the other armored car," one of the young soldiers said. He was looking out now through one of the weapons apertures from which their vehicle, although now disabled, could normally be defended. With the power off, the video screens were no longer working, but there was light both from the emergency lighting system and a narrow opening where a seam in the distorted roof had pulled apart.

As the soldier ceased speaking they could hear a rapid series of ticking noises, like an irregular drumroll on the side of their vehicle. The soldier ducked down, turning to look for instructions, or perhaps reassurance; the corporal in charge of their detail had struck his head in the fall, and was just starting to regain consciousness.

"Cone rifle fire," Bleys said; and Dahno sat back down.

"It can't possibly penetrate our armor," Bleys said reassuringly;

and at that moment they heard a renewed series of bolts from the power cannon of the armored car. The cone rifles went silent.

In a moment there came a loud rapping on the hatch of their vehicle. Bleys reached for the manual override.

"It'd better be our guys," Dahno muttered.

Bleys chose not to respond as the hatch unsealed, then popped forward in its track and slid to the side.

"Are you all right, sir?" It was the young lieutenant who had been refusing to speak with them, now looking in at them from the brightly sunlit gulley floor.

"Yes, Lieutenant, I think so," Bleys replied. "What's the situation, please?"

"We've been attacked," the young man replied. Then he blushed. "Of course you knew that . . . I'm sorry." He seemed, Bleys thought, to have loosened up with the action.

"Don't be," Toni said. "We're very glad you got to us before those people managed to open us up."

"Is anyone hurt in your carrier?" the young officer asked.

"I don't know about the people up front," Bleys said, "but your soldiers were tossed around, and the corporal's just coming to—"

"I'm fine, sir," the corporal said from somewhere behind Bleys.

"I'll take a report in a minute," the lieutenant said; and turned his gaze back to Bleys.

"I think this vehicle isn't going to be moving for a long time," Bleys said. "We need to transfer to another vehicle and get away from here, unless you're confident you've driven off whoever attacked us."

"That's not going to be easy," the young officer said. He seemed to have recovered his composure. "Our communications are jammed, and the only vehicle we have left is my armored car, which can't hold all of us."

"Where are the enemy?" Bleys asked.

"My sergeant is out scouting right now," the lieutenant said.

"Have you taken many casualties?" Toni asked.

"Yes," the officer said, his face tightening and turning a little pale. There was a sort of longing in his eyes as he looked at Bleys, as if he were wishing that the uncomfortable questions were coming from a superior officer rather than a female civilian. "They took out the lead armored car with some sort of rocket, and another one took off the back half of the other troop carrier. Sergeant Lemoyne got out of it, along with about a dozen men, a couple of them wounded. One of your staff people got out, too, but I'm afraid he ran right into the sights of the cone rifles."

"Oh, no . . . ," Toni said softly.

"What do you suggest we do?" Bleys felt he had to ask, despite being unsure of how much he could trust this young officer's judgment.

"Your party will get inside the armored car immediately," the lieutenant said. "We can get some, possibly all, of the wounded in with you. We'll have to take a chance and send the car off in whatever direction seems to be safest in light of my sergeant's report."

"And the rest of you?" Toni asked.

"That will depend on the situation." The lieutenant was evading her question, Bleys thought. His estimate of the young man began to rise a little.

"Meaning you intend to leave some of your force—including yourself, I suspect—behind," Toni said flatly.

"They may be needed to provide cover," the lieutenant said. "And the car would have to be slowed to a walking pace if it tried to stay with us. Speed is your best defense, I think."

"He's right, Toni," Dahno said. She looked dissatisfied, but had no response.

"Sergeant Lemoyne is coming back, sir," a soldier yelled down from above the gulley.

"In any case, let's get you up to the car," the officer said. As they scrambled out of the hatch he directed a couple of his men to help them climb the gulley side, using a narrow, less steep, connecting ravine.

Their escort, making use of power pistols to blast a series of shallow steps in the steeper parts of the slanting walls, soon had them up on the rolling grassy surface from which they had fallen. As Bleys, the last one up, came over the edge, he could see the smoldering wrecks of the two ruined vehicles, as well as several sprawled bodies. He also saw the lieutenant return a salute from his sergeant, who turned away and began organizing the nearby soldiers.

"If you would all get in the armored car, please?" the lieutenant said.

"What did your scouts find?" Bleys asked, ignoring the order for the moment while waving Toni and Dahno forward.

"The enemy seem to be in force back the way we came," the officer replied. "And we expect they'll be looking for us to continue on the shortest line toward protection—the way we were going, I mean."

"That's to be expected," Bleys nodded.

"Yes, sir," the lieutenant said. "So I'm sending the armored car on a perpendicular axis to the right of our line of travel. That will take you over the rise there—please don't look in that direction."

"You think someone might be watching us?" Bleys said.

"Frankly, I don't," the officer said. "But I'd rather not take chances."

Bleys nodded, impressed.

"Please continue," he said.

"This area was fought over last year," the lieutenant said. "That was before I was activated, but the sergeant went through this area during that campaign, and he believes there were some light fortifications in that direction. There might be a chance of finding some landlines we can tap into and call for help; and if nothing else, it might give us a place where those of us on foot can be under cover while the car moves on to send back help."

"All right, Lieutenant," Bleys said. "Tell us what you want us to do."

"Get into the car, please," the officer said.

"Are you coming with us?" Bleys said. He was pretty sure he knew the answer by now.

"No," the young man said. "I'll stay with my men."

"Aren't you afraid someone might say you should have stayed with the people you were assigned to protect?" Bleys was now genuinely curious, intrigued by the unexpected maturity he was seeing in this very young officer.

"No," the man said now. He looked at Bleys more closely. "I don't think you're asking that to try to get me to go with you, are you?" he said.

"No," Bleys said, "I'm not."

The young man nodded, seeming satisfied.

"We're leaving the car in the hands of its normal crew," he said. "The rest of us are going to fan out in a double arc to provide cover when the car takes off. I'll take charge on one side of the arc, Sergeant Lemoyne the other."

"I'll leave you to your work, then, Lieutenant," Bleys said. He nodded, and turned to climb into the armored car. In the doorway he paused, looking back at the young officer, who was already moving away.

CHAPTER 9

The inside of the armored car was crowded, and Bleys, Dahno and Toni, all wearing bulky blast protection jackets, were confined to the vehicle's central well. The two tall men had to stand, crouching under the hatch that opened to the car's topside. Toni had been given a padded helmet, but there were none large enough for the heads of the two men. Dahno's protective jacket would not close over his chest.

The six wounded soldiers had taken up so much space that the car's driver and one gunner were the only healthy soldiers who could be fitted in. The driver was carrying out his orders to move as fast as he could, with the result that everyone was tossed about, the conscious among the wounded crying out involuntarily at the worst bounces.

The speed did them no good. They had gotten less than a mile when an explosion tore up the front of the armored car, bringing it to a sudden halt that threw everyone around, and leaving it tilted sharply down toward the front.

Toni, who had been sitting awkwardly on the coated polyfiber floor at Bleys' feet, was pitched sideways into his legs, and he fell over her, taking a blow on the side of his head from the edge of the central well; but he managed to get his arms down as he fell, taking most of his weight on them rather than on her. The car began to fill with smoke.

Bleeding from a cut on the side of his head, Bleys regained his balance and pulled himself over Toni and between two of the wounded soldiers, who appeared to be unconscious. Reaching the hatch at the rear of the armored car, he threw it open and scrambled out, turning to help Toni, who had crawled right behind him and, lying on her stomach partially out of the car, was scrabbling to pull herself through the tilted hatchway. He set her on her feet and reached back to give Dahno a hand as he dragged an unconscious soldier to the opening.

"What about the rest of them?" Bleys asked.

"The driver's dead," Dahno replied, stooping forward to get his head out into the cleaner air. "And most of the others were closer to the driver's compartment and took more of the blast than we did . . . I think there can't be more than one or two still alive—" At that moment a secondary explosion rocked the vehicle again, pitching Dahno out the hatch onto Bleys, who, hampered by his hold on the wounded man, was knocked down again. A fresh wave of toxic smoke poured from the hatch.

"Forget it!" Dahno yelled now, struggling to his feet. "I think some ammunition went off, and between that and the smoke, no one can be alive in there anymore."

"Over here!" Bleys heard Toni call. He needed a moment to locate her.

She had found a cluster of low, flat rocks and was crouching in an opening between two of the largest of them, waving at them. Bleys and Dahno scrambled over the rough ground in her direction, struggling to carry the dead weight of the unconscious man between them; and threw themselves down into whatever low spots they could find among the rocks, just as cone rifle fire opened up from beyond the smoking ruin of the armored car.

"We're in trouble now!" Dahno gasped. Incredibly, he sounded almost cheerful about it. Even as he spoke there was a new burst of firing—this time from power weapons. They ducked as low as they could and kept quiet, but Bleys was unable to keep himself from trying to look in the direction from which the firing had come.

In a few minutes he was rewarded by the sight of soldiers led by the young lieutenant. They came on rapidly in a skirmish line that swept to and beyond the ruined vehicle, spreading out in a great arc about Bleys' position. The lieutenant turned and began to trot in Bleys' direction; but when he saw Bleys looking at him, he stopped and waved for them to move toward him, half-turning to point in the direction in which their vehicle had been heading, at a small ridge that made the horizon seem startlingly near.

"There's a trench and a bunker just over that rise," he yelled as Bleys stood up. The young officer had lost his helmet and his face was smeared and dirty, as if he had been thrown into the dirt repeatedly. The whites of his eyes stood out against the dirt, seeming to be wide-open and glaring. He turned to trot in the direction he had indicated.

"Come on!" Bleys said, turning to look for Toni. She was already up, and Dahno was rising, trying to pull the wounded soldier up with him. Bleys stepped over to help, and found himself interrupted as several more soldiers showed up, rounding the rocks to both sides of the civilians.

"Thank you, but we'll take care of him," one of the soldiers, a corporal, said. "Head for the lieutenant, there. We'll be behind you."

"Thank you," Toni said; and for a short instant Bleys marveled at the politeness everyone was displaying. Toni pulled at his arm, and he found himself running beside her. Turning his head, he saw Dahno—not exactly running, but moving at a fast walking pace that managed to cover ground effectively. He seemed to be breathing hard. The small group of soldiers behind them were also in motion, but more slowly.

The lieutenant and several of his men had stopped, crouching cautiously at the top of the rise and apparently trying to ascertain what might be on the other side. As Bleys ran he saw three of the soldiers get up, trot over the top of the rise, and disappear. Their officer waited, looking back as his three civilian charges neared, puffing.

"Just wait here for a moment," the lieutenant said. "My men are checking out the bunker ahead."

"Will we use that, if it's safe?" Toni asked.

"I don't think we have much choice," the lieutenant said, looking back in the direction from which they had come. They turned to look with him, in time to see a line of armed figures close in on . the armored car they had just left. Some of the figures raised long, slim weapons, and cones began whistling in their direction.

Bleys found himself being pushed backward, over the top of the rise; and looked to his side to see that the young lieutenant had him by one arm and was yelling at him . . . strangely, Bleys could not seem to understand what the man was saying.

That realization jolted his mind back into action, and he turned his back on the enemy and plunged ahead in great lunging strides that totally cleared much of the most uneven parts of the reverse slope. He could see Toni and Dahno a short distance ahead of him. Toni was looking back at him frequently as she ran, which slowed her down to Dahno's pace; and Bleys was catching up to them quickly.

"Keep your eyes forward," he yelled at her, waving one hand as if to push her faster. He wanted to tell her they could not afford it if she lost her footing, but he had no breath to spare.

The two ahead of him were nearing a kind of ditch, above which two soldiers were standing, waving them ahead.

Bleys had lost track of the lieutenant again, but another soldier, a very young woman, had caught up with him—he could hear her gasping as she ran, hampered by the kit that bounced at the top of her back every time a foot hit the ground. But she turned to look into his face as she drew ahead of him, and grinned. He realized he was grinning back.

Ahead of them, Toni and Dahno had reached a ramp that sloped down into the ditch. The two soldiers he had seen before were coming back in Bleys' direction, their weapons, held diagonally across the fronts of their bodies as they ran, looking like black slashes over their mud-stained gray-green uniforms. A third soldier had appeared, and seemed to be giving directions to Toni and Dahno as he headed back past them, toward Bleys. Toni and Dahno both stopped, looking back.

At that moment whistles ripped the air above him. He recognized them as a close hearing of the distinctive sounds made by the shaped propellants packed inside the long, slim, hollow needles fired by cone rifles. Something thumped the back of his blast jacket, and in-stinctively he tried to duck as he ran; but he lost his stride, almost falling sideways into a low patch of thorny brush. To his right and a bit ahead of him, the young soldier who had just passed him seemed to jerk in midstride, blossoms of bright red growing in two places on the back of her right thigh, below the hem of her uniform tunic. She buckled at the knees, and fell, her weapon flying off in front of her as if thrown, to tumble down the slope for a few feet, until its momentum died on the rough ground.

Bleys recovered his balance and lunged forward, reaching the young soldier even as the three soldiers who had passed Toni and Dahno ran, gasping, past him, heading back up the slope.

As he reached the wounded soldier, Bleys became aware he was winded, breathing now in great sucking gasps while clawing to clear sweat that was clouding his eyesight. He crouched beside the young woman and found her still conscious, and cursing. Her helmet had stayed on, but as he bent down one of her hands clawed at its catch, then threw it to the side before reaching back to paw futilely at the back of her thigh.

"Come on!" Bleys gasped, trying to yell. "You can't stay here!"

For a second she looked at him, her blue eyes wild and glaring; and then the skin around those eyes seemed to relax a little. She grinned again, and started to say something—but at that moment there was a loud outburst of power weapon fire behind them, and as one they looked back.

At the top of the slope behind them, a long line of their pursuers had appeared, strung out along the crest. Bleys did not try to count them, but he guessed there might be several dozen of them. He saw arms pointing in his direction, and then they leaped in pursuit down the slope . . . but now they had walked into an ambush themselves, as the young lieutenant and his men, using whatever cover they could find in the uneven terrain, had successfully avoided being noticed until the enemy had skylined themselves, within easy range.

"We've got to go!" Bleys yelled at the wounded soldier. It escaped his notice that his windedness of a few moments ago was gone. She turned to look back at him, and nodded; but when she tried to rise, she cried out, grimacing in pain.

Beyond her, Bleys saw, Toni was coming back toward them. He raised one arm and waved it, making a pushing motion as if trying to physically push her backward into the ditch. She stopped, and he rose up, pulling the young soldier with him by her shoulder, with a grip on the cloth of her uniform. The soldier cried out again, but then broke off the cry and pushed herself up from the ground; and together they began to stumble down the last portion of the slope toward the ramp.

Behind them, the power weapon fire had broken off; but he had no energy to spare for a look back. He was having to hold the soldier up as they moved, and she seemed near to passing out. Someone yelled behind him, and as he reflexively turned to look over his shoulder he lost his grip on the soldier; she slid down to the ground, giving a short cry.

Toni was running up the ramp as he reached down for the wounded woman, but even as he got a good grip on her weapons harness, Dahno appeared, seeming to pull the young woman up from the ground as effortlessly as some trained weightlifter might snatch a set of weights in a match.

"You're going to get us all killed yet!" he said; and turned, cursing, to stride down the ramp with the young woman in his arms. Toni reached Bleys and grabbed his arm.

"I'm fine!" he gasped. "I'm fine! Go!" He pushed at her, trying to turn her around and propel her ahead of him; but they ended up hurrying down the ramp and into the shelter of the ditch side by side. Ahead of them, Bleys could see his brother's broad back nearly filling the space between the vertical walls of what was, in fact, not a ditch at all, he realized, but the remains of a military entrenchment.

The soil that made up the walls of the trench was light in color, a sort of yellowish brown that he found distasteful. The floor of the trench was muddy, slippery and sticky.

Dahno had reached some sort of doorway set into the left side of the trench, in the middle of a stretch faced with crudely mortared rocks and logs. He seemed to be trying to turn in to the doorway, but was having trouble negotiating the turn, encumbered by the unwieldy form in his arms. He stopped, and started to shift the soldier's body into a more vertical position—and at that moment cones whistled from a point further down the trench. Dahno half-turned toward Toni and Bleys—and then fell backward, the young soldier sliding from his arms, down into the opening he had been trying to enter.

As he tried to throw himself to the ground, Bleys' feet slipped in the mud, and he fell sideways into the wall of the trench, his grip on Toni's arm pulling her with him, so that she fell on top of him.

Power rifles roared twice—three times—from behind them, and he saw a figure, beyond Dahno's body, tumble backward as if kicked in the stomach by some invisible god.

"Up!" he heard a voice yell; but he and Toni had already untangled themselves and begun to rise. They ran, crouching and gasping, to where Dahno lay, reaching him even as several soldiers came running up behind them.

"Get him inside!" Bleys heard the lieutenant order; and hands reached from behind him to take hold of Dahno's body. Toni stood up, and backed away.

"I think there's someone down in the doorway," Bleys yelled.

"Clear the doorway, Stanton," the lieutenant ordered. A soldier looked into the doorway, while the others lifted Dahno from the mud.

"Hurry!" the lieutenant yelled. Whistling noises punctuated his order, and two power rifle blasts could be heard from behind. Someone screamed shrilly—and then Bleys was at the doorway, Toni disappearing into it ahead of him.

He ducked his head to get under the wooden beam that formed the top of the entrance—and immediately found he had to take an unexpected long step downward just inside the doorway, only to be immediately faced with a wall of sandbags shaped by a timber frame. He turned right, to take two more deep downward steps into what appeared to be some sort of dugout bunker.

The bunker's roof was made of crudely cut logs of varying sizes, and the wall nearest the trench had been reinforced with stones and sandbags. The ceiling was uncomfortably close over his head, and his hair brushed against the widely spaced perpetual lightstrips that were providing their illumination—apparently no one had thought them worth scavenging after the local war had moved on.

The wounded soldier he had helped earlier was already lying on the floor halfway across the room, now with blood staining her uniform in several new places, and Toni was hurrying to kneel beside her. Two unwounded soldiers were coming back toward him, and he found himself virtually pushed into them as the party carrying Dahno managed, with a good deal of cursing, to guide his large frame through the doorway and the turn. Bleys stepped aside, and the soldiers, four of them, carried Dahno over near where Toni was checking on the wounded woman; and put him down gently. Bleys could see portions of several needles lodged in the fabric of the blast jacket Dahno was still wearing over his suit jacket, as well as bloodstains on his shirt, underneath both jackets.

The two other soldiers had gone back past Bleys and out the doorway, from which he could now hear some yelling mixed in with the whistles and roars of a skirmish apparently beginning to draw closer down the length of the trench. The four soldiers who had carried Dahno quickly passed by Bleys and went back through the doorway, but within seconds more soldiers were coming back into the bunker.

The first two were half-dragging a body, which was carried across the room and, as before, deposited near where the young woman was lying. Toni had left her and moved over to check on Dahno.

"Does anyone have any medical supplies?" Toni yelled. One of the soldiers, already moving back toward the doorway, checked long enough to uncouple a portion of his harness, from which depended several sealed pouches. He handed the entire harness to Toni, and she grabbed it and began to open the pouches, while the soldier headed back to the doorway.

Before he got there, more figures filled the entrance, again carrying a body. They carried the wounded man, this time, past Toni, putting him down, gently, in the far corner. As they turned away more figures entered, also carrying a body—and this time, the body was that of the young lieutenant.

Bleys felt a headache coming on.

CHAPTER 10

"Dahno's going to be all right," Toni said now, apparently still trying to give Bleys a better understanding of what had happened during his blackout. She shifted position slightly as she knelt beside one of the wounded soldiers, perhaps trying to ease the strain on her knees while she bent over to pry up the edge of an adhesive bandage and lean close, peering. Pushing herself back up, she nodded to the side and back, to indicate another body Bleys had not seen clearly up to this point. Bleys rose and stepped past her, to kneel beside his older half-brother.

"How're you doing, brother?" Bleys said.

"You heard Toni!" Dahno snapped testily. His face was pale and haggard, tired and sweaty and dirty. His white shirt was open down the front, with a bandage showing underneath; there was blood on the shirt. His brown jacket was rolled up under his head.

Bleys was reminded of a moment, years in the past, when he had come upon his brother, asleep, during a particularly stressful episode in their lives, and had seen the normally smiling, cheerful face showing deep exhaustion and worry.

"Two needles," Toni said, looking over her shoulder at them. "One's still inside his chest, where I think it was stopped by a rib, but I've controlled the bleeding."

"Don't worry," Bleys said to his brother. "I had worse than this on Newton."

"Maybe," said Dahno. "That doesn't help."

"We ran out of pain-blocks," Toni said. After a pause to adjust whatever she was working on, she spoke again: "My wristpad was damaged when I fell outside, but if you can try again to get through to Henry, he can bring more blocks with him when he gets here with the Soldiers." She was referring, he knew, to his bodyguards, rather than any military forces.

He also knew she was prompting him again, still trying to get him up to speed.

"I'll try again." He nodded at her. He didn't remember trying before, but her words told him he must have done so.

Bringing his left arm up as he moved across the room, he slid back the wide cuff of his dark gray jacket—now smeared with drying yellow mud—and looked at the control pad on his wrist. It was currently in a map-display mode; apparently he had been trying to determine their exact location. He did not remember doing that, either.

He reset the wristpad for communications, but found the usual channels jammed. He programmed the pad to run a continuous scan of the local channels, looking for an open one; and as he watched the rapidly shifting displays, he silently reviewed what he had learned about their situation.

Always, when he had emerged from a blackout, his memory of events leading up to it had been sharp and clear, right up to the point where he went blank—and while he had never recovered a memory of anything that occurred during a blackout, he had always awakened from them with his mind once more sharp and clear.

This time, his memory seemed sluggish, as if some part of his mind was unwilling to expend the energy required to drive the focal point of his consciousness through the murky haze that obscured events of—of how long? He could not even pin down where the hazy part of his memories began; he had a feeling it went back into a time before the actual blackout had begun.

Now, why did he think that? More accurately, why did he feel as if that was the case?

Willing his mind to focus on the problem, rather than give in to its apparent inclination to blend with the fog about it, he found there was a hidden part of himself that believed this particular blackout had begun very recently. But it seemed to have cast confusion over a longer stretch of his memory.

Kaj Menowsky, his personal medician, had told him that stress could not only retard his body's continuing efforts to heal itself from the effects of the Newtonians' attack on his DNA, but also trigger a blackout. And Kaj had warned him that any such retardation of his body's healing process would increase the period of time in which he would continue to be subject to such blackouts.

Kaj had also told him he could heal himself faster if he could find a way to harness his own creative powers, somehow—and in fact he had done so once, in the worst part of his bout with the DNA antagonist, working his way through a series of dreams that seemed to have somehow taught his body what needed to be done; at least, Kaj had been pleased with his progress after those dreams.

Could it be that his subconscious mind, unaffected by the blackouts, was trying to send messages to his conscious mind? Was this some new manifestation of those same creative powers Kaj had prompted him to work with? It occurred to him, for the first time, that the creative powers he had used might have been simply his subconscious mind at work.

It was clear he had been under a lot of stress, in the events—whatever they were—that had led to his current situation; he wondered now whether that same stress might have become so great that his subconscious mind could deal with it only by putting his consciousness back in charge. That might explain his unprecedented act of coming out of the blackout while awake, for instance. But if so, there was likely a price to be paid—Kaj would happily tell him so, if he were here—and possibly his current confusion was that price.

In that case, his subconscious mind had left him in a bad spot. It was going to be very hard for him to pull them all out of this when his memory was foggy about whatever had happened before his awakening. He needed information above all. So far he seemed unable to remember the recent past with any depth; he could only pull up particular memories when something triggered an association.

It seemed clear his party was under siege in something that appeared to be a primitive military fortification. The soldiers with them were certainly a military escort, so it was likely they had been on another visit to a unit of Friendly troops. But where were Henry and his Soldiers? Toni's words had suggested she thought they might be nearby—and with that thought, the memory of the events following their visit to Will's grave came back to him, suddenly and clearly.

Henry had realized, as soon as the local military officials had stepped in following the bombing, that military people were not likely to allow a group of armed civilians to convoy through their midst. So he had taken his Soldiers undercover, hoping to find some way to protect Bleys and his party from a distance, in the event the local military could not manage that.

The fact that the military had said Henry's people could not come along did not mean they weren't around somewhere.

Henry had never been one for obeying orders like some wide-eyed child; in fact, he had spent a portion of his earlier life fighting against the Militia on Association. He still had a low opinion of them, which he sometimes seemed to extend to all other formal military forces.

The question was how to make contact with Henry and his Soldiers. Bleys turned his attention back to his wristpad; Toni's had been damaged, and he guessed that Dahno's had been also; his appeared to be all right—

Abruptly, he noticed a small blue light on his pad's display face, one he had never seen there before. He queried the pad and—

"—me," a voice said.

The voice was female and seemed very soft, and Bleys realized that the pad's *HUSH* mode had somehow come on.

He tried to use the *SEND* control, but it seemed inoperable. Even as he tried it the voice resumed: "Eleven minutes and thirty seconds." It paused; then: "Do you hear me?"

The voice sounded familiar, with some of the Friendly intonations most of his Soldiers had. His Soldiers came from a variety of worlds, but most were from the Friendlies; and while none of those used the archaic-sounding canting speech of the ultra-religious, they generally had the distinct Friendly accent he was used to. He himself had taken voice training that, among other things, rid him of the few tinges of that accent he had picked up while spending his teenage years on Henry's farm.

In a few seconds the voice spoke again:

"Eleven minutes and twenty seconds. Do you hear me?"

As the voice continued to count down, Bleys tried to locate the channel the message was coming in on; but all the remainder of his communications system seemed to be cut out of whatever circuit this message was coming in on . . . and even as he futilely clicked *SEND* for the third time, the voice stopped at the ten-minute mark.

A new voice spoke—Henry's voice.

"Bleys," Henry said, "I don't know if you can hear this or not. Don't try to respond to this message. You can't; I'm using an emergency channel on a gravity band. Your pad can only receive, because a gravity transmitter is too bulky for any wristpad."

A gravity band would be unlikely to be either blocked or monitored, Bleys thought as Henry's voice continued softly. Leave it to Henry to have one more backup behind the backups. For a brief moment he felt a lightening of his spirit.

Maybe that's where Dahno gets it.

"This message is going to repeat at every one-minute mark of the countdown, from here on," Henry was continuing, his tempo speeding up, "because I can't stay here to keep talking. We know where you are, and we're behind the people who have you surrounded. There're a lot of them, but if we can take them by surprise we've got a good chance of getting you out of there."

Bleys found himself nodding as he listened, following Henry's thought. He glanced up, and found that everyone in the bunker— everyone who was conscious—was watching him. They probably couldn't hear anything with the *HUSH* setting activated, but he had their full attention anyway.

Toni was smiling broadly—*of course! Henry couldn't have added the gravity receiver to my pad without her knowledge.*

Not only was she generally in charge of Bleys' communications, but she and Henry had a bond of their own, and would likely have worked together on something like this.

"I have to ask you," Henry was continuing, "to try to find a way to attract the enemy's attention on the zero mark. Getting their attention could make all the difference, by letting us get right in on them before they notice us. Any sort of demonstration would help, and the louder the better." He paused.

"Bleys, anything you in there can do might save more than one of our lives."

The words reminded Bleys of the Soldiers who had died helping him escape from Newton. Toni had counseled him to find a way to say something to Henry about those men and women, but he never had . . . he just couldn't find the words.

The first voice he had heard resumed its countdown: "Nine minutes fifteen seconds," it said. Then: "Nine minutes ten seconds. . . ."

At the nine-minute mark Henry's words repeated themselves. Bleys, thinking furiously, listened through Henry's message again, and then set the pad to give him a visual countdown only. He looked about.

Everyone—except for the two wounded soldiers, who were unconscious—was still looking at him. He turned to face the soldiers grouped near the door, and then raised both arms, bringing his hands up to the level of his eyes, where they acted as a frame for his face. The soldiers seemed to cluster together about their sergeant, their eyes now all on his face.

Bleys faced them for a moment, silent and dramatic, with feet slightly apart; and then he paced—smoothly, with short, slow steps—toward them. Inside, he was wishing he had worn the black half-cape he used on public occasions, with its red, shiny lining intended to attract attention. Still, the situation had focused their attention on him in a way he had never experienced before—and certainly his need to be persuasive had never been stronger. . . .

"Now is the moment," he said. And he put into those words all the training he had used to make his voice strong and comforting, sure and mellow. "Now is *our* moment!"

He focused on the eyes of the shortest of the soldiers, a dark-skinned youth who had picked up a cut on his left cheek that left a thin dried ribbon of blood down the side of his face. The youth's eyes widened slightly as Bleys tried to pour his certainty down the channel between them.

"You've performed well," Bleys said, "all of you! No one would have expected you to hold off those people out there." Bleys' eyes moved to those of the tall man off to the side of the group; and that young man's eyes widened in turn, staring into Bleys' eyes. Bleys, his own vision focused tightly down, could see the pupils of the young soldier's eyes as they dilated slightly.

Bleys spoke on, capturing each soldier in turn with his eyes while he spoke of their bravery and worth, of the task that lay ahead, and of how their deeds would look to those who were coming to find them.

Their sergeant, he saw, had broken loose from the spell, and was now looking with a puzzled expression at the rapt faces of his men.

"Gather together," Bleys told the men, "and feel the trust of your companions. Each of them trusts *you*, as do I." He broke off, and gestured the sergeant forward with a short wave of his arm. As the man moved forward, Bleys extended the arm to drape it lightly on the man's shoulder, pulling him in toward Bleys' own body; and as he did so, Bleys himself pivoted, the action serving to pull the sergeant away from his men, who, oblivious, were gathering in a circle and speaking quietly and warmly to each other, joy on their faces.

"Sergeant," Bleys said, now stepping to the side, away from the man, "I know this seems strange to you." For the first time Bleys saw that the man was himself hurt, a red stain showing on his left side, just above hip level. The stain seemed large, but had been crudely bandaged and was hidden from normal view by the man's battle jacket. Now that he was paying attention, he also saw that the man seemed to be holding his left shoulder slightly hunched, as if it, too, had been injured.

"It did," the man said, in reply to Bleys' question. "Not now. Now I recognize what you're doing. You're one of those *New People* who can go around persuading people to do whatever you want."

A Dorsai!

It seemed strange to see a soldier from that planet, so renowned for the military abilities of its people, working as a simple noncommissioned officer in some little brushfire war.

That shows how bad things have become for them—they have to take any little job they can get.

"Some people call us that," Bleys said. "Or *Others*. Whatever the name, I am that. But you seem hostile; do you feel as if I've persuaded you—as you put it—against your will?"

"You tried," the sergeant said. "But you did it to my men!"

"Your men are needed, Sergeant," Bleys said. "There's a mission they have to carry out—one that will save our lives. I'm only trying to get them ready for it."

"You're going to send them out there? They'll be slaughtered! The enemy can fire down the length of the trench and there's no cover at all!"

"But they'll grab the enemy's attention for a few moments," Bleys said. "Someone's coming up behind them who'll use that inattention to get in on those people and remove them."

"But my men! They'll be dead!"

Before Bleys could answer, the man started to move forward—and quickly checked himself as Toni, stepping up from the side, pointed a power pistol at his head from a couple of feet away.

Sadly, Bleys shook his head, glancing quickly at the display on his wristpad.

"Maybe," he said. "Maybe not. They'll have a chance. It has to be done."

"It's not right!" the sergeant said. "You're sending them out there like they were in some kind of dream! You're not even giving them a choice!"

"*I* don't have a choice, either, and we have less than three minutes," Bleys said, reaching out to remove the power pistol from the sergeant's weapons belt. Taking the pistol off its safety, he pointed it at the Dorsai's stomach. "Turn to your left and kneel facing that wall. If you try anything, you won't be alive to help your men."

As Toni watched the kneeling man, Bleys returned to the rest of the soldiers. They were enthusiastic about his rejoining them, and seemed, in their captured state, not to have noticed the confrontation with their sergeant. Bleys took a moment to greet each one individually, as if they were all comrades together, and gathered their attention to himself once more. He spoke again.

In a few moments he had given them their instructions, and they turned to checking their weapons and arraying themselves on either side of the doorway.

"Remember," Bleys said, "don't move until I give the signal. Then get out the doorway fast, spreading out as you go. Put out as much fire as you can. You can break those people, I *know* it."

Eyes now fastened on the entranceway, they all nodded resolutely. Eighty seconds to go, Bleys saw.

At that point the sergeant, ignoring the gun Toni held on him, rose, pivoting—and moved toward him. Bleys raised the man's own pistol; but the sergeant slowed and splayed his arms to each side. One hand was bloody. He continued, however, moving toward his men, and Bleys understood suddenly.

"You don't have to go out there, you know," Bleys said. "Whatever you might think of me, I wouldn't make you do that." Over the sergeant's shoulder, Bleys could see Toni, still behind the man, with her gun on him. Dahno, off to the side, had pulled himself up onto an elbow and was now raising a pistol, his face ugly.

"No, Dahno!" Bleys said, raising a hand in a warding motion. Dahno, he was sure, was in the grip of emotion that wanted a violent outlet.

Bleys had no time to think about it; he was in the grip of his own emotional reaction—one he, too, could not control.

"I suppose I could take your word for that," the sergeant said. "It makes no difference." He paused; and while he did so, Bleys silently reversed the pistol and handed it back to him. The hand in which Dahno held his weapon seemed to jerk as he clenched his finger over the firing button—but nothing happened; the gun was empty.

The white-mind face Toni had been wearing—the inhumanly blank face that signaled a concentration state in someone who had attained a great mastery of the martial arts—changed, too, as her eyes narrowed and her lips curled in a grim half-smile. Bleys thought he caught a gleam from behind her lowered eyelids.

Bleys put his attention back on the sergeant.

"They're my men, you see," the man said, as if that explained it all. He holstered the pistol without looking at it; then turned and limped toward those same men, who had been chattering softly among themselves, as if blind and deaf to the drama behind them. The volume of their chatter rose for a moment as he joined them, but died out as he spoke softly among them. After a few sentences he took a moment to check each man individually, looking him in the eyes and asking a soft question or two. And in just a few more seconds, Bleys gave them an order as the countdown on his pad reached zero; and they burst through the doorway one at a time, the Dorsai leading.

Bleys felt himself frozen in place, listening to the eruption of sound from outside, the explosions of power weapons and the whistling of cones. Toni gripped his arm, pulling him toward Dahno.

"We've got to be ready to go," she said. "Help me with him. If Henry gets through to us, we may have only moments to get out before the opportunity passes."

As they got Dahno to his feet, silence fell outside. They waited tensely, eyes glued to the entrance; and in a few minutes Bleys heard Henry's voice call his name.

"We've got to go now," Toni said, quietly but intensely.

"Yes," Bleys said. He had to go. It would be too tragic a waste, otherwise. . . .

CHAPTER 11

The local sun was lowering toward the horizon line formed by the ridge to the west of Henry MacLean's position, the dimming of its light darkening the opposite sky as he, along with some of his Soldiers, walked across the field, pausing to check out each body they came to. To all sides more of their number were fanning out, alert for any further threat, and he could see another thin line of his people holding the crest of the ridge ahead of him.

This land had never been very productive—Henry's eye could still be that of a farmer—and having a war fought on it had made it rough and uneven, pitted and scabbed. There were no trees of any size nearby, he noted, although his Soldiers, in their attack, had made effective use of the scrubby trees and underbrush lining the small creek that curved around two sides of this position. He himself had walked out of that underbrush to move up the gentle slope.

It was no surprise to him that there were few trees in sight; trees were always casualties when war visited in one place for very long.

That setting star, which seemed small to his eyes, was called Tau Ceti. It was a strange name, he thought; and the paleness of its yellow light seemed strange, too—but he knew he felt that way out of his lifelong familiarity with the more orange light cast by Epsilon Eridanus, the star that shone on his home planet.

He had seen bodies lying about on Association, long in his past; and on Newton, too, more recently. The look of them never seemed to change, no matter the color of the light.

And something else hadn't changed: once dead, it did not matter whose side the body had been on.

He had been moving forward as he thought, part of a skirmish line of the former Soldiers of God he led. Now he stopped, as the change in his perspective revealed the lips of the trench that had been their objective. The entranceway to the bunker would be under the lip on the farther side, he knew; in a few more steps he would be able to see it.

Henry and his Soldiers had been approaching somewhat obliquely to the line of the trench, which now presented the appearance of a kind of scar cutting across the barren field. It didn't seem a very strong defensive position, he thought, but perhaps it hadn't needed to be. What little he had heard about the war that had been fought over this area suggested it hadn't been a serious contest. . . . He wondered if more people had not died here in this afternoon than in all of that war.

With a hand signal he started his Soldiers moving forward again, cautious as always. Those to his right had already reached the trench, and two of them stopped, covering down its length, while the other two leaped over it, to take up watch on the other side.

In a few steps more he, himself, could see down into the trench. There were more bodies here, these in uniform. From some distance back and at a different angle he had seen these young men burst out into the trench from the bunker, shouting and firing—and had seen them blasted down. Two had gotten a little distance down the trench, back the way he had just come, before falling into the greasy mud; and one had made it up over the edge of the trench, the move giving him enough time to put several bolts into the midst of the group of enemies that had been setting up a power cannon intended to blast Bleys and his party to pieces in their shelter.

It was that cannon that had forced Henry to decide on immediate action.

"Bleys? Are you here?" he called, directing his voice at the entrance across the trench. "Dahno? Toni?"

As he waited he shifted position, two strides taking him over to the body of the soldier who took out the cannon. The man was badly torn up, having taken a number of needles before bolts from power weapons had blasted him out of life. He had never dropped his pistol, though—his hand, curled in death, still held it firmly.

He appeared to be a little older than the others. But all of them, including this man's enemies, that Henry and his Soldiers had killed, and who now lay behind him—they were all too young.

He was reminded of Will, whose grave he had visited only two days ago. He thought someone must have looked down on his son in very much this same way . . . did that person feel then as he, Henry, did now?

"Bleys?" he called again. And he gave hand signals to his people to flank the position they were now watching.

Remembering Will, as usual, also made him remember Joshua, his other son, still living on the old farm on Association. In a very true sense, he realized now, Will had died so that Joshua would live. Joshua, and all their people.

And some of these young people had died so that Bleys could live—if he lived. The others, so that Bleys would die. Did they cancel each other out?

Not in God's arithmetic, he thought.

"Henry, we're here." It was Toni's voice, and he looked up to see her appear cautiously out of the bunker entrance, stepping down slightly into the mud while waving a white cloth of some sort; with her other arm she was trying to support Dahno, who was also being held up by Bleys, coming out behind him. Henry did not have to speak before several of his Soldiers leaped into the trench to help take Dahno's weight, as, refusing to sit down, he picked his way past a couple of bodies and trudged heavily toward a crude ramp that had been cut out of the side of the trench, farther down its length.

"Bleys, are you hurt?" Henry said. "Toni?"

"No, Uncle," Bleys said. "Dahno has two needles in him, but the rest of us are all right."

"Is there anyone else in the bunker?"

"A body or two," Bleys said, "and—"

"Two more wounded soldiers," Toni added. "Please get them help."

"Where is—" Henry began to call; and checked himself upon seeing that Mary Holzer, their lead medician, was already at Dahno's side as he reached the bottom of the ramp.

"I'll look him over," Mary said in her soft voice to James Cella, her number two. "Check inside, Jamie."

She tried to make Dahno lie down so that she could examine him, but he refused, insisting on getting up the ramp and out of the mud-bottomed trench.

Rather than taking the ramp, Bleys had vaulted out of the trench with the aid of cupped hands provided by one of the Soldiers; and now reached Henry. Toni had remained with Dahno.

"Thank you, Uncle," Bleys said as he came to a halt, looking back past Henry at the scattered bodies that had been their attackers. "I believe they might have gotten in on us before long."

"Probably not," Henry said. "They would not have needed to do so. They were setting up a power cannon that likely would have blown that place down on all of you."

"Do you know who they were?" Bleys asked.

"I have no idea," Henry said. "They aren't wearing uniforms."

"Are there any left alive?"

"Not so far," Henry said. "We need to get you out of here—no, don't argue. These people may have comrades; or if not, the army will soon discover how they were deceived and come back; we don't want them to find us with their own dead people."

"But I need to try to find out—"

"We'll check all the bodies and their equipment for anything that might tell us what you want to know," Henry said, "before the rest of us leave. But you and Toni are going now—" he pointed at a wide, high-riding vehicle approaching from an angle behind them, "—and Dahno, if he can travel."

The vehicle was one of a type commonly called a *vagen*, a civilian adaptation of a high-riding, boxy carrier used on many worlds to ferry small military units. It drew up beside them, angling in at the last moment so that its driver could be next to Henry as his window opened. Its fans threw up very little dust from the still-damp soil.

"John, are you ready to go?" Henry directed his question at the now-open window.

"Yes, Henry," John Colville said. Bleys happened to know that John's father had fought beside Henry years ago, when they were both Soldiers of God.

"Rolf and Kamala have had their wounds treated and are in the rear compartment," John was continuing. "They can shoot."

"Bleys, you get in beside John," Henry said. He turned slightly and raised his voice.

"Mary, can he be moved?" he called.

"Yes, Henry," the medician replied.

"Move over there, John," Henry directed. "Bleys and I will walk over there in a moment. Leave the front seat open for Bleys, and put Dahno, Toni and Mary in the middle compartment. Who's driving your escort?"

"Richard Nelson," said John; "and, yes, I've made sure he knows where we're going. He has Ben and Eli with him, as well as our other wounded."

He moved off toward the ramp, and Bleys and Henry followed on foot.

"How many have we lost?" Bleys asked after a silent moment.

"I don't know that yet," Henry replied. "We had to scatter our people to all sides and try to coordinate our attacks, and there's been no time to get the details. That's another thing I'll have to tell you later." He paused to think for a moment, still walking.

"God willing, I believe we have done better than I feared," he went on. "Those people were not properly alert to the possibility of trouble coming upon them."

They had almost caught up with the vagen now.

"God gives us a lesson in these people," Henry said, "one we would do well to heed: be prepared for the possibility of trouble. Thus, you must go ahead of us, now."

As Bleys still hesitated, Henry spoke more sharply: "Go! Get in!"

Abandoning argument, Bleys moved around the vehicle to its passenger side. Henry began to give more signals to those of his Soldiers who had held their positions farther out from the bunker.

By the time Bleys opened the door, Dahno and the rest had been loaded into the vagen from its far side, a process facilitated by the fact that the vagen was riding higher on its idling fans than did more usual vehicles. Bleys climbed in, finding that a deep well under the dashboard provided plenty of room for his legs.

As soon as Bleys was in, John put the vagen into motion, heading back the way he had come. Another, similar vehicle appeared from somewhere, to fall in behind them.

Looking back as they went, Dahno fidgeting and complaining beside her, Toni saw Henry watching them go.

It must be tearing him up inside, she thought. *I know he loves Bleys like another son—enough to risk his very soul to try to keep Bleys out of Satan's hands. But to do that he had to kill, which he believes—no, he knows, to the depths of his soul—is wrong.*

As a curve in their path put Henry out of her sight, she faced forward, then leaned back in her seat.

She had never forgotten that Henry had once admitted to her that he was prepared to kill Bleys himself, rather than let him, as he put it, fall into Satan's hands. She herself had resolved that would never happen.

At the same time, she had grown fond of Henry herself; and she recognized that if Henry ever came to that point—regardless of whether he succeeded in killing Bleys, or not—it would come as the result of an almost inconceivable state of pain and despair.

Spare him, Lord!

As she heard her inner self say those words, she knew she meant her prayer to encompass both men.

By the time the local sun set, their vehicle had made a rendezvous with a long-haul cargo carrier. Hidden inside one of the containers inside its streamlined shell, they almost backtracked the way they had just come, now traveling along a paved trafficway that passed about twenty kilometers to the west of the bunker. While they did so, the vehicles from which they had parted, now functioning as decoys, crossed the Nightfish River on their fans—avoiding the bridges— and sped toward Abbeyville, a city large enough to host a Friendly consulate.

Feverish and achy in the aftermath of the action and the black-out, Bleys drowsed on an air mattress inside their container, Toni sitting quietly beside him as she worked over her wrist control pad. Dahno, sedated, lay quietly on another mattress while the medician monitored his condition. The wounded Soldiers—six in total—had stayed with John Colville and his vehicles, adding to the authenticity of the decoy operation while speeding them toward more advanced medical care.

"I've missed something," Bleys said, lifting the arm he had draped across his brow; the lightstrips glued to the walls of their container seemed to be able to glare right through his eyelids. He rolled onto his side and propped himself up on one elbow, watching Toni as she monitored the displays on her wristpad.

"I deliberately set out to stir the pot on this planet," he went on, "thinking that if our Others were galvanized into action, they might unearth some clue to whoever these people are who've been working in secret here. Or perhaps those people would become aware of the increased activity, and react in some way that might lead us to them. But *this!* Two major attacks in two days, thousands of kilometers apart . . . ?"

He stopped himself from shaking his head, for fear that the lurking sense of discomfort in the center of his skull might blossom into a full-blown headache . . . he had come to be leery of headaches.

"I wanted to elicit some reaction," he said. "But if these attacks are that reaction, it's so far out of proportion to the situation as to be insane. So I must have missed something."

"We talked about this after the bombing," she said, "and you and Dahno agreed it must have been the work of that—that secret group you came here to look for."

"Only because we couldn't think of anyone else," he said. "But that conclusion only dodged the question of why they, or anyone on this planet, would want to attack us."

He held up a hand, stopping her reply while he thought.

"But maybe they don't have to be from Ceta at all," he went on after another moment. "We've made a lot of enemies elsewhere, certainly."

"Who out there could have reached down onto Ceta and set up not one, but two, attacks in such quick succession?" she asked.

He nodded at her objection.

"Generally, you're right," he said. "The only group really capable of being efficient enough to follow us to Ceta on short notice and then set up these attacks—only the Dorsai could do it."

"It's not the Dorsai," she said.

"I know you have Dorsai ancestry," he said. "Is there another reason to believe they couldn't do this?"

"It's not that they couldn't," she said. "It's that they wouldn't."

He was impressed by the firmness of her assertion.

"You're that sure?"

"Absolutely," she said. "I have Dorsai ancestry, yes, but that doesn't make me one of them. It does, however, make me sure that such an attack is something no true Dorsai would ever do."

"I'll admit it feels like a false idea," he said. "But who else could have done it?"

"Besides," she said, not ready to let go of her thought just yet, "no Dorsai-led group would have let itself be caught so off-guard by Henry and his Soldiers—no disrespect to Henry and his people. . . ."

"That's true, too." He grimaced and raised a hand to massage his forehead. "Who else is there? Who have I overlooked?"

"You're working now from the premise that the attack must have come from off-Ceta," she said. "But the logic only works if the premise is correct."

"You're right," he said. "I did start out by assuming there isn't anyone already on this planet who would have wanted to attack us—and who also could have done it. But I gather you're saying that I'm making a shaky assumption, there."

"Yes," she nodded. "If you think about it for a moment, what you really mean is that there's no one on this planet who would have done it, and could have done it, *that you know of.*"

"And where are you going with this?"

"You've already deduced the existence of an unknown—a hidden—group on this planet. But you know next to nothing about them, so how can you conclude that they couldn't have attacked us?"

"But that group, whoever they are, should not have had any reason to attack us," he said. "Yet."

"Go at this from the other side of the problem," she said. "Ask how they knew—not only that we were on the planet, but that we presented a threat of some sort to them. And then, ask how anyone could have known where we were going to be—not once, but twice."

He nodded. "I guess they've done us a favor."

She looked at him, interest in her face.

"You know perfectly well what I mean," he said. "We still don't know who those people are—but we definitely know there's someone out there!"

"More than that," she said. "We now know they have some sort of access to our plans."

"And that narrows the range we have to search quite a lot, doesn't it?"

"Yes," she said, looking more somber. "Our own people."

"Yes."

They talked on quietly for a time, as the night passed outside their container. Bleys slipped into an intermittent and unrestful nap, awakening each time the medician's *CALL* roused her for another check on Dahno's condition . . . and sometimes he woke for no reason that he could tell, as if he were seeking to escape some dream his waking mind could not remember.

Toni stayed awake, keeping her attention focused on the satellite news channel that beamed down steadily as they moved across the face of a continent.

"Are you all right?" she asked, finally, softly, a few hours later, when he had come uncomfortably awake once more.

He looked at her, wondering what she was referring to.

"I'm tired, and my head aches," he said warily. He kept his voice low, as she had. "But I'm not hurt."

He stopped, and flicked his eyes in the direction of their companions in the container.

"It's all right to talk," Toni said, still keeping her voice down. "Dahno is heavily sedated, and Mary's sound asleep."

"I've been waiting to see if I'm going to go into another black-out," he said, almost whispering. "But I'm not sure I'll know I'm doing so, until after I come out of it."

"You've certainly had enough stress to bring on two or three blackouts," she said, almost cheerfully. "We'll deal with that if it happens. But that wasn't what I was getting at."

"Then what were you asking about?"

"How are you doing, emotionally?" she said.

"Emotionally? What makes you ask that? Are you wondering if nearly being killed is going to make me break down?"

"Break down, no," she said. "But it's not unusual for people to have an emotional reaction of some kind after they get out of a bad situation. When we had to fight our way off Newton you were sick from the DNA poisoning, so I couldn't tell how you were doing otherwise. But it's occurred to me that, if you aren't already having some reaction, maybe you should be warned to expect one."

"I guess I know the kind of thing you mean," he said, remembering how he had felt the first time he killed a man—Dahno's old associate—back on Association. "So far there's no sign of anything like that."

"It may sneak up on you," she said. "Don't be surprised by it, and don't let it make you do something you'd regret."

"Are *you* having a reaction?"

"A little," she said. "But one as trained as I've been keeps her ki centered as a matter of habit; and that helps prevent her—me—from being thrown off balance."

"I don't know if that means you don't have a reaction to all those deaths, or if it means you have a way to cope with that kind of reaction."

"The latter," she said. "Being as trained as I am doesn't mean I don't feel."

"I didn't think otherwise," he said. "It's different with me, a little. I began to train myself, long ago, to prepare for the deaths that would be necessary . . . it doesn't mean I'm blind to them. But they can't throw me off stride."

Silence followed.

Finally, about seven hours after they had left the bunker, it came.

"It's Henry," Toni said. Bleys sat up, looking over at her control pad.

Determined to avoid being traced through their communications, Henry had instructed them to send out no messages, but to watch for his instructions to come in piggybacked on the signal from the broadcast satellite.

"My pad is still decoding—there!" she said. She took a moment to read the text message on her small screen.

"It's actually not for us," she said. "Our drivers are being given orders for a rendezvous in—let's see—just over three hours." She looked up as Bleys made a movement.

"Do we need to let the drivers know?" he asked.

"No." She shook her head. "They have their own pads—" she was interrupted by a soft double tone that seemed to emanate from the lightstrips inside their container.

"That would be them letting us know they've gotten instructions," she said. "Leave it in their hands."

"All right," he said. He settled back on the mattress. In a moment he spoke again from beneath the arm draped across his face.

"This is the hardest part."

"Delegation was never a strong suit for either you or Dahno," she said, smiling a little. "But you, at least, are learning. Now get some sleep."

"And you?"

"I may be a basket case tomorrow," she admitted. "All the more reason for you to be in top form."

Part of him was uneasy about doing as she instructed, but he could not come up with an objection that would not sound lame even in his own ears. He settled for closing his eyes again. He still wondered if he'd fall into a blackout now, or soon—or if not, whether he might wake up later without any memory of what had occurred today.

After a while, he fell into an uneasy sleep.

———

Unimaginably distant, the stars—maybe they were entire galaxies—were so faint that they would not be noticeable to any senses not sharpened by lifetimes spent in interstellar space. But as he watched, in his comfortable floating, those lights were a dazzling panoply of infinitely varying shades of red—the red of light so old it had gotten tired on the way to him.

He had been out here for so long that any time before was—not forgotten, but forgettable in its insignificance.

The black was cold but not unfriendly. It held him in its calm, strong embrace as comfortably as any warm ocean, rocking him gently as it drew him, in accordance with the immutable laws, to the end it had been ordained he would share with all the Universe, as it all came together in that final, gentle, terrible place that was the totality of the infinitely far future.

But there was a blur intruding on his solitary blackness, a barely sensed perturbation in his long, slow orbit, that incensed him with its wrongness . . . some intruder, out of place, or maybe just out of time. . . .

CHAPTER 12

Well before midnight the Friendly consulate in Abbeyville had received permission from its host state, the Lancastrian Commonwealth, for a detachment of Friendly troops to be brought in from one of the leased units Bleys had already visited, to increase security in the consulate compound. All parties were maintaining a strict silence about the day's events, and nothing had made it into the media, which was the way everyone preferred it.

The two vehicles in which Bleys and his party left the battlefield had proceeded to the city after transferring their passengers, and by mid-evening had sped into the consulate's inner courtyard. The subsequent arrival of the rest of Bleys' official party, along with an official request for a deployment of local forces to guard the consulate from the outside, seemed to make it clear that Bleys was in, and intended to stay in, the consulate's safe confines. But no official statements were issued, and communications in or out of the consulate were scant and tightly controlled.

The consulate had already been buttoned down for hours when Bleys and his companions arrived at the rendezvous with Henry and his Soldiers, nearly a thousand kilometers away. But none of them had any intention of locking themselves into a potential trap.

Instead, they all headed for a tiny regional landing pad, where two privately chartered suborbital shuttles awaited them; and within four hours Bleys, Dahno and Toni were smuggled aboard *Favored of God*, secreted in a load of supplies for the repairs that were supposedly in progress on the ship. *Favored* had been sitting quietly on the pad outside Ceta City since some days before Bleys' own arrival aboard *Burning Bush*, ostensibly awaiting the arrival of its charter party. *Favored* was listed, in the port records, as the *Konrad Macklin*, of Freiland registry.

Kaj Menowsky, the Exotic-trained medician who had killed off the genetic antagonist with which Bleys had been poisoned on Newton, was waiting for them, along with a few of the ship's personnel, as Bleys and Toni were released from the crates in which they had boarded the vessel.

"Kaj!" Toni exclaimed. "We were told you'd been hurt. How're you feeling?"

"I'm fine," the medician said shortly. Clearly feeling he had no time for being sociable, he immediately began making a quick check into the stability of Dahno's condition. "It was just a mild concussion," he added, almost grudgingly, without turning to look back at her.

After a very short time, though, he smiled; and directed that Dahno be conveyed to the ship's infirmary. Then he turned to Bleys and Toni.

"How are you two?" he asked.

"I'm fine," Toni said. "Just tired—we haven't slept much lately."

"I'm fine, too," Bleys said.

"Come with me," Kaj said to Bleys. "I want to check you over, too."

"No," Bleys said, more loudly than he had intended. "I'll answer as many questions as you want, but later! I have to have time to think and to get some things under way. And you have to take care of Dahno."

And I just can't take any of your incessant questions right now! he added to himself. The medician, for all his good work in combating the genetic attack on Bleys, at times made it seem as if keeping his patient talking was the key to his treatment.

"I've already confirmed that Mary did everything necessary to stabilize Dahno's condition," Kaj said. "It'll take only minutes to remove the needle still in his chest—in fact, Mary could have done that, even under field conditions, if the needle weren't lodged in a rib. But this ship has all the equipment we need, and I promise you

Dahno will be able to move about with very little constraint within three or four days, and will be completely recovered in less than two weeks. But—"

"No 'buts,'" Toni said firmly, taking Kaj by an elbow and rotating him so he could follow the crewmembers moving Dahno deeper into the ship. "There's an emergency situation still in progress, and we have things we have to get done right away." With a hand in the center of his back, she pushed him gently in the direction he was now facing.

"Again?" Kaj said; and then he shrugged, lengthening his stride and moving away from them in the direction of the ship's infirmary.

"Contact me in twenty minutes!" Toni called at his retreating back.

"I should have specialized in trauma . . ." they heard his voice trail off as he passed through the hatch.

"Bleys, this is the first officer, John Tindall," Toni said then, turning and indicating the middle-aged man who had supervised the gentle removal of Dahno from his crate—no small feat, given Dahno's size—and then come to stand silently nearby during the brief argument with the medician.

"I know we've met before, Mr. Tindall," Bleys said, offering his hand.

"We have, Great Teacher," the first officer said. "We've had the pleasure of your company on board *Favored of God* on a number of occasions, although at those times we were usually carrying other passengers as well."

"The pleasure has been mine," Bleys said. "I learned long ago I could feel safe and comfortable in the care of this ship and her people."

As the first officer beamed, Bleys continued: "How is Captain Broadus? I assume she's busy?"

"She is ashore, sir," said Tindall. "Henry MacLean indicated it was imperative that this ship appear to be on other business, as well as virtually deserted during repairs. Since repairs are customarily the first officer's province, the captain took rooms ashore—under a false name, of course."

"I see," Bleys nodded. "No one would think anything was going on aboard a ship whose captain was apparently taking a bit of recreational leave."

"Yes, sir," said the first officer. "The captain is unhappy about it, though."

"They also serve who only stand and wait," Bleys murmured.

"Yes, sir."

"I suspect, now we've come aboard, she'll find some reason for her own return," Toni said. Then, more briskly: "Mr. Tindall, can we arrange to have a work space set up for us?"

"Already done," the first officer said. "Please follow me."

"I need to know more about what's been going on," Bleys said, as he and Toni entered the ship's main lounge a few minutes later. "We still haven't figured out who our enemy is."

"Henry said we'd have nearly total communications available here—and I expect that would be you?" Toni said, addressing the question to two figures now rising from desks on the other side of the lounge.

"Yes," one of them said. He was short and muscular, with hair almost the same medium shade of brown as his skin.

"You're Walker Freas, I think," Toni said. "And you would be Sarah Kochan," she went on, turning to the second figure, a short, red-haired woman whose face carried an intense display of freckles.

The two Soldiers nodded. Their presence indicated they were members of the specialists among Henry's Soldiers—some of whom were technical specialists being trained in the skills of fighting, and the rest warriors being trained in technical skills. Bleys, when Henry had brought the idea of the dual force to him, had foreseen friction between the two groups, but the cross-training seemed to be paying off, as each side developed more respect for the other, having learned something of what the others had to know. . . .

"There are four more of us," Walker Freas said, "two on duty with the comms consoles, through that door there—" he pointed, "—and two catching some sleep."

"Henry gave me to understand you have landlines set up through the pad facilities, that can't be traced," Toni said.

"That's right," Sarah Kochan said. Her face lit in a toothy smile. "The line is shielded up to its junction with the public system, as is required by the interstellar compacts for spaceports."

She was referring, they all knew, to some of the legal niceties that gave all ships on spaceport pads the sovereignty of their home planets, and put them virtually beyond the control of whatever planet they might be on.

"And after that juncture, it becomes virtually anonymous in the midst of the public system," Sarah was continuing. "It's a permanently open connection, which means no initialization signals to attract attention—going to a safe house where we have all the standard comm security gear in place, as well as a nano-modulated—"

"What you're saying, I think," Toni interrupted what was clearly about to become much more of a technological lecture than Bleys wanted just now, "is that even if anyone traces calls to the safe house, they can't trace it back here."

"Oh, it could be done, I guess," Sarah said. "But not in any time frame I've been given to understand we have to worry about."

"Let's speak about this in more detail a little later," Toni said. "But for the moment we need to talk more about content than about systems."

"Do you want to ask us questions, or would you prefer our summary first?" Walker Freas asked. The unexpected aptitude the one-time mercenary had shown for intelligence collection activities had been very pleasing to Henry, Bleys remembered.

"Summary first, I think," Toni said, exchanging a glance with Bleys, who had already moved over to take a seat at one of the vacated desks, where he found already up and running a screen that accessed the ship's information storage. He entered the password needed to access the files from Others' headquarters that had been copied into the ship's computer before it left Association; and then looked up and nodded at Toni.

"We may ask questions as you go," Toni said to the two Soldiers.

"Of course," Walker Freas said. He turned and nodded to Sarah, who also sat down at a screen.

"Following your instructions," Walker Freas said now, "those of us who came in secretly on *Favored of God* set up covert surveillance on the Others' headquarters and its personnel, and two-person teams went out to surveil seven of the Others who primarily work elsewhere on the planet."

"Did you have information of some sort that led you to choose those seven?" Toni asked.

"No," Freas answered. "With nothing to go on, we simply chose seven at random."

"What did you find?"

"Up until your arrival, nothing untoward happened—except for one thing that didn't happen: our people couldn't locate one of the outlying seven Others."

"Which one?" Bleys asked.

"Stella Tanalingam," Walker Freas replied.

"Could she have been out on her route?"

"We don't think so," Walker said. "We had information on all the local Others' routes, of course, and our team followed along hers. As it happened, four of the other six outlying Others were also out on their routes, and the teams assigned to them had no trouble finding them."

"Could she have been on vacation, or ill, for instance?" Toni asked.

"Perhaps," the Soldier said. "But we don't think so, because there was another unexpected variation from pattern: her route was still being worked."

"Worked? You mean—" Toni began, but Bleys interrupted her.

"You mean someone else was out following up her normal contacts, don't you?" he said.

"Yes," Walker nodded. "Specifically, one of her staff members."

"You know that because it was someone listed in the table of organization you were given," Bleys said. "Which one?"

"Lester Parnell," Walker said. Bleys immediately called up the available information on that individual. He had thoroughly reviewed all such material already, but despite his retentive memory he took time to scan the file once more, while waving a hand for the summary to continue.

"In all other cases, the Others' staffs never acted on their own,"

Walker Freas said. "Generally the staff stays in the office, acting as liaison and so forth; if one of them goes out on a route, it's always in a position supporting the senior Other."

He fell silent, watching Bleys, who appeared intent over his screen. After a moment Toni spoke again.

"You've been telling us what you saw before our arrival," she said.

"Right," the Soldier said, and continued: "At what we now know was a short time after *Burning Bush* came out of its final shift, there was an explosion of activity in the headquarters here in Ceta City. None of it could be called suspicious, given the circumstances of your arrival. And within a short time, there was activity in all the outlying offices we were covering."

"All attributable to their seniors being instructed to come to Ceta City," Toni said.

Walker nodded.

"But in Stella Tanalingam's office?" Bleys asked, looking up now from his screen.

"Activity, yes," Walker said. "But no one went to Ceta City from that office. Rather, Parnell came back to the office immediately, and some sort of conference was held, involving two other members of the staff—and two persons unknown to us."

"There was no way to listen to that conference, or to any calls?" Bleys asked.

"No. Others' security is entirely too good to allow that. Perhaps we could have arranged something, with time, but—"

"Never mind," Bleys said. "Go on."

"As I said, we only had two people on the scene," Walker said. "When the conference broke up, they made the decision to split up. Elizabeth Kalra followed Coleman Jones, another of the staff at that meeting, and Ken Anderson went off after one of the unknowns." He stopped.

"And?" Toni prompted him.

"Coleman Jones merely went home," Walker said, "and has either stayed there or gone in to the office. Ken Anderson has not been heard from again."

CHAPTER 13

It was Bleys who finally interrupted the silence.

"Was there any unusual activity after we left the office here?" he asked.

"Not for some time, as far as we could tell—with one exception," Walker said.

"An exception arising after the bomb attack on our convoy," Bleys stated.

"Yes," Walker said; and Sarah nodded.

"What happened?" Toni asked.

"Pallas Salvador was at home—it was night here when that attack occurred," Sarah said. "Our estimate is that no one called her with the news for several hours. When she got the news, she went to the office immediately."

"And during that intervening period, the staff—what?" Bleys asked.

"Two staff members who are normally off-duty at night came to the headquarters less than an hour after the attack," Walker said. "Gelica Costanza and Susan Perry. During the following twenty minutes three unknown persons arrived, and remained there for over an hour, leaving about twenty minutes before Pallas Salvador arrived."

"Descriptions?" Bleys asked.

"Better than that," Sarah Kochan said. "Pictures."

"Pictures?" Toni asked. "I thought even the most conventional security equipment prevented that kind of thing?"

"Anti-eavesdropping equipment works by inhibiting electronic circuitry," Sarah said. She smiled. "We took non-electronic pictures as they entered and left the building."

"How—" Toni began.

"Mechanical cameras," Bleys interrupted her. "They use some sort of non-electronic recording medium with a simple mechanical lens—we don't have time to get sidetracked on that: where are those pictures?"

"I'm sending them to your screen now," Sarah said.

"I see," Bleys said after a moment. "Are these the same people who came to Parnell's office?"

"No."

"What descriptions do you have for those people?"

"A man and a woman," Walker Freas said. "Both estimated to be in their upper sixties in age. The man tall and muscular, with rosy white skin and graying brown hair, and the woman black-haired and brown-skinned, about six inches shorter than the man and unusually thin."

Toni, who had moved to look over Bleys' shoulder at the pictures from Ceta City while Walker gave the descriptions of the unphotographed people, looked up.

"There's a common denominator," she said.

"Yes," Bleys nodded. "They're all in the same age range."

"We noticed that, too," Walker Freas said. "And with only one exception it's the same age range as the staff members they conferred with. We don't think it could be a coincidence, but we don't have an explanation for it."

In the ensuing silence, Toni pointed out that tomorrow was the day the Others' leaders were scheduled to reconvene at the Ceta City headquarters.

"You're right," Bleys said. He paused to think for a moment.

"We need time," he said. "Get a message out postponing the meeting for seven days—route it through the consulate in Abbeyville, giving the impression it's coming from me there."

"All right," Toni said.

A moment later the door annunciator chimed. At a nod from Bleys, Sarah Kochan touched a control, and the door opened to reveal Kaj Menowsky. Toni held up a hand before he could speak.

"Bleys?" she said. Her tone got his attention.

"You need to go with Kaj now and let him look you over," she said.

Bleys looked at her, then at Kaj in the doorway. After a moment he stood up.

"We need to make this fast," he said to the medician.

Kaj only nodded, and backed out of the doorway as Bleys began to stride toward it. Bleys, however, stopped, and turned half around.

"Find me some experienced researchers," he said to the room in general. "I mean experienced in negotiating libraries and databases. I'd prefer they were our own people, but we can use locals for the sake of speed, if we can maintain security." He turned away but continued speaking over his shoulder as he walked toward the door.

"I think Henry called in some of the outlying teams to augment the force that screened us after the bombing," Bleys said. "Is anyone still out watching the outlying offices?"

"Yes," Walker Freas said. "Henry sent a few of the people who were originally with you to take over that surveillance."

"Probably thinking they were known to the local authorities in the area around us," Toni said. "They wouldn't have been known in the surveillance areas."

"Call them all in," Bleys said, "except for the ones watching Lester Parnell. We're going to need the rest here."

"The meeting's been postponed," Toni said when Bleys returned to the lounge less than an hour later. "What did Kaj have to say?"

"He said I'm fine."

"I'll check that with him later, you know."

"I knew that," Bleys said. "He wants to look you over, too, you know. In any case, he'll still tell you I'm fine, although he'll probably take longer than that to say it."

"And he thinks you should take a nap."

"How did you know that?"

"He always wants you to get more rest," she said, smiling.

"I'll admit to being tired," he said. "I'll get a nap in a minute."

"There's a bedroom right down the corridor," she pointed out. He nodded.

"Where is everybody?" he asked.

"In comms," she said, indicating the door that had been pointed out to him earlier. "I'm afraid the Soldiers don't run to research skills, so I've got them looking for suitable locals."

"Would any of our official party be likely to have such skills?" he asked.

"Yes," she said, nodding. "But they're all still in Abbeyville, pretending you're holed up there; and I thought it'd be best not to risk exposing that ruse."

"You're right," he said.

"Why don't you tell me what you want researched," she said. "Then you can catch a nap while I get it all in motion?"

"We want historical researchers," he said, "but I'm still trying to work the problem in my own head. . . . Let me sleep on it, and I'll have it by the time we have people ready to work. Besides, you need sleep even more than I do."

Things were quiet aboard *Favored of God* that evening. In fact, Bleys thought, it was almost like being in space, except there were fewer people around. He had napped for nearly four hours before getting up to have a small meal, which he prepared for himself in the ship's kitchen. Toni was still asleep.

He wished he could look out from the ship now, to see space as they passed through it—to look out at the stars, as he always tried to do when out among them . . . but then, it wasn't space he would see out there now. He could activate a sensor to watch the Cetan night sky from here in the lounge, but it would not be the same thing.

It was strange that he could feel so free, in a ship like this, when it was out among the stars, and yet feel so penned in—in the very same ship—when it was at rest on a planet's surface.

He had not really realized, until now, how much he had come to miss those visits with the stars. On his first interstellar trips with his mother he had gotten out from under the thumbs of the caretakers she set to watch him, by parking himself in the lounges of the various liners and watching the starscapes the vision screens presented. . . . Some of the better liners had even had wraparound effects that could make him feel as if he was floating in space without need for a ship. On later trips, when he was an adult traveling alone, solitary, that feeling of kinship with the stars had, if anything, grown stronger.

These years his trips were always made in the company of others—other people and other concerns ... so many of both, he could never seem to find the solitariness necessary to recapture that feeling of kinship.

Would he ever be that alone again? It seemed strange even to him, that he, who had felt loneliness so keenly all his life, should miss being alone.

It did not seem likely he would ever again be in a position to travel by himself, unburdened by the presence of others who could demand his time and attention.

—Maybe not. He remembered now, suddenly, that many years ago Donal Graeme, who had come as close as anyone ever had to being the ruler—no, make that *guardian*—of the entire race, had still managed to be alone in a ship, on that last trip when he had vanished, as sometimes occurred when a phase-shift went wrong.

Did Graeme travel by himself because of some similar desire to be close with the stars? Maybe he ought to look into more details of the man's life.

And maybe he could learn to handle a ship and go off on trips by himself. . . .

But then, he reminded himself, Graeme had been a Dorsai, an accomplished member of a people skilled in shiphandling. Still . . .

He shook his head. His mission was going to require all the lifetime he could manage to attain, and more besides.

A few hours later, Toni came into the lounge by way of the comms room.

"Henry's on the line," she said. "He wants to know if you have any new orders."

"He told us earlier that the Soldiers found no identification of any sort on the dead attackers around that bunker, but that they were going to try to analyze some of the clothing and equipment," Bleys said. "Did anything come of that?"

"The equipment and clothing are all locally produced," Toni

said. "Henry's reluctant to use official channels to follow up the serial numbers on the weapons, because that might tip someone off on what we're doing."

"He's correct," Bleys said, "but I don't think it could hurt us, as long as the request seems to come from the Abbeyville consultate—it would be normal for us to be trying to follow up the attack."

"It's still daylight in Abbeyville," Toni said. "I'll have Henry forward the information through the staff there. Is there anything else?"

"Not at the moment," Bleys said, "but there'll certainly be something for him to do tomorrow—maybe we should get him prepared for that. But what are you doing up? I thought you were sleeping?"

"I was," she said, "but I left instructions for them to wake me when Henry called. I'll be going back to bed soon. . . . As for Henry, I'd suggest we don't tell him anything about tomorrow, just now. Anything we have to tell him won't be hurt by waiting until morning—keep in mind, Henry has probably had even less sleep than we have, these last few days."

"You're right," Bleys said. "I should have remembered that."

"We can all use some more sleep," Toni said.

"I'm looking forward to it," he said. And he was, he realized, now that he had said it. Because sometimes his mind produced answers in his sleep.

"Don't let me sleep too long," he added, remembering that on those occasions when his mind had worked on a problem in his sleep, he had often slept for an inordinate length of time.

He stood up.

"How long is 'too long'?" Toni asked.

"Let's say—either when there's some unusual activity by the people we've been watching, or twelve hours."

"All right," she nodded.

"Are you coming to bed?"

"In a few minutes," she said. "Henry's waiting on the line; and I'd like to leave a few instructions with the duty people."

"All right," he said, and went through the door to the corridor. As Toni opened the door to the comms room, Bleys' head appeared in the other doorway again.

"Have there been any repercussions from all the bodies we left scattered in that field?" he asked.

"If you mean in the media, or in the form of any activity by our secret enemies—not that I've heard," she said. "Our diplomatic people informed the Solomonis that you managed to escape when your convoy was ambushed, and I'd guess they'll be embarrassed enough to keep the whole thing out of the media."

"Don't put out any feelers about it," he said. "But keep listening. Silence may lead our enemies to make a wrong move."

"I'll leave instructions on that, too."

He nodded, and vanished from sight again.

CHAPTER 14

Contrary to his own expectations, Bleys slept heavily and awoke early. Toni was not with him, and he wondered whether she might have chosen to sleep in another room; there were plenty available.

He lay in bed, half awake at best, cocooned in the force field that made up the sleeping surface. He had not turned on a light, but simply continued to lie there watching the simulated night sky to which the room's ceiling had been set. Turning his head to the right would have put his eyes on the time display that glowed in midair on that side of the bed, but he did not do that.

Part of him would have welcomed a longer time in the depths of unconsciousness, but he felt vaguely that further sleep would elude him. He would only drowse, tossing and turning; until, finally, he would rise to start his day feeling achey and unwell, his head thick and his emotional state depressed.

But he was also reluctant to start his day right away; and so he lay there in the darkness, probing lazily at the back of his own mind and waiting for something—anything—to happen. As far as he could tell, he had not dreamed. He was disappointed about that.

The star display on his ceiling was familiar, he realized idly; it was the night sky he had gazed at as a youth on Henry's farm—except there were more stars: this ceiling was showing him many of the faint stars not generally visible through Association's atmosphere. He speculated listlessly on whether this artificial sky included such faint stars in order to make the display more aesthetic . . . it did not really seem very gaudy.

Night skies were almost identical on all the human worlds, he knew. The worlds inhabited by the human race were not far enough apart for the differences in their locations to make for major changes in their starscapes, beyond the presence or absence of those worlds' own stars.

But there were differences nonetheless. He was able to pick out, in this instance, the bright light that was Association's sister planet, Harmony, as well as another, even brighter light that was—that represented, he corrected himself—Archangel, the great gas giant that shared Association's system, farther out from the star.

In every system in which he had ever watched the stars, the sky presented information that told just which system it was—and, often, evidences of the human presence . . . artificial satellite, spacecraft. . . . Only when he watched the stars from a starship in transit had his view been unobstructed, clean and clear and pure.

Was this a standard starscape entered in the ship's settings, to be seen by anyone who might use this room—the notion came to him out of nowhere—or had this view been specifically set for *his* eyes?

It would make sense for a ship based in the port of Association's capital city to reproduce the night sky from that viewpoint, but it might well be that a variety of skies—of viewpoints—were available for the programming.

—*Was someone programming his sky?*

His eyes closed, involuntarily, and he sat up in the darkness he had created with his eyelids. His hands clawed at the controls in the panel next to the bed, but he was fumbling, unable to manipulate them in his haste and with his lids clenched shut. He stood up, still self-blinded, and stumbled to the small bathroom, throwing himself into the shower in the darkness, not bothering to take off the shorts he always slept in.

After a while, the feeling of sickness passed; until at last he was able to open his eyes and stop the water beating down on him. It was water of the planet, piped on board from the port's facilities, and it was inadequate to its task: he still felt soiled, dirty.

Dried, he returned to his bed and experimented with the ceiling display. He had never paid much notice to the ceiling settings during his previous trips in this ship, perhaps because on real trips he could look out of the ship, at the real starscape between planetary systems, whenever he wanted . . . he was only interested in artificial skies when stuck on a planetary surface. . . .

Besides, he usually had other things on his mind.

He felt better, now, to learn that only the single display was available. He lay there and watched it, wondering if it would rotate to imitate Association's movement, as the displays in other rooms he had slept in had done. In time he drifted into a light, restless sleep.

When he awoke again, he could feel a small, lurking presence in his head, a hint of a headache waiting to be born. It made him uneasy; headaches were often precursors of his blackouts—signals, his medician had warned him, of the bad effects of some stressful situation.

To take his mind off the threat, he tried to force it into consideration of the problems he had been working on before going to sleep . . . and he began to realize there was a layer of irritation underlying his self-concern. Irritation over all the problems obstructing his course, irritation that his own mind and body should distract him from his task—even irritation that his unconscious mind had not, as he had hoped, solved any of his problems while he slept.

Recognizing his lack of focus, he dipped into his past training, and engaged in his breathing exercises; he had been introduced to them in Dahno's training program, and his workouts with Toni had reinforced that training. Within a short time he had turned himself around: the irritation, although not banished, had been embraced, used to get himself up and moving.

There was no food service in the ship, so Bleys made his way to the kitchen to find himself something to eat.

Ashore, he mused, moving down the corridor. He wondered how many people, these days, recognized that the term derived from the ancient days of ocean travel on Old Earth. Most of the Younger Worlds had their own oceans, but still . . . Nonetheless, it was clear that the mother planet's influence remained even in the language of her most distant children.

He was also one of few, he reflected as he entered the kitchen, who knew that such a room on an Old Earth ocean vessel had often been called a *galley*. Why had that term not been taken into space, when *ashore* had? It seemed haphazard, almost untidy, that some terms had emigrated while others had not . . . the person who guided a spaceship was not called a pilot anymore, he knew; to his mind the presently used term for that functionary, *driver*, was wildly inappropriate.

He put that train of thought aside to examine his choices in foodstuffs; and decided to settle for making himself a plate of toasted bread, cold chicken, cheese and fruit.

In a way, it made him feel more cheerful that he was getting his own breakfast. He had not had to do anything like that for a long time—where were the knives? *Ah!*

As his involvement with the Others' movement began to grow, back when he and Dahno still shared an apartment in Ecumeny, he had spent more and more of his time working with others, eating with others . . . and even when he was alone, his time had been too precious to be wasted on domestic chores.

But in this particular time and place, he felt good about fending for himself, as if somehow he was contributing to solving the race's problems—and at that moment the knife he had been laboriously pushing through a hard block of cheese seemed to jump in his hand as the resistance of the dense foodstuff ended abruptly; and the severed end of cheese skidded off the plate to fall to the floor.

And *that*, he thought, had not happened to him since sometime during those years when he lived with Henry and his sons on their farm.

"Oops," he heard Toni say, behind him. He turned to look at her.

"*There* you are," he said. "I thought maybe you were still asleep in some other room."

"What were you thinking, just now?" she asked, ignoring his comment. "You had such a distant look."

"I was remembering the first meal I ate when I came to live with Henry," he said. "Goat cheese, bread and a stew that was mostly vegetables, with a little bit of rabbit meat."

"A lot of people believe plain food is blessed in the eyes of the Lord," she said.

"It was all the farm could provide," he said, not intending any irony.

"It's that way for a lot of people on Association, even today," she said. "On Harmony, too. And these are good days, compared to those early years after the planets were first settled."

"On some of the other Younger Worlds, too," he said. He shook his head. "A lot of people have already suffered because of the decision to leave Old Earth."

He was conscious of her eyes on him, but he avoided looking directly into her gaze, and bent to pick up the cheese he had dropped. She got a treated cleaning cloth and wiped the floor surface; and then watched as, after starting to throw the fallen cheese away, he turned to the sink to rinse it off, before putting it on his plate.

"There are a lot of people who'd love to have that cheese," he said. "Even dirty."

"Something to drink?" she asked.

Back in the lounge that had been converted into an office for him, he put his plate and glass on his desk and pulled over a large, but light, float chair of the kind Others' ships always kept available for him. His finger reached out for the control that would give him access to the databanks, but then hesitated.

He was sitting in the same position, a distant frown on his face, when Toni walked into the room, carrying her own plate and glass. When she saw his face she walked across the room to her own desk, and put her plate down; and began to eat while catching up on the communications that had come in overnight.

Some minutes later, she pressed the *HUSH* control on her console, and opened an interior comm channel.

"Bridge here. What can I do for you, Antonia Lu?"

"Why, Captain—I didn't expect *you*! I thought you were out of the ship?"

"I came aboard last night," the deep female voice replied. "I couldn't stand it. And who else would be answering your call? The ship's nearly empty, since it's normal procedure for most of the crew to go ashore when repairs are in progress, which is the story we've given out."

"I know that's true," Toni said, "but it still surprised me to hear your voice."

"Someone has to do it, after all, and the First Officer is, I hope, sleeping—he was on watch for nearly twenty hours, since the few crew members left on board are working on the repairs and remodeling."

"They're actually repairing something? I thought that was only a story?"

"Well, it is," the captain said. "But the story won't look realistic if this ship doesn't send out discarded materials every now and then. We even have Cetan personnel coming aboard every day to do some of the work; but our crew is responsible for keeping them away from the areas where you and the First Elder might be seen. Now what can I do for you?"

"I'm afraid this puts me in an awkward position, Captain. I was hoping I could get a few bodies in here to help me move some furniture."

"Move furniture?"

"I'm afraid so. It's a matter of putting this lounge into a—a configuration that will facilitate our work." Toni knew it would be easier to explain what she wanted when she could simply point at things.

"Right now?" the captain asked.

"As soon as possible, at any rate, if it can be arranged."

"Give me a couple of minutes, please."

After the captain keyed off, Toni set the lounge's main door to stay open. In a few minutes the tall, stocky form of Captain Anita Broadus appeared in the doorway, followed by three crew members—two men and a woman; two of them appeared rumpled, as if they had just awakened, and one of the men was trying to stifle a yawn.

Upon seeing Bleys still apparently deep in thought, the captain turned her attention to Toni, who had walked across to meet her.

"Are we going to disturb the First Elder?" the captain asked— she was trying to whisper, Toni realized, but she was a large woman with a personality to match, and one used to command; even her whisper came out with a booming quality.

"No need to whisper, Captain," Toni said, using a normal tone of voice. "The First Elder is thinking, but we'd have to work pretty hard to disturb him."

The captain's nod seemed contrary to the skeptical look on her face.

"I appreciate your coming," Toni continued. "But I only meant for you to send someone—who's watching the bridge?"

"Oh, I woke the First Officer," the Captain said.

"Oh, no—I didn't mean for anything like that!" Toni said, her eyes widening. As she began to apologize, the captain interrupted her.

"Don't fret yourself over it," she said, her dark face lighting up with a broad smile. "That's what first officers are for! And John knows better than anyone we're down to a skeleton complement. Now tell me what you need."

Deciding that the best way to end everyone's inconvenience would be to put her project into action, Toni quickly explained her idea; within moments the tables and chairs not already being used by Bleys and Toni were being pushed aside, the entertainment consoles disconnected and unbolted from the floor—even the long bar was detached and pushed as far against the opposite wall of the lounge as it would go.

In less than fifteen minutes they had cleared an elongated open space down the longest axis of the lounge, its sides made up of two rows of easy chairs that faced the cleared space, as if awaiting an audience.

"Is this about what you had in mind, Antonia Lu?" the captain asked, handing a power wrench back to one of her crew. She had moved at least as much furniture as any of them.

"Yes it is, Captain," Toni said. "Thank you so much."

"Yes, thank you, Captain," Bleys said, his voice startling Toni as he moved quietly up behind them.

"I'm so sorry, First Elder—" the captain began; but Bleys stopped her with a raised hand and a smile.

"Please, Captain, don't be," he said. "I should be apologizing to you—I know our situation has created a lot of problems for you—"

This time it was the captain's turn to interrupt.

"That's nonsense, sir," she said. "I think you know the crew of

Favored of God is proud to do whatever it can to help you in your work." Her eyes were gleaming in her broad face, and her cheeks were bunched up in a great smile that showed large, gleaming white teeth.

Bleys was silent for a moment; then he spoke, more softly.

"And you do it very well, too."

The captain gave a nod, a kind of sideways dip of her head. There was silence for a moment, before she turned back to Toni.

"And is there anything else we can do?"

"No, Captain—thank you so much!" Toni said.

The captain waved one hand vaguely toward her head, as if faking a salute; and then put on her professionalism again, gathering her people and striding out the door.

"I'm sorry we disturbed you," Toni said to Bleys. "I hoped you were so deep in thought you wouldn't notice, and I was guessing you'd work better if you had a walkway like the one you use back home."

"It's a good idea," Bleys said. "I'm certain I'll be using it—I'd thought about walking in the corridor, but . . ."

"You seemed to be thinking hard," Toni said. "Is there anything I can help with?"

"Well, I can't answer that yet," he replied. "It's just that a bell seemed to ring inside me, while we were speaking about the cheese; and so far I'm having trouble pinning down whatever my mind's trying to tell me."

"The cheese?"

"I'll explain when I know," he said; and he shrugged and returned to the chair he had been sitting in.

"You never ate," she said, following him.

"I forgot," he said. He sat down and started in on his breakfast. In a moment, he looked back up at her.

"Thank you," he said.

Within fifteen minutes he was pacing rapidly up and down the length of the cleared space, one hand lightly slapping the surface of the bar each time he reached the far end of the room and made his turn.

Toni sat at her desk, keeping an eye on the occasional communication being silently fed to her screen.

The silence stretched out, punctuated only by the light *slap* of hand on bar.

As noon approached, Toni was starting to contemplate the idea of interrupting Bleys in his pacing. She had had to do so in the past, and she hated it—she thought of his walking as a form of meditation, and believed it was good for him.

On this occasion, however, the word *meditation* did not really seem to fit the exercise; there was something more driven, more keyed-up, about this particular session.

In any case, Bleys soon broke off on his own accord, immediately after making one of his turns at the bar; and stopped, looking down the length of the lounge at her.

"How long have I been at this?" he asked finally, breaking the silence.

"Just over four hours," she said. "Are you all right?"

"I'm all right," he said. He took a step toward her; then stopped. His face bore a strange look—on other people, she thought, it might have been shame, perhaps mixed with chagrin.

"I really am all right," he went on. "My headache is gone and my head feels clear. But it appears my physical conditioning has suffered since we came to this planet."

"Hardly unexpected, considering what we've been through," she said. She surprised herself by giving out a sort of throaty snort, and grinned. "I was going to suggest we get back to our exercises, but thought it best to take another day of rest."

"You were right," he said. He looked around. "Do you think we could work out in this space?"

"Easily," she replied. "Your control is more than adequate to keep you from falling over the furniture." She cocked her head slightly, looking at him sharply.

"What's wrong?" she asked.

"I think I gave myself blisters."

"*That* shouldn't have happened," she said, frowning. She rose from her desk and walked toward him. "What are you doing differently?"

"Nothing—that I know of," he said.

"No, of course not," she said. "If you knew what you were doing wrong, you wouldn't do it. Can I assume you're wearing your normal footgear?"

"Yes."

"Sit down in that closest chair, and I'll call Kaj to come up."

"It's not that bad—" he began, but she interrupted him.

"There's no point in trying to tough it out," she said, looking stern. "Trying to do that will cause you to make unconscious adjustments, and your whole body will end up out of balance. You know that."

"I know," he said, holding up a hand to stop her. "I know. I meant it's not necessary to call Kaj here—I can go to the infirmary."

"It'd be best," she said, nodding. "The equipment there can take care of your feet better than handheld tools down here . . . are you really up to it?"

"It's only a few blisters," he said.

"I didn't mean it that way," she said. "What I meant was, are you up to dealing with Kaj? You've been pretty short with him from the start, but . . ." She trailed off.

"I know," he said. "I think I'm past that now."

She looked at him silently for a moment.

"There's more going on here than I realized," she said finally. "But I can't believe you put in all that thought on your relationship with Kaj; so I think that's only a—a side effect."

"You're right," he said. "But let's not talk about it now. Call Kaj and see if he's free to see me."

"He will be," she said. "He doesn't let anything get in the way of his vocation."

"I know," Bleys said. "It's one of the things I've realized—that he's more like me than I knew."

She returned to her desk, a thoughtful look on her face, and made the call.

CHAPTER 15

When Bleys got back to the lounge an hour later, Toni was all business, giving him details on the results of the search for researchers. The list of candidates, although the joint project of the Soldiers here in the ship and the staff still locked up in the consulate, had, Bleys knew, been led and guided by Toni.

There was speculation in her expression now, as she looked at him across the space between their desks, but he was sure she would not try to probe into his thinking unless she believed he needed that, somehow.

"No one has made an approach to any of these researchers," she said. "So it's possible some of them can't, or won't, take on whatever project you have in mind. But we can pay well."

"We don't want to offer so much more than the market as to attract attention," he warned. "In any event, we won't need all of them, so there's plenty of leeway for refusals. I'm more concerned about their locations—I mean, I want to use people who are scattered about the planet, rather than concentrated in one place, such as here in Ceta City."

"I suppose you mean if they're dispersed, they're less likely to gossip with each other—people in a specialized field often know each other, after all—and perhaps get an idea of the extent of the project?"

"That, yes," he said. "But it would also increase the chances that each will have access to peculiarly local information not available in other parts of the planet."

He saw her visibly make an effort to stifle her questions as she returned to her briefing.

"I assume you have no intention of either bringing researchers here to the ship, or going out to see them," she said; "so we'll have to instruct our people outside to make the initial approaches to the researchers."

"That's right," he said. "We'll put together a prospectus for our people—by the way, they should be very clear that this is an undercover operation: they can't let the researchers know who they're working for . . . in fact, the researchers themselves would be wise not to let anyone know what project they're working on."

"We'll have to give some thought to which of our people to give this job to," Toni said. "Most of the staff aren't really geared up for—what did you call it?—'undercover' work."

"Run this through Henry," Bleys said. "He'll probably suggest using some of the Soldiers who were raised on this planet; they'll be more likely to have the right accents and mannerisms to be accepted as normal Cetans; with a suitable cover story, they'll raise less suspicion."

"You're worried that if the researchers talk about what they're doing, it may draw interest from the wrong quarter?"

"Certainly," he said. "But I also don't want the researchers to get themselves killed before they complete their work for us."

There was a short silence in the room, before Toni continued.

"So what is it you want researched?"

"Actually, you have one more data-sort to do," he said. "I want you to separate out researchers who seem to have familiarity with something like image alteration or image recognition software."

"That kind of information ought to be in their résumés."

"Then go through our files on the organization's personnel here on Ceta," Bleys said. "I mean the files we brought along with us, rather than those in the local offices. Copy the photos of every staffer over forty-five years of age. Give those photos to about a half dozen of the imaging-qualified researchers, scattered around the planet. Those researchers should not be given any other information—not even the names we have for those subjects. We want the researchers trying to identify the photos with no preconceptions—understood?"

"I see what you're saying," Toni said. "Could I suggest the researchers be told to think of the subjects as they were about twenty-five years ago?"

"You're proceeding on the assumption that those staff people would have been most active in whatever they've been up to, when they were in their thirties or so?" Bleys said, nodding. "I was coming to that, but don't let the researchers overlook checking on the current faces."

"I understand," Toni said. "And the other group of researchers?"

"Again, give them nothing to base a preconception on," he said. "Simply tell them to dig up any information they can on any secret, semi-secret, or underground organization on this planet during the period between fifteen and forty years ago—particularly focusing on the areas of finance and crime."

"That's a pretty broad mandate," she said. "It'll likely take weeks to get full results back."

"True," he said. "I don't think we have that much time, but we don't necessarily need the full details, either; I'll be satisfied with sketchy reports if they come quickly."

"Let me see if I can come up with some way to include in the package a requirement that the researchers report to the person who hired them once a day—it'll mean our people have to be reachable, somehow, which Henry won't like."

"Maybe the researchers ought to make themselves reachable at designated times each day," Bleys suggested. "Most of the good research facilities have excellent communications equipment, and I'm sure Ceta won't lag in that respect."

"Staggering the report times will make it possible for a single one of our people to deal with more than one researcher," she pointed out. "But would reports twice a day be better?"

"Yes," he said. "The researchers can be told their reports back will help narrow the field of the research—I mean, that with their reports we'll be able to send back suggestions on where to focus their efforts."

"All right," she said, nodding in her turn. "Anything more?"

"No."

"Then I'll get started."

"Cheese?" Her voice came out of the starlit darkness of the bedroom they were sharing.

"I wasn't really thinking about *cheese*," he said, turning his head in her direction. He could see a pale shadow that was her body, faintly lit by the artificial starlight.

"I knew *that!*" she said. "But if it's not too nosy, I'd like to know how that led you to—whatever it led you to."

"I don't mind," he said. "But it's going to sound silly—maybe flimsy."

"But you went somewhere with it, didn't you?"

"I just started from there," he said. "The thought of how hard life has been, for so many on the Younger Worlds, reminded me that life is much better—even luxurious—for me now. And for the Others we've been leading."

"I guess you could say you've raised the Others to an elite position," she said. "Is that bad?"

"It might be."

"You're saying we've been spoiled?"

"I know *I've* gotten too used to the good life." He raised himself on an elbow, turning his upper body slightly sideways to face her.

"That's not so—you work harder than anyone I know!"

"That's kind of you," he said. "And it may be true—but in any case, that's not exactly what I meant."

They were in a force bed, so he did not feel any movement when she sat up, but he could see her pale form rise a little, and loom closer. He rolled onto his back again.

"Then you have to explain what you mean," she said, settling down while leaning against his side. He had automatically raised his arm as she moved toward him, and now he brought it down behind her back as she raised her head to accommodate his shoulder.

"Life has been going well for us—for our Others," he explained. "It may have led us into a sort of spiritual contentment—which, I guess, can look like simple laziness in some contexts."

"How can you say that? The Others here on Ceta *do* work hard—they're always on the go!"

"Yes, they are," he said. "At least, it certainly looks like it, on the surface. But what if *they've* gotten complacent, too?"

"You mean, they've only been going through the motions?"

"Well, as I said, the cheese reminded me that life has gotten much better for us—at least in the ways most people measure that kind of thing. Two things are responsible for that: we Others learned to work together for a common end, and people who might have opposed us forgot how to do that . . . oddly enough, I was speaking to Dahno about something akin to this just a couple of weeks ago; but at the time I never thought to relate that discussion to me, to us."

"Us?"

"Look," he said, "I started this expedition to try to figure out why our Others on this planet had not reported on the unknown group—I dislike that term, the 'secret people'—on this planet. Whoever they are. I was assuming that either our people were working dependably but the unknowns were amazingly good at keeping their doings secret, or some, at least, of our Others had been brought over to helping them."

"Yes," she said. "I remember that the biggest obstacle to believing in the existence of these 'unknowns,' when you deduced it, was the fact it was so unlikely that a group that powerful could be so well hidden."

"Occam's razor," he said. "A simpler explanation is more likely to be correct—or, at least, useful as a starting point: that our people—and everyone else on the planet, for that matter—did a less than great job of observation."

"Hence the researchers you've commissioned."

"Yes," he said. "And until I get some feedback from them, I'm only able to make estimates on what's been happening, and on what it means for us."

She shifted position, rolling over to rest on his chest.

"Sorry," she said. "My arm was going to sleep. But can you give me some idea of what your 'estimates' are?"

"You mean you want my best guess."

"All right, yes," she said. "Disclaimer noted. Now what do you suspect?"

"Well, first," he said, "I think the Cetan organization—I mean our Others here—has been infiltrated. Not just manipulated from the outside, but infiltrated."

"Some of the staff people," she said.

"Why are you asking me what *my* guesses are?" he said. "You seem to be doing just as well as I am."

"Don't be coy. That much was fairly obvious from the Soldiers' observations."

"Which reminds me," he said: "the Soldiers have been very useful, working undercover, but I suspect they're limited in their abilities to carry out some kinds of tasks—we have to look into setting up some sort of independent group to handle such matters for us in the future."

"A kind of—what did they call it in the histories?—'intelligence service'?—no, 'counter-intelligence,' it was! That term made me laugh, I remember."

"I haven't thought this out enough to be able to say what we'll want such a group for," he said. "Just remind me, please, to think about it. Because I believe we're in a war—so far, just a sort of undercover war, perhaps, but we have to be as ready for this kind of war as for a more normal war of soldiers and ships . . . it's just that this kind of war starts earlier than the shooting war."

"All right. But back to the infiltration."

"Just knowing that our organization here has been infiltrated is not enough," he said. "We have to find a way to determine who's working for the unknowns, and who's only misled and manipulated."

"Particularly among the Others," she said. "But you know, some of the staff are likely innocent, as well."

"You told me earlier that that staff person Pallas Salvador provided—Sandra Rossoy—had been unable to find the nine missing Others."

"Yes, she reported on that even before we left Ceta City."

"I know she did. But what did you think of her?"

"Do you mean, do I think she's working for the unknowns? I do not."

"Why not?"

"She's much younger than the staff people we've had reason to suspect," she answered.

"That's not—"

"I know, I know, that's not much by way of proof. But it's corroborated by my reading of her character."

"That was unfair of me," he said. "I only asked what you thought of her, and you could hardly be expected to provide proof of anything, at this point. But I think you liked her."

"I did," Toni said. "She's a young mother who's put aside her career—or at least taken a step down—for her family, and she showed no bitterness at all. In fact, in the brief time we worked together I found her to be almost idealistic. I think she firmly believes in the Others, and is proud to be associated with us. I think it was only shyness, and maybe a sense of reserve, or dignity, that kept her from bubbling over about having met you."

"I have another reason to believe in her loyalty," Bleys said.

"What's that?"

"Remember what Pallas Salvador said? That Sandra had been her most valuable assistant until she had to move when her husband was transferred?"

"Yes, I remember."

"Her husband's transfer opened up the place for Gelica Constanza to take over as Pallas Salvador's assistant, didn't it?"

Toni was silent for a long moment.

"I see," she said at last. "That's a little frightening."

"It might be that," Bleys said. "It shouldn't surprise us, though, to find that these unknowns have the power to get Sandra's husband transferred; they've already shown they have a lot of power on this planet—but at the same time, that deduction gives us one more piece of information to use in filling out the picture of who those people might be."

She was silent for another long moment.

"The vanished Others are probably dead, aren't they?" she said at last.

"It's likely," he said. "I think they're the only ones among the Others here that we can know remained loyal. It probably killed them."

"That's sad," she said. "It's as if there's been a war going on, and we never even knew it. Some of our people died, and we never knew it until we stumbled on it by accident."

"Well, there *is* a war going on," Bleys said. "There has been for a long time now, I think."

Toni was silent for a long moment.

"You're not talking about these people here on Ceta, are you?" she said at last.

"No," he said. He sighed, feeling, suddenly, immensely weary.

"War is a conflict of opposing forces," he went on. "I believe we're caught in the conflict of *historical* forces—a conflict that's been going on for a long, long time."

"You've mentioned these historical forces before," she said. "It makes me feel as if you think we're slaves to some—some invisible thing we can't even see. Do you feel that way?"

"Do you feel as if you're a helpless slave to gravity?" he asked.

She took a moment to think that over; and then pushed herself up, to lean over him, propped on one arm.

"Or the laws of physics or chemistry?" she said. "Or even time?"

"I hadn't thought of time," he said. "That may be a very good analogy."

Her elbow moved sideways, leaving her to fall on him, her chin thumping into his chest.

"Sorry!" she said; but her apology was ruined by a giggle. "It's that gravity thing again!"

He put the edge of his hand under her chin, and lifted it; and she lifted her face to meet his.

CHAPTER 16

They were both sitting up, their backs against the wall at the head of the bed.

"I didn't mean to distract you," Toni said. "You were talking about war and the historical forces." She was tucked under his arm and leaning into him, cheek against his chest.

"I never realized my mentions of the historical forces raised such bad connotations for you," Bleys said. "To me they're just a neutral force in the background of life. I was surprised when you talked about being a slave to the forces—that's impossible, you know."

"Well, you changed my feelings when you mentioned gravity," she said. "I understood it right away, and it made me feel silly about my earlier reaction." She moved her arm out across his chest, and hugged him.

"Slavery is something only people can create," he said, smoothing her hair gently. "It shouldn't be a worry for you; you just don't have it in you to be a slave."

"I think that's true," she said. "Just being with you has shown me how powerful I am in my own right—and that everybody can be just as powerful if only they're set free to see the possibilities in them."

"You had it in you before we ever met," he said. "It's a spirit of self-reliance, or maybe just self-responsibility . . . a lot of people seem to have at least some of it, but I want everyone to have it."

"Why do some have it, while others don't?"

"I don't have a complete answer for that," he said. "It seems to come from the way people are raised, but I'm not sure that's the whole answer. From what I've read, the Dorsai seem to produce a lot of individuals with that sense of responsibility—maybe you have your Dorsai ancestor to thank."

"I *do* thank her," Toni said. "She was an important person in my life. But it's more than that; my non-Dorsai ancestors could never have been enslaved, either."

"I believe that," he said. "And I know there are Friendlies like that, too." He shrugged. "Whatever it takes to produce that completely free, responsible, strong individual, our societies don't seem to have it—not enough of it. That's why I think the race needs to go back to Old Earth and retrench—look into itself until it finds the way to be mature adults."

"Is that what you believe the historical forces want?"

"I don't think the forces have any *wants* at all," he said. "They're just *there*."

"Like gravity, you said."

"We never were completely independent entities, any of us," he said. "We never will be. We're like fish: we swim in an ocean of forces—even matter is really a function of forces—and we have no prospect of ever being in a position to order the ocean itself. But that doesn't lessen us; in fact, we *need* the forces—it's like the ocean: if it weren't there, we could never swim at all.

"Hello?" he asked, after a long moment of silence.

"I haven't gone to sleep," she said. "I was thinking about a cosmology class I took once, long ago."

"What about it?"

"Well, I remember we explored speculations people have had over the centuries, as to what makes up what we call the 'fabric of space.' I had trouble with the idea, I remember, because I'd always understood space to be—well, empty. Nothingness! And yet using the term 'fabric' seemed to me to imply there was—is—something out there with a texture . . . something that can be touched. Or at least sensed, in some way."

"The physicists," Bleys said, "have largely accepted that even though we lack the senses necessary even to perceive that 'fabric,' as you called it, there must be something like it, to hold everything together. My thought is there's something like that going on with history . . . or maybe with time."

"Are you saying you have some sort of perception of these historical forces?"

"Not at all," he said. "All I have is a construction—a sort of fictional picture in my mind, that sometimes I can use to help me envision what's going on in the Universe."

"Would you tell me about it? Do you mind?"

"I don't mind," he said. "But I've never tried to describe it to anyone before; so bear with me if this seems a little vague."

He paused for a moment.

"You mentioned the 'fabric of space,'" he said. "Now try to imagine a kind of fabric that flows through time."

"A fabric of time?"

"I don't necessarily mean it in the sense of something that holds time together," he said. "What I'm thinking of is more like a ribbon, or even a tapestry—a tapestry made up of threads that each represents the life of a human being, as that life moves through time, so that the entire tapestry runs from the beginning of the race on into the future, indicating the direction the whole race is moving."

"So this tapestry is, in a way, telling you a story—the story of the human race?"

"Yes," he said. "That's why *tapestry* may be a better word than *ribbon*, even though the length of the thing is more ribbonlike. I sometimes imagine the threads are all of different colors, and I can pick out my own and those of some other people. I imagine that the great moments of the race are represented when threads of similar color begin to run together—which means some great idea has arisen and begun to influence more and more people."

"Do some people's threads—their lives—have more weight in determining the direction of the tapestry than do others'?" Toni asked.

"People, no," he said. "It's the ideas they hold that gives the weight. Or maybe *weight* is the wrong word; maybe *color* or *direction* would be better."

"I think I get the idea," she said.

"I know these threads aren't real," he said. "It's just a picture, a symbol in my mind, that puts my own position and plans into a form I can think about more easily. I've found that meditating on the image sometimes seems to lead me to answers for some problems . . . perhaps it's a channel into my subconscious mind, that uses my own creative abilities to analyze situations on a level below my conscious mind, when that consciousness is having trouble.

"Sometimes I feel I can see the direction the threads are going, into the future. I'm sure they're not real, but just projections from my mind's calculations—or guesses. But sometimes seeing them gives me ideas for things to do, as if I were looking at a map."

"And where do the historical forces come into this?" she asked.

"They don't, really, in any physical sense," he said. "But the forces are made up of the energies of the life-threads, and the ideas that motivate them. When a large number of people want a particular future for the race—even if they never think of what they want as influencing the race's future—their threads run together. Together they have a kind of—let's use *weight* for this—weight that bends the tapestry of the entire race's future in their particular direction. If other people have different ideas, their weight tends to lead the tapestry in a different direction . . . so that the tapestry of the future is being tugged in, at a minimum, two different directions."

"So maybe *war* isn't a good word for the reconciliation of these historical forces," she said.

"Perhaps not, as applied to the forces themselves," he said. "When water is released from a dam and flows down to a lower-lying body of water, it's not a war—it's only a righting of things that have been out of balance . . . a simple search for a state of equilibrium."

"This feels very right to me," Toni said. "It fits with the importance of *balance* in the martial arts, for one thing. And I recall, too, that some of the masters suggested that the true martial artist should be like water—be infinitely flexible, able to adapt and flow without effort."

"It sounds like the opposite of war," he admitted.

"You said yourself, a while ago, that war is a conflict of opposing forces," she said. "But our art seeks to flow *with* an opposing force, rather than entering into open conflict with it."

"That's right," he said. "I spoke too loosely. Maybe it would be more accurate to say that although the historical forces don't go to war with each other—people do. *War* is always a subjective phenomenon; it's only accurately used when it's applied to the way the forces work themselves out in human lives."

It took her a moment to reply.

"What it seems to come down to, if I understand you correctly, is that the historical forces themselves are largely irrelevant to the average woman or man. And if a war comes out of those forces—"

"I suspect *all* wars grow out of those forces," he said. "Sorry—I interrupted you."

"Well, if a war comes, it doesn't matter to the average person whether it's the result of historical forces, or not," she said.

"For the average person, it seldom matters *what* causes a war," he said. "It's like a storm that blows up in the late afternoon. To all intents and purposes, it's just something that happens, that the person being rained on didn't cause, didn't ask for, and didn't want—but has to endure."

"And you, knowing about these historical forces—you don't feel like you're a slave to them?"

"No," he said. "Maybe an ally. All I'm really trying to do is save the human race; and if that purpose happens to facilitate the working out of some conflict between the forces—so be it. I'm not doing what I'm doing for the sake of the forces, but for myself and for the race."

"So maybe the best analogy might be that you're trying to guide the race through that storm?"

"I like that one," he said.

Again, she was silent; and finally he spoke again.

"It *is* sad that some of our Others have been killed," he said. "I'd've prevented that if I'd seen it coming. But in the course of events, many more are certain to be killed, both Others and ordinary people, before the race is placed firmly on its path to safety. Many of those will die because they oppose what I'm doing, and some will die to support it—and the only difference between them may be that the latter die out of loyalty to a better cause . . . even though many on both sides will never know exactly what it is their struggles and deaths are supporting."

"You said it, a few minutes ago," Toni said: "The Others who've been killed here on Ceta were probably killed for their loyalty."

"Yes."

"The converse of that idea is that any of the Others—or the staff, for that matter—who are still alive may have been corrupted."

"It may be," he said, "although I find it highly unlikely that so many could have been diverted from their loyalties. During our first meeting here, I really felt I was seeing people genuinely committed to our organization. Those Others in that meeting seemed interested, even eager, to work on our plan—and, yes, I realize I've just done exactly what you did, a few minutes ago, in talking about your ·reaction to Sandra Rossoy."

"They may not all be corrupted yet," she said. "On the other hand, the eagerness you saw might have been just interest in getting something from us."

"It's not necessarily the case that *any* of them are, as you say, 'corrupted,'" Bleys said.

"But if they're not cooperating with our unknown enemies, then they're dupes."

"In any case, we're still facing the problem of what to do about it," he said. "We can be pretty sure of the identity of at least some of the infiltrators. But we can't have them arrested, and there's no way to guarantee they'd tell us anything if we confronted them."

"We could grab some and interrogate them," she said, a questioning tone in her voice.

"That could be a very dangerous move," Bleys said. "Remember, we still don't know the extent of their power and influence here. We know that some of our enemies have taken positions on the Cetan Others' staffs, but we also know they have confederates who aren't on the staffs—and we have no idea who those people are or how many of them there might be."

"Could you try to use your persuasive power to get one or more of the ones we know of, to cooperate?"

"I could try it," he said. "There's no guarantee it would work—remember, there are people who seem to be immune to that particular ability."

"All right, I see that," she said. "But if you're right about them, what are you going to do?"

"What exactly are you asking?"

"Well, just going by the number of staff people over forty years of age—even though we don't know exactly why age might make a difference—and knowing they have confederates who aren't staff members, it seems likely we face a large number of enemies. We can't arrest them . . . can you settle for just *firing* them?"

"It may be that will be all we can do," he said. "I'd rather find another way."

"Another way to what?" she said. "I don't think you're clear, in your own mind, as to what you want to do—I mean, not just as to what the next step would be, after you've identified those people, but what you want to happen beyond that. Are you?"

Her voice had risen in tone as she spoke, speeding up; and even before he could answer she had turned, to poke him on the chest with a finger.

"*That's* why you got those blisters when you were walking!" she said, emphasizing her words with another poke. "You know it from your own martial arts work—your thinking was out of balance, and that affected the balance of your body. Mind and body are all tied together, you know that!"

He looked at her, stunned.

"I'm sorry," she said, more softly. "I didn't mean to poke you so hard—"

"It's not that," he said, recovering from the rush of thoughts that had briefly immobilized him. "It's just that—well, of course I've been told about balance, and about the link between body and mind, but it never came home to me until now!"

He put his hand on her shoulder, excited.

"Do you remember Kaj telling me, when I was very ill from the DNA antagonist, about harnessing my creative powers to heal myself?"

"I remember something about that, yes."

"He was talking about the same thing!" Bleys said. "It all fits together!"

He laughed aloud.

"It *does* all fit together—mind and body!"

"All right," she said, "I think I see: you got the blisters, indirectly, because your thinking was out of balance, so that was your mind affecting your body."

"Maybe it would be more accurate to say it was the body *mirroring* the mind," he said. "I wonder if anyone has ever tried to study that kind of mind-body relationship?"

"Are you sure, now, that you've balanced your thinking?"

"You're trying to remind me to keep my eye on my overall mission," he said. "I haven't forgotten it. But you're right, at least to the extent that I've been concentrating on finding out who the enemy are, and not thinking about what comes after that."

"Sometimes there are advantages to working like that," she said. "I can't say this isn't one of those times when a problem works itself out if you just let it run. But I've been wondering what would happen next, and I thought I'd ask what you thought about that end of it."

"I've got a few ideas," he said. "I need a lot more information before I can act on any of them."

"So we're back to the problem of obtaining information," she said. "Any plan we make might blow up in our faces if we can't base it on concrete information."

"Our problem, on the initial level at least, has two possible answers," he responded. "On the one hand, the simplest—or at least most certain—way to handle this might be to just dump the entire organization here on Ceta; but that would come at a devastating cost in the money and people we've put into this organization, as well as the influence we've built up with power-brokers on this planet."

"And the other solution is to find a way to prove whether the individual Others—and their staff people—are loyal," she said; "once sorted, you can fire just the disloyal."

"That would be preferable," he said, "if we can figure out how to do it. But even then, we're still left with people working for us who were fooled."

"There are worse crimes than being deceived," she said. "And speaking of crimes, I noticed that one thing you wanted the researchers to seek was undercover groups in the financial and criminal areas—how did you get to that?"

"Oh, that," he said. "I don't know if you'd call it a process of elimination, or just extrapolation, but if you look at what we *do* know about what those unknowns have been doing—manipulating markets and economies, arranging assassinations—they're good at those kinds of things. They must have had practice."

"Well, then," Toni said, "that brings up another question: why would professional criminals go through all the trouble of working for the Others? Some of them have been with us for years, although it doesn't strike me as the kind of life that appeals to criminals . . . and I can't think of a lot they could gain by doing so, either."

"Yes," he said, frowning in the darkness, "that's another question."

He slid back down from the wall, to lie flat.

"We have a lot more to learn," he said.

"Not now," she said, moving down herself. "You need your sleep."

She laughed.

"I'm getting to sound like Kaj."

In the morning Toni was out of the bedroom before Bleys was ready, insisting she would prepare a hot breakfast.

"We've been badly off-schedule," she said. "A return to our usual routine will make us feel better, which means we'll think better. When you're ready, come to the kitchen and help me."

"I should check on what's been happening overnight," he said.

"By the time you get to the kitchen, I'll have breakfast ready. You can help me carry it to our desks, and you can do your checking while you eat."

Reports had already begun to come in from the researchers—most, so far, relayed from the other side of the planet, where the first day of researches had just ended.

"This is puzzling," Toni said, forwarding a new batch of reports to Bleys' screen. "I'm not sure this is of any use, but you said you wanted to see everything."

Bleys only nodded, his eyes glued on his screen while he ate largely by feel.

"A bit later, we'll get back to our workouts," Toni said. She had to repeat herself to get his attention.

Late in the afternoon, Bleys looked up from his screen as Toni appeared in the lounge, her hair still slightly damp—the two of them had completed a short but vigorous workout only a short time before, and Bleys had rushed right to his screen while she went off to their quarters.

"You need to shower," she said.

"I'll go in a moment," he said. "I needed to look at the data right away, to see how it fits with an idea I got while we were working out."

"I could tell you were distracted," she said. "Remember, you have to be able to let go of the world."

"I know," he said. "I just couldn't do it. . . . Anyway, I think I'm starting to see a pattern—or maybe two patterns."

"Two? What do you mean?"

"Let me think about it while I shower," he said. "If it holds up, I'll explain—and maybe we'll have some planning to do."

"Is there anything I should look into while you're gone?"

He sat silent, thinking.

"I'm working on another plan," he said at last. "It'll need a few of Henry's people, and I'm afraid it'll involve actions he might not be happy about."

"Will anyone get hurt?" Toni asked.

"No."

"Then—" she began; but he interrupted her.

"Not immediately," he added.

"All right," she said. "What else do you need?"

"A medician," he said. "One with advanced pharmacological experience."

She eyed him for a long moment.

"And you don't think Kaj will do it," she said at last.

He nodded.

"Can you locate someone like that?" he said.

"No," she said, "I don't think I can. At least, not quickly. But a couple of the Soldiers are originally from this planet . . . I'll ask." She paused.

"Quietly," she added.

CHAPTER 17

Three days later another delivery of supplies, packed into several container shells, was loaded onto the conveyor belt that slanted up from the spaceport pad into the depths of the ship known as the *Konrad Macklin*. Within minutes after they had vanished into the ship, the belt began to move in the opposite direction, and shortly thereafter a sealed utility bin, of the kind used to hold waste and construction debris, rode down the belt. Even before it reached bottom a pair of mechanical arms had risen from the cargo vehicle that had delivered the supplies; less than a minute later the vehicle was moving off in the direction of the Customs Office, where the contents of the bin would be reviewed before it was allowed to proceed into the Cetan economy through the commercial exit gates.

The containers that had entered the *Konrad Macklin* had not been so inspected; most planets worried more about what might come onto their surface than about what might be leaving.

By that time the second of the newly arrived containers had been opened in a small room just off the ship's cargo hold. A layer of sound-deadening adhesive flooring, each section in its individual carton and all of them stacked on end, was removed, revealing, under a false bottom, the still form of a blond woman dressed in a loose, off-white shift—Pallas Salvador. She was removed to a bed in a stateroom, where she was left to waken naturally, monitored by medical sensors and a video port.

Her waking was slow, a ragged alternation of approaches to consciousness and relapses into darkness; but eventually her mind responded to the urge to push through the blackness, and shortly thereafter her eyes opened to a dimly lit, utilitarian room that she fuzzily recognized, from its architecture, as being in a spaceship.

Even dim, the light caused the headache with which she had awakened to bloom with an increased intensity. She closed her eyelids, hoping the pain would ease enough that she could think, at least a little; and after a few minutes, it did—a little.

She tried to sit up, knowing she would have to pay for the effort with pain. On her second attempt she managed to push herself back enough that she could sit upright, propped against the coated wall at the head of the bed; and she sat there for some minutes, her head down on raised knees while her hands massaged her temples. She attempted to think about her situation, but it was hard to stay on any line of thought when she hurt so much.

A few minutes later the door opened, and she looked up to see Antonia Lu looking in at her.

"Are you all right?" Toni asked, stepping in from the corridor and letting the door close behind her.

Grateful that the light from the corridor—a glare in comparison to the room's subdued lighting—had been shut off, Pallas Salvador started to nod; but hastily aborted the movement as her head threatened to split open from temple to temple.

"I don't know," she said, trying to keep her voice down so as to minimize the pain. "I guess so." Beneath the pain a tide of irritation was rising: she had always hated appearing weak, and she was certain the tears in her eyes would be interpreted in that fashion.

"I know your head is hurting quite a lot," Toni said, her voice soft and sympathetic. "It's an unavoidable side effect of the drugs used on you."

"Drugs?" Pallas asked, unthinkingly throwing her head back; she winced and clamped her eyes shut.

"I'm afraid so," Toni said. She was smiling in sympathy when Pallas opened her eyes again "We think we know which drugs you were given, and we believe we have something to counteract the aftereffects you're feeling." She held up a slim silvery tube.

"May I inject you with this?"

"Yes," Pallas Salvador said. "No! Wait—" She shook her head; and then hissed an intake of air through clenched teeth, clutching at her head as her eyes snapped shut, tears pooling at the bases of her lashes.

"It hurts even to look at you," Toni said. "You don't have to take this if you don't want to, of course. Would you prefer I left you alone for a while, to sort things out?"

The blond woman lowered an arm and forced her eyes open, looking upward at Toni through the blur of the moisture beaded on her lashes.

"No," she said, keeping her voice low. "Give it to me."

Toni held the end of the tube to the inside of the other's wrist; and for the briefest of instants Pallas heard a tiny hissing sound, while her wrist seemed to feel a cool breath.

"You should feel better quickly," Toni said as she pulled her hand back.

"Thank you," Pallas said in a low voice. "Where are we?"

"On one of our ships," Toni said. "But don't speak for a few minutes—just close your eyes and try to relax; it'll speed your recovery."

"But—"

"Don't speak," Toni said. "Please. I'm going to get you something to eat—we think you've been unconscious for quite a while, so as you start to feel more like your usual self you'll probably begin to think you're starving. I'll be back in a couple of minutes."

And she was gone.

Already Pallas could feel the headache easing, and with it the muscle tenseness that had been making her grimace and clench her teeth. She eased herself back against the wall, grateful for the change—and also grateful to find herself able to think more clearly.

How had she gotten on a ship? Antonia Lu's words suggested that she, Pallas, had been drugged by someone before she arrived here. What had happened? She instinctively began inventorying the sensations of her body, a little afraid of what she might find. She was wearing one of her nightgowns, with no underwear beneath it, which suggested that whatever had happened had occurred while she was sleeping; but she could find nothing unusual in how her body felt to itself—at least, nothing that could not be attributed to the drugs she had been dosed with. But she needed to use the bathroom.

She was struggling with her memory when Antonia Lu came back into the room, smiling and carrying a light paper-material tray.

"Here's a little breakfast," she said, placing the tray gently on Pallas' hastily lowered knees and then pulling a cloth napkin out from where it had been tucked into the self-belt of her cherry-red blouse. "Our medician suggested you eat very lightly and slowly for the moment, so we'll see how this poached egg and toast goes down; I'll get you some more when you're up to it."

"That sounds like a good idea," Pallas said. "I didn't really notice how my stomach was feeling when my head hurt so much, but now I guess I'm a little queasy. But I'm thirsty."

"That's what Kaj expected—that's our medician, Kaj Menowsky," Toni said. "He also said he wants to check you over after you've eaten and rested a bit."

"Check me?" Pallas asked. "Is there something wrong?"

"No, no," Toni raised one hand a little. "He ran some tests on you when you first got here, and didn't find anything more than the effects of the drug. But Kaj was Exotic-trained, and he isn't happy unless he can—well, let's say he's really thorough . . . now eat! That container holds a pint of a sweetened tea."

"It's good," Pallas said in a few minutes. "And I think it's going to stay down."

"That's good," Toni said. "Now why don't I leave you alone to get a little more down, and get some rest? You can call me anytime you want, using the control pad on the wall there—I've coded my number into it."

"I think I've had enough, and I *am* tired," Pallas said. "I feel as if I've been wrung out. But what happened to me? How did I get here?"

"I can't tell you much," Toni said, "and I should probably let someone who knows more talk to you about that. All I know is that our security people stopped a group of people who were apparently trying to kidnap you."

"*Kidnap* me!" The blond woman's eyes opened wide and she sat up, swinging her feet off the bed and having to clutch at the tray to keep it from sliding to the floor. "Who would do that?"

"As I said, we don't know much. Our people have been investigating, but I haven't heard what, if anything, they've found."

"Am I still in danger?"

"Absolutely not," Toni said. "That's why we're on our ship—no one can get to you here."

"But—"

"No more questions!" Toni said, softening the imperative words with another sympathetic smile. "Rest! If you don't call me before then, I'll wake you in a couple of hours. Then, if you're up to it, you'll eat a little more, Kaj will look you over—and maybe by that time we'll have more to tell you. Now just relax. You know where the room controls are."

"All right," Pallas nodded. Fatigue was winning out over the remains of her fear and anger.

Somewhat more than three hours later, Pallas Salvador, now dressed in dark blue ship's coveralls, was sitting back in one of the easy chairs in *Favored of God*'s lounge, the remains of a light lunch still resting on the small auxiliary table next to her. She had not eaten much of it. She was trying to make herself relax.

For the entire time she had been sitting there, she had played with her food, unsuccessfully trying to avoid watching Bleys Ahrens, who was working quietly at a desk on the other side of a long clear space that bisected the large room. He had insisted, when Toni led Pallas into the room, that Pallas eat and relax before they talked; and now she was eager to talk with him, but also—what? Afraid?

"Bleys, are you free to talk with Pallas Salvador?" Toni asked now. Pallas knew Toni had been keeping an attentive eye on her, from her own desk. Bleys looked up from the display on his screen.

"Certainly," he said, his voice, low and calm, soothing her anxiety a little. "No, don't get up, please. We'll both be more comfortable if I come over there."

He walked across to her, his long legs in their dark gray trousers and black boots covering the distance quickly even though he was pulling his oversize chair with him. He placed the chair in a position to her left front, a move Pallas recognized, from her training at Others' headquarters on Association, as designed to avoid the confrontational connotations of a face-to-face situation.

"I won't ask how you're feeling," he said, smiling at her. His white teeth gleamed out of the lightly tanned face beneath his dark hair, and the collar of his white work shirt was open. Even seated, he seemed to tower above her. "Not because I don't care, but because I know what Kaj Menowsky has learned about you, and what you've told Toni."

She found herself relaxing. She really could use a little more sleep, she thought. That slight accent that colored his speech pattern was quite pleasant to listen to . . .

"Everyone assures me you haven't been damaged," Bleys Ahrens was continuing, "and that you've been making a solid and fast recovery. We're all glad to hear it, and we're determined to make sure that whatever happened to you doesn't happen to you—or to anyone else among our people—ever again." His last words had taken on a cold tone, while his eyes seemed suddenly to become hard, his jaw muscles to tighten.

Pallas' eyes opened wide, and she sat up in her chair. She had not been thinking in terms of anger, but Bleys' words seemed to fan some hidden ember inside her.

"What *did* happen to me?" she asked. "And who did it? I don't remember anything at all, and Antonia Lu said she didn't know much—"

"And we don't know much," Bleys said, his voice again low and calm, soothing. In response, he noted, her breathing slowed, the skin around her eyes loosening a little. The purposeful manipulation of her emotions into a series of quick variations would, he knew, leave her more susceptible to his suggestions than she might otherwise be.

"I'm going to tell you everything we've learned so far," he went on, putting just a hint of a smile on the edge of his serious, determined expression. "I'd like you to listen carefully, and tell me whenever you hear something you think is incorrect, or whenever you remember anything—anything at all. Will you do that?"

"Of course," she said. Her chin lifted slightly as her voice became a little stronger. "You can count on me."

"I thought so," he said, looking pleased.

Immediately, his trained perceptions noted that she was reacting positively to his approval. He leaned forward in his chair, an action that had the twin effects of bringing his eyes down to the level of hers and moving his face closer to hers. He could see the pupils of her eyes dilating in response to the increased sense of intimacy he had evoked.

"As you know," he began, "there were two attacks on my party while we were on tour." She nodded, her eyes, large and grave, focused on his face.

"Of course, we let you know we were all right." She nodded again.

"What we didn't tell you," he continued, "was that after thinking about the implications of the attack, we became concerned that you yourself"—her head drew back a little—"as well as your colleagues, might be in some danger, too."

"I think I see what you're saying," she said, her words quiet and timid at first, but strengthening and coming faster as she continued: "You're suggesting that the attack on you might not have been due to your position as a Friendly official, but to your work as—as one of us."

"Exactly," he said, smiling at her. "Of course we didn't know the reason for the attack, since the people who planted the bomb weren't found; but we decided to take no chances, and I ordered some of my security people to stand guard over your offices—and over you personally."

"But why didn't you tell me?" Pallas said. "I could certainly have—"

"That was a hard decision," he interrupted her, "but one I made personally." He paused to look her straight in the eye, as if offering her a chance to challenge him.

"That's what my main job in this organization is," he said. "I make decisions. Every organization has to have someone to do that—someone who *can* do it, and do it well, even when the situation is . . . difficult."

He smiled at her again.

"You weren't in charge here the last time I was on Ceta," he went on, "and I haven't had time to get to know you very well. But I made a decision to trust you would understand, later. . . . I thought I'd be able to count on your agreeing—as all of our Others have always agreed—to put yourself at the disposal of our movement."

"But of course!" she said. "You *can't* doubt—"

"—and I didn't," he interrupted again. "I did not doubt at all; and so I did what was best for our movement." He smiled again, almost shyly.

"In short," he went on, "I used you."

" 'Used' me?"

"Used you," he said, nodding. "I used you as bait. I had to find out who was behind the attack on me—I had to know if it was part of an attack on our movement. So I set our people to observe whether any further attacks were made—which meant they had to watch you, because you were the next most obvious target, if the attacks were in fact aimed at our Others."

"Yes, I see that," she said. "But why didn't you tell me?"

"I had several reasons for that," he said. "For one, it was possible that if you knew our people were watching, you might change your behavior—and our success depended on you continuing to follow your usual routines."

She started to object, but he interrupted once more.

"The other reason was perhaps less obvious," he said, "but was more fundamental: we had no safe way to let you know what we thought might be going on."

"I don't understand!"

"Remember, we were on the other side of the planet," he said, "in the Friendly consulate in Abbeyville."

She nodded, recalling his messages from that location.

"At that point," Bleys continued, "we were unable to communicate safely with you anymore."

" 'Safely'?" She blinked.

"Yes," he said. "If you think about it, you'll realize that in both attacks, the attackers had to have been informed of our exact itinerary." He held up a hand, forestalling her exclamation.

"In short, we believe someone is able to intercept our communications to you," he said.

"I see!" She nearly yelled it. Recovering herself, she continued in a lower tone: "I *do* see . . . but I thought our communications were secure—" There was now a question in her tone.

"So did we," he said, a rueful look on his face. "But now you'll realize, we couldn't safely let you know what was happening, because whoever was reading our messages—"

"—would know we were on to them!"

He smiled at her.

"So we trusted you would understand later," he said. "And I see you do."

She smiled back. It seemed so clear and right, the way he explained it.

"Oh, yes," she murmured.

For a few moments there was silence in the lounge.

Eventually Pallas was led back to her room. She was sleepy, but filled with a kind of exhilaration. She felt she had a heightened understanding of the unity of the Others—*her* Others—under Bleys' leadership, and of the rightness of their work. She drifted into sleep on a slow, smooth tide of warm feelings that she hugged to herself, smiling.

Meanwhile, Bleys was telling Toni, back in the lounge, that he was now convinced that Pallas Salvador was not one of their unknown enemies.

"I agree," Toni said. "That doesn't mean she's entirely without fault here."

"As head of the organization on this planet, she's of course ultimately responsible for everything," Bleys said. "Or did you have something more specific in mind?"

"Put that way—no," she said. "I'm the one who said being deceived is no crime. But maybe being the leader of a group who were deceived so badly requires a certain—well, penalty."

"As a kind of organizational imperative?" he asked. "I mean, as an example?"

She paused, thinking.

"No, I guess I don't mean it that way," she said finally. "It might be good for the organization to impose some sort of punishment—*pour encourager les autres*, as they used to say; but any major sanction placed on her would be disproportionate to her actual culpability."

"I don't understand that phrase you used," Bleys said. "What was that, Old Earth French?"

"Sorry," she said. "French, yes—I don't speak the language, but I found the phrase in a book spool that my Dorsai grandmother owned, when I was small. It was Cletus Grahame's *Tactics of Mistake*. She told me it meant something like *as an incentive to everyone else*. I loved the liquid sound of the phrase when she told me how to pronounce it, and it stuck with me."

"You're concerned about the fairness of punishing Pallas Salvador," Bleys said.

"I guess I am, yes," she replied, "even though I feel there's something wrong if she isn't somehow made to pay for what's happened here—I mean, she didn't even know that nine of her people had gone missing!"

"We don't yet know the full details of what's happened here," he said, "nor the extent of any deficiencies in her operation. But I'm beginning to believe Pallas Salvador has a lot left to give to our organization. Dahno and I, just on the basis of the reports we saw coming from Ceta a few years ago, made her the top person here despite knowing she wasn't the most adept person we have, as far as the ability to persuade and convince goes—because she was showing a lot of administrative ability, which the wide dispersal of power on this planet seemed to demand. But now, with this example in the back of her mind, it's possible she'll become a great administrator and organizer—in the particular situation of this planet now, coordination may be as necessary as persuasive abilities."

"You know I don't see the reports that come in from Ceta," Toni said, "but just from our time spent in her offices, and conversing with her staff, I'd say she's been walking a narrow line between being a productive leader, or a tyrant who could alienate her people. It might be better if she were—well, not punished, but put in another, less supervisory position."

"Keep in mind the fragile position of our organization on this planet right now," Bleys said. "If Pallas Salvador isn't particularly liable for having been deceived, then neither are her subordinate Others or their staffs. But I think that when they're apprised of this plot, those Others—and their staffs—will be left feeling very guilty, even if we never give a hint we're holding anything against them."

"And seeing Pallas Salvador disciplined—no matter how lightly— would weigh on them, and affect their morale and performance," she said. "I see."

"The organization here, I now believe, is about to enter a period of major change," Bley said. "None of these Others seem to be extraordinary at their jobs, but I've seen things that suggest that many have a good deal of ability. And for us, in this place and time, quantity may be more important than quality."

"And we don't have enough spare personnel to step in if we removed them," she said, thoughtfully. "Not right now. We could do it over time, though."

"But time has suddenly become very important, here," he said.

"What do you mean?"

"I came here with a made-up tale that we were about to take major action to seize control of this planet," he said. "It was only intended to shock the local organization, giving us a chance to watch their reactions and learn who had other loyalties. I had no serious belief we could do much more than fix our problem and continue silently building for the future. But now, I'm beginning to have other ideas."

"What've you seen that tells you that?"

"I'd rather not say," he said. "It's not much more than a feeling, at this point; I need a lot more information."

"Are you saying a patched-up organization, led by someone who let her organization be hijacked, can carry out a program to take control of this planet?"

"They might have some help," Bleys said.

He refused to provide any further information; and in the dissatisfied silence that followed, he was saved by Kaj Menowsky, who called from the infirmary to report that Dahno was demanding to see Bleys.

"I've been waiting for him to come out of his shell," Bleys told Toni. "He's been recovering well, physically, but he's been withdrawn."

"I know," she said. "I stopped by to see how he was doing, yesterday, and he was barely polite—I think he's sulking about something."

"I don't believe he's ever been hurt before," Bleys said. "I think he's been getting used to the concept, and it's making him rethink things."

She looked at him for a long moment, a thoughtful look on her face; until, finally, she smiled.

"Most people would be wondering what he'll decide to do," she said. "You already know, don't you?"

"I have some ideas," he said. Then he shook his head.

"Oh, not in any detail," he went on. "That depends on how things play out for a while. But if you're talking about the short run—he'll want to go back to Association right away."

"Is he afraid he might get hurt again?"

"Not in the sense you mean," Bleys said. "No, he'll just want to be able to get off where he can think and plan."

"How can we send him back without risking letting people know you're not really hiding in Abbeyville?"

"We'll figure something out. . . . I'd better go see him now."

CHAPTER 18

Henry was the third to go through the frosted-glass doors of the main entrance to the Others' offices, behind two of his Soldiers. Even though the external foyer's surveillance system had been disabled, here on the nineteenth floor of the building, their void pistols were kept out of sight until they were through the doors.

By the time Bleys entered, behind two more Soldiers and ahead of Toni and the last two Soldiers, the two women in the reception area were on their feet. The younger one, the same receptionist Bleys had met briefly on his prior visit, seemed to be trying—and in danger of failing—to present a calm demeanor; she was unable to keep her stare from returning, again and again, to the weapons now carried openly by Henry and the first two Soldiers—who were already past the two women and covering the interior doorways.

The second person in the reception area was the same stocky older woman Bleys had invited to sit in on the previous meeting—Pallas Salvador's administrative assistant, Gelica Costanza. She seemed calm and alert, although her lips were held a little tightly. She was, Bleys thought, a professional at maintaining a professional expression.

Already she had dismissed any concern for the men behind her, and focused her attention on Bleys. He played to that as if her gaze were a spotlight, pinning his own gaze on her and moving up to face her, almost bending as he looked down into her eyes. He could see those eyes widen, and as he drew nearer her pupils dilated a little; but even as he halted in front of her, they shrank to normal size.

"We hope you'll forgive us for this melodramatic entrance, Gelica Costanza," he said, keeping his voice quiet and pleasant. "I presume you're aware there've been several attacks aimed at our party." He was sure she was sharp enough to notice he was consistently using a plural form, rather than speaking of himself; he hoped it would alter her thinking, just a little.

"We've all been very concerned, Great Teacher," she said. "Frankly, it's made it very difficult to keep our minds on our work." Bleys could see no falseness in her smile, and he noted that she had used his honorific title, rather than his name.

I have to be very, very careful with this one, he told himself. *She's as good as anyone I've ever met.*

"We've been having that problem ourselves," he responded, putting a smile of shared comradeship on his own face. Then he made a show of becoming serious, even throwing his shoulders back slightly.

"Our work must go on," he said. "That's why we must have the extra security." She nodded, giving every appearance of understanding that need.

He leaned forward, speaking in a confidential tone.

"I hate it," he said. "But apparently it's become necessary."

She produced a sympathetic smile. Watching it, he knew she had not weakened her defenses. But he had not really expected her to be beaten so easily.

"Please accept our apologies, as well," Bleys went on, "for the fact that we've arrived a good deal earlier than you were expecting us—we'd built extra time into the schedule to allow for mishaps during our trip here from Abbeyville, but everything went perfectly." Again he smiled, almost apologetically, before straightening to his full height and turning to glance about the room.

"Are all our people here, then?" he asked. For a moment he thought she was about to say something else, but she responded to his question.

"Everyone who was here for the previous convocation," she said, "except for Pallas Salvador herself. She messaged us that she wanted everyone here early, well before your scheduled arrival— she said there was some preliminary work to do—but we've been waiting for her, and she hasn't arrived herself." Her voice had gotten deeper as she spoke, and more resonant than at any time since Bleys had met her. He wondered if she had not just made a slip.

"She will not be here today," he told her; and her face said she had caught the formality of his language. That face, which had been broadcasting the attentiveness appropriate to a subordinate, now displayed a certainty that, curiously, seemed to relax her.

"For the moment, at least, assume you're in charge here," he said, returning to a more comradely informality.

Her face recovered its professional blandness, but it took her a moment to respond.

"All right," she said, finally. "What do you need?"

"You can start by leading the way to the conference room."

He gestured for her to precede him, and then followed her down the short, plushly carpeted corridor. Watching her as they walked, he caught a slight anomaly in her movements, as her right arm seemed to stiffen from its normal swinging motion, and shorten. Bleys realized she had bent the arm at the elbow, reaching across her front— and the arm of one of the Soldiers behind him reached past Bleys, holding a pistol pointed directly at Gelica's back. Bleys gave a silent *hold* signal.

On Gelica's left side, her loose beige jacket twisted slightly, as if something had pulled on that side of its fabric. Immediately, Toni, directly behind Bleys, tapped once on the side of his left arm, without speaking; and pushed her left arm into his view as he looked sideways. Her wrist control pad was indicating that a very brief electromagnetic impulse had just been intercepted, its origin very near. He nodded, and signaled for the Soldier pointing the gun at Gelica to drop back.

"You'll chair the meeting," he said to the back of Gelica's head.

"May I point out that I'm only staff?" she said, looking back at him now. "And even among the staff, there are others here senior to me."

"I know," he said, as she halted before the closed double door and turned sideways to look at him. He stepped to his right, rather than moving up beside her, and she took a step backward to keep him in view. "And if one of them," he continued, "or a junior, for that matter, is shown to be abler, you may be moved to other duties. But for the moment, the job is yours."

She nodded, and then darted a glance at Toni—and her eyes widened a little as four of the Soldiers, their void pistols carried at a high ready position, moved quickly past her to the door. One placed a hand on the right-hand knob and glanced a question at Bleys. Bleys nodded.

In seconds both doors were open and all four Soldiers were inside, their pistols now down and pointing in the general direction of the milling crowd before them. The chatter in the room died down almost as quickly, as the Soldiers moved to and down the length of the side wall, the lead Soldier proceeding almost to the other end of the room, where the serving tables—not yet set up—were waiting.

"Go," Bleys said; and Gelica moved ahead of him into the room.

All the conference attendees, Bleys saw, were on their feet and facing the armed Soldiers, even as they unconsciously backed away from them and toward each other, as if trying to stand back-to-back in the face of danger. None of them, he noted, were tripping over chairs.

"Sit," he said, and eyes flickered toward him.

"Sit," he repeated, only a little more loudly. This time, they did.

They sorted themselves out quickly, most taking whatever seat was closest—although a few, he saw, seemed to seek out the seats closest to the emergency exit near the back of the room. Once seated, all kept their eyes on Bleys, seemingly ignoring the armed men.

Bleys had reached the head table before most of the conference attendees had managed to seat themselves. As he seated himself in the middle, larger seat, Toni took the chair to his immediate left, and then pulled a small electronic device from a thigh pocket, placing it on the table. Gelica, on Bleys' right side, stood behind the chair at her place without speaking, for long enough to grab the attention of the audience. When at last she spoke, her voice projected through the room without seeming overly loud.

"Bleys Ahrens will address you now," she said; and turned to look at him.

Momentarily startled, Bleys recovered rapidly. He had not been expecting her to be so succinct.

It was a good idea, though, he thought; *these people are too edgy for any ordinary speech.*

"Our apologies for startling you like this"—he gestured at the

Soldier-lined wall as he spoke—"but it was necessary. Because we've been betrayed."

In the dead silence that followed, he turned his head to look at Gelica, now settling herself into her seat next to him.

"Have the missing nine been located?"

"No," she said, her eyes narrowing slightly as she looked back up at him. "No. We sent staff—"

Bleys cut her off as he turned to the rest.

"You're shocked," he told them. "Get over it. The harmless little games you've all been playing have turned into a war, and there've already been casualties. It's time for you all to begin using those minds you've been gifted with."

The faces before him were largely blank, but it was hard to tell whether it was the blankness of shock, or camouflage.

"Think about this," he said, "if you want to stay alive: someone wants to kill us."

Before him, a couple of faces seemed to go slack for a moment; but most continued to display intense concentration. A few of his audience seemed to square their shoulders a little, and there was a good deal of resetting of feet—enough to produce a small rustling sound.

"You're all among the best the human race has to offer," he told them, seeking out faces with which to make eye-to-eye contact. "Most of you have received the very best training we could give you—training, in particular, to help you use the talent you've been gifted with, to persuade and lead. You've become trusted members of our family"—it registered on him that Gelica was reacting to something at that point, but he continued—"and then you were sent to this world for the purpose of using those talents, to gain influence and power here, as your fellow Others have done on other planets, for the benefit of all of us, and of the entire human race.

"I know some of you haven't had the training I mentioned," he continued, and smiled at a couple of the staff people he saw near the front of his audience. "We simply haven't had time to give every Other the training we'd like them to have. Nonetheless, you, too, are Others, and members of our family."

He paused for a moment, scanning the faces as if he were about to smile. But he did not smile at all.

"So it is a great sorrow to me to have to say that some of you, at least, have let all the rest of us down."

He gave them a moment to react to, and recover from, that statement, and then continued.

"We have long known that our persuasive skills seem not to work on everyone," he said, "and particularly not on the Exotics and the Dorsai. Am I right?"

A few among them nodded, but he ignored them and plowed on.

"We have discovered—never mind how—that the Exotics and the Dorsai have been the targets of a secretive economic attack for a long time—decades, in fact."

He went on to lay out for them the basics of what he had learned about the Ceta-based attacks on those two Splinter Cultures.

"The proof is indirect," he said, "but while a certain amount of those three planets' bad economic situation can be blamed on historical forces and the general decline of the old order, which have resulted in changing political, military and social conditions making for more competition for those planets, and less of a market for their products and experts, it is nonetheless true that a lot of their declining economic situation is the result of outside factors." He was, he suddenly realized, keyed up—he was feeling embarrassed at the droning, pedantic language he had begun to use. But it was a planned tactic, chosen because he knew the boring style would be reassuring to the nervous ones in the crowd.

"Exotic ships," he was continuing, "which once—leaving out Old Earth—dominated interstellar trade, don't get as great a percentage as they used to, of the cargoes and passengers going off-world from all the planets. Who do you think has benefited from that?

"People on other worlds buy less of the Exotic specialty exports—medical technologies, environmental tools and so on—" He broke off, purposely leaving a hanging silence.

"A lot of this can be traced here," he said. "I mean, to Ceta. Why didn't you tell us?"

There was silence in the room for a long moment. Most of the faces in front of Bleys were stunned and dismayed, but there were a few that were reacting in wariness and fear . . . and most of those faces were seated as a group in the back of the gathering.

"It was your job to further the progress of our movement," he went on, "by extending our influence on this planet and sending back to the rest of us information that would be of use to us all in furthering our work elsewhere. But it's impossible to believe that none of you managed to pick up on the fact that a large and powerful group on this planet was exerting its efforts to alter the balance of interstellar relationships."

He paused again, to let them draw the inevitable conclusion for themselves—and just as he was about to resume, a tiny rivet set in the underside of his wrist control pad vibrated silently against his skin in three short bursts.

Bleys broke off his remarks and turned to Toni, on his right.

"Toni," he said, "would you go out to Henry and ask him for the disk I left with him?"

As Toni nodded and rose from her seat, Bleys turned back to his audience.

"We have a recording that will illustrate what I'm talking about," he said—and in that moment Toni, who had been passing behind the head table on her way to the door, produced a small needle pistol and laid its muzzle softly against Gelica Costanza's temple, whispering something that caused the woman to freeze her startled reaction.

At the same moment the four Soldiers placed along the wall brought their void pistols back up, to point directly at Bleys' audience—and Bleys noticed that three of the four were concentrating their attention, and their aims, in the area of the group that he himself had earlier noticed.

Bleys kept his attention on the audience while this action occurred, watching their reactions, and was pleased to note that only a few showed signs of disabling shock. They might have gotten complacent over the course of their long, quiet term on this planet, but for the most part they seemed—given the upset that had marked the last few weeks—to be recovering the abilities they had been schooled in during their training.

A few of the audience had also noted where the attention of the Soldiers was directed; those Others were holding themselves very still, he saw, but several were unobtrusively bringing their feet into a position of readiness. He made a note of their faces.

"Stay calm," he said now to the whole room, projecting his voice to reflect authority; and then repeated the command in a quieter, soothing tone, making a slow, downward patting motion with his left hand.

As he spoke, his right hand had been under the table, unclipping a void pistol that had been stealthily placed there the preceding night. He had not wanted to bring it in himself—void pistols, although silent weapons that killed without leaving a mark on a body, were necessarily rather large—but he wanted this one for the immense psychological weight it would lend him. Everyone knew that the charge emitted by the long, coil-wrapped barrel was almost invariably fatal.

He swiveled in his seat and pointed the pistol at Gelica from a distance of less than a foot. Her eyes fastened on his face, but she made no move.

"I've got her," Bleys said softly to Toni. "Watch the seats."

Toni pulled her small pistol away from Gelica's head and stepped quickly to her left, passing behind Bleys and around the end of the head table to take up a position against the wall and near the front of the seating area. From there she pointed her pistol in the direction of the same group the Soldiers were watching from their places along the opposite wall.

"Sit absolutely still, all of you," Bleys said to the room at large. He put into those words every ounce of the ability he had developed to project a feeling of authority, but he never took his eyes off Gelica. "Make no sounds at all."

"You know what this pistol is," he said, now speaking softly to the woman beside him. "A void pistol doesn't wound."

He gave her a moment, and then ordered her to raise her hands and rise slowly from her seat, taking care to touch nothing, including the table and her chair.

"I want you to back up," he said, "always keeping your hands in the air."

In a moment her back was against the wall behind the table. Bleys had risen to move with her, and now, from a position slightly to her side and a half-arm's length away, he placed the pistol at her temple.

"We know your people have entered the building," he told her now, speaking loudly enough that everyone in the room could hear him. "But if you, or your people here in this room, make any move to reach for a weapon, or to communicate, you'll all be killed instantly."

He took a moment to speak more loudly, never taking his eyes off Gelica.

"You in the seats should know that not only are there five weapons aimed in your direction, but they're held by people very skilled at observing and interpreting the slightest movement that might hint of danger. If you want to live, sit still."

There was a dead silence in the room behind him. Gelica's eyes remained fixed on his, a hint of extra redness showing in her face.

"We began to suspect you some time ago," Bleys told her, now speaking in a much lower voice. "Now we've baited a trap for your friends."

"There're too many of them for you," she said, her voice husky. There was a hint of moisture in her eyes, but he did not make the mistake of taking that as a sign of weakness.

"I don't think so," he told her. "We knew that by scheduling this appointment, we'd give you an appealing target. But we have many more Soldiers here than you saw. Some of them entered this building and even these offices, last night—they planted this pistol for me—and have been hiding nearby, waiting for our signal—"

He broke off; his wristpad had once more prodded him, in a series of short coded touches.

"Your people have gotten on the elevators," he told her. "Our Soldiers now hold the lobby behind them, and will disable the elevators once your people get to this floor. When your people get off the elevators, they'll be trapped in the foyer and covered from all sides by experienced fighters firing from good cover."

He gave her a few seconds to think about it.

"It would be a futile slaughter," he said. "Will you call it off?"

The door to the conference room opened, and Henry stuck his head inside.

"There are sixteen of them," he reported, after taking a moment to assess the situation in the room. "They're on two elevators that should arrive at just about the same time, and they're not carrying their weapons in sight."

"Which gives us a further advantage," Bleys said to Gelica. "What about it?"

She looked up into his face, the moisture gone from her eyes and her color back to normal.

"Will you trust me to call them?" she asked.

"What will you say?"

"I'll tell them to stay in the foyer with their hands in the air, and wait to be disarmed," she said. "But I can't promise you they'll obey me—they aren't my people, and I don't think they'll want to give themselves up to you."

"They don't have to," Bleys replied. "We don't demand they give themselves into our power. Once disarmed, they can simply leave, if they wish, and we won't hurt them." He paused to emphasize his next words.

"It would be good if they knew we could have killed them."

She looked at him for a moment, her eyes assessing him anew.

"You have to hurry," he pointed out.

"Yes," she said. As her hand began to reach toward her jacket, his left hand reached out and pulled one side of her jacket open, exposing a harness that held a pistol holster under her right arm, balanced by a small electronic device on the other side. She smiled at him, and carefully pulled out the electronic device; then she activated it, tapping out a series of numbers on its pad before raising it to her lips. She explained the situation and gave the instructions just as Bleys had dictated them.

"Henry—" Bleys began—

"I heard," Henry said; and the door closed behind him.

"They don't like it," Gelica said a minute later. The communication device evidently had a *HUSH* function, which was logical considering its clandestine purpose—he had not heard any response to her words.

"Will they do it?"

"Yes," she said. "They've reached the foyer and have seen enough to be convinced this won't be the walkover they were expecting."

"Now tell your people here in this room to raise their own hands," Bleys said.

She hesitated.

"We think we know who they are," Bleys said, looking into her eyes. "In any case, we have no more reason to kill them than we'd have to kill your allies in the foyer."

After a moment she nodded.

"Do as he says," she called down the length of the room. "Let yourselves be disarmed. We gain nothing by getting ourselves killed here."

As movement began behind him, Bleys kept his attention on Gelica. She smiled once more, and wordlessly, slowly, reached under her jacket again, being careful to use only the thumb and forefinger of her right hand—her arm had to bend awkwardly—to pull her small pistol from its holster. As she pulled it out it swung like a small pendulum from her two-fingered grip, its unbalanced weight almost pulling it from her fingers. Bleys reached out with his free hand and took it from her.

"Would you take your pistol away from my head now?" she asked, after a moment.

"You know I can't," he said. "You're too clever. You just might have some other surprise. Let's just relax and wait for Henry."

They did just that, while Gelica's self-identified confederates in the room were disarmed and lined up, kneeling, along the side wall.

"The rest of you remain in your seats," Toni announced to the remaining group of conference attendees. "We can't be sure we've gotten all of them yet, so we have to keep you all where we can watch you, until we can finish sorting you all out."

Eventually, they *were* all sorted out.

CHAPTER 19

"Would you tell me your real name?" Bleys asked, looking across the length of Pallas Salvador's office from his seat at the absent Other's desk. He and the woman he had known as Gelica Costanza had moved there for privacy, leaving her friends, the Others and the Soldiers behind.

The woman, who had been standing with her back to him, turned, and looked at him for a long moment.

"Deborah," she said quietly, finally. "Only Deborah."

"Then you really *are* an Exotic," he said, referring to that culture's tendency to use single names.

"Of sorts," she said. "And from Kultis rather than Mara."

"You're also an Other, I think," he said.

"No," she said. "Not as you now use the term."

"What do you mean?"

"Like you, I'm a crossbreed," she said, "as are all of my comrades—"

"Exotic," he interrupted, "and—Dorsai?"

"That's the sort of deduction I'd expect you to make," she said, sounding exasperated. "I know about your bunch by now: you only anoint people as 'Others' if they're crossbreeds from the three main Splinter Cultures, the Exotics, the Friendlies or the Dorsai."

"'Anoint'?" he said. "Why the hostility?"

"As it happens," she said, ignoring his question, "I was raised on Kultis, but my mother was actually from Newton."

"And your father?"

"I never knew him," she said. "He was a wanderer, and he vanished soon after I was born." The words were delivered expressionlessly, without defiance or challenge, but he felt as if she had spit them into his face.

"I never knew my father, either," he said. "But I don't think that's what you're upset about."

She only looked at him.

"We don't designate—'anoint,' as you put it—Others, by their ancestry," he went on. "You've repeated a common misconception."

She rolled her eyes upward for a brief moment, as if disgusted.

"I never said—"

"For us," he said, overriding whatever she had been about to say, "'Others' are *cultural* crossbreeds."

"All right," she said, after a moment, "I'll accept the correction. It makes little difference."

"That's true, too," he said, nodding. She started to say something more, but stopped herself.

"Being 'Other' is a state of mind," he explained. "And it's a state you and I have in common."

"You're trying to butter me up," she said.

"If trying to get you to listen to me with an open mind amounts to buttering you up, then yes," he said. "But right now your thinking is being influenced by your reaction to what's just happened to you and your people—can you listen from beneath that?"

Her eyes narrowed, and he thought he detected a glint from beneath their lids; but after a moment some of the tension went out of her.

"All right," she said. "I suppose there's a chance you have something worth hearing. Go ahead."

"You were raised on Kultis," he said, "so you probably were put through some of those tests the Exotics like to measure people with."

"Yes, I was." Her expression had hardened slightly at his mention of the tests.

"They didn't say you tested out as full Exotic, did they?"

"They didn't tell me anything," she said. "They told my mother I tested at about forty percent Exotic."

"And the rest?"

"*Undifferentiated* was the term they used," she said. The hostility was still there, he thought, but she was hiding it better.

"What they said makes little difference," he replied.

"What do *you* know about not fitting in?"

"Everything," he said. "I know everything about not fitting in. That's the state of mind I was talking about."

She moved over to a chair; but rather than seating herself, she turned to look at him again.

"All right, maybe I've underestimated you," she said.

"Again," he said.

"Again, yes."

He rose and walked across the room, trying to keep his body language unthreatening; and sat in the chair next to the one before which she was standing. He looked up at her, still on her feet and looking down at him. Her eyes were narrowed; but even as he watched, her face recovered its neutral expression. After a moment she sat next to him, turning at an angle so she could look directly at him.

"You're one of the original Others," he said. "And you're all angry at those of us who've appropriated your name."

"Oh, not really," she said, almost sighing. Her shoulders slumped a little, and he reminded himself she was a good deal older than he.

"I suspect you know perfectly well," she was continuing, "that the Others groups you and your brother took over were only what they seemed—social clubs of sorts."

"But they were set up by you and your friends," Bleys said. "To cover your own activities."

"How much do you know?"

"Not everything, by any means," he said. "But I know you and your friends formed the nucleus of a criminal syndicate on this planet, thirty years ago and more."

He was watching for a reaction to his use of the word *criminal*, but she gave him nothing but her words.

"All right," she said, "suppose that's true: so what?"

"You did a very good job, once you decided to cover your tracks," he said. "But I know your group started here on Ceta, and was always strongest here."

"Well, it was natural," she said. "Ceta's where the money is—it's been a major center for interstellar banking and commerce for generations."

"How did you, personally, get involved in the Others?" he asked.

"'Involved'?" She grinned, and he found the sudden change from her usual imperturbability—which had kept him searching her face for the smallest of clues—a little shocking. But there was little humor in her grin.

"I *started* the group," she said; and laughed. The laugh had a slight edge to it, and he had to restrain his sudden inclination to lean back, away from her.

"We were on the outside, wherever we were," she continued after a moment, more quietly. "That's what Dan and I had in common. We got the idea to find others facing the same kind of life; and together we all found that, with that shared apartness, we could be loyal to each other—we didn't have to be loyal to any state, planet, or company." This time her smile was relaxed and natural.

"It brought us freedom. It was a natural step from there, to start putting people we could trust inside various organizations—it gave us opportunities we never had before."

"It worked very well, didn't it?"

"*Very* well. We could work in secret to help each other—at first, just to help each other get jobs, or do business, but later we helped our friends take advantage of information we had access to, or make decisions that helped each other—and in time, we took control of some companies, and used those to branch out into other fields . . . some people would have said we were guilty of everything from smuggling to securities fraud." She shook her head. "We weren't a gang that coordinated our actions for a single purpose. We were just independent actors who knew there were people they could count on for help if needed."

"So the stories about a secret criminal organization—"

"Exaggerations," she said. "Rumors about our existence began to show up, and we ended up getting blamed for things other people did. At first that was disconcerting—we didn't really see ourselves as *bad* people—but in the end we decided that our best interest lay in sticking together. . . . The rumors even turned out to work to our advantage, in some dealings. We prospered."

"Because you all worked together, and you trusted each other."

"You're right," she said. "But it's also true we were smart."

"And you were motivated."

" 'Motivated'?"

"I mean, you were all hungry," he said. "You all grew up feeling alienated, as if you were outsiders on the various worlds you lived on. You resented that."

"I hadn't thought of it quite that way," she said. "But you're right: we were angry, and we were united in that feeling. It made us *family!*"

"I know that feeling, too," he said.

She calmed, looking across at him.

"I believe you," she said. "You're telling me that your Others are like my Others."

"At least in some ways," he said, nodding. "But then what happened?"

"We did *too* well," she said. "People started noticing, and investigations were suggested."

"Did you make enough mistakes to make investigations dangerous?"

"I don't think so," she said. "But it's possible we made a few— we started when we were young, and we were inventing our roles as we went along."

"Then what was the problem?"

"We were getting older," she said. "We'd been successful, and we wanted to enjoy what we'd earned without having to worry about outsiders interfering with our lives. Some of us had children . . ."

"And you were still unsatisfied," Bleys said.

"What do you mean?"

"It wasn't as good as you thought it would be, being rich and powerful," he said.

"How can you *possibly* know that?"

"It's the way Ceta works," he said. "This planet is dominated by old money; they'd never have accepted you newcomers."

"You're making it too complicated," she said. "We were just tired."

"So you went underground?"

"We were always underground," she said. "Maybe we went further underground. But, yes. Some of us just retired—a few even moved off-planet. Those who stayed active made more use of surrogates. And over time, the name 'Others' began to fade from sight."

"Aided by the innocence of those social clubs you set up," he said.

"Yes. Anyone investigating the Others had to stumble on those groups. They could investigate the clubs all they wanted, because there was nothing there to find—until you and your brother came along, and all of a sudden the social clubs were being looked at by outsiders again."

"So you infiltrated *our* Others," he said. "Why?"

"At first, just to find out what you were up to," she said.

"What did you think about what you found?"

"It was interesting," she said. "We'd only been looking for money but we learned you people have more than that in mind."

"So you decided you wanted to get in on that, too?"

"Maybe," she said. She shook her head, a small smile on her face.

"We were divided on whether we could even take part," she continued. "It seemed clear you were a lot more dangerous than the organizations we'd infiltrated in the past. We were still undecided what to do—we were just going along for the ride to see where it would take us—when you came along and ripped the whole thing open."

"So why didn't you just join us openly? Why try to manipulate our people?"

"Remember who we are," she said. "Most of us—those from our original group—are older. It's true we have some younger people, largely the children of some of our original members, but the heart of our group lies in the original members; the younger ones, with a few exceptions, just don't seem to have the same drive we did. . . . Maybe it's just they didn't have the same kind of lives we had." She looked a little sad for a moment, but then seemed to shake it off.

"But we of the original group—the older ones—we'd been to-gether for decades, and we couldn't break away from each other, to try to join some larger group. Besides, we were too old to be accepted in your training program. All your people would have given us were subordinate positions."

"Subordinate positions were what you started with, back when you first started working together," he said. "That was right up your alley—you all know exactly how to take advantage of such positions."

"You mean, how to take advantage of the people who employ us to carry out part of their work," she said.

He nodded.

"Yes," she said. "We found those of your people who were lazy, who would be happy to let us take over part of their work. And we learned how to do it."

"So you let your bosses live the good life, while you and your people wrote the reports that were being sent to us."

"Yes."

Suddenly, he felt as if something had changed—as if she had tightened up inside. He had seen no alteration in her face or her body language—at least, not one he could recall noticing—so he had no idea what signal had come to the attention of his subconscious. But he knew he had stumbled on something that was important—important, at least, to her.

For a long moment he only looked at her, silently. Then he raised his head, emphasizing his advantage in size; and when he spoke, the sympathy was gone from his tones, replaced by an authoritative voice that he had learned while growing up exposed to the leader-oriented religious culture of the Friendly planets.

"Tell me why you did that," he ordered.

She seemed to recoil a little.

"Did what?" she asked. "I already explained—"

He interrupted her harshly.

"The reports," he said. "Why was it important to you to have control of their writing?"

She seemed now to be at a loss for words. He let the silence drag on, openly watching her face. It seemed to fluster her.

After another moment he leaned back in his chair, altering his body language and tone of voice to project an impression of sympathy.

"Then let me answer that," he said. He smiled at her, a smile that held just a hint of sadness.

"You wanted to control as many of the reports as possible," he said, "because you wanted to try to stop certain things from being reported off-planet."

"That's absurd!" she said, seeming to recover her strength. "What could we be trying to hide?"

"What, indeed?" he said. "You're about to repeat to me that you and your people have no loyalty to anyone on this planet but yourselves, aren't you?"

"That's right," she said, defiance in her voice. "We were just criminals who preyed on these people. What do we care whether you find out—anything—about any of them?"

He nodded, maintaining his smile in silence. The defiance faded from her face, to be replaced only by a neutral expression. And the silence dragged on in a contest of their wills.

It was Bleys who relented, after some minutes.

"By now you, and your friends back in the conference room, are probably wondering what we've got planned for you," he said, his smile becoming broader and showing a certain wryness. But she showed no reaction to that implied threat.

"Nothing," he said.

As her silence continued, his smile softened, and he went on.

"It took us only a couple of days of research to figure out who you were," he said. "Your people did a good job of hiding their tracks, and yours; but they couldn't completely erase the historical records— for that matter, when they *did* manage to erase historical records, the process left holes that were themselves evidence of your group."

Now her face registered a slight apprehensiveness.

"We think we'll be able to track down every member of your group who's become a member of our staff," he said. "All staff members have to submit résumés, identification, and photographs, and all of you did. But the staff members we checked on, including you, didn't show up more than a few times in this planet's records of three decades ago—not even in the most innocent of ways—and not much in the time since."

He shook his head.

"You erased too much, too well," he said. "So well that we've come to understand that we can probably trust any staff members who *do* show up in the local records—because if they were members of your group, their records would have vanished, too."

"So you can take us all, then?"

"We could—although not those of your people who never came to work for us," he said. "But as I said, we won't. You'll all be allowed to go."

Now her face was puzzled.

"Why? We infiltrated your organization, took advantage of your people—learned what you're up to—and you expect me to believe you'll just stand back and let us walk away?"

"You forgot to mention the nine of our Others who have vanished," Bleys said. "They're dead, aren't they?"

Her face froze.

"I think so," she said softly, after a moment. Her voice rose just a little as she continued. "But *we* didn't do it!"

"Your allies, again? The people you insist don't exist, for you to have loyalty to? The people who sent the armed men we just disarmed in the foyer, that you said weren't yours to control?"

Her lips twitched, but she said nothing.

"You can still go," he said, more softly.

"Why?" she asked once more, her quiet voice carrying a freight of intensity. "Why would you do that?"

"What would we do with you?" Bleys said, spreading his hands as if dropping a burden. "We have no jails, and no desire to get caught up in the public legal process that would have to result if we accused you, to the authorities, of some crime, or tried to take some sort of fraud-based civil legal action."

He could see she had already thought of the only other alternative.

"We don't want to kill you all, either," he said, nodding to show her he understood what she was thinking. "It would make no sense.

You and your people no longer present a danger to us, and killing you all would be risky, in a number of ways. We're averse to taking risks to no purpose."

"Aren't you worried we might expose you to—to the governments here on Ceta? Or the media?"

He shrugged.

"What would that gain you?" he said. "Beyond revenge, of course—and I don't think that kind of pettiness is part of your character."

He smiled again.

"And, of course, there's the fact you couldn't credibly expose us without exposing yourselves. . . ."

She looked at him silently. He thought she was evaluating both his words and the intent behind them.

"All right," she said, finally. "I believe you."

She smiled now, herself, a little archly.

"I have to say, you're as logical a thinker as anyone I've ever met," she went on. "Most people would've gotten their blood up, wanting action of some sort."

"Even Dan?"

"You picked up on that, then," she said. "It was a mistake to mention him, I admit it. But I doubt it can hurt me—hurt us."

"Dan was a partner of yours when you started your Others?"

"Yes," she said.

"Where is he?"

"I don't know," she said. "He vanished—it must be fifteen years ago or more." She shook her head.

"Our relationship had soured, and he was restless. He'd always been a risk-taker, wanting to push for something else, something more—he couldn't stand being retired, or even semi-retired. He was always impetuous; so when he vanished, one day, we weren't surprised. But we never heard from him again."

"Are you telling me," Bleys asked, "that he constitutes no danger to us—that he's not among those of your Others who didn't try to become staff here, but are still waiting out in the Cetan population, unknown to us?"

"He's not, as you put it, 'waiting' out there," she said, showing a little amusement. "And you know very well I'm not telling you he's no danger to you. . . . Who knows what might be in the mind of someone who hasn't been on the scene for fifteen years?"

She became more serious.

"As far as I know, he doesn't—assuming he's even still alive—know anything about your Others. He hasn't been here to learn about you." She looked into his eyes.

"You'll have to take my word on that," she said. "There's just no way I can prove it."

He studied her for a moment.

"I think I'll believe you," he said.

"So can I gather up my people and leave?"

"You can," he said. "I'll walk you out to ensure your safety—if that's what you want."

She looked at him, once more puzzled.

"What are you suggesting?"

"When you leave here, I suppose you'll just go back into retirement," he said. "Were you enjoying that life?"

She took a long moment before replying.

"Are you offering me a job?" she said at last, disbelief in her tone.

"Maybe," he said. "Go ahead and leave now. But I'll be here on the planet for a bit longer, if you want to come back and talk."

"You're amazing," she said, after another long moment; and turned, to walk to the door.

CHAPTER 20

Two days later Gelica, now Deborah, came back, and she and Bleys talked for a long time.

She was back the following day, accompanied by three of her old comrades; and this time Toni sat in on their conversation. Two days after that, sixteen of Deborah's people, accompanied by eight other people, came to Others' headquarters.

"We thank you for agreeing to come here," Bleys said. He was standing behind the same head table in the conference room, but the room itself had been reconfigured since the last meeting. Now the head table was closer to the center of the room, and two lines of four tables each extended from its ends, to form a large U shape. Eight seats were placed along the outside of each of those lines, so that their occupants faced each other across the width of two tables and the open space between them.

On one side of the U a second row of chairs had been placed behind the seats at the tables; another row of chairs was ranged along the back wall, behind the head table itself.

Bleys' large chair occupied the middle place at the head table; and he was flanked by Toni and Pallas Salvador. Seated in the row of chairs behind them were a half-dozen of the Cetan-based Others.

"Peace talks," Toni murmured softly. Only Bleys heard her.

No staff or Soldiers were in the room, and the bodyguards who had accompanied Bleys' guests were stationed out in the hallway and the reception area, where they were trading stares with the Soldiers. All the staff, as well as the non-attending Others, had been exiled to the second, lower floor of the office suite.

There had been a noticeable lack of conversation as the various attendees entered and were directed to seats, and the silence continued after everyone had been seated; until, just before the most nervous attendee would have begun to fidget, Bleys stood up.

The backs of his knees pushed his chair back as he rose, and every eye in the room—at least, those that had not been on him already—moved to him. The first real sound came when some of the guests began to realize just how tall their host was.

Bleys paused for a moment after his opening remark, openly looking at each of the guests in turn. Deborah and her comrades, when they arrived at the meeting, had been accompanied by eight people who were members of a group that had been referred to by Deborah, in previous conversations, as *the Families*. Six of the eight were obviously elderly, older even than Deborah and her comrades, and the remaining two were about Deborah's age.

Deborah's people and the delegation from the Families had arrived together, but it was the togetherness of hostage-takers and hostages. Bleys had watched silently from his place as the parties sorted themselves out—after all had been checked for weapons. Deborah and her comrades had led the newcomers to the side of the table that was farthest from the doors; and then separated, to take their own seats on the other side of the U.

Bleys was sure the newcomers—the Families—would not take offense at his scrutiny; they were examining him just as openly. He did not really need to look at them, but he intended to give them an initial impression of openness, which was a good way to open any negotiation session.

There came, finally, a moment when they were all ready to move on; and Bleys, sensing it, sat down. Somehow, the atmosphere in the room had changed, he was sure. He glanced sideways at Toni, and she gave him an open nod.

He turned his eyes back to the tables in front of him.

"The person we've known as Gelica Costanza is the common element here," he said to the room at large. "I suggest that she begin these proceedings."

From the seat closest to the head table, on her side, Deborah rose, to stand for a moment without saying a word. Her body language said she was no longer Gelica Costanza—she seemed to be standing taller and straighter, with her head thrown back—and she reinforced that impression with her first words.

"My name is Deborah," she said. She smiled—but there was nothing pleasant in her face. Her smile was a bared-teeth affront to those across the table.

Directly opposite her an elderly woman stiffened, her mouth opening; but before she could say anything, the slightly younger woman next to her put out a hand to gently touch the older woman's forearm. The older woman looked sideways at her companion, and then past her at the other six people on her side of the table. None said a word, but at least three made slight movements of head or eye.

"I, and my companions," Deborah said, gesturing to her side of the table and in the direction of those seated behind her, "are all members of an association that has been called the *Others* or the *New People*—an association that for many years has been subverting a variety of commercial and financial entities—primarily, although not exclusively, on this planet—for our own purposes."

She paused now, to turn her now-neutral gaze on Bleys.

"I won't introduce all of my companions at this time," she said. "We don't intend to be deceptive, and you may ask any of us to identify ourselves further, at any time." She nodded, as if silently emphasizing some point to herself; and then turned her attention back to the people across the tables.

"As I told you in preparation for this meeting," she said, her eyes now on the elderly woman directly across from her, "the people at the head table are, in order, Pallas Salvador, Bleys Ahrens and Antonia Lu—all of whom have been mentioned in the reports you've gotten from us."

Her eyes moved along the row of faces opposite her as if she were ticking them off a list.

"Behind the head table," she continued, "are a group of Others—members of the Others' organization led by Bleys Ahrens. For the sake of clarity, I will refer to their group as Others, and to my own group as New People. Bleys Ahrens speaks for his group."

Now she turned slightly, to look directly at Bleys. The elderly woman stiffened again, but made no sound.

"Across from me," she said, "are representatives of an informal group that we—I mean, the New People—have come to call the Families. They are, as a group, largely unknown to outsiders."

Now her smile contained an edge of anger.

"They've been blackmailing the New People for several decades."

There was a stir in several portions of the room, but Bleys forestalled any other comment by leaning forward to look directly into Deborah's face.

"Deborah," he said, his tone stern and authoritative, "you need to control yourself. If you continue to try to antagonize our guests, you—and your people—will be removed from this meeting, and the rest of us will continue without you."

Deborah was silent for a moment, her face blank; but then she spoke once more, seeming to adopt once again the professional manner Bleys had come to expect from Gelica Costanza.

"I apologize if my tone was offensive," she said. "The facts I mentioned were correct, which I believe these members of the Families will verify." Across the table the elderly woman was now openly glaring at her.

"The lady across from me is Serafina Leng," Deborah said. "In order down the table beyond her are her sister, Camille Porter, Paul Tombas, Coley Milan, Fallon Porter, Bree Somosa, Melin Somosa, and John Haroun. Together, they represent—"

"That is enough, Deborah," Camille Porter interrupted her. "We can speak for ourselves."

She turned at an angle, so that she could look directly at Bleys across the front of her sister.

"Deborah has some resentment for us," Camille Porter said; "it's justified, but it can be ignored for the moment."

At that, her sister made a noise, as if about to protest, but then subsided. Further down the table, Coley Milan was not bothering to hide his amusement. Ignoring them all, Camille Porter continued, looking straight at Bleys.

"We here are indeed members of a group that the so-called New People have referred to as the Families," she said. "It's an appropriate enough term that even some of the younger members of our group began, some time ago, to use it. But the fact is that the *group*, as I referred to it, actually has no name, for the simple reason that it has never had any sort of formal structure. Rather, we are merely members of various Cetan families who have found reason to work together—and you should be aware of the fact that none of us has any power to speak for, or commit to, anyone else."

Bleys nodded gravely, looking the woman in the eye; but he said nothing. After a moment Camille Porter spoke again.

"Implicit in our lack of any representational capacity," she said, "is a question as to the usefulness of having this meeting at all." Her comment was clearly directed at Bleys, and he responded.

"You're asking what the point is in having *negotiations*, when one *side*—allow me to use those terms for the sake of brevity, please—can't deliver on anything agreed upon," he said. He nodded, putting on a face of serious consideration.

"We're aware of that potential problem," he said. He had decided, on the spur of the moment, to try to match Camille Porter's pontifical speaking style. "But the same lack of any representational capacity you allude to also makes apparently impractical any other form of communication with your Families. Yet we feel that opening up some form of communication between our sides is vital."

"Vital to you, maybe!" Serafina Leng burst out.

"Vital to the Families as well, I think," Bleys said mildly. "If any of you think such a thing is totally impossible, then may I ask why you've chosen to come here at all?"

In the ensuing silence, Bleys swept his eyes down the line on Serafina Leng's side of the table.

"We're the ones who asked for this meeting," he went on, finally, in a more conciliatory tone, "and we recognize that places us in a somewhat supplicatory posture—particularly in light of the fact that we're the ones who are new to this planet. However, any lack of seniority on our part should not be taken to mean we have nothing of value to offer you."

" 'Offer'?" Paul Tombas spoke up. "In exchange for what? I can't think of anything you could offer us that would be worth our giving you control of our planet."

"I could contest your implication that your Families 'control' Ceta," Bleys said, "but I won't. Because it's irrelevant to the point of this discussion."

There were frowns among the members of the Families; and in the silence Camille Porter spoke up once again.

"Then what *is* that point?" she said. "Deborah, in acting as your emissary to suggest this meeting, told us she believed you had something to say that would be worth the hearing. We were unable to conceive of what that might be, but Deborah has proven intelligent and useful in the past, and we were willing to explore the situation. However, thus far we've seen nothing to back up her claims for you."

"Deborah was proceeding on the basis of the things I told her, after we captured her," Bleys said. "Moreover, I'm sure she's capable of making deductions from her observations; and she may have told you some of that, as well." He smiled.

"But can you possibly believe I would share, either with her or with you, everything we have?"

"Still just talk," Paul Tombas said.

"We believed Deborah," Camille Porter cut in, "when she told us you were here to take Ceta away from us—it fits with what you've done on other planets."

"She told you just what I told her, along with others," Bleys said. "It was a ruse, designed to flush out whoever had prevented the proper functioning of our organization here."

"Are you saying you don't want to take control of Ceta?" Camille Porter asked.

"Of course we did," Bleys said. "But we couldn't see any feasible path to that outcome, and so we weren't very serious about it. In any case, we had no idea someone else was already in charge here . . . that information totally altered the situation as we had analyzed it."

"'In charge' is perhaps not an accurate description," Camille Porter said. "Nor do we pretend to completely rule this planet. But our forebears gave us a position that allowed us to have a large, but quiet, influence on matters here, and we have been careful to maintain that heritage."

"It was that 'position' of yours that the New People ran afoul of, when they orchestrated their scheme to defraud some Cetan institutions, then?"

"More to the point, it was our experience with them that led us to place a watch on your own Others," Camille Porter said.

"By that time, of course," Bleys said, looking thoughtful, "the New People had been under your control for a long time." He looked across at her. "Under threat of exposure, I presume?"

"Among other things," she said, her tone carrying a dry humor.

"So although Deborah tried to convince me that the New People infiltrated our Others for their own purposes, she and her people were really working for you?"

"There may have been a certain confluence of interests in the matter," Camille Porter said. "Please don't get the notion that we enslaved the so-called New People. We treated them well, and allowed them to keep many of the rewards they had accumulated from their efforts."

"But they were controlled."

"What alternative was there? Uncontrolled, they were dangerous."

Bleys looked along the row of faces flanking Camille Porter.

"Is that what you think of us, too?" he asked.

"Do you take us for complete idiots?" she responded.

Bleys put a wry grin on his face.

"Not in the least," he said. "That's why I asked for this meeting."

"You're still offering some sort of deal, then," Paul Tombas said. "Did you not understand that we're not going to give you our control of Ceta?"

"Oh, I understood that, all right," Bleys said. "That's not what I'm asking."

The eight faces he was watching showed a variety of reactions, ranging from puzzlement to irritation to interest. He let them think about his words for a few seconds longer, and then dropped his bombshell.

"I offer you our help in destroying the Exotics and the Dorsai," he said at last.

Startlement showed on some of the faces; the rest shut down, trying to show no reaction at all.

"I don't understand what you mean by those words," Melin Somosa said finally, her tone making it a question.

Bleys simply smiled at her, and said nothing.

"What could *you* offer to do against the Dorsai and the Exotics?" Serafina Leng spoke up sharply. "—no, don't stop me, Camille! It's clear this man knows more than we thought, and there's no point in playing games with him!" She turned back to Bleys.

"How much do you know?" she asked.

"Only a little," he answered. "I know that you've been working to undermine the economies of three planets, with the intent of destroying their ability to survive." He shrugged.

"Exactly how you do it, I don't know," he went on. "You can't possibly have enough wealth to carry out a scheme like that by yourselves, so my guess is you're leveraging your assets somehow— perhaps by subverting influential decision-makers in important commercial and governmental positions . . . a campaign of small steps, I suppose; but you've had decades to work on it, and moving by small steps over a long period of time actually works to your advantage, by making your actions less noticeable."

He stopped, but no one answered.

"The details don't matter," he went on finally, "although you may not be willing to believe me on that." He smiled, shaking his head just a little.

"But I haven't come up with a reason why you should be taking such actions—it has to have been expensive . . . I confess to being intrigued and puzzled."

"Even if what you say is true, I can't think why we should tell you our reasons!" Camille Porter said.

"That would be one of the prices of our help," Bleys said quietly.

"Help? What can *you* do to help us?"

"More importantly, *why* would you want to help us?" Paul Tombas said. "I can't think what would be in this for you."

"It's really quite simple," Bleys said. "It would get those two peoples off our backs."

"How are they *on* your backs?" Tombas asked, apparently intrigued.

"Please don't take us for fools," Bleys said. "You know perfectly well we've taken controlling positions on five of the Younger Worlds"—there were several nods in response to that—"and it doesn't take much insight to realize that the Exotics won't stand for that situation for very long."

"Of course you mean that your group's position now represents a threat to the Exotics," Tombas said. He glanced to his left, at Coley Milan or the people beyond him. "And if threatened, you feel the Exotics would set the Dorsai on you."

"Yes," Bleys said.

"That might very well be so," Camille Porter said. "But why should we care what happens to you and your Others?"

"You don't, of course," Bleys said. "That's a good business position to take—if all you want is to maintain the status quo."

"What does *that* mean?" Camille Porter said.

"We want revenge!" her sister cut in. "No, I will *not* keep quiet, Camille! I'm getting too old to play games, and if we have a chance to strike a deciding blow in my lifetime, I want to do it!" She glared at her sister, a glare that perhaps included the rest of her companions, although at the end of the line Melin Somosa and John Haroun, apparently the two youngest on that side of the table, were nodding at her.

"Did you ever hear of William of Ceta?" she asked, turning her face back to Bleys.

"Of course I have," Bleys said. She was referring to a Cetan entrepreneur of nearly a century ago, who had very nearly succeeded in a complicated scheme to corner the interstellar market in employment contracts—a plan that more liberal historians still contended would have resulted in the virtual enslavement of the working and professional classes.

"The Prince," Bleys said. The response was simple, and it was all they needed.

"That's right," she said, nodding. "If you know his story, you know he was on the verge of taking control of all the Younger Worlds, until that Dorsai Donal Graeme interfered!" An angry tone was rising in her voice as she spoke.

"Graeme and his Dorsai used military force to stop Prince William, and they broke him—broke his spirit and broke his fortune." She paused. "Even broke his mind."

She glared at Bleys.

"The Prince was ahead of the whole human race at every turn," she said harshly. "He played by the rules of business, and when his opponents couldn't defeat him, they turned to military force!" She subsided in her seat, as if worn out.

"It was vile!" Her voice was quieter, disgusted.

For a moment, there was silence in the room.

"I don't believe William had any family," Bleys said finally. Before he could continue, Melin Somosa interrupted him.

"That's according to the official records," she said. "There're some who say they're of the Prince's blood."

"The Families?" Bleys asked.

"Not all of us," Camille Porter interjected, apparently resigned now to having everything come out.

Toni, Bleys saw, was now wearing an expression very akin to her white-mind face. He suspected it was an attempt to conceal her thoughts, and he hoped no one among the Families was adept in the martial arts.

Toni held her peace until they were back in *Favored*'s lounge; and even then her voice was quiet.

"You must be aware that those people are insane," she said. "Did you know about them going into that meeting?"

"I knew who they were, from Deborah," he said. "She wasn't aware of their enmity against the Exotics and Dorsai, and I think she was as surprised as we were to learn that those people are consumed by their families' involvements with Prince William's downfall."

"Their fortunes were built on his rise, I gather," she said.

"William was a mercantile manipulator," Bleys said, "and anyone who followed his lead probably made huge fortunes. Donal Graeme was only interested in stopping William himself, and I suspect no one tried to take away the assets of his followers—they were likely well-entrenched in the planet's economy by then, and taking them down might well have caused a depression here." He thought for a brief moment. "And like many plutocrats before them, they probably had come to believe that other sorts of power were their right."

"But how could an attitude like that—and a resentment like that—have lasted down decades, and generations?"

"The Families, I suspect," Bleys said, "were so wealthy they never had to deal with the rest of the world. Their children lived in a world in which they dealt only with each other—intermarrying would have been prized, since it would strengthen the connections between the various families even more. In an atmosphere like that, the paranoid views of the parents were reinforced . . . views like that are always emotionally powerful—particularly if they're not countered by exposure to reality."

"You can't trust them," Toni said.

"Of course not," he replied. "And they won't trust me. That won't matter."

"I think I see," she said. "It's like working with fanatics like that Militia officer you had chasing Hal Mayne."

"Barbage," Bleys reminded her. "Yes. As long as I know what they want, I can trust them to try to do exactly that."

"It only works as long as what they want matches what you want," she said.

"I know," he said. "It becomes my job to remain aware of exactly when our interests will diverge."

As they were eating, later, Toni spoke up again.

"I still don't see how they could have had the power to have such a great effect on the situation of the Dorsai and the Exotics," she said. "Planetary economies are just too large for individuals to have much force against them."

"Which is the kind of thing I told you, earlier, about the historical forces," he said. "And you're right—"

"Oh, I see!" she exclaimed, interrupting him. "Because you've been thinking about the historical forces for so long, you had a—a mental framework that helped you see how to handle the Families, too!"

"In a way," he said. "You probably noticed that when we got into our substantive discussions with them, I purposely fed their perceptions of their own strength—it's the kind of thing rich people hear all their lives: how right they are. But as it happens, they *did* have some effect on their enemies—because it just happened that the interstellar economic system was going in the same direction they were . . . they couldn't have stopped it if they'd tried; and instead, they rode with it."

"So in fact they didn't have the effect you found, that brought you here?"

"Not directly," Bleys said. "You're correct to say that individuals can't have such effects on planetary scales. But it's also true that every organization—every government and business—can only act if the individual people running them take some action . . . otherwise, they're just dead social machinery."

She frowned, thinking.

"I don't understand," she said at last.

"Let me give you an example," he said. "I don't know exactly what they did, but it must have been close to this . . . ." He paused, thinking.

"Suppose you have one hundred million interstellar credits to spend on trying to ruin Exotic trade with Freiland," he said finally. "That amount won't go far, if applied directly. But if you use it to bribe key Freilander officials, the effect of that sum can be multiplied, since such officials usually have control over even larger economic and political capital. . . . For instance, a bribe of five million credits to a Freiland Space Force procurement officer might lead him to give billions of credits' worth of contracts—for supplies, for ships, for military consultants—to someone other than the Exotics and the Dorsai."

"I see!" she said. "That's what you meant when you referred to 'leveraging their positions,' earlier."

"Yes," he said. He smiled. "Do you see something familiar in that concept?"

"Yes," she said, thoughtfully. "It's exactly what you've been doing to take over the worlds."

"But in more ways than economic," he said, nodding.

"Economic assets were all they had," she said.

"That's right," he said. "Again, they were in the right place at the right time: they were in a position to corrupt individuals in positions of power, during an era in which the interstellar system was decaying."

"The only thing that can really stop such corruption is an overriding sense of morality," she said, "and you've been saying for some time that that's been dying away."

"Corruption multiplies itself," he said. "The race has been under stress ever since it went into space, and the resulting corruption will kill it unless I can lead it back to Old Earth and make it face the need to renew its sense of morality and responsibility."

"So you'll be using their corruption to fight future corruption," she said. "It's a concept the aikido masters would have recognized."

CHAPTER 21

The first thing Bleys did, upon arrival back on Association, was to check the great Mayne-map, as Dahno called it, on the wall of his private lounge. He realized immediately it had been updated in his absence.

"The Dorsai!" he exclaimed, more to himself than to Toni, entering the room behind him. "I should have known he'd go there next—he's been making the rounds of all the groups that aren't in our camp." He raised a hand to massage the side of his head.

"Well, that seems logical," Toni said. "But why didn't he stay with the Exotics longer? Surely that would have been safer?"

"In the short run, perhaps," Bleys said. "But this is no longer about safety—Hal Mayne's or anyone else's. I told Dahno that Hal Mayne is actively campaigning against us, and this proves it."

"How?"

"The only reason for him to go to the Dorsai would be to try to enlist them in the fight against us," Bleys said.

"Is it likely the Dorsai would listen to a lone and unknown young man?" she asked. "They have a reputation for being pretty hard-headed."

Bleys remembered again that she was partly Dorsai herself.

"You haven't met Hal Mayne, have you?" he said. "I wouldn't put it past him to be able to get the Dorsai to listen very seriously to him. And they'd be right to see us as a threat to them. But in any case, I don't think he went there entirely by himself."

"You mean someone from the Exotics is traveling with him?"

"In a way, perhaps," Bleys said. "I don't know that. But I think he went with, at a minimum, their blessings. In fact"—he nodded to himself, the idea catching fire in his head even as he spoke it—"I'd say it's probable he carried some kind of introduction or message from the Exotics, asking the Dorsai to take him seriously."

"I see your thinking," she said. "We know the Exotics are inclined to help him because they've already done so—and if they weren't agreed on the need to take some sort of action together, he'd still be there, trying to move them."

"Exactly," Bleys said. He turned to a desk, where he could use a screen to get access to all of the Others' information files, including data that had arrived while he was off-planet.

"Let's see if we have any more detail."

"We were lucky to learn of Mayne's trip at all," he told Toni a short time later. "One of our people going to Sainte Marie was making a connection at a pad on Mara, and just happened to see Mayne passing through. He managed to observe which ship Mayne boarded. Sheer accident."

He paused to think for a moment, massaging his temples, his eyes closed.

"We need to be able to monitor travelers better," he said. "We haven't had any need for that up to now, except for trying to track Mayne himself—for that matter, we haven't had the people to put into a time-consuming effort like that. But we're entering a new stage, and we're soon going to have more of that kind of resource."

"So now we'll try to watch for him to leave the Dorsai?" she said.

"We will, yes," Bleys said. "But I'd say he's already left there."

"What makes you say that?"

"He only had one thing to do on the Dorsai," Bleys said, opening his eyes. "And he's busy."

She raised an eyebrow.

"He's taken the next step," Bleys explained, his eyes returning to the great map. "Now he's recruiting his army. The war is on."

Later that day Dahno appeared. He had been back on Association for more than two weeks, and was fully recovered from his wounds. But Bleys had been quietly told that his brother, on his arrival back at Others' headquarters, had sequestered himself in his suite.

"Come up if you'd like," Toni said when Dahno called. "But Bleys is asleep and I won't wake him."

Dahno came up anyway, arriving via the interior float elevator within minutes, his face petulant. Toni thought he looked a bit drawn, underneath a layer of irritation.

"Why can't I see him?" Dahno barked. "He shouldn't be asleep. I checked to see if your flight resulted in any transit-lag, and none of you should be having that problem! *I'm* not tired!"

She refrained from commenting on his logic.

"He's got one of those headaches he gets ever since he was damaged by the Newtonians," she said. "They nearly blind him with pain, but he won't use blocks."

"War!" Dahno jumped as the door behind Toni was thrown open, the single word seeming to leap out at them. They saw Bleys framed in the doorway, draped in shadow; behind him the hallway that led to his bedroom seemed like some ancient cave.

Clad only in a pair of the shorts he habitually slept in, Bleys stumbled through the doorway into the light of the lounge, eyes half-closed. His forehead seemed moist and creased, and his jaw muscles were tightened.

"It's going to be war," he said, more quietly. "Would you close the curtains and dial down the lights, please?"

While Toni did what he asked, Bleys walked across the room to take his seat in front of the Mayne-map. His movements seemed stiff, but after he had looked up at the map for a few moments, his voice was calm when he spoke.

"Dahno, we've spoken in the past about using military force to get what we need from the Exotics," he said. "But we haven't gotten around to really thinking about building up forces like that."

"You know I'm against it," Dahno said, his voice louder than it needed to be. "Why should we bother? We can get more than we need to overawe the Exotics from the armed forces of the planets we control."

"Don't you see, that won't be enough," Bleys replied.

"Why not? The Exotics have no military of their own."

"But what have they always done in the past, when they were threatened?"

"They hired the Dorsai, of course," Dahno said. "But they haven't—" He broke off as his eyes, following Bleys' gaze, fastened on the new line on the Mayne-map.

"Yes," Bleys said. "I thought the Exotics probably asked the Dorsai to listen to Hal Mayne, but I was a little slow off the mark—in fact, they probably had him carry a message asking for the Dorsai's help."

Dahno stepped over to look down at his brother.

"Are you sure?" he said. His voice was low and serious; but without waiting for an answer, he raised it in protest: "We can't fight that. That's not our game!"

"I told Toni, earlier, that I thought Hal Mayne went to the Dorsai to try to recruit them," Bleys said. "But I didn't really believe they would respond quickly—not until it was too late; and so I didn't think it through far enough."

"What do you mean?" Toni asked.

"You yourself told me the Dorsai are—I think you said 'hard-headed,'" Bleys said. "I assumed that while they might well listen to Mayne, they wouldn't take any sort of action on the basis of his word alone. But if the Exotics have made some sort of financial offer to the Dorsai—for instance, if they've agreed to underwrite some action Mayne might propose to them—then it's suddenly a much more dangerous situation for us."

"It certainly is!" Dahno said. "War is nothing I ever intended! And particularly not war with the Dorsai—no one can beat them!"

"Well, let's stop and look the situation over," Bleys said mildly, looking up at his brother. He had not seen Dahno since his brother left *Favored of God* three weeks earlier, and what he saw—now that he took a moment to look more closely into his brother's face—startled him. But Bleys showed no reaction.

"What's there to think about?" Dahno said, his voice rising. "We can't match the Dorsai!"

"Why not?"

Dahno looked at his brother, silent, as if unable even to comprehend the question.

"Why not?" Bleys repeated; and he sat up straighter, his movements more fluid and all signs of pain erased from his face and posture.

"Brother," Bleys said, "we knew all along the Exotics and the Dorsai would never give in to our leadership, even in the face of the greatest economic and political pressures we could muster. But our planning was based on the assumption we could neutralize the abilities of those three planets to oppose us on the other Younger Worlds—in other words, that they would play the game on the field we chose—and let time work for us."

"Yes," Dahno said, his voice not as loud as a moment before, but still carrying an edge. "I even talked about using force to take whatever resources the Exotics might deny us—but I was talking about some time well in the future. If the Dorsai come into this on the Exotics' side, we can't ever do that, and might very well lose our control of the planets we've already got!"

"You mean it might scare our allies into deserting us," Bleys said.

"I'd say that's a certainty!"

"You're no military expert, brother," Bleys said. "Neither am I, for that matter. But everything I've ever read tells me that no military force—even the Dorsai—can just pick up and launch an attack without a certain amount of preparation time. We've got time, at the very least."

"Time to what?"

"Time to build up our own forces," Bleys said.

"You want to raise an army to oppose the Dorsai?" Dahno said, his voice incredulous. "That's insane! How many people would ever join us to do that?"

"Oh, it would be a mistake to *tell* them, ahead of time, what we're doing," Bleys said. "Nor do I mean we just raise an army and space force and nothing more. No."

He leaned back in his chair, looking at the Mayne-map, which also doubled as a map of the whole of human civilization.

"In fact, we're merely elaborating on our original plan," he went on. His voice was still quiet, almost detached. "Even if the entire population of the Dorsai came out in force, it couldn't really stand up to the combined opposition of, say, nine worlds."

"*Nine* worlds?" Dahno asked. "You're including—let's see—Ceta, Freiland, Sainte Marie, and, um, Coby?—with the five worlds we already control?"

"Right," Bleys said.

"It doesn't *matter!*" Dahno said, his voice, recovered from his momentary startlement, again loud, and edgy. "Can't you *see* that? Even if we *did* manage to get control of nine worlds, and even if that control didn't disintegrate at the first threat of a war with the Dorsai—" He stopped for a moment, as if the words were exploding out of his mind so fast that he had lost his place in the argument. He took a deep breath.

"Bleys," he said—his voice was lower and softer, as if he had remembered finally to employ the persuasiveness that had been surprised out of him earlier—"even if we *could* raise enough of a military force to beat the Dorsai, it would ruin us!"

"I'd rather not get into a shooting war with anyone," Bleys said. "And I really believe our nonmilitary assets will assure us of victory, and an overwhelming one—to the point where realism will make our opponents lay down their arms."

"The Dorsai don't surrender," Dahno said, scowling.

"Even if that were true," Bleys said, "they've never had to fight a war in which they didn't have a place to stand."

He swiveled in his chair, to an angle from which he could look at both of his companions. Toni and Dahno, he saw, each wore a puzzled frown, yet he perceived a vast difference in the unspoken message each face was conveying.

"One thing the Dorsai have never adapted to," Bleys continued, "is nonmilitary conflict. We aren't armies in the field, trying to take and hold territory, so we don't present a military target along the lines of anything they've had to deal with before. Whatever action they take will have to be outside their experience."

"What kinds of actions are you suggesting they might try?" Toni asked.

"Oh, perhaps precision preemptive attacks on military bases of the planets we control," Bleys said. "But that would alienate the populations of those worlds, which would be a great plus for us. I think they'll realize that—and if they don't, the Exotics certainly will."

"What does that leave?"

"Not much," Bleys said. "Underground actions, such as sabotage. Or even assassination campaigns."

"*Are you serious?*" Dahno yelled, shaken.

"They wouldn't go in for assassination," Toni said calmly.

"Perhaps. Perhaps not," Bleys said. "People always tend to throw their principles aside when they feel sufficiently threatened. But it's not going to be a real danger to us in any case, because we'll be well protected."

"By who?" Dahno asked.

"By the peoples of the worlds we control," Bleys replied. "We, and all of our Others, can have so many bodyguards it would take a heavily armed military unit to break through them. And any attempt to try that would be dealing us a winning political position."

Dahno looked sour.

"How do you reach that conclusion?" he said.

"Think about it," Bleys answered. "They can't act for a while yet. In the meantime, we'll be convincing the peoples of the Younger Worlds that we're peaceful philosophers seeking only the good of mankind—that's what I've been doing on my speaking tours for years. You know we can persuade at least a fair portion of the masses of that notion, especially if we tie it to something else they want, like a bigger piece of their planets' economic pies or to stick a finger in the eye of Old Earth."

"Oh, we can do *that*, all right," Dahno said. "Most of our top Others already have major establishments and sizable personal followings of their own . . . but how does that help if the Dorsai decide, say, to come after you—or me, or any of our top people?"

"The Dorsai aren't fools," Bleys said. "They can't afford to be seen as aggressors, and they'll know that being seen attempting to kill us would energize those who believe in us, and swing a lot of those on the fence over to our side. And if the Dorsai have any doubts on that score, the Exotics would certainly confirm it for them—because, after all, it's true." He paused as a new thought came to him.

"In fact," he continued, "we may want to think about manufacturing an assassination attempt . . . at the right time, of course."

"Will a few economic incentives, even coupled with jealousy, work on enough people?" Dahno asked, ignoring Bleys' speculation. "People are complex, you know that; and many of them have totally differing motivations."

"That's certainly true," said Bleys. "But it was never my intention we would stop with such a simplistic program."

He stood up, and strode over to the Mayne-map, looking up at it from its left side.

"There are all these worlds full of people," he said, "and it seems like a huge task to try to motivate them all, I know. But in fact, we don't have to motivate them *all*."

He looked sideways as Dahno approached the other side of the map. Toni kept her station in the middle of the room, watching.

"There are all sorts of keys to those people," Bleys said, "and we can use them all, trying one key after another until enough of them are emotionally aroused and intellectually confused to follow our lead—because whether they're motivated by simple greed, or religious fanaticism, or jealousy, all of it comes down to the desire to believe that they're better than the people on the other side, who they want to believe are undeserving of their luck, or crafty conspirators, or disbelievers. . . ." He waved a hand across the face of the map.

"That's not the only weapon we can create," he went on. "We can add fear to the mix . . . fear that the peoples they already hate will come and take what little they already have."

"You mean you think we can convince the peoples of nine worlds that the Exotics and the Dorsai are planning to attack *them?*"

"We can make it look even worse than that, just by adding Old Earth to the mix," Bleys said.

"But a lot of people on the Younger Worlds look up to Old Earth," Dahno said.

"True," Bleys said. "But 'looking up' to the mother planet doesn't necessarily equate to loving her; and people on pedestals make the best targets. In any case, we don't have to convince everyone on the Younger Worlds . . . only enough to be a substantial—but loud—minority. In practice, a loud minority usually controls a society, because when they yell loud enough, it stampedes others, or at least makes them pause before going into open opposition . . . that's how it always works."

Dahno shook his head, as if denying he had even heard Bleys' words.

"There are other things we need to do, too," Bleys added before his brother could speak.

"After all, a shooting war may yet develop—not necessarily against the Dorsai—and it'd be a good idea to be prepared. So we need to take control of those Younger Worlds we don't yet have, as quickly as possible, while consolidating our positions on the five we've already got. If you think about it, the resources of nine worlds, when properly mobilized, will give us a large and powerful military force, which I suspect the Dorsai would rather not face."

He paused for a moment.

"Old Earth herself probably couldn't resist that. With nine worlds under our control, and the Exotics and the Dorsai neutralized, the mother planet would be alone and friendless."

"*Old Earth?*" Dahno said. "What are you *saying?*"

"Just thinking ahead," Bleys said. He looked about. "I'm hungry."

CHAPTER 22

"I think we can get the rest of the Younger Worlds into our camp fairly quickly," Bleys said later; he was dressed now, and working his way through an omelet and a stack of toast, even though it was midafternoon. He had asked Toni to prepare the meal, rather than having it sent up from the kitchens lower in the building; she had a way with breakfasts.

"Our people," he went on, "have been working to gain influence with the power brokers on those planets for years—something those societies are particularly vulnerable to, since they're all decaying societies with a lot of internal conflicts. That's the kind of situation in which we can work internally without appearing to be nosing into local affairs; any major conflict that breaks out will seem to be totally a local phenomenon, and won't raise any alarm bells in other places."

He paused to take another forkful, following it with a bite of toast; and chewed while thinking. No one interrupted him.

"It's all there in history," he went on. "Whenever a society begins to deteriorate, its most powerful people always decide they need to take control. Usually they start by telling themselves it's necessary to take action not just for their own protection, but to protect the society itself; because they always believe that their society's only working if it's reflecting their own beliefs and desires."

"Don't I remember some old philosopher saying that the rich always seem to believe they got that way because they were morally better than the poor?" Toni said. "Of course, once they get to that attitude, it's only a small step to deciding they have a moral right to control everyone else."

"We never did get rid of slavery," Dahno said. The venom in his voice was not directed at his brother, and his gaze seemed to be focused inward. While Bleys had dressed, Dahno had refused Toni's offer of food, but had accepted a drink, and then another; he had seemed calmer, until this subject came up.

"We just got better at disguising it," he finished.

"We've never been fully civilized," Bleys said. "That's one of the reasons I've been telling you the race needs to grow up."

Dahno subsided, almost sulking, but nodding his head a little. Toni smiled quietly, and Bleys smiled back at her over his brother's head.

"You were talking about the power-holders—I guess you'd call them that," she said.

"So I was," Bleys said. "In fact, I was about to say that they're usually smart enough to realize they can't sell a program like the one I just spoke of to the masses." He put his fork down absently. "So they work in secret, using their money and power to buy the people already in positions of influence, while using propaganda to portray the positions they favor in a positive light."

"Which of course is exactly what we've been doing," Dahno said, a sour look again on his face.

"That's what I've been saying," Bleys said. "We'll use our persuasive powers to get control of those same influence brokers on each planet—the systems and the secrecy are already in place, and we only have to insert ourselves into the picture . . . the beauty of it is, the details of our control can be kept secret, because the lack of openness is already accepted in those systems.

"It's ideal for us! We can be philosophers and philanthropists for public consumption, which adds to our political clout—and the less attractive things we have to do can remain out of sight."

"All right," Dahno said, sounding rather grumpy, "you make it sound like just more of what we've been doing. But the devil is in the details—none of those planets is going to just fall into our hands overnight."

"No," Bleys said, "but we've got more leverage than we've ever had, now that a large portion of Ceta's power is aligned with us."

"Ceta?" Dahno said. "What do you mean?"

"I'm sorry, brother," Bleys said, "I forgot we haven't spoken since you left Ceta."

"Something happened after I left?"

"Yes," Bleys said. "A lot happened." He went on to outline how he had located the unknown force on Ceta whose existence he had deduced.

"So I bargained with them," he continued. "They only want one thing, and I promised our help in getting their revenge on the Exotics and the Dorsai."

"It still seems impossible that they could have been so powerful."

"Oh, it is," Bleys said. "But they got lucky, too: what they wanted just happened to move in the same direction as the forces of history. Do you remember that huge storm we saw while we were hiding on that mountain on New Earth?"

"Oh, I remember," Dahno said. "What does that have to do with this?"

"I think you understand no single thing can create a storm like that," Bleys said. "They result when a large number of factors all fall out in the exact way needed . . . and that's what I'm talking about: over the last sixty years, the positions of the Exotics and the Dorsai got weaker while the rest of the Younger Worlds became more competitive—and at the same time the whole system became more corrupt."

"You still haven't said what we're getting back for helping these Families," Dahno said.

"Entry," Bleys said. "They're using their influence on Ceta, and a few other planets, both to help our people get access to more of the power brokers, and to facilitate our efforts to gain control of other elements on Ceta."

"I suppose they think if we get control of people not already under *their* power, that will help *them*," Dahno said. "Are they really that blind?"

"They're really that obsessed," Bleys said. "Their parents and grandparents raised them on the belief that they had been unjustly deprived of their rightful place; it warped them. They're so strongly focused on revenge they don't worry about what it costs—"

"They've never had to worry about the cost of anything at all, in their entire lives," Toni interrupted.

"Right," Bleys said. "They've come to believe they're invincible . . . it's a little like an economic version of how the Elect among the Friendlies feel about themselves."

"We've never been able to make any headway with the religious fanatics," Dahno warned.

"True," Bleys said. "But we've managed to work with some of them, just by giving them what they want in return for getting what we want."

"If true, that makes them good candidates for our people to work on," Dahno said, grudgingly.

"It's even better than that," Bleys said. "This situation is made to order, because when we get quick results—and we will—the Families will become even more open to listening to us—"

"—And before long they'll be completely in our hands," Dahno finished, his grouchiness apparently forgotten. He looked interestedly at his brother.

"You've already got something in mind to give them those 'quick results,' haven't you?"

"I told them that if they get us access to top power holders not already in their camp, we can persuade them to help our program of taking business away from the Exotics. They liked that idea: our persuasion doesn't cost them as much as the money they've been spending on bribes."

"Well, even if it all works," Dahno said, "how does that help us get the remaining Younger Worlds into our camp?"

"I think our people are more efficient than the Families, and more organized. We'll soon have results, using just the tools the Families are giving us access to—results that will make it even more obvious that the Exotics are getting less of a share of Ceta's trade. Any Cetan groups not already on our side will see there's something to gain in going along with our program, and in turn, with their support, we can guarantee that Exotic ships get even fewer cargoes, and even fewer Exotic experts are hired."

"How can you guarantee something like that?" Dahno asked.

"With the help of the worlds we've already got in our pockets,"

Bleys said. "Any faction on Ceta not initially willing to go along with us will likely jump at the chance to get a larger share of trade with, say, Newton. In fact, we can probably encourage the growth of a planetary government on Ceta—which would make our control less complicated—by using whole-planet most-favored-nation sorts of incentives."

Dahno looked unconvinced. "What you're saying," he said, "is going to cost a lot of money, because most of those actions will be running a deficit."

"What kind of deficit?" Toni asked.

"Those kinds of trade manipulations have always been carried out only by governments seeking political gains," Dahno said. "Which is of course exactly what we'd be doing, too. But that kind of manipulation almost always runs counter to the normal workings of trade, and results in making everything more expensive for everybody. What Bleys is suggesting is that we draw on the resources of the planets we control to artificially deprive the Exotics and the Dorsai of wealth, a kind of economic warfare."

"I think what you're saying," Toni said thoughtfully, "is that we'd be using the capital built up on the worlds under our control to change the normal ebb and flow of trade—as if we were building a breakwater along a beach—"

"A breakwater made of bales of old-fashioned money," Dahno said.

"Well, I can see how that will take trade away from the Exotics and the Dorsai, and hurt them," Toni said. "But how does that help put those other planets into our camp?"

"On every planet there are always people who instantly understand that a program like that means the goods are being made to go elsewhere only because government money is pushing them about, and they'll want a piece of that money," Dahno replied. He seemed to have forgotten his earlier skepticism, and to be wrapped up in contemplation of the strategy he was exploring.

"They'd sell their souls for opportunities like that," he went on, "and turning their planets over to us, to get those opportunities, won't worry them until later, if at all."

"We can afford it if the Younger Worlds we control begin to run big deficits," Bleys said, "if in the short run it helps us get the uncontrolled worlds under our thumbs—because in the long run it won't matter."

"It ultimately comes out of the pockets of the people," Dahno said. "In the mid-term, that might be very unpopular."

"There will be ways to handle that, once we're firmly in control," Bleys said. "And we can alleviate those effects a bit by forcing the Exotics—and the Dorsai, too—to pay even more ruinous prices for the things they need to import. That will recover some of our losses, while impoverishing them . . . for them, it will seem as if a depression has set in."

"We'll have to be very, very adroit to carry out a complicated scheme like that," Dahno said, shaking his head. "You're essentially buying the support of some elements on each planet by surreptitiously robbing other elements on those, and other, planets, as well as the Exotics and the Dorsai. It's a bit of a house of cards, don't you think?"

"If we were only engaging in the financial manipulations, it might well be prone to fall apart," Bleys said. "But that would be only one of our tactics, and not the major one, either. And they're all worth it if they help us further consolidate our control on the five worlds we have, and gain the other four worlds. The same trade considerations I suggested for Ceta will pull Freiland into our camp, too—they won't want to be the odd man out when it looks like the other planets are getting good deals."

"What other tactics can we use?" Dahno asked.

"Big lies," Bleys said. "All the planets have some tinge of jealousy and hatred for the Dorsai, the Exotics and Old Earth herself, and I've already laid the groundwork, in my talks and recorded lectures over the last few years, to get people to dwell on such things. There's a well of emotion ready under the surface of many of those people, that we can open up with a whispering campaign, saying that those three groups have been secretly working together to try to take control of the rest of the planets.

"We'll also tell them that Old Earth, using the facilities of the

Final Encyclopedia, has been secretly working to develop super-weapons to be used in its campaign to take back control of the colonies it once lost."

"Won't that bring Old Earth in against us?" Dahno asked, his voice challenging.

"Not for a long time, if at all," Bleys replied. "That planet is totally splintered, and it's an enormous and time-consuming task to bring those people into any sort of alignment . . . but probably that question won't even arise, because most Earthmen won't notice what we're saying about them—the mother planet tends not to pay too much attention to the Younger Worlds, after all."

Bleys stood up, his napkin, forgotten like the rest of his meal, falling to the floor as he turned his back on the table and strode over to the gigantic map.

"All of this," he said, waving an arm before the map, "should be powerful enough to at least give our people on the uncontrolled planets a start. If we can fan the conflicts properly, we can only gain politically. If civil wars break out, we can send in peacekeepers, voluntarily provided, out of fellow feeling, by the planets we already control." He turned to look back at Toni and Dahno.

"Coby won't be a big problem," he said, pointing without looking over his shoulder; "it's the greatest source of metals in the Younger Worlds, and once we control it, a lot of the planets will tend to go along with us just because they need metals so much."

"But Coby doesn't even *have* a government we can take over," Dahno said. "It's owned by a consortium of commercial enterprises that won't be susceptible to our normal tactics." He walked over to join Bleys at the map. "The consortium's control has always been totalitarian, and the people there have no power."

"Even easier for us," Bleys said; "we won't have to try to raise popular support there. We'll simply give the owners and managers of those companies a quiet word that if they don't cooperate, we'll make all sorts of trouble that will cut into their profits." He turned back to the map, and reached up to point to the Procyon system.

"The Exotics, living in the same system, of course have always owned a large slice of the shares in Coby. But they can be outvoted by the other owners." He turned back from the map.

"Both the people on Coby and the companies that control every aspect of their lives have essentially cut their ties with or citizenship in any other world. The people are the only ones who're willing to work there: the outcasts of the other worlds. They're virtually slaves already; they won't even notice when we take over. And the owners?" He shrugged.

"The owners long ago learned their profits increased if they cut their ties with their native planets; they didn't have to pay taxes, and no other planet has ever been willing to interfere with how they treated their people—it would threaten their access to Coby's metals—allowing the owners to pay low wages to workers with no political voice at all. They may regret that strategy when they find they have no offworld friends to rescue them from us—all we have to do is threaten to take everything if they don't give us control."

"Which we could make palatable by leaving them large and secure incomes," Dahno nodded.

"For the moment, anyway."

"What . . . ? What did you just say?" Bleys asked, late that night. "I'm sorry; I was thinking. . . . I guess I was far away."

"Do you want to talk?" Toni repeated. She was lying on her side facing him, her head propped up by one arm.

He looked at her for a moment. She did not usually probe at him like this.

"What's on your mind?" he said.

"Tell me about Hal Mayne," she said.

"Hal Mayne? I've talked about him before."

"You have, yes," she said. "But mostly you're talking to Dahno about how dangerous Hal Mayne is, and I only happen to be in the room."

"I guess that's so," he said. "I'm sorry; I don't mean to be leaving you out."

"I know you don't," she said. "And you're not, really. It's not so much that you're not telling me—something—about Hal Mayne, as that I can see there's something about your reaction to him—or maybe your feelings for him—that I can see the edges of, but you never talk about."

He found himself at a loss for words, and the silence stretched long enough that it was she who finally broke it.

"Maybe it's something you haven't even thought about, your-self," she said. "So let me tell you what it looks like to me." She paused to raise herself off her arm and move the pillow her elbow had been nestling in to his stomach; and then rolled onto it, so that she could look down into his face.

"To me it looks as if you react to Hal Mayne in some way you never react to anyone else—no, wait!—that's not exactly what I mean." She took another moment to think.

"Something about him makes you sad," she continued. "Not the way a person would feel about an enemy." Her finger was poking lightly at his chest. "I know you're sad a lot, but this is different. . . . Do you understand what I'm getting at?"

"Well . . . ," he said, stretching the word out a little. "I guess I'm disappointed."

She looked at him, simply waiting for him to continue.

"I think you know—" He stopped. *This is hard! Why do I keep running into these hard places?* "—no, I know you know," he went on, "that I've always felt I can never have a friend." He was looking now at the ceiling of his bedroom, which as usual was set to display the starry night sky. Like the sky, he was oblivious to her reactions.

"I know that. I've always known it," he went on. "I accepted it as the way of my life, long ago. But for some reason I don't fully un-derstand, when I learned about him, and even more when I met him, some part of me insisted that this man could be the friend I never thought I could have."

"Could be—but isn't?"

"Yes." He exhaled, a release of tension almost loud enough to be a sigh. "Instead of my friend, he's become my enemy—and the most dangerous possible enemy. There are already people who are beginning to pay attention to him, like the Exotics."

"Are you sad because he refuses to be your friend—or because he's your enemy?"

"I don't know how to answer that," he said, looking back to her face, framed by her black hair.

"Then let me ask this," she said: "if Hal Mayne were to become your friend, would you turn back from your plans, from your goal in life?"

He looked at her for a long moment.

"No," he said, finally. "I think I see what you're getting at—I can't very well expect him to give up his goals for my friendship, when I would never do the same."

"That's not what I'm saying," she said. "I'm saying you already have a friend, one so big there's no room for another . . . I mean the purpose you've devoted your life to."

For a long moment he just looked at her.

"I've been blind," he said then. "How do you handle it?"

"I knew what I was getting into when I joined you," she replied, a fist thumping him on the sternum. "But what do you think about what I just said?"

"I believe you're right," he said, after taking a brief moment to think. "I tell myself frequently that my—my purpose—is more important than everything else—"

She interrupted him.

"You mean you *need* to remind yourself frequently, because—because other things in life distract you?"

"Let's say: because sometimes the things I may be required to do are too hard."

"I'm sorry; I interrupted you," she said. "Go on with what you were saying, please."

"I was saying that I tell myself, frequently, that my purpose is more important than anything else," he said. "But I hadn't thought, until now, to relate that to Hal Mayne." He stopped for another moment, thinking.

"I guess subconsciously I interpreted his escapes—first from his estate and then from that prison cell—as a personal rejection of me, and of my offer of friendship. Of course that's a stupid reaction on my part." He shook his head.

"That reaction—my reaction, I mean—was a mistake in itself. It was a weakening of my resolve. And that applies regardless of whether Hal Mayne rejects me as a friend, or accepts me."

He stopped, looking into her blue eyes.

"I used to worry," he said, "that you'd reject me, too, once you learned enough about my plans." He shook his head. "We're beyond that now, aren't we?"

She closed her eyes, and lowered her head to his chest; and held him.

CHAPTER 23

Bleys keyed off the circuit over which he had been talking with the Others' personnel office, six stories below him; and leaned back in his chair, looking down the length of the lounge at the great map he used to keep track of his nemesis. Years of self-control kept him from grimacing.

Dahno would not have hesitated to express his scorn, if he were here and Bleys had mentioned that word, *nemesis*. There was little concrete evidence to speak for Mayne's dangerousness.

Yet Bleys remained convinced Hal Mayne was the biggest single danger to his plans.

In a way, Mayne was irrelevant—no single human being, including Bleys himself, carried sufficient historical mass to control the direction of those threads of historical forces Bleys had pictured for Toni, that night on Ceta.

But those forces were closely balanced; just a small weight, added to one side or subtracted from the other, could alter their direction— alter it enough to change the course of the human race, as a puff of wind could alter the flight of a bullet.

The historical forces, that he pictured as a many-threaded tapestry flowing through time, were made up of all the decisions ever made by human beings, across the entire span of the race's history; and so they had a weight, an inertia, no single person could turn aside.

So his task was not to shift the forces himself, but to move members of the human race—convince them that his was the correct path. If enough people went along with him, their combined weight could dominate the direction of the forces . . . within himself he felt a feeling of familiarity, as if what he had just thought echoed something he had heard, or thought, or seen—somewhere before . . . he could not pin it down.

On the other hand, if Hal Mayne convinced enough people not to go in the direction Bleys knew was needed to save the human race, the forces might tend to the other direction.

It saddened Bleys to think that the entire future of the race depended on unknowing decisions made by the totally ignorant, but he could not tell them—not yet—that the very future of humankind was at stake in this conflict. They would not believe it. They would find it unlikely, ludicrous—too far from their own personal lives to be accorded either credibility or interest.

It was yet another sad fact about the human race, he thought: most did not think ahead far enough to imagine a future beyond the lives of their grandchildren—more accurately: to care about such a future time.

It had taken him years to learn that fact about his fellow humans. When he was much younger he had occasionally tried to bring conversations around to considerations of the far future and the destiny of the race; but most of those around him seemed to lack interest in such concepts.

Eventually, he had theorized that those reactions resulted from a strange kind of fear—that most people were very uncomfortable dealing with the concept of a world in which they, or something they had created, no longer existed.

Bleys was utterly sure Hal Mayne thought that far ahead. Bleys did not know why he knew that, but he knew it. Which meant that Hal Mayne must feel something like the same sadness, the same loneliness, of being almost the only one he knew who saw what he saw.

In an attenuated way, that was what had made Bleys so sad, on that day when he first met Hal Mayne, in his prison cell, and offered him friendship. At the time Bleys himself had not really fully understood how deeply similar their situations were . . . perhaps Hal Mayne, too, had not really understood he was being offered the gift of an understanding friend.

Will he come to see it, someday? When will it be too late for even that understanding to change things between us?

Toni had made him articulate it: Bleys could never give up his mission, even if it cost him everything else he wanted out of life. He wondered if Hal Mayne felt the same way . . . but how could he, when his side of the struggle was so clearly wrong?

No one else understood the race's peril as Bleys did. Not even Hal Mayne.

He reached for a piece of the fine paper kept in a small box on his desk. It was expensive paper, a linen blend that felt good under his fingers when he chose, as he did now, to write to himself. He could, and often did, use any available paper for such writings— when the urge was on him the writing was all that mattered. Still, there was a pleasure of creation that came with using an antique-style pen to put his words on the finest of papers . . . it was a kind of art, he felt.

He had thought idly, now and then, of studying calligraphy; but he had never done so. Art was not the point of his writings.

I never really knew how lonely I was, until I started to imagine what Hal Mayne must feel, *he wrote*. He's been taken in by the Final Encyclopedia; I wonder if he's lonely there?

He paused, looking at the words. He had no real need to write such notes; and in a way it made little sense to do so; the words, although encoded as he wrote, were never seen by anyone else, but destroyed as soon as he had finished writing.

He smiled, almost shyly; and skipped down the page a little, to write again:

Do I use these notes as a substitute for having a friend?

He looked at the words for a moment, the smile fading; and then fed the sheet into the slot in his desk that, using a variation of the phase-field technology that was the basis of both interstellar travel and the panels that shielded the Final Encyclopedia, disintegrated the sheet totally, spreading its component subatomic parts evenly throughout the universe and placing it forever beyond recovery. He pulled out another sheet of paper, and wrote.

In my youthful, failed attempts to find God, I read all the holy books. In some there's a story that tells how Jesus, before his crucifixion, asked if the burden God had given him could be taken away. But it could not be. Not if Jesus was to do his job.

I have the burden of knowing the danger the human race is in, and of being the only one who can see that danger, and a way out of it . . . and because I'm the only one who can see it, I can't shift my burden to someone else.

If I truly believed in God, perhaps I could forget the danger, and just leave it to Him to take care of His children. But I was never able to develop the faith such an abdication would require. So I have no one to pass the cup to.

It's up to me. Even though *I* might not be up to *it*.

Me. Alone.

He sat back, looking down at the paper but not really seeing it.

He must lead, then, even from his position of weakness. *He* must lead, because no one else saw the danger.

He would have to do it through lies, because few would believe the truth. Dahno did not; and even Toni—the only other person to whom he had explained his vision—even she had only accepted what he said, as if tucking it away to think about later.

He was committed to a course of trying to break down what was needed, into a series of steps; and then to finding a way to make each step so attractive a lot of people would want to take it.

His future would be long and arduous, as he tried to lead his blind species along those steps.

Would he ever be in a position to explain the end?

Somehow, he would have to find that position; because he could not live long enough to carry the race through to its maturation.

One step at a time, he told himself.

He fed the second sheet into the disposal slot, and then keyed the internal comm circuit for Toni; and asked her to find Amyth Barbage, and have him come.

After he finished speaking, he looked again at the slot he had just trusted to destroy two sheets of paper. He said no word, made no motion that might betray the suspicion that had risen in him—but for a moment the hairs on the back of his neck stood up.

Have I been overlooking a danger?

He spent the rest of the day pacing, until Toni came to make him work out. By then, he was impatient for it.

Neither of them was yet back in optimum condition, but they had managed to get in a martial arts workout every day since their return from Ceta, and they were not as far off their marks as before.

On this occasion, though, Toni was startled when, in the midst of the dance-like movements of their exercise, Bleys surreptitiously began to communicate with her, using the touch-language her own family had developed over generations, which she had taught him.

"Why?" she communicated. Bleys understood she was asking why he was using this secret form of communication, here inside the secure bounds of Others' headquarters.

It was a disadvantage that their workouts, which were primarily based on judo and an extended form of aikido, included only brief moments of contact through which they could touch and communicate, as they maneuvered about each other, each attempting to reach the point of being able to use the other's ki against him or her, and thus throw the other.

Ki was what their workouts were really all about. *Ki* was the Japanese word that described the centering of the body's energy flows; and the point of aikido was to blend oneself with the opponent's ki, so as to be able to redirect it without having to oppose it—and to do so without losing one's own centeredness.

"Brother," he told her, his fingers answering her question in a series of taps, pressures and pulls delivered as he took a momentary grip on the lapel of her exercise jacket—her gi—before their movements took them apart again.

"Listening?" she asked, when next they came together; and in the same moment he was signaling *"Assume listening."*

"Danger?"

"Always."—And they moved apart again, to keep up the integrity of the exercise.

Over the next hour, bit by bit, Bleys told her—using abbreviations and skipping a lot of the unimportant words, and trusting she would pick up meanings from bits and pieces—that he had always known that Dahno thought he, Bleys, might be insane. Dahno had gone along with Bleys' plan to alter the purpose of the organization Dahno had built, from simply seeking money and power, to seeking to control the human race, only because Bleys had shown his brother, in a time when Dahno's world was beginning to crumble around him, that he really had no choice.

"That explains a lot," Toni communicated, with the left hand that pulled his arm while her right arm swept him into an uncontrolled plunge across the room. . . . Bleys, in his effort to communicate, had lost his focus for a moment.

Back on his feet and gripping her sleeve, he told her he had nothing specific to go on, but he was sure Dahno was working on some plan of his own.

"Until he was wounded, he always felt invulnerable . . . but since we returned, he's been showing a pattern of alternating opposition and acquiescence."

"How does that evince treachery?" she communicated.

"It's not that it proves he intends to betray me. It's that it proves he's not thinking like himself—like the Dahno who created and ran the organization so successfully. This is the pattern he was showing when he got into trouble and left Association, leaving me to deal with that trouble . . . he would oppose me, just out of his normal habit—but then, remembering he had a new plan, give in to me . . ." Bleys paused, using a hand signal to tell her that he needed to catch his breath—he really *was* out of shape.

"And if he isn't planning something," he continued when they resumed their exercises, *"what I tell him tomorrow may make it so."*

"Tomorrow?"

"Brother can be a great help to me," Bleys explained—referring to Dahno as *brother* was faster than going through the laborious spelling process. *"Has been. But if he intends to oppose me, I have to stop him."*

"How can you decide what to do if you don't know what he's planning?"

"I can't afford to waste much time and energy on what is, essentially, a sideshow. I'll have to simply try to disrupt whatever his plans are. And I may be able to do that while also getting some use out of his talents."

"What do you want me to do?"

"Tomorrow I'll propose calling a convocation of all our top Others, telling you to call them in, and to have them arrive here on Association in three weeks. Instead, you'll tell certain ones to come secretly to my offices on Harmony, four days earlier than the three weeks."

"Which to Harmony?"

"Will signal names during tomorrow's exercise."

"Tell me what you're planning?"

"Too long and complicated. You'll hear most tomorrow."

Soon after that they finished with their workout. On his way to the shower, Bleys turned back, as if a thought had just struck him.

"Have you located Barbage yet?"

"The message went out," Toni said. "I haven't had a response yet."

"Send an amendment," Bleys said. "Tell him not to come to Association, but to wait for me to leave him a message at my offices on Harmony."

"You're going to Harmony?" she asked, giving no sign of their silent conversation . . . he had been sure she would not fumble before any unseen listeners.

"I wasn't," he said. "I just decided on it while we were working out. Harmony is where Hal Mayne was, until the Exotics got him away; and I think there's some follow-up to be done there."

"It won't hurt to look in on McKae, either," she said, continuing their charade. "I know you don't like the kinds of things First Elders have to do, but there's much to be gained from keeping your hand active in the government."

"I wish I could consider McKae reliable," Bleys said. "His personality seems to have been deteriorating, but I can't discount the chance he'll rebel sometime."

"You can afford a certain amount of protocol," she said. "It reassures him, and that helps you get our people into all levels of the government."

There was no charade in that statement.

"The latest reports are in from Ceta," Dahno said, stepping off the disk of the float elevator later that day. His broad face shone with cheerfulness and he was moving quickly, more energetic than at any time since his injury.

"I've had them scanned in so you can look them over on your screen," he added, waving a hand in the direction of Bleys' desk.

"I will," Bleys said, smiling back at his brother, "but why don't you summarize it for me, first?"

"The Families are sending six of their young people here to us for training," Dahno said, grinning. "They're convinced of our abilities and they think they can learn them. It'll be a great opportunity for us to set up future control of the Families."

"It'll be interesting to meet them," Bleys said. "I've believed for some time that the reason the Families are ruled by their elderly members is because the younger generations don't care about what happened to Prince William. We'll make good use of them."

"Also," Dahno continued, "they've given Pallas Salvador the chair of the Malik Shipping Line, as well as directorships in three other major companies; and they've placed more of our Others into nine other directorships in five other major companies. Pallas Salvador says it's no gesture on their part: she's already moved Others into a number of key positions in several of those companies—enough that we're running short of people."

"I presume Pallas Salvador is carrying out our end of our bargain?"

"She says she's already given orders to divert three shipments of metals intended for the Dorsai—they'll be 'lost,' officially, and the shipping company's records will only show that the cargoes left Coby on Malik vessels and haven't been heard of since. Meanwhile, the Dorsai's escrow will be frozen until the matter is cleared up—which will drag out for a very long time. . . . The Families are very pleased; it's something they never thought of."

"How did she manage to set that up so quickly?" Toni asked.

"Pallas Salvador is neither innovative nor particularly persuasive," Bleys said, "but she can be an efficient administrator, once she's given the outline of a plan."

"She's going to have her hands full," Dahno said. "We'll probably need to put someone else in to run the organization there."

"No," Bleys said. "She's possessive. I don't think she'd react well to that. We'll give her several more deputies, but we have to make it clear to her she's still in charge."

"Overly possessive subordinates grow to be a problem," Dahno pointed out, oblivious of his own shortcomings.

"That's true," Bleys said, "but for the moment—and probably for a long time to come—we'll need her efficiency to cement the alliance—"

"By giving the Families everything they want, of course," Dahno interrupted.

"For now."

"All right." Dahno nodded. "But those people are smart, and I don't want us overlooking something, and finding we've been gulled. Going along with them makes sense for now, if you think she can be depended on not to try to push too far—the Families'll be watching for tricks."

"Pallas Salvador has strict orders not to take any action that might spook them," Bleys said, "and I'll be watching her closely. For the moment, doing exactly what the Families want—weakening the Dorsai and the Exotics—is just what we want; so we lose nothing by seeming to cooperate, and in fact we gain from use of their power and connections."

"Can you keep close tabs on Pallas Salvador and still run the rest of the organization? Or do you want me to take an extra hand?"

"We'll all be taking those 'extra hands,'" Bleys said. "Our plan is growing faster than expected, and we'll all have to take on more work—become more efficient."

"The only reason I'm not fighting you over this alliance," Dahno said, "is because I don't see how its failure can hurt us. I don't trust the Families—I know you don't either—and they don't trust us. But if this deal falls apart all we lose is our organization on Ceta, and we can live with that." He had regained some of his apparent cheerfulness.

"Are you trying to warn me about something?"

"Maybe I am," Dahno said. "I've said it before: you've taken this organization very far, very quickly. But this unrestrained growth is dangerous! We're far short of the trained people we need just to keep control of what we've gained, and I just don't see any way the two of us—even with Toni's more-than-able assistance—can keep everything going . . . it's becoming a gigantic juggling act, and you and I can't be everywhere at once, making every decision and keeping an eye on every one of our people."

"You're absolutely right," Bleys said. "But there are a few things we can do to take some of the load off ourselves."

"I don't think I like the sound of that," Dahno said, his eyes narrowing. "Come out with it: what've you decided to do without telling me, *this* time?"

"It takes too much time to pump out well-trained Others from your training program," Bleys said. "You've produced able people who've served us well, but we're short on numbers."

"We can't change that!" Dahno protested. "We've expanded the program as far as it can go without being diluted by the lack of individualized attention."

"I'm not so sure about that," Bleys said. "But you're right about one thing: whether we can expand the program or not, it would take time to build the system, and we just don't have it."

"We can't speed up the process," Dahno said; "what's in the pipeline is what we'll have, for a while."

"That means we have to compensate for the lack of trained Others," Bleys said, "by making our trained people work harder, and moving the untrained recruits into more responsible positions."

"How can you get our people to work harder?"

"You should know, brother," Bleys said. "You're the one who taught them all to be ambitious."

"Ambition? You mean you have something more to appeal to them with?"

"Certainly: more power."

"What kind of power?"

"More control on their worlds," Bleys said. "More worlds to control. And more of a voice in running our organization."

"You can't be suggesting we give up our control!"

"I am," Bleys said. "Some of it, anyway."

As his brother remained silent, Bleys spoke again, more softly.

"War is coming," he said. "Under the surface, it's already here. It won't necessarily be a war of soldiers and ships; but it's going to be a war of ideas. It'll be a war between Hal Mayne and myself—and the peoples lined up with each of us—and it'll be a war for the minds of every other human being."

He paused, turning to look briefly at Toni, and then looked back at his brother.

"I know you don't believe it. But this war has already started, and I have to do everything I can. I have to rush my side into getting ready. Because Hal Mayne's already out there setting up, and he's going to be hard enough to beat without giving him a head start. He's going to be a very dangerous foe once he builds his side to its full strength."

Dahno was not through with his opposition to Bleys' ideas, but by the next morning he seemed to change his stance; and he agreed readily to Bleys' proposal for another convocation of the senior Others' leadership.

"Firdos, would you send me all the files on our own people?" Bleys said.

"Do you want just the files on the people who've passed through training here?" the staffer asked. "Or do you want the information on the other-planet recruits, too?"

"All of them, I think," Bleys said. "I know there'll be a lot of them, but I need to find particular sorts of people."

"We have more information on those who went through our training course here, of course," the staffer replied. "And that includes some psychological profiles—is that the kind of thing you're after?"

"It's not the only information I need," Bleys said, "but it'd be very useful."

"We won't have as much information on the people recruited by the off-planet organizations," Firdos pointed out. "But we could tell them to send more information, if you'd like."

"Yes, would you do that, please?"

—

CHAPTER 24

The holder of the position of First Elder of the Government of the United Sects of Harmony and Association, like his superior, the Eldest, had his own official offices and official residences—to be exact, one on each of the two planets.

In the political life of the Friendly worlds, more often than not there was no Eldest to rule both planets—that political phenomenon required that the same candidate receive a majority of the votes cast on each of the two planets. In those periods in which no candidate received such a double majority, the two planets were individually governed by the candidate who had received the plurality of the votes cast on that world, and matters affecting both planets were—in theory—handled by the two planetary governments working as a team.

Both planets had a capital city, along with official residences and government office buildings; and on the infrequent occasions when an Eldest ruled both worlds, he and his government generally moved back and forth between the two planets, spreading his presence to both worlds in the most expedient political fashion. There were plenty of available facilities, since residences and offices on each world had been emptied by the last election and were available at the Eldest's discretion.

Since his election Eldest Darrell McKae had chosen to spend most of his time on Harmony, even though his career had begun on Association. The reason for this was unclear, but some suggested that the Eldest, feeling Harmony was the weak point in his electoral base, was intent on strengthening his hand on that planet.

Bleys, however, suspected McKae was avoiding Association both to cut down on encounters with his original supporters—since his

election the Eldest had become more open in his taste for wine—
and to avoid having to face his failure to curb the activities of the
First Elder he had appointed. And Bleys was sure McKae preferred
to avoid that First Elder, Bleys himself—who was more often on Association than on Harmony.

On those occasions when Bleys came to Harmony he had no
need to find either accommodations or working space, since each
planet had a complete set of offices for both the Eldest and the First
Elder. However, there were things Bleys preferred not to do within
the confines of government-provided facilities; and on this trip he
delayed only long enough, after his arrival on the pad in Citadel, for
a trip to the Others' Harmony offices, before traveling to Healing
Waters.

Healing Waters was a small city that nestled between two small
rivers at the point where they nearly joined before emptying into
Revelation Bay, a shallow, island-dotted body of water largely useless for ordinary commercial purposes. It was a picturesque warm-
zone city given over to vacationers—to the limited extent the
Friendly planets had citizens wealthy enough to afford that luxury.
This gave Bleys an excuse to be there—need for a restful vacation—
as well as the insulating effect of distance from the capital and any
who might be interested in his doings.

As the time for Amyth Barbage's appointment neared, Bleys was
sitting under an awning at a large table that had been moved to the
deck of the penthouse suite of the city's most luxurious hotel. He
had chosen this hotel because he expected to be joined by the senior Others he had secretly invited to a meeting that might well be
critical to his plans.

Being on the hotel's roof minimized the risk of being overheard
in his dealings. He had been able to bring only one of the security
technicians who normally scanned any room he stayed in for listening devices; to bring a larger staff on a supposedly routine and restful trip might have attracted Dahno's notice.

In the past, Bleys had always been able to persuade his fellow
Others to go along with his ideas; that was, in fact, the base on
which his control rested. He anticipated no difficulty now in persuading his invitees to support him in the plan he intended to

present—to the select group here and now, and to the larger group that would be attending the meeting that was to start next week on Association.

But he had never had to try to create such a consensus of opinion in the face of active opposition from his half-brother.

Whenever their ideas had conflicted in the past, Bleys had managed to work in secret well enough to present Dahno with a situation in which their subordinate Others were already in strong agreement with Bleys' ideas, leaving Dahno little option except to go along. But open opposition by Dahno at the meeting on Association would present the gravest of dangers to Bleys' plans: no matter how well Bleys persuaded the Others at this secret meeting to take his side, it was more than possible his brother, with a few days to work on them, could turn them around. For it was Dahno who had recruited and trained them; it was Dahno who had managed to win some sort of place in their hearts.

Bleys had an unrivaled ability to show people how going along with him would benefit them, but Dahno had the better ability to get people to follow him just because they liked him.

On the lower floors of the hotel, suites had been emptied in preparation for the arrival of the invited leaders, but none had shown up yet; Toni was back in Citadel, waiting to meet them on arrival, to divert them here.

"The Militia officer Captain Amyth Barbage is in the foyer, Great Teacher," a voice said over the intercom speaker. The voice belonged to one of the staff people from the Harmony Others' offices. Having brought only a skeleton staff on this trip, Bleys had been forced to coopt a few people from the Harmony office—but he was finding that strange voices on the intercom, and strange faces carrying out his orders, made him a bit uneasy. It seemed unlikely that mere staff people would somehow decide to report to Dahno on what little they might learn about Bleys' doings here; but Bleys had to question everyone's loyalties, if Dahno had had time to work on them.

The leader of Harmony's Others, Kinkaka Goodfellow, was also a possible danger. He had spent his whole career here, on a planet always in easy observation range of the Others' home office on Association; it was more than possible his first loyalty was to Dahno. Bleys had diverted the Harmony leader by tasking him with preparation of a delicate report to be presented at the coming meeting on Association. It was Bleys' belief that Goodfellow would be intensely preoccupied for the entire time before that meeting: Kinkaka Goodfellow was a consummate bureaucrat.

Bleys could perhaps have borrowed people from the First Elder's offices here on Harmony, but he had even less reason to be sure of their loyalty—here came Barbage now.

The man looked, if anything, even thinner and colder than when Bleys last saw him, in the cells in Ahruma, less than six months ago. Bleys had been wondering how Barbage might have been affected by Hal Mayne's escape. Most men would have been humiliated by that unfortunate event, but Bleys was somehow sure Amyth Barbage would never be humiliated by anything at all.

"I am here at thy command, Bleys Ahrens," Barbage said, as always using the antique-sounding canting speech practiced by certain of the ultra-religious on the two Friendly planets. He had stopped three meters from the table and come to attention, which Bleys knew was a deliberate reminder that Bleys, as an officer high in the government, was one of Barbage's superior officers, and thus able to command him regardless of Bleys' own merits. In the captain's twisted logic, a reminder to a superior officer that his rank was all that required Barbage to obey him always carried the hidden message that Barbage was superior in nonmilitary matters; for Barbage considered himself to be one of the Elect, those guaranteed salvation and special consideration by God.

At the same time, Bleys found it meaningful that the Militia officer had not used Bleys' title, but addressed him by name. Barbage seemed to be presenting a mixed message, and Bleys decided that it was some kind of challenge.

"Be at ease, Amyth Barbage," Bleys said. In turn he had used the Militia officer's name rather than his rank, believing it would remind the man that for all his high political rank, Bleys professed to hold an even higher position—one Barbage himself had seemed to acknowledge in the past, when he had addressed Bleys as *Great Teacher*.

Barbage, however, provided Bleys with no hint of a reaction to Bleys' words, but merely snapped crisply from his position of *attention* to a position of *at ease* that in fact displayed no hint of actual relaxation, but looked like the previous stiffness, differently arranged.

There's no point in sparring with this man. He's as harsh and unsparing as ever, and there's no forgiveness in him, whether for others or for himself.

Bleys wondered briefly whether Barbage might think he had just won a point from Bleys; but he shrugged, mentally, and set the idea aside. He was not playing any game in which points mattered.

"Would you like something to drink, Captain?" Bleys asked mildly. "Or even something to eat?—I'm not sure how far you've had to come today."

"I have not come far," Barbage said. His words seemed to be a refusal of any refreshment, which was hardly surprising, coming from this ascetic individual. Barbage's eyes were held level, his gaze passing over Bleys' head, as if he refused to recognize the First Elder. "I have been awaiting thy arrival in this fleshpot of a city for two days."

A reproof! This is progress, of a sort.

"I know you would never approve of a city of pleasure like this, Captain," Bleys continued, his tone as mild and unreproachful as before. "But I didn't call you here to afflict you with the atmosphere in this place. Rather, my duties have required that I come here, and it was efficient to call you to me here."

"I am always at thy command, Great Teacher," Barbage said, "and of course at the call of the First Elder, as well."

That's as much as he can possibly unbend, Bleys thought, eyeing the officer. *Yes. He will do it.*

"I called you here, Captain," Bleys said, "because there is a need for you—one I felt it best to convey to you in person. And I've chosen you because I'm convinced you're the best man for this task—not only because of your own abilities, but because of your past history with and knowledge of Hal Mayne."

With that Barbage's eyes came down, to focus, burning, on Bleys' face, an intensity in them that would have made other people want to raise their hands.

"Surely he hath left this planet, Great Teacher," Barbage said. He spoke slowly, but there was an edge to his voice. "Is it that he hath gone to Association—"

"No, Captain," Bleys said, interrupting the question. "He's now well beyond your reach." He gazed directly into the officer's black eyes. "But a way to reach him may yet be available to us, if you can carry out the task I have in mind."

"What is that task, then, Great Teacher?" Barbage's head had drawn back just a little, as if he were preparing to spring forward and bite Bleys.

"Hal Mayne is gone, Captain," Bleys repeated, "but the outlaws of his Command are, I think, still at large."

And now Bleys saw a light kindle behind those dark eyes.

"I shall find them for thee, Great Teacher," Barbage said. His eyes turned down for an instant; then rose to look at Bleys directly once more.

"Alive?" he asked, his light baritone voice carrying a cold message.

"Alive," Bleys said. "Particularly their leader, the woman Rukh Tamani. But I warn you to be very careful of her: I have met her, and I tell you she is dangerous."

"I know of the woman," Barbage said. "She is indeed strong in her evil. It will avail her nothing." The look in his eyes was ugly to see.

"Nevertheless, I will give you some help," Bleys said, reverting to a more formal tone. "You will shortly receive notice that you've been promoted, and given command of three companies of Militia and the authority to commandeer any Militia forces in areas into which your pursuit may take you."

Several of the senior Others arrived over the course of the next few hours, sent along by Toni after she had met them in Citadel and peeled them away from their entourages.

Bleys had asked Toni to meet the invitees because he had confidence in her ability to smooth over hurt feelings that might result from the unexpected change in their plans. The leaders would almost all be arriving in their own ships—a sign of the wealth and power they were becoming used to—and they would not have been expecting to be separated from their staffs and households; nor to have their entourages confined to their ships, incommunicado, for the duration of this secret conclave.

Bleys found he need not have worried about Johann Wilter's reaction. The leader of the Cassida organization looked as dapper as ever, but his gaze was still steady and he brushed aside Bleys' apologies for the methods used, saying he was certain that whatever Bleys planned would be well worth any inconvenience. This man, Bleys saw, was not going to let himself be distracted by a momentary infringement on his status.

Wilter was accompanied by Support Hayakawa, an Association-born Other who, although Wilter's senior deputy, was clearly under his boss's thumb.

Ana Wasserlied, leader of the New Earth organization, was another matter entirely. She had come without any of her deputies, and her angular body, superbly dressed as always, was radiating resentment over having been met by Toni, separated from her entourage, and made to come around the planet in a rented shuttle.

"Ana, thank you for coming," Bleys said, offering his hand. "I apologize for making you uncomfortable with this alteration in your schedule, but when you hear what I've brought you here to discuss, I believe you'll understand."

The woman uttered polite reassurances, but her blue eyes burned and her posture remained stiff and unforgiving.

By the end of the following day, six more leaders had arrived: Hammer Martin from Freiland, and two of his deputies, Joachim Suslov and Aries Foley; Kim Wallech and Astrid Croce from Sainte Marie; and Pallas Salvador from Ceta. Only Pallas Salvador had come in on commercial transportation.

Each was greeted personally, and warmly, by Bleys, and encouraged to simply relax and enjoy the facilities of a city meant for diversions, while they acclimated to a different time frame. Most seemed happy to do so, but Johann Wilter and Hammer Martin, although compliant, displayed a certain impatient eagerness to get on with whatever they had been called here for.

"They're going to be our best allies," Bleys told Toni, who had come in along with Pallas Salvador after meeting the Cetan leader when she disembarked in Citadel. "They live for their jobs and their power, and they'll be eager to expand. But we'll have to do something about Ana Wasserlied, and I might need you to help me distract her."

"Distract her? Are you planning to replace her?"

"I think that may have become necessary. But I can't do it before this meeting, and probably not before the one on Association. I made a mistake in calling her here, I'm afraid." He shook his head. "I still believe she'd be willing to go along with my plans, under ordinary circumstances, but she's allowing her resentment over what she sees as an imposition on her status—being brought here in the way she was—to blind her."

"In other words, she's lost sight of the overall plan," Toni said.

"Yes. We'll have to come up with a list of possible replacements," Bleys said. "But the priority now is to keep her from learning the purpose of this meeting—I can't count on her not to talk about what I want to do here."

"To Dahno, you mean."

Bleys nodded.

"Perhaps a couple of innocent meetings, apparently in preparation for the more formal meeting on Association," Toni suggested. "You could say your idea was to bring our most important Others here so they could get to know each other better, in a pleasant, relaxing setting—it would fit with your acknowledged intention to set up a group leadership structure. And there's the fact that Pallas Salvador, who isn't well known to any of the others, has suddenly become an important figure; this could be presented as a way to let the top people get to know her."

"And with a couple of joint meetings out of the way," Bleys said, "I could have individual meetings—and have Ana's first. I'll set her up with some plausible story, tell her she'll be contacted further; and then send her back to New Earth."

"Leaving her out of the Association meeting altogether?"

"Yes," Bleys said.

"Won't that seem strange to the rest of the leaders?" Toni asked. "And suspicious to Dahno?"

"Can you think of an alternative?"

"Well, it's possible," Toni said, looking thoughtful, "that a few days of special treatment here—particularly some special attentions from the other leaders—might make her more amenable . . . there's a plausible basis for a plan like that in the fact that she was invited here at all. A few days of feeling she's part of the elite group might work wonders on her."

"That's a good idea," Bleys said. "She's always been able, and if we can just get around her attitude problem, she could continue to be useful. But that kind of plan would require, among other things, enlisting the other leaders in our little act." He paused, thinking.

"Come to think of it, that could even be made to work to our advantage—once they're enlisted in working together on one objective, they'll be more amenable to working together on other things."

"It'll give them a sense of having gained additional power already," Toni said. "That'll make them more supportive, too."

"Yes," Bleys said. "The more they feel they have to gain by going along with me, the less likely it becomes they can be persuaded otherwise by Dahno."

Two days later, during a break in his meeting schedule, Bleys unobtrusively left the hotel, traveling across town in an automated cab to a small restaurant. He got out of the cab there, but did not enter the restaurant; rather, he signaled for another such cab; and by the time it arrived, the woman he had once known as Gelica Costanza had emerged from the restaurant to join him.

"Thank you for coming, Deborah," Bleys said, while programming the cab to head for a destination on the other side of the city. Locked in a small, moving room, they talked without fear of observation.

"Are things going well on Ceta?" Deborah asked.

"Very well," Bleys said. "You played your part to perfection at the meeting with the Families, even to setting yourself up for a reprimand. I can't thank you enough."

"Believe me, it was my pleasure," Deborah said. "Or I should say, our pleasure. All of my Others—sorry, *New People*—were happy to have a chance to strike back at the Families; and your deal with them allowed us to finally leave the planet, and with enough resources to be able to set up comfortably elsewhere."

"It may not look like much of a 'strike' at the Families," Bleys said. "Anyone looking at the situation would say we've given the Families just what they want."

"We know better," Deborah said. "We've been inside your organization; we know we've fed the Families a poison pill."

"You have an interesting way with words, Deborah," Bleys said.

"I doubt I hurt your feelings," she said. "Remember, I've seen close up how logical a thinker you are. You're not the kind to let an emotional reaction alter your plans."

"You don't have very much experience to base that judgment on," Bleys said.

"Oh, I'm not calling you an unemotional machine," she said. "But I'm confident I've seen the truth."

"Are you interested in seeing more?"

She smiled.

"I figured you had another job for me," she said. "Tell me about it."

"Are you sure you want to hear it?" Bleys said. "The last time you helped us, you and your friends ended up having to leave Ceta, losing your careers and a lot of your assets."

"We'd wanted to leave, anyway," she said. "We were never really at home there, particularly after the Families began leaning on us. No more than we'd ever been anywhere else."

"I know you've settled on New Earth, now," Bleys said. "Are all of your New People comrades there with you?"

"Almost all of them," she said. "We've been family for a long time, and we're looking for a way to keep working together—my generation, anyway. The younger ones are a little restless."

"No retirement?"

"Not us," she said. She smiled. "Are *you* going to give us that work?"

"Maybe," he said.

He was still explaining what he had in mind when their cab reached its programmed destination, so he reprogrammed it for a trip back across town.

They talked on, through trip after trip across the small city.

CHAPTER 25

Most of the Others who had been called back to Association had not been on the planet since their graduation from Dahno's training program, and they seemed to revel in returning as wealthy, elite members of interstellar society; until they came to Dahno, most had been young, poor, and without useful social or political ties.

They were impressed by the fleet of spacecraft now owned by the organization, as well as by the luxurious facilities Dahno and Bleys had moved the organization into. They all well remembered the elderly building in which they had once been trained and lodged.

Invitees began arriving a couple of days before the conference's scheduled beginning, and Bleys, Dahno and their staff were kept busy finding ways to make their guests' stays as enjoyable as possible; Association's entertainment facilities were limited at best.

Eventually all were on hand, and the meeting could begin.

On the evening before the official opening of the convocation, Bleys hosted a small party for a group of the invitees, people he had picked, after dealing with them for a day or two, as most likely to be influenced by what he had to say. All were second- or third-level Others.

Late in the evening, when most had taken enough food and drink to become congenial, but not yet drunk, Bleys, holding a brandy snifter, moved across the room to settle himself on a sofa near which several conversations had been taking place. The conversations died away even though he spoke no word; their eyes were all on him.

"Please, you shouldn't call me *Great Teacher,*" Bleys said, in response to a question from Prosper Fulton, one of the delegation from Cassida. "We Others are all, in our way, family, and I like to think of us as brothers and sisters."

That drew smiles, and there was some movement, as if they all felt a momentary impulse to draw together in a closer group.

"It's a family, then, that I'm proud to be a part of," Fulton said now, glancing about the circle of Others who had gathered around Bleys. "But if you don't mind, I feel you and Dahno are the elder brothers of our family. I know both of you have different tasks than those of us who spend our time on the worlds we've been sent to . . . I guess I just wanted to ask for some idea of what you see as our current situation, and where you think we're headed."

Eyes in the circle became serious above their smiles, but Bleys laughed.

"You're trying to get a preview of my speech for tomorrow morning's opening," he said. "Were you planning to sleep in?"

"I think what Prosper may be asking," Ameena Williams said, from her place behind the sofa where Prosper was sitting, "is for something personal from you—I mean, I've heard you speak many times, during your visits to New Earth, about our abilities as leaders of the human race, and the importance of our task of taking up that leadership position and using it to lead the race to greatness. But when it's put that way, it seems a little cold, or maybe distant; so we'd like to hear something from you about your own personal vision: about what you personally want, and why you personally are involved in this."

Bleys frowned down at the snifter in his hand, as if trying to see a vision in the brandy there. The silence held, and at last he looked up.

"I have been blessed," he said at last in a formal tone; and as he looked up into their faces he could see that the words chimed agreeably with most of them. All of those here had been raised on one of the Friendly planets, and found religiously themed speech comfortable and familiar.

He looked back down into his snifter, giving the impression of one too shy to let his soul show from his eyes.

"I'm just like most of you," he went on. "I grew up a virtual out-sider on this very planet, feeling that no one understood me, that I didn't belong. But I was lucky to have a brother who felt much the same way, and then doubly lucky—or blessed—to find a group of people who understood how I felt." He looked up, to see their emo-tions naked before him.

"At first I thought of us all as a kind of large family," he went on; "a family that would care, and would take care of each other." He cautiously scanned them as he spoke, trying to judge the effects of his words.

"But I think I've learned of something even larger, even better," he continued. "I've learned that we Others aren't really completely separate from the rest of the human race. Yes, we have abilities they don't have, and we see things a bit more clearly than they do. Above all, we have a unity of purpose they've never had, or perhaps once had, but lost." He shook his head.

"My own 'personal vision,' I think you called, it, Ameena? I guess I'd have to say it's to know that every person I will ever meet is as able and competent as we Others are—to let the entire human race have a feeling of comradeship and caring like that we feel when we're among ourselves."

"Is that even possible?" Peter Cossey said from the end of the couch. "Isn't it true we're so advanced over the average human be-ing we can never be completely on a level with them?"

"That may be," Bleys said. "For now. I think that will change over the course of time—if we're willing to reach in that direction."

"Are you suggesting we need to change what we've been aiming to do?" Prosper Fulton said now.

"No, I don't think so," Bleys said. "In fact, I think it's a natural outcome of what we've been doing."

"You mean," Ameena Williams said, "you believe our leadership of the race will over the long term result in all of them lifting them-selves up to our level?"

"That's exactly what I think," Bleys said. And he watched a few tentative smiles blossom.

"Well, then," Ameena said, her dark face displaying puzzlement, "am I wrong in thinking that many of the rest of the race are opposed to us, and may even be prepared to fight us?" Eyes swung to Bleys for an answer.

"You're not wrong," he said. "In fact, some are already preparing for war."

"War?" someone asked from the other side of the room. "How can we deal with that? And how does that help us do what we want to do?"

"War is certainly the last thing we want," Bleys said. "Please don't take my words to mean I'm seeking out anything like that. But I think you all know that war often results when people have conflicting ideas. I suspect you've all seen that in your own lifetimes—" They all nodded. "—and sometimes it's just unavoidable."

"War—with who?" Prosper Fulton asked.

"War, I suspect, on multiple levels," Bleys said. He looked about the circle once more, checking for emotions that could give him feedback on the effectiveness of his words.

"Most of you are working on worlds already under our leadership," he went on. "On those worlds you're finding that some are beginning to resort to force to resist the direction in which we're trying to lead their societies . . . but it may well go beyond that." He paused, as if thinking. "They're finding allies in the Exotics and the Dorsai."

"The Exotics and the Dorsai?" Burton Taney asked, as if appalled.

"Those, yes," Bleys said. "Those two cultures—I'm sorry to say I don't see any way they can ever be brought to see what we're trying to do . . . it's as if they have their own visions for the future of the race, and they're incompatible with ours."

"But we can't win a war against the Dorsai!" Sami DeLong said.

"On the contrary," Bleys said, "they can't win a war with us." There were murmurs of puzzlement all about him.

"You're all remembering the old stories about the Dorsai, and how they're unbeatable in battle," he went on. "They're mostly just that—stories—now; because times have changed, and changed in our favor." There were some mutterings on the edges of the circle, but he ignored those, seeking to supplant their concerns, while they were still young, with his own words.

"If the Dorsai were able to conquer all the Younger Worlds, they'd have done it long ago," he said. "They never even tried. Remember, they have the smallest population of any of the worlds. We have all the advantages: population, resources . . . and most of all, a clarity of purpose."

"'Clarity of purpose'?" Prosper Fulton asked, frowning.

"It's the main thing our leadership gives the Younger Worlds," Bleys said. "We know what we want. The peoples of those Younger Worlds not under our leadership are confused, preoccupied with the details of their own lives; because of that, they're divided among themselves. That goes for the Exotics and the Dorsai—divided, they'll never be a serious threat to us. Just as, divided, they can never amount to anything in any other endeavor."

He paused, and looked about the circle once more, pulling their attention back to himself, away from their fears.

"It's as simple as this," he continued after a moment: "People *want* to be led. Most of them lack the confidence to deal with anything outside the scope of the way they've always led their lives—when something unusual happens, they become frightened and want someone to hold their hands and tell them they're in the right and everything will be fine if they just do what they're told."

"And that's what we'll do," Ameena Williams said, nodding.

"Until they're able to take care of themselves," Bleys said. "It's a tremendous responsibility, as I think you realize. But it becomes our mission simply because we're the only ones able to deal with the unexpected, with change—it's an ability we have because we grew up outside the usual mold of society. It's not just that we're generally more intelligent than most of the race; it's that we're able to see how to use what we've got to achieve our goals."

"But *war*," Sami DeLong said softly, a troubled frown still on her face.

"Oh, we'll do everything we can to avoid it," Bleys said, his voice filled with confidence. "We'll build up a military force of our own, one so powerful no one in their right mind would try to fight us—that's the best way to avoid having a war at all." He paused to take a small sip from his snifter.

"But war might come, anyway," he went on. "People aren't always sensible." There were troubled nods about the circle.

"We'll make sure it's not fought on our own planets," he said. "That's one of our responsibilities as leaders."

"But what about Old Earth?" Prosper Fulton said.

"What about it?"

"Won't Old Earth be likely to want to—well, to stop us, when they see what we're doing?"

"Now you're getting into matters I planned to discuss during the course of our meetings," Bleys said. "Believe me, I've been thinking about this for a long time." He paused, projecting seriousness.

"We'll talk more about this later, I promise," he went on. "But I firmly believe we're more likely to fall into commercial, rather than military, conflicts with Old Earth." He smiled at them. "After all, the mother planet doesn't really care much who rules the Younger Worlds, does she?"

The nods around the circle were slight, hesitant.

"I think you all know Old Earth doesn't really pay much attention to the Younger Worlds," Bleys went on. "She doesn't have to. Old Earth is too involved in her own internal conflicts, and her citizens worry more about living their own good lives . . . and in the end, remember: if war should come, are those spoiled, pampered Earthmen likely to come out from their planet and fight very hard?"

He looked about.

"I don't think so," he finished. "But that doesn't mean we won't have conflict with them."

"You mentioned a 'commercial' sort of conflict," someone said from the back of the circle, a question in his voice.

"Well, it's possible," Bleys said. "If we weld a unified community out of the Younger Worlds, we'll automatically be forming a commercial entity that could conflict with Old Earth's own interests, eventually. But my hope instead is that when we become a commercial equal, we can deal with them as equals—and eventually our community will expand to include them." He took the last sip from his brandy.

"There are many forms of conflict," he said, his gaze circling among their faces. "We have the advantage in all of them." He smiled.

"It's true Old Earth's population is the equal of all our Younger Worlds combined. In both military and economic conflicts, any battle would be a hard one—particularly because we can't wait another few hundred years for our population to grow. And waiting won't increase the natural resources of our planets." He put his empty snifter down.

"If you've studied history," he went on, leaning back, "you'll understand that in any sort of conflict with Old Earth, we'll be under the disadvantage of being able to bring only a fraction of our people into contact with them, across the long lines of space transportation—while the mother planet would only have to operate just outside its own atmosphere, with the advantages of interior lines of communications and having its largest markets within its own sphere."

"You seem to be assuming such a war would be fought near Old Earth," Peter Cossey said.

"I guess I am," Bleys replied. "And that's because of something I mentioned earlier: they have no clarity of purpose—but we do. That gives us what military science calls the *initiative*."

"You implied other forms of conflict might occur," Ameena Williams said.

"Yes," Bleys said. "In fact, I consider them much more likely." He looked about the circle once more.

"I'm talking about a conflict of ideas," he said. "I'm talking about our vision of a future for the entire human race coming up against their own vision."

"Do they *have* some sort of vision for the race?" Sami DeLong asked.

"A very good question," Bleys said, smiling. "The answer is: probably not—not in any terms we've been thinking about." He shook his head, looking sad.

"The fact is, Earthmen don't think about the future any more than do the people on our own Younger Worlds. The closest they might come to it is this: they generally have an attitude—maybe you could call it a series of unspoken assumptions—about the future. And if you think about your history, you know what those are: they believe that Old Earth's way is the best way, and that Old Earth is destined to be the natural leader of the human race for all time.

"What we're going to do will change that," he went on, "for all time. It will take time, but it will happen."

He paused again; and then leaned forward, raising his hands before his chest as if placing something before them, for them to look at.

"So," he went on, "we should look beyond the actual confrontation time, when it comes, to what we want to accomplish. What we really want is to end Old Earth's attempts at dominating us. These days, those are very underground, very subtle; but they're still there, a hidden motivation for that planet's behavior, and the energy behind the attitudes of most of those on Old Earth toward all of us on the Younger Worlds. As if we were a lesser people.

"What we're really up against is the task of changing the mental attitudes of half the members of the human race—their attitudes toward us.

"I'm confident there will come a real victory, in the form of a real change in the way they think. That's why we've had to start on our own worlds—as you did in the organizations you lead—in changing the mental attitudes of our own peoples, to a form that will allow them to shed their blinders about the mother planet. And *that* is going to be a large part of your jobs, in the future."

He paused for a longer period. He wanted to let them think, to let his message sink in.

"Remember this," he said finally: "the real battle now, and to come, is between two different mind-sets. It's a battle of attitudes and beliefs. We can't hope to *make* them adopt ours. Never in history has that been possible; we'll never be able to impose our mind-set on them. What we have to do is expose our mind-set to them, until they begin to find—" he paused, apparently groping for the right words, "—elements, yes, in it, that are attractive or useful to them."

"You make it sound as if we're all going to become philosophers, and teachers," Prosper Fulton said.

"It's unavoidable," Bleys said, nodding. "Because you—each and every one of you—either already are a leader, on your planets, or will be soon. Leaders always teach things to their followers, even if unconsciously. You'll be teachers simply because those who follow you will be looking at you, watching what you do and thinking about what you say—every single thing you do or say will be a lecture, a lesson."

"I don't know if I'm ready for this," Sami DeLong said softly.

"But how did you think you were going to help lead your planet?" Bleys asked her, his voice low and quiet. "Surely you didn't think you'd simply give the occasional order, and it would be obeyed without anyone being changed in any way?"

"No," she said, softly. "No, I guess not . . . I just hadn't thought about it that way."

"But you don't feel ready to be an example," Ameena Williams said, looking across the circle at Sami.

"Of course she doesn't," Bleys said. "I wouldn't want her to feel otherwise. That's the path of arrogance; it's dangerous and leads to major mistakes." He shook his head.

"We're not prophets," he went on. "We're just particularly gifted human beings trying to make life better for everyone else. I don't want you to tell people they should be something else that's better than what they are now. They should be whatever they are now, whatever they've chosen to be—but a better, stronger, more capable version of it. And they should find their own ways to reach out to that chosen state."

He leaned back in his chair once more, looking at the ceiling.

"You asked me, Ameena, about my own 'personal vision,' as you called it, for the future: if it were possible in this present time, when we're spread over a number of worlds widely separated among the stars, I'd like to see you all go forth in a robe with a begging bowl in your hand, and wander with that message, as individuals once wandered across the face of Old Earth in those pre-space travel days.

"Remember, we won't suggest they change, that they make themselves different. We wish them to stay as they are and improve into a better version of themselves, continuing as whatever identity they've picked out in life. Whatever role they've chosen, in society, in life—they should stay in that role. Provided it's the role they want. If it's not, they should seek the role they want and grow into it, improve into it—headed toward a state in which they'll be more powerful and more responsible, and will have effort and mind and body and strength left over for helping all others be better in their roles, in turn."

Shortly after that Toni appeared, making the noises a hostess makes to politely herd her guests to the door; and the group, with thoughtful looks on their faces, gave their thanks and left, talking quietly. Bleys knew a few of them, at least, would gather elsewhere, to discuss among themselves what he had said.

As Bleys had expected, the assembled Others were enthusiastic over the prospect of greater power and influence, not only on their own planets, but within the Others' organization. As with any group of people, however, their motivations and views varied widely, and it took weeks to hammer out a pattern for the future workings of the organization. Always, up to now, they had simply followed orders, whether from Dahno or Bleys, or from the nominal superiors appointed by Dahno and Bleys; suddenly thrust into the position of having much more of a voice in the workings of the organization, almost every one of them found an opinion, or two.

It was necessary, if tedious, Bleys supposed; they were having to grow into new roles.

Bleys did not tell them he and Dahno could no longer do it all themselves; rather, he told them, in essence, that they had graduated to the next level, that they were coming into their kingdom.

Dahno watched his brother's performance, and kept his silence.

Few noticed. Those Bleys had won over during the secret conclave on Harmony found their plan to stampede the gathering largely unneeded; the Others who had not been at that gathering quickly embraced Bleys' vision. They didn't even bother with a vote; up to now, the organization had never taken one, and so no one thought of it.

Still, it took time to hammer out an outline for the new organization, and there was a lot of infighting when it came to picking which Others would sit on the Council. Bleys knew it could all have been accomplished in much less time if he had simply stepped in to tell them how it should be; but that would have deprived them of the proprietary feeling—the feeling of ownership of the organization— that was the main thing he had wanted to see come out of this meeting.

He was pleased to find, too, that they all still recognized that Bleys—and, they thought, his brother—were the ones who had gotten them this far. That spirit of deference and cooperation would not last, he knew. But it would last for a while—long enough for him to lead them all in the beginnings of the direction he wanted.

Once set on the course he desired, they would find it difficult to move in another direction.

He would deal with the coming problems when he had to— before their future opposition became strong enough to beat him.

CHAPTER 26

From his place at the dais, Bleys silently watched as the Others at the tables ranked before him chattered together in small groups. This was the last day of the convocation which had so dramatically altered the structure of the Others' organization. Throughout the weeks here, personal alliances and enmities had been created, and had shifted; boredom had set in, to be relieved by renewed enthusiasm; and even a few romances had bloomed, distracting the concerned parties—all exactly the sort of doings to be expected in any large gathering of people away from their usual routines.

In the end, he believed, he had prevailed, at least enough that his plan could go forward. Some of those before him were exulting at the vision of wealth and power placed before them, and for the moment they credited Bleys with turning it over to them, and were committed to supporting his plans to subjugate the Dorsai and the Exotics, and to unite the Younger Worlds in a power bloc that would ultimately be capable of standing up to Old Earth.

Some had other motivations, such as those he had provided to the gathering of idealists; they, too, were coming out of this gathering with something to prize.

What might happen when all of them became used to their gains was a subject none bothered to worry about. Indeed, some would never worry about more than their rosy present; and as for those who were of the sort that would, before long, look for more—he had a little time yet in which he could count on them giving him what he asked for.

Now, as he maintained his silence, one by one the faces turned in his direction, the chatter dying away.

"—what I say!" As usual, the last voice to continue speaking stood out, shockingly noticeable in the new silence. Bleys waited several beats more, before speaking.

"I have one more item," he said, "which you'll have noted as the last thing on the agenda—the matter of making some of your people available for a new assignment."

Skepticism showed on more than a few of their faces.

"We were informed people would be wanted," Hammer Martin said. "But since you didn't tell us what the mission was to be, I, at least—" He looked about as if seeking evidence of solidarity. "—I couldn't be sure just what sort of people were wanted." He paused, as if expecting an answer; when none came, he continued, a certain belligerence in his voice.

"So I sent for a half-dozen of my people, who have a varying mix of skills," Hammer concluded. "If you'll tell me what you're looking for, I can name the ones who match your needs."

"We'll take them all," Bleys said. He moved his gaze about the long room, projecting calm in the face of a rising tide of protest.

"We're going to need all the people you've selected for us," he said, "and more besides. Messages have already gone out to your home offices, naming people we selected in our analyses of your tables of organization; in fact, some of those people are probably already on their way here."

Like any managers of bureaucratic organizations, the leaders before him, Bleys believed, had probably chosen to select for his use people they felt they could do without—the lazy, the inefficient, the inept, and the flawed. He knew these leaders would now take his words very much like a slap in the face. It was a breach of the unspoken protocols normal to any large organization—even though the Others' organization, up until this meeting, in fact had no protocols beyond obedience to Dahno and Bleys. But Bleys was confident he could bring them past their outrage.

Beside Bleys, Dahno shifted slightly in his chair, where he had been lounging back, as if disconnected from the meeting, for some time. Dahno had argued with Bleys about this project, when Bleys suggested it.

Is he pouting? Bleys wondered. *Or is he worried about their reaction?*

Bleys did not need to be told he had just thrown metaphorical

cold water on the people before him; he had, after all, not only diminished their individual kingdoms, but rubbed their noses in the
fact that he had the power to do so. These were people who had become used to occupying positions of considerable influence, if not
control, on entire planets—people who, moreover, had just been
handed visions of power on an interstellar scale. They had become
subject to the same effect power has on most people: they had very
high opinions of their own importance.

On the other hand, they had already received a large trade-off, in
the promised increase in their individual power.

It was not his intention to alienate them—not as long as they did
their jobs as he required. So it was time to reconcile them to their
losses.

"We know this hurts your efforts on your individual planets," he
said now, in a soothing tone. "You've been doing good work—we
know that, and you know that."

He put a little more authority into his tone now.

"But the work we've all been doing is not confined to your single
planets—you know that as well."

He smiled at them, just a little.

"None of us can ever make the mistake of losing sight of the overall situation," he went on. "In fact, that's exactly what the Chairman
and I are for: to not let the view from one planet obscure our organization's aims on all the worlds."

Dahno had sold these people, when he recruited them, on the
idea that they were superior to ordinary people and really deserved
to rule the worlds. Dahno had not really intended to seek that ruling position, but Bleys had risen to supplant him, in all but title,
precisely because he had revived that notion, reinforced it in their
minds, and given them reason to believe it could be done.

Behind Bleys they had risen to positions of wealth and power;
and like most people who attain those things, they wanted more.
They would, he knew, do whatever he wanted—even forget sub-
tractions from their organizational domains—if they believed he
could lead them even higher.

By giving them what they wanted, he would get what he wanted.
The results he was aiming for would not at all be something these

people would be very happy about, but that did not matter, because by the time they realized where he was going—if they ever did—it would be much too late.

"We've spent almost a Standard month here," he went on, "discussing the next major steps of our program—steps that will bring four more worlds under our control and neutralize any possible threat from the Exotics and the Dorsai." He was settling into his planned exposition now, and, all unconsciously, they were sensing that, and setting in their turns into a more businesslike frame of mind.

"Three worlds remain to be considered," he said. "Well, four, if you count Dunnin's World, but—" He dismissed that most marginal of planets with a short wave; and saw unease come to faces that had calculated exactly which worlds he was referring to.

"Yes," he said. "Venus, Mars—and Old Earth."

They were stirring about a little now, as the goats had, in their pens back on Henry's farm, when someone came near in the night. He could hear an undercurrent of comment, and beside him Dahno seemed to be studiously concentrating on the data display embedded in the tabletop.

"*Old Earth?*" Ana Wasserlied said, her voice a little shrill. "Even if—" He cut her off.

"I know," he said, once more calm and soothing. "You were about to remind us that the population of Old Earth is about the size of that of all the Younger Worlds put together, and that we have barely enough people to do our work on those worlds as it is, without subtracting more from their ranks—and that we couldn't possibly send enough to make even a dent in Old Earth's politics." He smiled at her.

"We all know all that," he said. "Don't worry; that's not what we have in mind."

He left the podium and moved back to his chair, where he sat down, leaning across the table as if ready to take part in a serious discussion among equals.

"Really," he said, "when you think about it, what we're proposing is nothing more than a bit of preventive maintenance." He took a moment to let that innocuous term's connotations sink into their minds.

"The prospectus for this conference contained a brief summary of the political and economic situations on all the worlds," he went on after that moment, "but we know you had no particular reason to pay much attention to what our research staff had to say about Old Earth. You're all probably aware of the basic facts: Old Earth is the richest, most populous and most technologically advanced of all the planets, it's true. But it continues to be, as it has always been, a planet so disorganized as to make Ceta look simple." He smiled, and got low laughs as a reward.

"Old Earth's power structure is a maze of competing and conflicting political, economic and societal entities, consisting of everything from the remnants of ancient nation-states to independent undersea, orbital, and lunar installations, multinational economic entities, and cross-boundary social alliances." He shook his head.

"They haven't united on anything at all since the days when Dow deCastries led them to try to rule the Younger Worlds," he continued. "All we want to do is keep it that way."

He could see that the unease in their faces was being replaced by curiosity.

"So far," he said, rising to his feet once more, "Old Earth has paid little attention to what we've been doing on the Younger Worlds. But some elements there might become alarmed as our power continues to grow—within a short time we could be in control of nine worlds, after all—and we don't want the old planet to be concerned."

He looked about the room as if challenging them to dispute his argument. It was a tactic they had all been taught to use themselves, intended to convince an audience of the speaker's own certainty of the truth of what he was saying; it was a common human reaction to feel that people who were so deeply certain about a belief as to be emotional about it were probably right. Bleys knew they would recognize the tactic, but he believed that very recognition would disarm their instinctive fear reaction.

"As I mentioned some weeks ago," he went on, now in a softer, calmer voice, "we believe the Exotics have been aware of our movement for quite a while. Whether they initially confused us with the original Others group makes no difference: regardless of what went before, they're certainly aware that our plans for the Younger Worlds can only threaten them. It's predictable they'll try to raise an alarm on Old Earth, hoping to rouse it enough to provide some sort of counter-vailing force against us."

He moved to the podium again, shaking his head.

"It will do them little good," he said, "because they can't unite that planet any more than we can. Nonetheless, we'd be wise to try to smother that effort."

He raised a hand, as if reaching out to pull in their understanding.

"*That's* why we need to take some of your people," he said. "We want to send them to Old Earth—not to try to take it over, but only to counteract—to kill at birth—any impulse to take action, of any sort, against us."

Some were nodding now.

"We'd like your personal input, all of you," he continued, "as to possible leaders for this mission—in fact, if one of you would, your-self, feel particularly qualified for the task, please—"

Beside Bleys, Dahno sat up straighter in his chair; and at the same time Hammer Martin spoke up.

"It should be me," Hammer said. "This job demands the skills of someone experienced in starting a whole organization from scratch; and among those of us who were sent out to do just that on our vari-ous worlds, I'm senior." Again he wore a somewhat belligerent look on his face.

"Wait," Dahno said. He was rising to his feet, looking at Bleys.

"It's my job," he said. He turned to look out over the audience.

"I've got the skills needed to analyze the situations we find there," he said. "You know that, brother—" He looked back at Bleys for an instant. "—it's been vital to our work on the Younger Worlds."

Bleys nodded, cautiously. Dahno had surprised him on several oc-casions, and he had an uncomfortable feeling it was happening again.

"I know how to find the best people to cultivate," Dahno went on, again addressing the whole gathering. "And I've been on Old Earth before and have contacts already in place."

Low, approving murmurs began to arise in the room, but Bleys voiced a further objection: "You're a sitting member of the governing body on Association," he said. "More than that, you're a large part of our control on these two worlds—"

"We've got a firm controlling structure in place here," Dahno said. "We had to ensure that from early on, if only because you and I had to spend so much time off-planet. And the Eldest, McKae, is your own particular creature, you know that."

"But there's been a growing insurgency on both these planets for some time," Bleys said.

Dahno dismissed that with a wave of his hand.

"That's nothing," he said. "There're dissenters on the other planets we control, too, but none are much of a threat. And here on the Friendlies, your position as First Elder, along with your control of McKae, gives us complete control of the armed forces of the two worlds—the strongest armed force on any of the Younger Worlds, leaving out the Dorsai."

"Beyond these Friendly planets," Bleys said, "we also need you in the work we've planned for Ceta and the others—"

"Again, you don't need me for that," Dahno said. "Our people here"—he swept a hand across the room—"have surprised us both in how much they've learned and the abilities they've shown to control the powerful on their planets."

He looked across the head table, beaming with pride at the Others before him, every one of whom had been trained in the program he had established. Bleys followed his eyes, and saw that those looking up at them were responding to his brother.

Dahno had won them totally. Bleys had been waiting, all through the convocation, for his brother to speak up in opposition—but now that it had happened, he, Bleys, had still been surprised.

"You forget, brother," Dahno was going on, "I was the one who organized all this in the first instance. I was the one who found and recruited these people who've proven to have so much ability. And organization, above all, is what's going to be needed on Old Earth."

He looked back at Bleys.

"You won't find anyone better, brother," he said. And the faces Bleys saw behind the ranks of tables were nodding, certain.

"That's true," Bleys said.

I'll have to let this one go, he thought, *but what does he have planned?*

"You six were sent to me," Bleys said, "to carry out a specialized task." The meeting with the Others' leaders had ended a week ago, and the lower-ranked Others he had sent for had largely arrived at headquarters and were being trained to accompany Dahno to Old Earth.

Bleys had been watching for certain of them to arrive, however; and now he had half a dozen of them with him in a small meeting room.

While he spoke, Bleys looked with interest at the six, seated close to him around a small table. All were men, which was not surprising considering the personalities he had been looking for; but he had, he now realized, unconsciously been expecting they would look different from other people . . . somehow. They didn't, really.

"We want you to put together a special weapon for us," he went on.

None of them reacted at all, that he could see. But then, that seemed to be one index of the kind of people he'd calculated could do this job.

"To be more specific," he continued, "we want you to find us the right kind of people—people who can be depended on to carry out certain kinds of actions—and then to train them, and lead them to perform certain special tasks for us."

He paused again, looking for some kind of reaction. He got only silence.

"It was almost painful," he wrote in a note to his memory late that night. He was, unconsciously, shaking his head as he did so; and he was doing it in darkness, making it impossible for anyone else—or himself—to see what he was writing.

I never realized how much I depend on getting feedback when I speak—even if it's only from the technicians recording one of my talks. But those people today were the human equivalent of white noise.

The sheet of paper under his hands was unsympathetic.

I was looking for a particular kind of sociopath, he wrote on. The kind who can function within a system. I should not have expected them to be normal.

And I didn't. Not really. But these were all people who had learned to counterfeit normal human behavior enough to fit in—for the most part—in some societal niche. But they weren't even trying, this time, to seem human.

He paused, looking down the length of his lounge in the direction of the Mayne-map, which he could not see; and then he bent over the unseen paper, and continued writing.

And yet, when I first met with them individually, and again after the meeting, I thought they seemed close to normal. I'm still reacting to that impression.

On reflection, I think it's because initially I gave them the kind of encounter they were more or less used to—in other words, they had an idea what sort of behavior was expected of them. But when I presented a deliberately vague summary of what I want them to do, I presented them with a situation they had never encountered; and, not knowing the right pattern to adopt, they could only wait for some cue to tell them what pattern might be right.

He stopped, to look down at the paper as if rereading what he could not see; and then felt for the disposal slot and fed it in. Then he pulled out a new, blank sheet.

When the job is creating and leading assassins, I don't want people who might have second thoughts.

Will I be the one having second thoughts?

CHAPTER 27

The air was bitter in the uplands that marked the border between the two major sections of Harmony's largest continent, where Rukh Tamani's Command was snowbound in the variform conifer forest just below the pass known as the High Walk.

It was not that her followers were completely unable to move through the snow between the trees; but they were exhausted, having been harried from shelter to haven for months by a seemingly energized Militia.

Tired, they were nonetheless able and willing to move. But Rukh knew that her people—now numbering less than sixty—needed to rest. This seemed like a good time to take that rest, since the snow that had fallen in the mountains for the past day and a half had covered their tracks.

If they did not move, they would make no new tracks.

Armed opposition had been Rukh's way of life since her childhood ended in terror and death; opposition, at first, to the hypocritical religious tyranny of Harmony's governing cliques, and, later, to the insidious persuasions of the Belial-spawn, who had come to control that government—those called the *Others* on the rest of the Younger Worlds.

Unlike many of those in her Command—and unlike most of those Harmonyites who, though not in open rebellion, nonetheless secretly sympathized with anyone courageous enough to take up arms—Rukh had no dreams of a life of peace, nor any illusions about the likelihood of living to some older age. Yet she was not unhappy at all, and could frequently be observed, in less pensive moments, with a quiet, soft smile on her dark, and strikingly beautiful, face.

She knew some had compared her beauty to that of one or another of the queens captured in onyx in Old Earth's ancient land of Egypt, that land so often mentioned in the Bible. The idea neither pleased nor displeased her, for she knew that whatever beauty she had, had been a gift from her God, and was not of her earning.

The beauty was an ephemeral thing, and could be taken from her in an instant. Her mother had been beautiful, too; but Rukh had seen her mother's body burned and torn, and knew that beauty meant little.

The one thing she possessed that was hers alone was her soul; and while it could never be taken from her, she had given it willingly to her God. And since that day on which she had dedicated her soul, and all its worldly trappings—possessions, body and mind—to her God, she had never been afraid.

It seemed so clear, to her, that she wondered at times why other people were afraid—of injury, or of death. No foe could reach into or damage her soul; it was God's, and He was beyond fear or death. Whatever might be done to the body was a transient thing, that would pass and be forgotten in what would be, in God's time, only the shortest of instants.

She wondered why more people did not reach out to their God, to trade their cares for peace and joy. Occasionally she had succeeded in telling them, in showing them, that road; but it seemed it was her work that reached people most easily, most surely . . . as if words, so easy to use, were also so easy to forget.

Still a young woman, she had already put many long years into carrying out her task. There had been great successes, that confounded the enemies of God and drove their slave-soldiers back in confusion and despair—successes that made her name one that rang for those who still had the clarity of purpose to fight for the Lord.

In odd moments she wondered if that was truly her purpose in life. However, she was not much given to ponderings on purposes, and was content to wait for God's plan to be revealed to her, so that she could follow it.

Usually, that plan seemed to be just to keep her Command alive and functioning; and moving it about to give hope to the Lord's people . . . and, once in a while, to take advantage of some opportunity to cripple the forces of their enemy, by belying their blasphemous claim to be themselves doing the Lord's work.

Such an opportunity had come her way a few years ago, when God had led her to allow the young Earthman, Hal Mayne, to join her Command. The youngster had made no pretense of being of their faith, yet he seemed to her to have a comparable strength of moral purpose.

For all that Hal Mayne appeared, physically, to be tall, strong and rugged, she had seen, in that first meeting, that he was still a boy, still open and trusting, even naive—and one who had been badly hurt inside. But the Earthman had proven to have iron inside him also; few others had ever dared to stand up to her now much missed Lieutenant, James Child-of-God.

In the end Hal Mayne had saved her Command, by disobeying her orders and stealing the explosive materials they had been guarding as they fled from the Militia, moving them to where they could be used.

No longer burdened by those materials, the Command had been set free to vanish into the rugged countryside, finally evading the Militia pressing them. After that, they had been able to re-form and use those materials to badly damage the great Core Tap project near the city of Ahruma.

She had not seen Hal Mayne since he left the Command, but she had learned that his actions, in saving both her Command and the explosives, had caused him to be captured and imprisoned.

She had carried out the Lord's mission, though; and afterward found out that Hal had been able to escape from the Militia. She did not know where he had gone.

The enemy had apparently been taken aback by the bombing, and the Command had been granted a much needed period of rest and recuperation, which allowed many of its sick and wounded to recover in hiding.

But that respite had ended, less than a Standard year ago, as the same Militia officer who had once harried them nearly to their destruction returned to the field, armed with higher rank and more soldiers and resources.

The Lord giveth, and the Lord taketh away, she thought, wryly. For just as Hal Mayne had rescued her Command and her mission, so he had somehow been the factor that caused the officer Barbage to hound them. Barbage had a past history with the young Earthman, that apparently energized him far beyond any Militia officer the Command had faced in the past.

One resource Barbage had been given, that past Militia pursuers had lacked, was aerial reconnaissance. Satellites capable of close-resolution viewing, and aircraft capable of similar tasks, were exceedingly rare on the Younger Worlds; they were too expensive, in terms of metal, fuel and manufacturing capability, to be easily purchased. Most Younger World military establishments were not willing to spend their scarce resources on a tool so little needed and so easily destroyed by anyone with access to any of a variety of cheap, easy-to-obtain anti-aircraft weapons.

But Barbage had a few aircraft, and she believed that if the Command tried to move on through this freshly fallen snow, its tracks might be easily spotted from above, setting the pursuit back on their trail.

So they would rest, waiting out their enemy, who might become distracted or confused, or shift his attentions elsewhere.

The Command was in much better condition sixteen days later, when it reached the head of Esther's Valley, a broad reach of stony soil whose farmer inhabitants were largely sympathetic to the idea of rebellion. The Command intended to split into small, harmless-appearing groups that, traveling openly, could filter down to the valley's lower end, where they would rendezvous briefly before splitting up once more, to head out across the plains toward their intended target, the Militia arsenal at Gracegiven.

But even before the Command reached a likely place in which to stop and sort itself into smaller units, one of the scouts returned from the valley, to report there were two white shirts and a gray shirt—the latter with a large triangular burn mark on it—drying on a clothesline outside the first house they had come to. It was a signal known among the Commands: there was important news to be had.

"Two weeks without a sign of the Accursed," the youngster Mose Palomares said. "I knew it couldn't last."

Behind him, Joralmon Troy, one of Rukh's veterans, did not even try to suppress a laugh. Mose had proclaimed, just last night, that this time they had well and truly shaken the Militia off their trail. Mose was more than a little mercurial in temperament, Joralmon knew, but in action he became cool and steady; so his comrades accepted his other vagaries for their entertainment value.

Inside the farmhouse, Avila Cotter, an older woman with a burn scar on the left side of her face, told Rukh that the news had been spread throughout the land, in hopes it would get to Rukh soon; for she was the one most concerned with it, because it involved the Core Tap in Ahruma, the one her people had damaged so badly: the Accursed of God had completed their repairs to the Tap's infrastructure.

Work on the Tap itself would soon resume.

"It's likely a trap," Tommy Molson said that evening, the serious expression on his normally cheerful face displaying the lines of his age. He had only recently been made the Command's Lieutenant, Rukh's second-in-command. It was a position of trust, and the promotion was an impressive achievement for one who had been with the Command for such a short time.

Tommy Molson had shown up two months after the successful sabotage mission, asking to be accepted into the Command. Reluctance, on the part of Rukh's veterans, to accept a newcomer was only to be expected; and yet Tommy was known to them by reputation as the canny leader of a very small Command that had operated far to the north of Rukh's usual range. Moreover, he had brought with him a half-score of his own warriors, bringing them to a Command whose veterans were acutely aware their own numbers had been significantly diminished in their last campaign.

Tommy had eased possible frictions by joining the Command as an unranked member, and his experience and leadership abilities, along with his willingness to work and good nature, had won him steady movement toward greater responsibility.

No one criticized his movement up the Command's somewhat informal rank structure; the stress of life in a Command could teach a Warrior of God more about his fellows in one month than most people would be able to learn in a lifetime.

Tommy was quite aware, as the Command's senior leadership gathered about the communal fire to discuss the news, that none of the veterans here could hear his voice without remembering the nearly legendary James Child-of-God, who had been Lieutenant until shortly before the sabotage. But Tommy would not let that stop him from doing his duty; all here knew that, having seen that he had proceeded about his new job in a quiet and humble fashion. It had not led his new comrades to forget James, but it nonetheless earned him their respect.

"It may well be so, Tommy," Rukh replied. "All places are possible traps for us, you know that."

There were quiet nods among the veterans.

"First of all, what do we know of this Avila Cotter?" Tommy asked. "Are you sure we can trust what she says?"

"I never met her before," Rukh said. She looked about the circle. "Anyone?"

There was no reply.

Nonetheless, it was not unusual for the Command to obtain information from someone they did not know—or supplies, or shelter. Avila, however, was in fact known—by location and description although not by name—to many senior Command leaders, for she functioned as part of the informational network the Commands had no choice but to rely on.

They all knew that Avila Cotter and her kind lived in as much danger as any active Command member—but without the option of being able to move about and lose themselves in the countryside. It was vital to the Commands, as they roamed, to be able to check in with known, and trusted, local contacts, but those contacts themselves were always in grave danger of being detected by the government; they could not perform their self-appointed tasks if they went elsewhere.

So where the active members of a Command enjoyed nearly hero status among the faithful, their stationary contacts had to try to maintain as much anonymity as possible.

"It makes little difference whether her information is trustworthy, or not," Rukh said. "I believe it is, but it remains our responsibility to verify it."

"What about our plans for Gracegiven?" Tommy asked. "We have need of the ammunition and other supplies we can get there."

"Gracegiven is a ripe plum," Rukh said. "Go and pluck it."

"You're leaving us, then?" There were shiftings among the veterans.

"I shall go to Ahruma and look into the report," Rukh said. "If it's true, I'll send word to you, and wait for you to come. The supplies you get in Gracegiven will help us with this new mission, if mission it is."

"By yourself?" The protest came from Tallah, the Command's chief cook, treasured by all for her versatility and common sense. Other voices echoed her protest.

"Tallah, you must realize that if this news is indeed a trap, they'll be looking for us to come in a body," Rukh said. "Traveling alone, I'm much less likely to be noticed." She looked at the faces about her.

"Nor can I depend on others for confirmation," she added, more softly, but with a steel they recognized in her voice. "I must see this for myself. Moreover, it may take some time to come up with a plan of action, and the danger of detection will be much higher for a large group than for one person."

Fourteen days later Rukh stepped out of a patch of brush as a man she recognized left his little house to begin the day's chores. She had worked with him in the past, and knew him as a station-keeper, one of those who functioned much as Avila Cotter did.

Bernard Farmer was a tall, thin, brown-skinned man in his late middle years; and also the Shepherd of a small temple that served a rural community. He was thrilled to see her.

"The work of Rukh Tamani in Ahruma is known to all," he said, smiling. "Not only among the Faithful, in joy, but among the Accursed—although to them the knowledge brings a vastly different emotion."

"All of us work equally to confound God's betrayers," Rukh said. "I do no more than He bids me, as do all of us."

"Forgive me," Farmer said. "It was no more than my enthusiasm speaking. The news from the Core Tap has saddened all of us here. To have one of God's Captains return to afflict the ungodly gives us heart."

He smiled.

"Of course, a Shepherd should not need to be told that our belief in our God gives us heart if we are true, regardless of whether a Commander comes by, or not," he went on. "Nonetheless, I hope you won't be embarrassed."

"There is no embarrassment in doing the Lord's work," Rukh said.

The Shepherd nodded.

"Some of the Old Prophets would have little good to say about such human weaknesses," he said. "I honor those men and women for their strength. But in our little community, we are not Old Prophets, but only human beings who seek to serve the Lord despite our weaknesses."

His words brought back Rukh's memories of James Child-of-God, who had died not far from this area. The old man had raised her after her parents had been killed; and she knew in her heart that he had loved her as if she were his own daughter . . . and yet even that love, as everything else about him, had been of the implacable sort that marked the true example of those stalwart souls the Friendly culture called *Old Prophets*.

She turned the conversation back to the subject of the Core Tap; and within moments Farmer was able to give her leads to other people who might be able to provide more information.

CHAPTER 28

The tone that sounded in the meeting room was quiet but rich, a mellow sound that evoked a fruity ripeness, as if a gong had been sounded that was made of a softer metal than most. Until its sounding, this room, the informal meeting place of the Laboratories Review Council that ran Newton, had been silent as a tomb.

Five Council members were present, scattered about the large room as if wary of each other. At the tone the Council President, a slim, elderly man named Half-Thunder, reflexively reached to the control pad on the arm of his float chair. His hand stopped, however, before actually touching the controls, and after a moment another hand activated other controls.

The surface of the gigantic mural that dominated the wall behind Half-Thunder shimmered, its depiction of the major events in the life of Sir Isaac Newton resolving into a complicated three-dimensional schematic that flickered with continuous minute changes. Every eye in the room ignored those, focusing only on the bright red bars that slashed across the display in six places.

Those eyes were practiced, and it took only seconds for the body language of four of those present to change.

"It's clear," an inhuman voice said. The voice emanated from one of the seated Council members, and its mechanical, sexless quality was a result of the same disguising effect that caused the figure's head to appear as a blur of pale blue light.

"Perhaps," Din Su said. "Perhaps not."

Her voice was soft, and would have seemed gentle had it not carried an edge of clinical rationality that contrasted sharply with her plump, grandmotherly appearance. As she spoke she touched a control on her chair, and it glided across the room to a position midway between Half-Thunder and the figure with the blurred face, and halted in that position. She lifted a hand, to hold it poised over the arm of her chair, index finger extended as if awaiting an order to push a button, and looked expectantly at Half-Thunder.

As he watched her actions, the President's face lost its bleak look, and he moved his own chair closer to hers. At the same time there was movement in the far corner of the room, where Iban, a woman with a fine-boned face who had been standing alone near an interior door, seemed to gather herself, lifting a hand to pat at the black hair held tightly in place by colorful combs. Her austere clothing seemed almost an affront to her elegant, delicate beauty, but her movements were precise and firm as she walked across the room to take the vacant seat near Half-Thunder.

"Georges?" Din Su said, looking over her shoulder at the transparent door that opened onto the balcony, where another figure slouched against the glass, crushing the filmy drapes that obscured any view from outside. It was dark out there, and a heavy rain was falling, one that had been required by climatic considerations despite the weather-control fields that normally shielded the entire city of Woolsthorpe.

For a moment Georges Lemair seemed to ignore Din Su's words. His expression was sour and truculent under his overly long red hair, and his rumpled, casual clothing appeared badly out of place amid the sophisticated dress of the room's other occupants. But after a moment he shrugged, the movement of his shoulders seeming to push him away from the window; and he moved forward to take a vacant chair near the disguised figure.

As he seated himself, Din Su touched the arm of her chair, and a transparent blue bubble blossomed from the end of that arm, growing until it surrounded all of the Council members.

"What's the point of using the security bubble?" the blur-headed figure asked in its machine-like voice. "The election results we just saw show that three of you have been voted out of office, by margins far too wide for any challenge to be feasible. Until your successors arrive—along with the newly elected replacements for Ahmed Bahadur and the late Anita delle Santos—this Council has no quorum, and no business to discuss."

"The power's in our hands," Din Su said, "until we voluntarily yield it. And there are things we can do."

"Illegal things," the disguised voice responded.

"Illegality is what we say it is—" she said.

"That's easy for *you* to say, Gentleman!" Half-Thunder's voice cut across Din Su's words, shrill and angry, as if the gates of a dam holding back his anger had broken open, to pour it all into their midst. "You never have to stand for reelection, and no one even knows who you are! In fact—" He produced a void pistol, smaller than the usual run of such weapons, and pointed it at the disguised figure he had just named. "—in fact, I think we have no further need of you!"

Georges Lemair started at the sight of the pistol; but then subsided, saying nothing. Half-Thunder raked the other Council members with his gaze, his face flushed.

"You all know it!" he said loudly. "He talked us into an alliance with that Bleys Ahrens, telling us without it we'd lose our influence with New Earth—telling us it was necessary for us to stay in office, and necessary to keep Newton on top of the rest of the Younger Worlds—but it was a mistake!"

"Mister President—" Iban began; but she stopped as he glared at her, his pistol swinging wildly in her direction for a moment.

"What kind of fools have we become!" he said loudly; but no one took the words as a question. "We were set to be the supreme voice in the Younger Worlds, until we let this—this—" He stopped, almost incoherent with the rage he had seemed to stoke with his own words, and waved the pistol once more at the disguised figure.

"Half-Thunder," Din Su said softly. The President subsided, his glare losing focus, as if he were looking inward to wonder at his anger.

"Half-Thunder," she said again, more firmly," control yourself!"

His face reflected an effort to gather himself, and his eyes refocused on her face.

"You know we never got rid of the Gentleman before only because he represents elements of the population that didn't have the vote but were necessary for the planet's functioning," Din Su continued. "Our predecessors chose him as a way to gain the necessary cooperation of those elements."

She smiled.

"Of course, now that we've consolidated power in our own hands, those elements need no longer concern us." She turned to look at the Gentleman.

"Kill him," she said to Half-Thunder, watching the target of her command.

Her eyes were still on the Gentleman, so she did not realize that Half-Thunder had fallen back in his chair, the hand that had been holding the pistol now on his lap, and sliding from it—until gravity pulled it down and the pistol dropped to the floor.

She turned at the sound of the pistol hitting the carpeted surface, and saw Half-Thunder's head lolling backward, empty gaze directed at the ceiling. Her eyes went quickly to Iban, now holding another small pistol pointed at Din Su.

"So," Din Su said; and looked away from Iban, at the Gentleman. But she checked her next words, and in a moment turned back to look at Iban.

"Go ahead then," she said.

Iban did.

Despite the initial delegation of many administrative responsibilities to members of the Others' top leadership, Bleys had found, over the year that followed the reorganization, that his workload was steadily increasing. With Dahno gone, responsibility for the program that trained newly recruited Others had been taken up by Bleys—largely because he did not feel he could trust someone else with it.

That fact finally brought home to him a realization of how much the entire Others' organization—and therefore his whole plan—was dependent on the individual Others' loyalties to each other, and most of all to him. Always, when the idea had come to him in the past, he had pushed it aside, telling himself he would deal with it when the need arose. But now his mind was telling him that that time was almost here.

"What if one, or more, of the top Others' leaders rebelled?" he said to Toni one night, right after *Favored of God* had come out of a phase-shift, returning to Association from his latest inspection trip.

Over time, technology and pharmacology had combined to make

the experience of a phase-shift no longer the sickening, frightening, paralyzing thing it had been as recently as in Donal Graeme's time. But however little travelers might be physically affected by the experience, few of them could approach a shift without recalling the small, but very real, chance that their component particles, once scattered throughout the universe, might never be reassembled.

Contemplation of that reality was known to cause people to think a second time about their futures. Bleys sometimes wondered how professional spacecrew handled that particular vision. It might be that crew developed the happy-go-lucky personalities they were known for in self-defense—or perhaps the spacegoing life rapidly sorted out and drove away those who lacked an optimistic outlook.

Toni initially had nothing to say in response to Bleys' question. She had, now he thought of it, an attitude toward life that was completely different from that of the stereotypical spacecrew he had just been contemplating; and yet he was very sure she, too, could handle the prospect of a lifetime of phase-shifts without being affected in any way.

So could he, he thought. But that was because of his mission, which was so important it dwarfed all dangers; he realized now that if some accident, such as the proverbial shift to nothingness that had once taken Donal Graeme, should kill him, it would also kill his mission, and with it hope for the human race—because there was no one else with the strength and vision to carry it on.

"Hal Mayne could," he told himself. "But he wouldn't. He's blind . . ."

"What?" Toni asked; and Bleys realized he had uttered his last thought out loud.

"Just thinking," he said.

Toni was something else entirely. More than almost anyone he had ever known, she was a whole person, complete within herself. At her core lay a confident certainty, a sureness about herself, that made her imperturbable—it was, he suspected, the essence of her family's heritage of training in the martial arts, distilled through generations.

He wondered if she might not be more Dorsai, in attitude at least, than she herself realized.

Did other members of her family have a similar core? He had never met any of them, although Toni had mentioned once that a brother had gone through the Others' training program. Bleys did not remember him, so that must have been before he himself had become actively involved with Dahno's organization.

Where was that brother? Toni had never mentioned him again, although she had spoken about her father. Now that he thought of it, Bleys realized that in his frequent examinations of the Others' personnel files and reports, he had never noticed someone who could be that brother.

"Why would any of them rebel?" Toni spoke up, finally, interrupting his train of thought—which, Bleys realized, he had managed to sidetrack. "You've given them all they ever dreamed of, and more, and no one else can offer them anything better—why would they want to replace you?"

"Just because I'm here," he said, pushing himself into a sitting position with his back against the wall at the head of the bed. Still lying down, she rolled over so she could tilt her head and look at him.

"Like the mountain," she said after a moment.

"Mountain?"

"Some people have to climb them—to conquer them—just because they're there. So far, you're the mountain in their lives. So I suppose it's possible."

"More than possible," he said. "Over the long run, it's certain, because that's the way people are."

"Can't you use your persuasive abilities to keep them loyal?"

"That's what I've been doing," he said. "Every time I meet with some of them, I do everything I can to persuade them everything they want lies with me. So far it's worked: they seem to go away enthusiastic for the vision I create in their minds."

He sighed.

"But it never lasts," he said. "While I can persuade people—many people, not all—to believe what I tell them, it doesn't last. If they have any solid core to their personalities, their unconscious minds seem to return them to their old selves. Many of our Others—and most of the top ones—have the same persuasive ability themselves;

and I suspect what success I've had with them stems largely from the fact that what I tell them agrees with what they want, anyway. But that won't be the case forever."

"Which is why we have to keep making the rounds of the leadership," she said. "You have to keep refreshing their convictions." She sat up.

"I knew you were doing that," she said. "But I hadn't thought it out enough to realize the implications. You're killing yourself, trying to keep ahead of them, and the more Others are recruited, the more you have to do."

"Well, I don't have to work on all of our people," Bleys said. "Those of our Others who have the persuasive power exert it to keep their own followers in line—which is fine as long as the top people support me. But it's all a gigantic pyramid scheme."

"You're letting yourself become depressed," she said. "Stop it! Remember how far you've already come."

Both of them were silent for some moments.

"It's sad," she said finally. "It's like having to be suspicious of your own family."

He sensed, somehow, that her feelings ran deeper than her simple words indicated.

Two days after they got back to Association, word came that Ana Wasserlied, the top Other on New Earth, had been assassinated.

CHAPTER 29

By the time Bleys got to New Earth, Ana Wasserlied's deputies had already publicly placed blame for her murder on unidentified off-worlders; but there was a quiet war of succession going on, and Bleys discovered, as he had expected, that he was looked to as the kingmaker.

Having had time to think the situation over, he had already made his choice of a successor. However, he avoided announcing that choice for some days, using the time to watch the candidates in action.

As if unaware that the top Others on the planet were in an agonized limbo, Bleys spent an afternoon with Marshal Cuslow Damar, commander of the Friendly troops who enforced the Bleys-created truce that had averted a Bleys-induced civil war on New Earth—thus effectively giving Bleys control of the planet. Marshal Damar, Bleys knew, was no fool, and might have some useful ideas.

Much of what the Marshal had to say was confirmed when, on Bleys' fifth day on the planet, he kept a quiet rendezvous, once again using an automated taxi as a mobile meeting room. He had not, this time, been able to get away from his hotel totally unnoticed, but he was sure he had not been pursued closely enough for anyone to see and understand what he was doing.

"I can't prove it," Deborah said, "but I'm sure the assassination is connected to someone inside your Others' organization. My people here haven't had enough time to get high in the local organization, but we've had a lot of experience in learning things from subordinate positions—and your Others are generally pretty negligent in their security."

"Just here on New Earth?" Bleys asked. Deborah smiled.

"No," she said. "They're pretty bad on most of the other Younger Worlds, too—except for Newton and Cassida."

"That might be a legacy of the era when the organizations on those worlds were forced to operate underground," Bleys mused. "But in any case, I don't want them to be too good at protecting themselves—not just yet."

"Because it would make it a lot harder for you to keep an eye on them, through my people," Deborah said. She smiled again.

"Don't you worry about trusting me?" she asked.

"A little," Bleys said. "You're the most calculated risk I've ever taken."

"But *calculated* is the operative word here, isn't it?" she replied. "I've always liked the analytical way you approach problems. And I think you've recognized that my people wouldn't gain much if we betrayed you."

"That's one way to put it," Bleys said. "You might gain a little wealth by trading me for another employer, but I think that's nothing that's likely to motivate your people, or yourself."

"You're right—at least so long as you pay us well enough to satisfy our needs."

"Are you having any problems in that area?"

"No," she said. "You've been generous enough—again, you're smart enough to see it never pays to try to shortchange people you depend on. Besides, we know if we betrayed you, we could never manage to take over your empire and run it for ourselves."

"But I'd still be wise to avoid antagonizing you."

"That goes without saying." For a moment they were both silent.

"So what else do you have for me?" Bleys asked at last.

"I don't know what it means, but there's been some unusual traffic between Freiland, Cassida and New Earth over the last six months. I don't know if it's associated with the assassination. And I can't tell you if there's been any involvement of the Newton organization."

"What kind of traffic?"

"Just as one example, three Others from the Cassida organization—one a key deputy to Johann Wilter—have made five round trips to

New Earth in the last six months, traveling under false identifications on commercial transport, and while here they made no attempt to contact the New Earth organization."

"What did they do here?"

"I don't know," she said. "We here never knew they were coming, on any of the trips, until we got the word from our people on Cassida that they had already left there—because of the Cassidan organization's security, our people there weren't in a position to know about the trips ahead of time—but our people on the staff here would have known if the Cassidans made any contact with the New Earth offices."

"All right," Bleys said. He paused to think for a moment.

"Is there any asset I could get you that might have enabled you to learn more about this?"

"Not really," she said. "The problem is that our information about such a trip can't reach here before the Cassidans themselves get here—interstellar communications are still limited to the speed of a ship. If we had higher positions in the Cassidan organization it's possible we might learn something well enough in advance to send word on an earlier ship—but that seems unlikely.

"The only other possibility would be to have an organization that can check on every person who comes through a spaceport," she went on, "but that makes for other problems that I don't think are really in my line."

"You're right," he said. "But if you think of something else, let me know. Anything else?"

"Other unusual traffic," she said. "Not involving New Earth. Johann Wilter has made two trips to Freiland, and Hammer Martin has made two trips to Cassida, all of them kept—not secret, but at least low-profile. We can't say what we may have missed."

"I see," Bleys said. "It makes for an interesting pattern."

"There's more," she said. "We think there have been several quiet trips between Freiland and Old Earth, too—but since there isn't an Others organization on Old Earth, we can't say much more than that they left Freiland—"

" 'They'?"

"In the trips we know of, five different Others from the Freiland organization," she said. "Usually only two or three on a trip, always including one or two of Hammer Martin's top deputies." She shrugged. "That's it."

"All right," he said. "Have you gotten anywhere on Old Earth itself?"

"We've gotten one person into your brother's underground organization there. The organization seems to be avoiding hiring off-worlders, but because our person is the granddaughter of one of our New People who retired to Old Earth sixteen years ago—taking his family with him—she was apparently accepted as a native of that planet, slipping by your brother's checks. . . . Your brother is much better on organizational security than your Others on the Younger Worlds, by the way."

"That doesn't surprise me," Bleys said.

"Unusually so, in fact," Deborah said.

"Oh?"

"Even though we haven't been able to get into your brother's organization, we've tried to watch it from outside—details are on this chip—" She handed him a small envelope. "—and I'm told your brother is keeping more of a low profile than seems necessary."

"Of course," Bleys said, "he can't maintain his own identity there—"

"It's more than that," she said. "It's more like he's hiding. He has no permanent residence, he moves around a lot, and he seems to vanish at odd moments with no warning. He makes no appointments, and conducts most of his business at a distance."

"Do you have any idea what it means?" Bleys asked. "Dahno's said nothing in his reports to reflect anything like that."

"I've got nothing to base this on," Deborah said, "but my people say it looks as if he's on the run."

"From whom? Old Earth authorities?"

"We've seen no indication they know he's there."

"Not even the Final Encyclopedia?"

"It's always possible," Deborah said. "All I can really say is we've never seen anything that even hints at anyone knowing he's there."

"Except our people," he said. "Again."

"'Again'?"

"Never mind," he said. "Listen, I'm going to send some of my Soldiers to Old Earth to look into this." He stopped again to think.

"I don't intend for you to be working for them," he went on, "and they won't be working for you. I'm only telling you so your people won't be surprised when my people show up. All right?"

"You know we prefer to be independent," she said, "so that's fine. But I have one more item: two members of the Laboratories Review Council—both of them defeated in the recent elections—have vanished. We don't know what it means, but we thought you should know."

"And you were correct," Bleys said. "As it happens, I already know about that. It's nothing for you to worry about."

It'll be good for our relationship if she realizes I have other resources, he thought.

Of the six Soldiers Bleys sent to Old Earth, two had vanished within two weeks—mysteriously, and with no sign of any involvement by any Old Earth authority.

"I don't think you should go," Toni said.

"It's necessary," Bleys said. "I don't know what's happening, but it's clearly a threat to the organization, and that means it's a threat to my plans."

"You said it yourself, a while ago," she said: "your death would be the end of your plans."

"My plans could die even if I live," he said. "Whether the organization lives on is less important—it's always been just a tool." He smiled.

"In fact," he said, "the organization is likely to live longer than all of us, because it's a creature of the historical forces . . . I've told you before that no one individual is important to the movement of those forces, and that includes me."

"So the organization arose only because it was, historically, time?"

"Yes," he said. "If it hadn't been the Others, some other group would have stepped into the place the forces had left open—even without me, and without Dahno. But it's precisely because of those forces that the organization—working through people in it—is pushing at me. The organization is a kind of movement of the historical moment, and it's got a momentum of its own, that I can't stop."

"You *can't* mean your plans have been doomed from the start!"

"By no means," he said. "Think of it like this: I can't change the forces, but I can ride them. And if in doing so I can change the minds of people, those small changes, aggregated over a long time, will slowly alter the direction of the forces themselves."

"Doesn't it matter where the organization goes?"

"A little," he said. He shrugged. "It doesn't matter to me exactly which road the organization takes; because a lot of roads go in the direction I want . . . anything that will push the race off the Younger Worlds and back to Old Earth is a step in the right direction."

"You've spoken of war," she said. "Won't it threaten your plans if Old Earth wins that war?"

"I'm no longer so sure of that," he said. "No matter who wins, if there's a war it'll be so large that the economies of all the Younger Worlds will be bled white. If the organization wins that war, it'll gravitate naturally to the only place with a viable economy—Old Earth; and if Old Earth wins, it will turn its back on colonization for a long time."

"Can you just sit back, then, and let things play themselves out?"

"No," he said. "To ensure the success of my plans, I have to be able to gather the ablest elements of the Younger Worlds and establish them on Old Earth in positions from which they can begin pushing the race in the direction it needs to go—the direction of inner moral development, that will help it see the futility and danger in acting on the immature whims of random excitable individuals."

"I thought you weren't really important in the scheme of history?"

"I'm not," he said. "Not as an individual. But if I can influence enough people to see things the way I do, the sum of us can become important."

"And that's what you've been doing, in all those years of speeches and recorded talks," she said. "Bringing people around to your point of view."

"I wish it were as easy as you make it sound."

"I must go," Henry MacLean insisted later that day, even though Bleys had already refused to let his uncle investigate the lost Soldiers. "They were my people."

"And they were mine, Uncle Henry," Bleys said, speaking softly but firmly.

"Bleys, you can't go running off every time one of our people gets killed," Toni said, even more softly. "You know that—it's part of the price of your position."

She had already used up her other arguments, in private.

"I agree," Bleys said, looking at her with a slight smile, but not budging. "But this isn't a normal situation. This is Dahno. If he's doing something that endangers my plans, we have to know it."

He turned his eyes back to Henry.

"You have to agree with this, Uncle," he said. "No one else—not even you—can see through Dahno like I can."

"I cannot argue with you on that point, Bleys," Henry said. "But you must let me make a few suggestions, at least."

CHAPTER 30

There were just over ninety passengers aboard the shuttle that came down to Famagusta, one early spring day, from the *Sesostris II*. They had filled out the necessary customs forms while still aboard the passenger liner, and had been vouched for by the shipping line; the only remaining barrier was a passage through electronic inspection of their persons and belongings. When no untoward metal objects or unorthodox circuitry or chemicals were found, they were released to Old Earth's soil.

Passengers arriving on an Old Earth–owned liner generally received a substantial amount of deference, since they were highly likely to be well-off and well-connected. Indeed, most of the new arrivals were met and escorted from the spaceport, to be conveyed to their destinations in North Africa, southern Europe or eastern Asia.

Among the few not so greeted was a tall man with blond-brown hair that was graying at the temples. His skin was deeply tanned, but he seemed to suffer from a dermal affliction that created a nasty-looking rash and an accretion of random bumps and pitting. People winced internally when they saw his face, then politely averted their eyes.

Space travel was expensive, and seasoned interstellar travelers packed lightly, knowing it was cheaper to buy most items on arrival than to pay their luggage charges. The tall man with the unsightly face had only a tiny bag as he strolled through the terminal to the area reserved for taxis.

Out on the curb, his attention was caught by the tall palm trees that lined a nearby parking area. There were variform palms on some of the Younger Worlds, varieties genetically altered to fit those planets; but he had not seen a real one since his mother took him along on a trip to Old Earth. He remembered being fascinated by their prehistoric appearance; at the time he had just discovered picture books about dinosaurs, and those amazing creatures had been depicted moving among palmlike plants.

He would have liked to walk over and take a closer look, perhaps even feel one of those trunks, that looked so reptilian. But that would make him conspicuous; so he put the past out of his mind and walked toward the head of the cab rank.

At the Mediterranean shore north of the city he boarded an old-fashioned seaplane, carefully maneuvering his long frame into its cramped interior. He was startled when the lone pilot handed out foam earplugs to the passengers, but soon found himself grateful: they not only blocked out most of the noise inside the small craft, but also squelched any necessity to make polite conversation with his fellow passengers—or with the pilot, who had been showing signs of wanting to chat, before they were waved away from the dock.

The tall man had to crane his neck to look out the tiny window, but he rapidly found himself almost hypnotized by the water rushing away beneath them, close enough that he could see the scalloped white line that occasionally marked a wave crest. He was intrigued by the boats below; the seaplane flew low enough that he could easily make out the figures of people on their decks.

Within a short time the water lightened in color, taking on a greenish hue; he deduced it was getting shallower as they approached the Asian shore at Beirut—and then, as the plane banked into a turn, they began to parallel the wide sandy beach. Beyond it the ancient buildings of an old city rose in cluttered stacks, close enough to see laundry drying on balconies and rooftops, interspersed with communications arrays. In what appeared to be a small park, people were dancing in an intricate, figured pattern he had no time to figure out.

Most people of the Younger Worlds never got to Old Earth; like them, he tended to forget that it, too, was just another planet, rather than some fabled land of milk and honey—to use a figure out of his religious teachings. On Old Earth, too, there was dust in some places, mud in others—and always, people. Just regular people.

Beirut, he remembered, perched on one edge of Old Earth's largest continent. From his small window he could not estimate the city's size. It appeared to be strung out along the sea, penned between forested mountains and the pale beaches that stretched into the glaring, hazy sunlight in both directions.

As they taxied across an artificial harbor toward the little industrial dock that was home for the seaplane, he could see more palm trees in the distance. None were close enough to be examined.

Before he boarded the regional shuttle flight to Roma his face was smooth again; and by the time he left his hotel the next morning, his coloration seemed to have faded to only a moderate tan. Only his height would make him stand out on the streets of Wien, when he got there.

It took Bleys a day and a half to make contact with Dahno, and it was another day before his half-brother showed up on the street outside his hotel, driving a four-wheeled vehicle propelled by what was apparently a very silent motor.

"I apologize for the size of this thing," Dahno said, as Bleys carefully folded his length into the cramped passenger seat. "They frown on larger vehicles in these old cities—I think it's partly a political issue, but the streets *are* pretty narrow, at times."

"But you like the challenge of handling a vehicle in these streets, don't you?" Bleys said.

Dahno gave a short bark of a laugh as the wheels double-thumped over a set of parallel metal rails set into the middle of the street they were crossing.

"You felt that!" he said. "It's like being in touch with the ground. I'd forgotten the feeling of direct contact, after all these years of the fans or mag-levs we've been used to."

"Doesn't it distract you?" Bleys asked. "If you had someone driving, you'd have time to get things done—"

"Did you expect me to pull up in the back of a chauffered limousine?" Dahno said.

"Of course not," Bleys said. He was disturbed by an aggressively sarcastic tone he heard in his brother's voice—it was not Dahno's usual manner.

"You know conditions here much better than I do," Bleys continued; "you've been here for almost a year now, after all. But I'd have been perfectly happy to hire a taxi and come to you, you know that."

"I never tell anyone where to find me."

"All right. Where are we going?"

"On a tour, of sorts," Dahno said, sounding more cheerful. "It'll give you some idea of what I've been up to. Then we'll grab a bite to eat."

"All right, brother," Bleys said. "Show me."

Twenty minutes later they pulled up across the street from an ancient gray-brick building in a close-in suburb. The top two floors contained apartments, while the ground floor was given over to a few modest commercial establishments, the largest being a café that made a small terrace out of the sidewalk. Two doors down from the café, Dahno pointed out, was a freshly painted storefront that appeared to be the office of some sort of political movement.

"The signs in the window give the name of the organization sponsoring this office," Dahno said. "In several languages—this planet seems to cling to those old languages. It's one of those generic names that become anonymous when you take your eyes off it. But it's headquarters for a few idealistic volunteers who make phone calls, put out press releases and walk the streets handing out leaflets and talking to people."

"What do they say?"

"So far it's totally innocuous," Dahno said. "With variations from place to place, we're basically taking the side of the underdogs in actual, ongoing local controversies. We're establishing our credentials as idealists, against the day we can credibly protest that the Younger Worlds are getting treated badly by Earth."

Bleys thought about asking his brother if that was all there was to the effort, but decided not to push a confrontation just yet. Dahno, seeming to sense what his brother was thinking, spoke up again.

"All we want at this point," he said, sounding almost defensive, "is to prepare to ramp up to a 'hands off the Younger Worlds' message."

"When will that happen?"

"Not before we need it," Dahno said. "We need something specific, and controversial, to point to; so we're waiting for the right moment."

"Can I assume there're more than just this one office?"

"Oh, absolutely!" Dahno almost crowed. Bleys was beginning to find the rapid changes in his brother's mood disconcerting. "We've got seven offices like this one scattered about Europe, and similar—although apparently independent—organizations are doing the same kind of public relations on every continent. But this is only the most obvious aspect of the work we're doing."

He paused, turning to watch over his shoulder for an opportunity to pull out into the traffic rushing by.

"This was just about the hardest thing to get used to," he said offhandedly. "About being on Earth, I mean. The traffic here is almost always a constant stream."

"The Younger Worlds, and particularly Association and Harmony, have never been able to afford a lot of traffic," Bleys said. "I see what you mean."

He tucked that idea into the back of his head, thinking it might be useful one day.

"We're heading back to the center of the old city," Dahno said, swinging smoothly around the next corner and slipping into a slot in the flow of a more major street. "I won't be able to show you much on a drive-by, but we've got two more sophisticated operations working out of modern offices there. These are newer than the kind of storefront operation you just saw, and so far they haven't done much."

"What will they do, when they get up to speed?"

"What we're *already* starting to do," Dahno said, emphasizing his point with the tone of his voice, "is look for weaknesses in Earth's leadership structure—" Bleys noted that Dahno now spoke of the planet simply as *Earth*, rather than as *Old Earth*, in the Younger Worlds way. "—anything we can expose to the media as corruption."

"Again, giving your people credibility," Bleys said.

"Yes. Of course, all our organizations claim to be independent, and to be motivated only by an interest in the public good."

"And of course they really can't be connected to any Old Earth political group," Bleys said. "I see."

"Well, that's true," Dahno said, a note of caution in his voice. "The problem is, I can't have the Others you gave me noticeably involved with these organizations—it would be bad if someone noticed offworlders getting into Earth politics. So we've had to recruit locals to handle everything but the most hidden parts of our agenda."

"What're you doing with our Others, then?"

"That depends on their skills," Dahno said. "Some are handling the details of administering the organization, others are out fundraising. The smoothest are mingling with powerful people, making friends—and a few, the best speakers, have been getting involved in anything that'll give them a chance to make speeches . . . mostly religious bodies, although those seem to be harder to rise in than we're used to seeing on Association."

"Oh," said Bleys, returning to the previous subject, "I believe I see what you were starting to say: while your organizations can't be connected to any Old Earth political faction, some of your 'volunteers' can be."

"They're not with any other faction, *now*," Dahno said. "But with only a few exceptions, the kind of people willing to do the jobs my 'public interest' groups take on turn out to be just the people who were already involved in local politics, in some form or another."

"So you have to make sure, when you recruit them, not only that they're no longer working for someone else—but that their past history contains nothing that might come back to haunt us."

"Right," said Dahno. "We don't want to find ourselves tarred with somebody else's brush."

It took Bleys a moment to figure out the meaning of the figure of speech his brother had just used; but he thought, finally, he understood. His brother was apparently taking on Old Earth customs quickly.

In the meantime, Dahno had continued.

"We don't have any targets yet," he said. "But we've been making some useful contacts, and we're beginning to learn some unsavory secrets. When things start heating up here with concern over what the Others are doing on the New Worlds, we'll be in a position to discredit some of the people who want Earth to act against us."

"I presume that applies even if you haven't found anything to use against particular people?"

"If necessary," Dahno said. "But of course it's always more effective if there's actually some truth in the story."

"You sound hesitant about using this tactic," Bleys said.

"It's not the tactic, it's the targets," Dahno said. He shook his head, his eyes watching the traffic.

"We've got two strings to our bow," he went on—Bleys noted his brother's use of yet another strange Old Earth adage—"and I don't want to accidentally break one."

"What do you mean?"

"Well, as we discussed before I came here, my brief is to find ways to disarm any potential movement to mobilize Earth against the Others," Dahno said. "There are two ways I can do that, and I have to be careful to keep one tactic from disarming the other."

"You mean that in some way attempts to discredit Old Earth leaders—"

"I mean I have to be careful which leaders to discredit," Dahno said. "Because the dirt that I get on some of them, that might be useful to discredit them, also might be useful to make them lean in our direction when making certain decisions."

"I see," Bleys said. "And if you use the 'dirt,' as you call it, to discredit any particular leader, it won't be possible to use it to blackmail him or her."

"That's right," Dahno said; there was an involved, lively gleam in his eyes. "But there's another convolution to consider."

"And that is?"

"We still can't tell which way most of these leaders might hop— and I'm not referring only to political leaders, by the way—if the matter of the Others suddenly came to a head in Earth politics," Dahno said. "Some might be inclined to favor us, or have other motives for leaving us alone; since the matter hasn't come up, I can't tell yet exactly which ones are the enemies we'll want to get out of the way."

"So you need to learn more about all these people," Bleys said. "On a planet this large, that will be a gigantic task."

"True," Dahno said. "Can you imagine how stupid we'd feel if we destroyed the career of some politician who, it later turned out, would have been on our side anyway?"

"That might be," Bleys said, "but we'd probably never know it. In any case, I doubt you can get a dependable reading on how any one of them is liable to vote. There're just too many variables."

"Yes, that's it exactly," Dahno nodded.

"The most important thing is to build up the credibility of your groups," Bleys said. "I'd suggest you need to pick someone— probably more than one someone—to destroy. You can't wait much longer to find out where they might sit on some theoretical crisis in the future."

"That's true, too."

"At the same time," Bleys mused, fruitlessly pushing his long legs against the front wall of the vehicle—he felt cramped, and suddenly wanted very much to get out of the vehicle and pace up and down one of the streets they were passing—"you'd better be sure your first couple of exposés are dead on target."

"Absolutely! It's necessary that the first ones not only be big news, but confirmable."

"With a few correct reports giving you credibility," Bleys said, "your later accusations will have more staying power even if they can't be easily confirmed."

"In any case, it'll take time to debunk any that we manufacture," Dahno nodded again. "And in the meantime, the political process will be slowed down, maybe even paralyzed."

"It becomes a nice question of timing, then," Bleys said. "I'm sure you understand that."

"You know I do, brother."

CHAPTER 31

There was silence in the car for several minutes, until finally Dahno indicated a modern office building that fronted on a tree-lined mall; and, three minutes later, another, similar building whose ground floor held the offices of a broadcast media organization. Then he took them to a restaurant, leaving the vehicle running where he had stopped it in the street and leading Bleys inside without looking back.

Bleys, thinking he knew his brother's tastes, expected to be taken to an private upstairs dining room; instead Dahno led him straight through the restaurant and out a narrow, too-low back door that opened on an interior courtyard. Eight metal-wire tables were widely spaced about the courtyard, standing on pebble-surfaced concrete islands in a sea of vegetation. The season was early enough that the grass was dried and pale; the tiny, pale green leaves on the branches of the bushes and trees seemed inadequate to their future task of growth and display.

Unthinkingly, Bleys had expected Old Earth to be in a perpetual summer, but the earliness of the season was clear here in this courtyard. He regretted it; Europe's colorful gardens were known throughout all the Younger Worlds, and he would have liked to enjoy them. There was a single variety of flower here, that he could see, blooming in tidy rows against the wall of the building, where they got the sunlight. They had produced large, cup-shaped blossoms in a variety of colors, that opened to the sky from the tops of thin tubular stems.

Now that they were out of the vehicle, Bleys observed that his brother seemed to have gained some weight.

Dahno led Bleys to a table in the far corner of the courtyard, that was tucked behind trees and bushes, bare though they were. Two very large chairs awaited them there, the harshness of the metal-wire shapes softened by wine-red cushioning.

A black-haired woman in a patterned green-and-gold dress, which Bleys believed to be a modern version of an ancient oriental style, was already there, seated in one of the chairs. She stood up as they neared and took off her sunglasses. Her eyes were violet in color, he noted, and they had an epicanthic fold although her skin was pale.

Dahno did not introduce them.

"It's safe," she said to Dahno; as she continued speaking to him, her eyes turned to Bleys.

"All the anti-surveillance gear is working, there's a vapor barrier over the top of the wall to inhibit pressure-sensing devices and blur out optical systems—and all the people at these tables are ours."

"And the staff?" Dahno said. She turned her attention back to him.

"They won't get close to you," she said.

At Dahno's nod, she turned and walked away, gathering up the occupants of the other tables as she went.

"And is *she* safe?" Bleys said softly.

"Yes," said Dahno. "She's one of the Others I brought with me. You don't know her because she went through training before you did."

"Then why don't I recognize her from our files?" Bleys asked. Dahno grinned.

"She's had her appearance edited," he said.

"All right," Bleys said; and before his brother could act, he took the chair that allowed him to sit with his back to the courtyard wall, allowing him to peer through the branches at the door to the restaurant.

Dahno grinned again, and reached for the second chair, pulling it around the table so that he, too, could sit with his back to the wall.

Are we just squabbling over seats? Bleys wondered. *Or is it more than that?*

It did not escape his notice that by making them sit side by side, his brother had made it harder for either of them to look into the other's face.

"I've already ordered for both of us," Dahno said. "I didn't think you'd mind, since this is work, after all, rather than a dining experience."

"Knowing you, it'll be a fine meal in any case," Bleys said. "Did you order juice for me?"

"Several varieties," Dahno said. "You know it won't taste the same, here on Earth. I'd have gotten you Association orange juice, but I don't think anyone here imports it." He laughed.

"I also ordered several wines," he went on. "You can try them or not, as you choose. I know you don't care for alcoholic beverages much, but you might want to taste some of these—this is Earth, after all, where wine was born."

"I've tasted Old Earth wines," Bleys reminded his brother. "I've been on this planet before, remember."

"Right," Dahno said. "That was our meeting in—" He paused. "—you remember. But that was half the world away and years ago."

"Oh, I'll try some," Bleys said, relenting. "In fact, I look for you to give me a recommendation or two."

"Count on it," Dahno said. "I've learned a lot in my year here."

As he spoke a serving cart holding a series of shiny metal coverings was pushed through the restaurant door, to be immediately intercepted by the woman who had just left them. She took its control from the server who had brought it out and began to push it, floating above the grass, toward Bleys and Dahno. She was now wearing a costume nearly identical to that worn by the server she had replaced—black trousers and a frilly white shirt set off by a small black cravat held in place by a pearl stickpin.

By unspoken agreement, Bleys and Dahno suspended meaningful conversation as the woman approached and began serving them, elegantly lifting the shiny covers to reveal two large china plates filled with a breaded meat that had been topped with a brown sauce, along with carrots, broccoli and a white substance that looked almost, but not quite, like mashed potatoes.

"How is Henry?" Dahno asked. "I got your note that Joshua had a daughter some months back, and I've been wondering how Henry reacted to that."

"They named her Miriam, by the way," Bleys said. "But you know Uncle Henry's not much for letting his reactions show." He paused to watch the woman as she reached into the cloth-obscured lower portion of the cart to produce an ice bucket, half a dozen wineglasses of varying sizes and three antique-looking bottles with paper labels.

"He planned to take a week off to go back to the farm," Bleys continued, "but he wanted to wait until Ruth's mother left—she'd come over to help out; there wouldn't have been room otherwise. But that took about a month, and if I didn't know better, I'd say Uncle Henry was on pins and needles the whole time."

"I can't even imagine it," Dahno said.

The woman, Bleys saw, was having difficulty with the corkscrew. It was not surprising; cork was largely unknown on the Younger Worlds, where all bottled products were sealed by molded caps, on which a very different implement was used. Dahno, still cheerful, reached over and gave her a demonstration on how to handle the corkscrew.

When they had been served the woman withdrew with the cart.

"Is there anything else you haven't told me about your organization?" Bleys asked as he took a forkful of the white substance; it was mildly spicy.

"Well, at another level up," his brother said, "we've been cultivating people who already have credentials in the academic and journalistic fields. We've got a few on the payroll already, people who will slant their reports and conclusions just a little to our side, when the time is right for that."

"How far will they go for you?"

"So far—not far," Dahno answered. "But time will pass while they earn their money fairly easily; and eventually they'll find it difficult to cut themselves off when the earning gets harder."

"I suspect there's more to it than that," Bleys said.

"True," Dahno answered. "On the one hand, we're going to have them all make the occasional small statement they wouldn't normally make—not as something we need them to say, but only to make it harder for them to backtrack on their records if the spirit of rebellion ever rises up in them."

He paused to cut off another portion of his entrée and raise it to his mouth.

"Of course, people who can be bought so easily have likely been bought, in one way or another, in the past; so we're quietly digging into their histories. I believe we'll eventually have blackmail material on most of them."

"Sometimes blackmail just makes people angry," Bleys said. "That can lead to even bigger trouble."

"I know that," Dahno said, a hint of asperity in his voice. "Blackmail won't even be hinted at, except as a last resort." He paused, thinking as he chewed.

"My own belief," he went on, the touch of emotion gone, "is that people who'd let us influence what they say aren't particularly concerned for the integrity of their work anyway."

"What about my idea of trying to infiltrate the Final Encyclopedia?" Bleys asked.

"It's difficult," Dahno said. "Those people really restrict access." He smiled. "But I did it," he said.

"*You?*"

"No, I don't mean me personally," Dahno said. "It's not likely I could fool them as to who I was, even with the best phony documentation. But I've got two people in already."

"As staff?"

"No," Dahno said. "I got a couple of our pet academics accepted as visiting scholars."

"That's probably not as useful as a staff position," Bleys said, "but I'm willing to bet anyone who joins that staff is thoroughly checked."

"You know it," Dahno said. "And there's not much turnover, either." He cut into the remains of his veal.

"Your friend Hal Mayne seems to still be there," he said casually.

A bit later Bleys leaned back in his chair. He had tried the coffee Dahno pressed on him, a very different beverage from the coffee he had drunk on this planet before. It was an old regional specialty, his brother had explained, for which he had developed a taste; but Bleys found he did not care for its thick sweetness, and so had been sipping lightly from a glass of a red wine whose name—*Chateau La Fleur St. Bonnet*—Dahno tossed off lightly.

"The fountainhead of wines, France," Dahno said, apparently in an expansive mood once more.

"Really?"

"No, not really. Not in the sense of—say, having invented the idea. But the French vineyards—some of them—still rate as legendary names."

Dahno was swirling a large amount of cognac in a huge round glass, pausing now and then to raise it before his nose, before taking a small drink.

"You picked out a fine meal, brother," Bleys said now. "I appreciate it. But we need to do some serious talking, including going over our plans in more depth, and I don't feel comfortable talking in the open—do you have a safe place we can go?"

"We could go to your hotel room," Dahno said. He shrugged. "Or we could pick some other hotel . . . with a random choice of hotels and our technology, we'd be safe enough."

Startled by his brother's sudden casualness, Bleys agreed when Dahno suggested that he, Bleys, go back to his hotel first; Dahno himself had an errand to take care of, he told Bleys, but he would be along shortly.

Bleys had been in his room for more than two hours when the room communicator beeped. It was conveying a printed message from Dahno, saying that something had come up.

"Take a flight to Nairobi," the message said. *"There's a room waiting for you in the Sandman Hotel. I'll come to you there."*

With little choice, Bleys did as Dahno directed, pausing only to send a message from a public kiosk in the terminal; but he ended up waiting in his room in Nairobi for nearly a full day, until finally another message appeared, sending him to South America.

CHAPTER 32

The brothers finally came together again three days later, shortly before noon on a thinly grassed plaza set high in the Andes. On three sides of the plaza the gray stones of a small and ancient city's low buildings were forgiven by pastel-washed trimmings and the gaily-colored clothing of the citizens. The fourth side was a laid-stone walkway that overlooked a deep drop to the floor of a valley. From their seats at an elderly wooden table on the grass Bleys and Dahno, protected from the cold wind by a small weather buffer, could look over and beyond that walkway, across the distance-misted valley, at farther ranges of mountains layered blue and purple before the jagged horizon.

"I think this is my favorite spot on the whole planet," Dahno said, his gaze directed out into the great chasm. "Sometimes you can look down on the eagles."

He brought his eyes back to his brother.

"You know about eagles, don't you?" he said. "I know you've always liked to read about Earth's animals. This whole trip ought to be a treat for you."

"It is," said Bleys. "I even went to the animal park outside Nairobi before my shuttle left for Buenos Aires."

"One of the great things about Earth," Dahno said, seeming to have dropped into a more contemplative mood, "is that the animals are different from continent to continent. Africa is famous for its animals, of course, but Asia and the Americas have their own, very different, animal populations. On the Younger Worlds the only variances across planets are climatic."

"Old Earth has the advantage of a biosphere established through millions of years of evolution," Bleys pointed out. "The Younger

Worlds can't match that in only a handful of centuries, particularly when they're limited to the commercially viable breeding stocks that can be transported over interstellar distances."

"I imagine you saw elephants and lions in Africa," Dahno said. "Wait until we get to North America, where you can see a grizzly bear in its habitat—*that* is the undisputed king!"

Bleys kept up his side of the conversation until they were interrupted by a waiter who came walking over from a small bistro Bleys had not previously noticed, tucked in as it was on the ground floor of one of the elderly buildings on the south side of the plaza. Bleys wondered what security measures Dahno could have taken in this setting; he was sure there must be something—just as he was sure he had his own measures in place.

Once more Dahno displayed an intimate knowledge of the menu and an easy familiarity with the waiter, insisting on doing the ordering for them both.

He's nervous, Bleys thought, as he watched his brother discussing with the waiter minute details of their meals to come. *That kind of conversation isn't his style.*

The only times Bleys had ever seen his brother act in what could be described as a mercurial fashion had been those periods when Dahno had been under great stress. The spectacle disturbed him: the nervousness he believed he was seeing made him question how well he knew his brother, and that unexpected flaw in his perception, when combined with the fact that there must be something going on to make Dahno act this way . . . suddenly Bleys found himself in unfamiliar territory.

Abruptly, he was on his feet and striding toward the cliff's edge only a few meters away, leaving Dahno and the waiter deep in the subject of wines. That edge was guarded by a low stone wall, from the top of which a black-enameled iron rail grew to a height just below his waist.

He looked over that edge, as if daring himself to be uncomfortable with the height. Was he becoming nervous himself? he wondered. He had not planned the move that took him away from the table; he had been on his feet and in motion before he thought about it at all. It was unlike him to react like that.

What was he reacting to, after all? He had only been thinking that his brother was acting unusually, but what did that mean? No human being ever really got to know another so well that he could never be surprised.

Behind him, discussion ceased, and Bleys heard the sound of a chair being pushed back. Dahno would be walking up behind him in a moment.

Suddenly, Bleys was very conscious that he was standing at the edge of a great chasm, his back to a brother who had become a stranger. Unbidden, his left hand tightened on the iron railing in front of him . . . he could hear steps approaching from behind. . . .

Ridiculous! he thought; and made himself hold his position.

"It *is* spectacular, isn't it?" Dahno said, coming up on Bleys' right.

Bleys realized that his eyes were looking out, unseeing, across the great deep drop, at the nearest range of mountains. He slowly tilted his head downward, feeling the muscles around his eyes relaxing as they refocused on the winding silver thread that was a river far below, shrouded in the hazy shadows below the mountains.

He leaned forward a little, to look over the railing and straight down from the edge of the cliff, conscious all the while that his brother's eyes might be on him. The uneven rock face below him was pitted and scarred, and there were remnants of alien-seeming blue, red and white patches, as if someone had once painted some sort of sign on the top of the cliff. Below that, the rock of the mountain bulged outward, blocking his view of the place in the valley below where the river passed closest.

"I've never seen anything like this," Bleys said, still looking down.

Although the food was good—at least to Bleys' indifferent palate—the meal was a disaster. Dahno tried to keep a conversation going, jumping from subject to subject, but well before the after-dinner drinks came he had lapsed into a moody silence.

"I've enjoyed what I've seen of this planet," Bleys said, finally determining to get to the point. "And what you've told me of the projects you've gotten up and running already—it's impressive. You've certainly done exactly what you were sent here to do."

Dahno's head came up, eyes focusing on Bleys. His expression was bleak as he waited for Bleys to continue.

"I think you know what I'm about to ask, brother," Bleys went on. "There's something else going on, that you don't want to tell me about. And it's important enough that you're not your usual self. I think you must know I can see that in you."

Dahno looked back across the table at him for a long, silent moment.

"All right," he said finally, his broad face grimacing in distaste. "All right. I knew you couldn't be easily taken in, but I had to try it." He shrugged. "Because I didn't like any of the other alternatives.

"I guess you could call me a bit of a coward," he went on. "But I've been trying to avoid having to have this discussion. You're the only family I've got, aside from Henry and Joshua, and whether you believe it or not, that's important to me."

"I believe it," Bleys said. "I have similar feelings, I think."

"I know you do," Dahno said. "But I don't delude myself into believing those feelings would keep you from throwing me overboard if your plans required it."

His face had hardened as he spoke, his jaw setting. The hand that had been holding his glass clenched—and then opened spasmodically, the glass dropping to spill its contents on the tabletop.

"*Throw you overboard?*" Bleys said. "What brought *that* into your head? I told you, when you signed on with me, that you'd always have a place with me, and that if you didn't want it, you could retire in comfort." He put his own glass down and raised both hands slightly, holding them in the air above the table, demonstrating openness.

"You know about my long-range mission," he went on. "It's all-important, because it's aimed at saving the human race. But you're no threat to that plan, brother—in fact, you've been a great help to me, and still are, as far as I can tell. Why would I want to get rid of you?"

"That's just what I've been wondering," Dahno said. His face was, once more, bleak; and Bleys reminded himself that his brother was a consummate actor.

"I know you believe in your plan—your *mission*," Dahno went on, speaking before Bleys could respond. He shook his head.

"But *I* don't believe in it! I don't believe in this danger you see threatening the whole race. And I don't want to die for some theory I don't even believe in."

Bleys looked at his brother for a long moment, before replying.

"Is this because you got hurt on Ceta?"

"No!" Dahno said. He paused.

"No," he said again, more quietly. "Although maybe you could say that injury opened my eyes, made me think a little more. But past is past, and doesn't worry me. The future, though, is another matter."

"And the future now looks different to you? Different from how you used to see it?"

"Yes," Dahno said. "You think long-term—I know that. And I think short- and medium-term—you've always known that."

"But you've gotten more than you ever thought possible—you told me that yourself—by joining me," Bleys said. "And the long-term results you don't believe in can only come about long after we're both dead and forgotten. . . . It's the chance of war, isn't it?"

"In a way," Dahno said. "I'll admit that when you first estimated that the Exotics would hire the Dorsai to oppose us, it frightened me. But I began to realize you could be right—that the rest of the Younger Worlds could successfully oppose the Dorsai, and possibly Old Earth as well."

"But?"

"But even victory in your war would destroy the whole structure of the Worlds as we know them," Dahno said. He shook his head, as if trying to scatter some haze obstructing his vision.

"I know you probably think I've always been motivated only by money and power," he went on—and then, unexpectedly, he chuckled. "Even I believed that, until I was forced to think about the situation. But I realized, lying there recovering in *Favored of God*, that I wanted more than that."

"So what else do you want?"

"Do you know—I'm still not sure," Dahno said. His smile became somewhat sheepish. "Put that way, I guess I sound pretty confused. But I'm starting to think I need to find some other purpose in life."

Bleys looked at him for a long moment.

"And my purposes aren't good enough for you?" he said at last.

"I just said I don't believe in them!" Dahno said, his smile fading.

"All right, all right," Bleys said, raising a hand as if holding his brother off. "I can't say you didn't give my way a try. So what do you want to do?"

"I want out," Dahno said.

"What does *that* mean?"

"I just want out of my responsibilities to the Others," Dahno said. "I want to just be able to go off and do whatever strikes me as interesting." He smiled. "And I want to take enough credit to let me do what I want."

His expression became more serious.

"I brought in a lot of that credit, after all."

"Yes, you did," Bleys said. He shook his head, but he did not mean the motion as a negation.

"I think you're making a mistake," he said. "But if that's what you want, I'll go along with it—as long as I can be sure you won't interfere with what I'm doing."

Dahno laughed.

"What could I ever say that would make a guarantee you'd believe?" he said. "You know me better than anyone, after all."

Bleys just watched his face.

"But because you know me," Dahno went on, "don't you know that I don't want to play in your league?"

Another one of his Old Earth expressions?

"But my 'league,' as you call it, includes *everything*, don't you see that?" Bleys said. "I can't help that. It's just the way it is."

"But you can leave me alone, can't you?" Dahno asked.

"I said earlier you're no threat to my plans," Bleys said. He shook his head. "I think even if you were trying to oppose me, it wouldn't make much difference."

Dahno raised his head, his eyes narrowing, but Bleys held up a hand to stop him.

"I know how that sounds," he said; "I didn't mean it as an insult. I was speaking in terms of the historical forces—I've told you about them before."

"I know," Dahno said, subsiding. "You're reminding me again that none of us really has much weight when it comes to those forces of yours."

A small bell tinkled from across the plaza, and Dahno raised his head and looked behind him.

"I've got to go," he said, rising abruptly to his feet.

As he strode away he looked back over his shoulder. His face was veiled and distant.

CHAPTER 33

Bleys lay on his bed in a Lima hotel room, in a darkness relieved only by the ceiling's artificial starscape. This ceiling was unusual, because it offered him not just a variety of clear sky settings, but also clouds; and he had chosen a sky that included the planet's moon, Luna, as a thin crescent passing between and behind occasional thin clouds.

This was the kind of sky his distant ancestors had slept under. He wondered what influence skies like this might have had on the way humanity developed; perhaps they encouraged people to wonder, to dream, to imagine.

It didn't help him sleep, though; and after a while he rose. Although his mind was churning with the need to articulate some of his thoughts, he was unable to write. He sat there for a long moment, looking at the piece of hotel stationery before him.

Was someone watching him, even now?

Since the day he realized that anyone with the proper equipment to penetrate his security could read his thoughts in his notes, he had not often indulged his habit of writing notes to his own memory, even though he always coded the notes as he wrote them. Any code could be broken eventually.

Still, the process had been soothing to him, as if it allowed him to get a grasp on situations his mind was having trouble dealing with.

His hand put the stylus back down, atop the paper. All the best hotels pledged that their rooms were checked frequently for spy devices; but hotels were not likely to be watching for someone as clever as Dahno. It did not escape Bleys' memory that it was Dahno who had made all of Bleys' travel arrangements.

Pulling on a casual evening suit, Bleys went down to the street, hoping to elude any surprised pursuit by hypothetical watchers. He pointed his wristpad at an automated taxi just dropping a fare at an entertainment facility down the block, calling it to him; and went to another luxury-class hotel. There he checked into a single room, explaining that his luggage would be along shortly and paying the bill in advance. Dahno would be able to trace his use of the credit chip, but not quickly enough to set up surveillance inside the room.

In the room, with a glass of ginger ale already forgotten at his elbow, he began to write.

I'm surprised to find that I still haven't figured out what Dahno is up to. I came to Old Earth suspecting him of clandestine dealings with some of my Others—dealings perhaps as simple as efforts to safeguard himself from possible future dangers. Those would not concern me overmuch: if Dahno, or others in the organization, want more power, more wealth, it doesn't matter, as long as it doesn't endanger my own plans.

The problem is, I have no way of determining what my brother's motives really are—because I can't rely on anything he lets me see.

I'm used to seeing my brother displaying reactions; in almost every case, they're covering his true motives, his real plans.

He can't ever be completely open—I think because he can never bring himself to trust anyone. His obsession with ensuring his own independence demands that he always have an ace in the hole—which means that no matter what motive or plan he may reveal, there's always a deeper layer.

When he tells me he merely wants to retire, and that he's no danger to my plans, it's only part of the truth. Which may as well be a lie.

He tells me he cares for me, his brother; I know he's telling the truth, but it's not the whole truth—he's shown before that in time of crisis he'll abandon me to save himself.

Bleys paused, rereading his encoded thoughts on the paper before him. He wondered if he had not just written an epitaph for a portion of his life.

For all that he alluded to a need to have some purpose in his life, I don't think Dahno has yet seen that the weakness in his character is that he has no goals, no purpose. In his deep-rooted selfishness, he lives only for the near-term; he thinks farther into the future only in terms of its potential for danger, and he has no room or time or concern for others.

I say this knowing full well that at times he has displayed generosity, and has even risked his life to help someone else. But my brother is a complex person, and while the cheerful, charming Dahno is a real person, so is the Dahno who cares only to get his own way, in everything.

He has always insisted that he's nothing like our mother, but in fact, he's very like her, and only seeks to gratify his own needs.

His needs are for autonomy, which requires power and wealth, and a challenge, a game he can play to test himself against life. He's too intelligent to be truly sybaritic, to be lured by fame, money, sex, or the more normal vices.

Perhaps it would be accurate to say that he's lured by the feeling that comes when one plays God. But at the same time, he's careful to avoid taking on so great a challenge that he'd be likely to lose. Losing isn't godlike.

In short, Dahno would like to live in a world in which he's perpetually manipulating people, sitting at the center of his spider's web and controlling events by the strings he pulls in secret. And he's too short-sighted to see that even that must grow wearying, eventually— and that there's nothing more behind it.

Without realizing the full implications of what I was doing, when I took control of the organization he had built, I took away his main tool. His only real choices were to contest my control, or move to a new field.

Old Earth may be that new field. He's leaving the Younger Worlds behind.

The problem for both of us is that Old Earth has to be involved in my plans.

Dahno wants his own kingdom of challenges and rewards. He feels like a god, and I'm the other god in the mix (he thinks; he doesn't believe in Hal Mayne). So I must represent a threat to him.

Bleys wrote on, the words pouring out from his subconscious, as if they had been penned in there. The bubbles in the ginger ale were slowing down.

Within his range, my brother is a deep thinker. He'll have planned well, and set up plans and sub-plans, layer upon layer—I may never know all the contingencies he's prepared for, all the details. But I see now why he was so diligent about carrying out that program of disinformation, by which I thought we were deceiving the Exotics, the Final Encyclopedia, and any other interested party, about our true origins and our intentions. Even years ago he was looking ahead, looking at the possibility he might want to bury his past in confusion and start over.

The muscles of his hand were tired and stiff from the precision with which he had formed the block capitals he generally used for his notes. He felt drained, as if he had managed to sweat some fever out of his system.

He leaned back in his chair and reached for the glass of ginger ale. It had gone flat, but he had written so quickly the ice had not completely melted. He drained the glass, feeling its coolness pass down his throat and pool in his stomach.

He rose from the chair and stretched, yawning in a release from tension. Suddenly he felt he could sleep. He fed the sheets of paper into the disposal slot, and turned to leave; and paused—and sat down once more, picking up another sheet.

I've missed writing these notes. Perhaps the stress of being isolated, in a dangerous situation, makes me need to do so again.

Until this evening, I had no trouble suppressing the habit. That may be due to my evolving relationship with Toni: I'm talking with her more and more—and with myself, less and less.

This suggests a potential problem. My resolve has always been that no emotional involvement or other human failing would be allowed to divert me from my life's work. Toni seems to have no intention of diverting me from that purpose, but the danger of that happening really lies less in her than in myself—the danger that I might let myself weaken.

I told her once I had moments of weakening. What I didn't tell her was that she was partly the cause of some of them.

It took this trip, with its separation from Toni, and Henry, and all the others who revolve around me—and the smell of danger—to open my eyes.

I tell myself there's no need to drive any of them away, that I'm strong enough to keep my inner self controlled—but am I deceiving myself with wishful thinking, when I say that?

I can trust Toni, and Henry. I can even trust Dahno, within limits.

It's myself I have to guard against.

Before he left the room, Bleys wrote another, shorter note—one he did not destroy. Rather, he folded it over several times; and then carried it with him as he descended to the street. He made two calls from a public terminal, one of which brought him another automated cab.

Back in front of his original hotel, the folded paper was lying on the floor of the cab as Bleys stepped out; and as he did so, a blond woman in evening dress hurried up to engage the cab. Bleys politely held the door for her before entering his hotel.

When Dahno showed up the following morning, Bleys insisted on going someplace where they could talk safely; and after a certain amount of verbal sparring, Bleys eventually found himself sitting on a patch of bare dirt in a small park, his back to the trunk of a large tree. A small part of his mind registered, and regretted, that it was not a palm tree, but he dismissed the thought.

Two meters in front of him Dahno, still on his feet, leaned against the back of an ancient stone monument, the meaning of which Bleys had not attempted to figure out. At one time the monument might have been the only feature standing out on this piece of ground, but the tree that had gained a start near it now overshadowed it completely, and under its branches, between its trunk and the monument, the brothers were, in effect, in a small room of their own.

Dahno had not been willing to sit on the ground; and in fact, Bleys thought, he looked uncomfortable even standing.

"Thanks for agreeing to talk, brother," Bleys said. "Can anyone overhear us?"

"How can *I* tell?" Dahno said, apparently sulking. "You insisted on finding a place neither of us could have rigged in advance, but that means none of our security gear is here."

"Except what we're both carrying," Bleys said. "I didn't want to risk trying to bring the Newtonians' bubble device through customs—but you know I was asking who you have out there."

"All right," Dahno said, after a short silence. "I do have people 'out there,' as you put it. I'm not sure how many actually managed to keep up with our movements, but I'm sure some made it, at least." He smiled wryly, and stood upright, as if he had forgotten his discomfort.

"I don't know where they are, though."

"Will you send them away?" Bleys asked.

"I don't think so," Dahno said, his eyes narrowing a little. Then he smiled again.

"You wouldn't believe me even if I said I would, so what's the point?" He laughed.

"Any more than I'll believe it if you tell me you don't have anyone out there," he went on, "so why don't we just get to it?"

"Because neither of us wants anyone else to hear what we're going to talk about," Bleys said.

For a long moment Dahno just looked across at Bleys, an abstracted look on his face—behind which, Bleys knew, his brother's mind was racing.

"I don't think I want to hear it," Dahno said, finally.

"I don't think you can afford not to," Bleys said. "You're too smart to turn down information."

"You've got information for me?"

"If you're willing to trade."

"Trade?" Dahno paused. "What do you want to know?"

"As a preliminary matter," Bleys said, "what happened to you when we were on Ceta?"

"I got shot!"

"I'm not talking about that," Bleys said. "I mean, when that armored car was burned, you tried to get those wounded soldiers out.

And then you came back into the line of fire to pick up that wounded soldier I'd been helping. . . ."

Dahno was silent.

"Tell me why," Bleys said finally.

"I don't remember why," Dahno said at last. "I barely remember it at all."

In California that night, in a hotel room he had picked, Bleys wrote his mind to himself once more.

He was lying. More to himself than to me.

I thought I knew my brother, and so I tried to pick at the motivations for his humane acts, figuring he might be disarmed, and reveal something more about himself. But there was another layer of him I hadn't seen before. I'd known for years that the Dahno who is a massive, jolly giant who cares for nobody, for nothing, was a mask, and that there were other Dahnos beneath it. But I never realized until today that those other Dahnos are tormented—tormented by the fact that they're *not* the uncaring giant.

Under stress, Dahno himself saw that the other Dahno was a fraud. And now he's having trouble finding out what he is.

There was no talking to him, after I pressed him.

CHAPTER 34

It was just after two in the morning when the small rivet in the underside of Bleys' wrist control pad extended itself from its socket, to press against his skin. It began to vibrate silently, but did so for less than three seconds before Bleys' right hand had reached across to stop it.

Before the rivet had retracted itself Bleys was moving across the bedroom of his hotel suite, seeing only by the light of the city's sky-glow beyond the windows. He snatched up a small cloth bag with twin handles as he moved through the lounge to the suite's main door.

He paused before the door only long enough to reach up and de-press a tiny button on a device he had earlier inserted into the socket of a wall-mounted light. The thin line of light at the bottom of the door vanished; and when he silently opened that door, the hallway was pitch black—not even the emergency lights were on.

He already knew how many paces would take him to the corner to his right; once there he turned and then opened the first door, which let him into the emergency stairwell. He knew that the stairs came down to the landing on one side, and continued downward on the other, but he wasn't concerned with that, but stepped straight forward, cautious in the darkness, until he bumped into the railing that shielded the long drop down the central part of the stairwell.

There he finally stopped long enough to reach into the bag and pull out, and don, trousers and a short-sleeved shirt. From the trouser pockets he pulled out gloves and slippers made of an unusual, plastic-feeling material, and he put them on as well. Slipping his arms through the straps of the cloth bag, so that he wore it like a miniature backpack, he reached out into the darkness before him and swept with both arms, as if trying to pull the air in toward his chest.

He was immediately rewarded as his right arm brushed something, and he quickly had both gloved hands on a light, thin cord that was dangling down the stairwell. He could not feel the cord itself through the gloves, but they reacted to the cord's touch by generating a sensation like a hot wire.

Bleys pulled the cord in to locate the hardened loop at its end. He gripped the cord with his left hand and pulled at the loop with his right, but he found no hint of weakness. He pulled down on the cord, hard; and got an answering tug.

Imagining the long, invisible drop before him, he refused to let himself pause, but swung his right leg over the railing; and guided his slippered foot into the loop, so that he was standing in it as if it were a stirrup.

Still straddling the railing, he straightened that leg while reaching above his head to twine the still-loose cord about his gloved right hand and through his fingers. As the cord took his weight, he lifted his left leg over the railing; and in a moment he was dangling silently in the darkness.

He reached out with his left hand, to grasp at the cord at a place above his right hand; and plucked at it as if it were a guitar string. The cord vibrated, and he felt the edge of fear; but he clamped down on himself harshly.

With his free left arm he reached out and found the side of the stairs that came down from above; and even as he did so, the stairs began to move upward under his fingers, telling him that the cord had begun to lower him. He had only his body's sense of space to tell him that he was moving, unless perhaps there was some faint passage of air across his skin.

Up to now he had been in constant motion since his abrupt awakening; but now he had nothing to do but hang in the silent darkness, and he found himself possessed by an urge to sneeze, to cough, even to yell—anything to make some kind of impression on the dark nothingness.

His shoulder brushed against something, and he was surprised by the depth of the relief that rose in him, at this fleeting touch of solidity. He realized he must be rotating as he dangled on the cord, and that he had brushed against the side of a set of stairs—but on which side, he could no longer tell.

He was not sure exactly how much open space there was between the courses of stairs that made their way to ground level; but it could not be much. He raised his free left arm again before his blind face, as a man walking in a dark forest at night will instinctively raise an arm to shield his eyes from unseen branches; and slowly extended it.

For a few long moments he felt nothing, and he had to force himself to refrain from lunging outward in an effort to find some sort of solid surface. But after a few more seconds his hand met a downward-sloping piece of metal, which he identified as the railing shielding another course of the stairs.

How far had he come? With the railing to touch, he could gauge his speed as fairly fast: already the rail was gone into the darkness above him, and his hand was grasping one of the vertical members that held it—there was a word for those things, what were they called? But that, too, slipped away from him in the darkness, and his hands bumped the edge of the stair before sliding down its side and finding nothing more to touch in the darkness.

He reached behind himself, somewhat awkwardly, and found an identical-feeling stair on the other side, this one slanting in the opposite direction, but at the same time slipping silently away above him. And so he found a routine, reaching eagerly for each new set of stairs as it rose to meet him; and losing them in the darkness, only to be replaced.

There came a moment when his hand, reaching out in the rhythm he had fallen into, found nothing but air. He reached out farther, thinking he might have twisted as he fell, and swept the hand about him; but there was nothing.

He quelled an impulse to activate the control that would light the face of his wrist control pad, knowing that the pulse he had sent out from his room would have killed the pad. His mind wanted to reproach him for not having brought some non-electronic light source; but he thrust those thoughts from him.

But he could not avoid thinking of the possibility that something had gone wrong, that he was still dangling in the darkness high above the floor of the stairwell. The cord he was suspended on was a monomolecular fiber—so strong it could easily carry his weight, but so thin he had to use the gloves to keep it from slicing through his flesh. Could it have damaged the descent mechanism, somehow?

Or had he reached the bottom? He simply could not tell.

He reached out with his free arm, sweeping it about him; but again he found nothing, and his movements set him rotating and swinging as he hung there, like some great pendulum . . . until the absurdity of that image made him control his body's frightened instincts.

—And there came a noise in the darkness, a kind of double-click and a tiny *creak*; and the stairwell, which up to that point had been totally silent, seemed now to explode into noise.

A door had opened, and through it came a buzz he recognized as the rising and falling of voices—voices that were generally angry, but now and then held a high pitch that spoke of fear.

As if that noise had broken a spell in the stairwell itself, he heard a thump high above him; and more voices began to echo down the stairwell.

Within seconds, more of the stairwell doors were thrown open. He hung in place, furious that he could no longer use his ears to try to discover what was happening about him. The hotel's guests, he supposed—those awake enough to have noticed the outage—had concluded there might be danger in this blackout, or perhaps they had simply been overtaken by an instinctive dread of the darkness. But he now had no way to tell whether the danger he had been sig-naled to run from might be pursuing him down the stairwell.

The lower half-dozen floors of the hotel were largely given over to businesses, which were presumably closed for the night; so if he had made it to the bottom of the stairwell, he had a few minutes before the guests from above could make their faltering ways down in the darkness.

He heard cries from above, and what sounded like a fight—and then a scream.

He shut his eyes. There was nothing to see in this darkness, but closing his eyes would help him concentrate.

He hung there, trying not to reach out, but only to receive. And

in a moment he felt a small stir of pleasure awakening inside him—
a pleasure that seemed to radiate from a source outside his body. He
recognized it as the kind of reaction his brain had been trained to
give when his tactile senses were detecting a nearby heat source.

His brain was registering the heat reaction the cord raised in the
glove that held it, but there was another source nearby—a human
body, silent in the darkness but surely there. Its presence gave him
a reference point against which to gauge his existence.

"Are you all right?" a voice asked softly. He recognized it. As instructed, the man was not using his name.

"Yes," Bleys answered, also keeping his voice low. The voices
from higher in the stairwell continued, coming slowly nearer. "I'm
not sure how far above the floor I am," he said.

The heat source strengthened on his left side, and in a moment a
hand touched his leg.

"You're about a meter above the floor," the voice said. "Put your
free foot in my cupped hands and you can step out of the loop and
let yourself down."

In a moment Bleys was solidly on the hard floor.

"Now close your eyes," his companion said; and Bleys had barely
done so before he heard a small *click*, and a flash of light penetrated
his eyelids like a bright bolt of lightning. Cries sounded from above
them.

"I broke the cord's molecular bonds," Bleys' unseen ally said in
explanation. "We need to go. I have light-enhancing goggles, but
they're not working very well in this stairwell; put a hand on my
shoulder and try to stay directly behind me. They'll already be
breaking out portable emergency lighting, which may or may not
have been affected by the pulse that killed the circuits; it'd be a
good idea to pass through the lobby before they do that."

"Do we have to pass through the lobby?" Bleys asked. "There
must be an emergency exit opening directly off this stairwell."

"We're heading for a side door," the other said. "We'd been planning on using the emergency exit, but it's too dangerous now."

"What's the danger?"

"Police," the other said. "They were setting out to block the
emergency exits just before the lights went out."

"Police?" Bleys said. "Why are they here? Is that the reason for the alarm?"

"We don't know why they came," the other said, "but Henry ordered us to take no unnecessary chances. But please, now—no more talking. I'm going to try to guide us past all the people stumbling around in the darkness, and while it won't surprise anybody to hear someone speaking nearby, your voice is very distinctive."

He chuckled.

"What?" Bleys asked.

"Sorry," the other said. "I was just thinking about all those people out in the lobby, stumbling around in the darkness and cursing—it reminds me of something I heard in church—here's the door: silence, now, unless you *have* to speak for some reason. And if you do speak, keep your voice as low as possible, and say as little as possible—and here we go."

His companion seemed to be a bit of an apostate, Bleys thought. It reassured him, with its implicit message of confidence.

The door opened.

All artificial lighting was out in a large area around the hotel, but once they were outside there was illumination from the city's lights, still on beyond the affected area. Bleys and his companion were met just outside the hotel. His first guide vanished, and Bleys found himself walking into the darkness between two shadowy forms. He was led away from the hotel through a parking lot and then across grass and between bushes and trees; once his face brushed a branch; he started at the touch, and the person in front of him apologized softly.

Noise was rising behind them, but they were well away from it; and now Bleys could see the lights of vehicles moving in streams on distant streets—vehicles that had evidently been far enough away to not be affected by the electromagnetic pulse, but were now moving into the affected area.

One vehicle turned their way, and Bleys instinctively started to duck to the side.

"It's all right," a voice said; "it's ours."

In moments Bleys was in the back of a silent float vehicle, its lights dimmed as it moved through a park toward an area where the nighttime lights were still on; until at last, turning on its lights, it slid over the edge of a trafficway to join the stream of vehicles. The lights in this area were on; and, looking back, Bleys could see what appeared to be a pocket of blackness surrounded by the city's night lights.

In another twenty minutes they reached a private landing pad, where the float drove right up to the side of a space-capable shuttle. As the vehicle settled to the ground, and the panel separating Bleys from the driver's compartment opened, a face he knew smiled at him: the face of one of Henry's Soldiers.

"The shuttle will take you up to a low-orbit transit station, sir," the Soldier said. "You'll get there in time to board a jitney that'll take you to High Africa—that's a high-orbit station—where you can catch a ride to your ship. Everything you need's in this packet—" She passed it over to Bleys. "But—" She stopped.

"Well?" Bleys said, after a moment.

"Sorry," the Soldier said. "I'm getting a message—you need to get on board right away."

"I was told it was police who came after me," Bleys said. "Do you know why they'd be interested in me?"

"No," the Soldier said. "We alerted you as soon as John saw them arrive and begin blocking exits."

It had been John Colville's voice that Bleys had recognized in the stairwell.

"Then you don't know it was me they were after?" Bleys asked.

"No, sir," she said.

"But Henry's people take no chances," Bleys said, a little grimly. He wondered if he had not made that long drop in the darkness to no purpose.

They had reached the ramp at the shuttle's side, and the Soldier lifted a hand to an ear, listening; and then smiled.

"Our people say the police have made their way to your floor," she said. "You need to be in the air before an alarm goes out."

———

Rather than making his way through the corridors of High Africa, Bleys had the jitney's crew call for a shuttle to meet the craft as it docked. It was not so unusual a request as to raise suspicion: any traveler well-off enough to be embarking on an interstellar voyage would likely also be both able to afford the cost of a little extra service, and in a hurry to make a connection.

Thus, while the rest of the jitney's passengers made their way through the craft's main passenger hatch, now securely docked at the station's main concourse, Bleys was climbing down through a smaller hatch in the jitney's belly, to which the shuttle he had called for had locked itself. It took only a few moments for Bleys to give the shuttle driver the data for the orbital slot that *Favored of God*—once again traveling under a false name—was parked in; and they were undocked and on their way before the last of the jitney's other passengers had reached the concourse.

Wary of the possibility that any radioed message might be intercepted, Bleys had not spoken directly to *Favored of God* himself, but only had the shuttle driver call ahead to tell the ship that one of her passengers was coming aboard—Bleys had been provided with a false identity, and that was the name the driver gave to *Favored of God*.

Despite his discretion, Bleys found himself greeted by Captain Anita Broadus herself, her beaming dark countenance appearing, to his eyes, very like an emblem of safety. He could not prevent himself from smiling back.

"Great Teacher, it is so good to see you." The captain's voice fairly boomed throughout the entry corridor. "We were all hoping, when we were sent here, that we would be able to help you in some way!"

"Why, Captain," Bleys said, "surely you know by now that wherever you're sent, it's for our work?"

"That is my wish, of course, Great Teacher, and that of all my crew. But you must forgive me: Antonia Lu and Henry MacLean never tell us more than we must know to carry out our task, and in the times of silent waiting—as we have waited quietly in this boring orbit for three weeks now—sometimes we feel we are pushed to the side and forgotten. But please do not misunderstand me, Great Teacher—we are always faithful!"

"Of course you are!" Bleys said. "But everyone's mind plays the devil's tricks on them in those hours when there's nothing to do but wait. My uncle Henry will tell you that's the very time when faith and courage are most needed."

"And most hard to find," the captain said. "It can be a hard lesson."

'That's so," Bleys said. "I think you're aware that you're sometimes sent off to wait because I foresee the possibility of some need for you. But you must steel yourself to the fact that sometimes that need simply will not come about, and you'll be unused. But that doesn't mean the trip was taken for nothing. Simply in knowing you're near while I undertake some important work, I'm comforted."

The captain's smile blossomed once more, belying the seriousness of their conversation.

"Come, Great Teacher—would you like to rest? Or perhaps a meal? What would you like?" Without really waiting for a reply, the captain waved a hand, and a young crewwoman stepped out of the background, all but coming to attention at the captain's side.

"Shira will take you to your quarters, Great Teacher," the captain said. Although her words were a simple statement to Bleys, they were clearly an order for the crewwoman.

"Have there been any messages for me, Captain?" Bleys asked; and the crewwoman, who had already turned away, stopped, looking over her shoulder.

"Nothing by radio, of course, Great Teacher," the captain said. "But we've had four courier deliveries in the weeks we've been here. They await you in the same lounge you used before, and your stateroom is nearby."

She waved the crewwoman on her way, and Bleys followed.

By the time Bleys had worked his way through the messages, Shira had reappeared. Perhaps emboldened by some prodding from the captain, she was carrying a tray laden with a large meal and several beverage containers.

As she silently put the tray down on the desk, Bleys looked at it distrustfully; but then his nostrils picked up the scent of some tangy spice, and he suddenly realized he was starving.

He looked up at Shira—she was short enough that he did not have to look very far up—and she interrupted her silent backing away.

"Did you prepare this, Shira?" he asked.

"Yes, Great Teacher," she said, her voice tiny in the large room.

"You're new on *Favored of God*, are you not?"

"Yes, Great Teacher," she said again. "I graduated from the crew training facility at New Earth City two months ago, and the captain hired me for my first job."

"I think you're originally from one of the Friendlies?" he asked. "Your voice tells me so."

"I was raised on Harmony by my grandparents after my mother and father died," she said. "But I was born on Mara and spent the first part of my life there."

"I'm sorry to hear about your parents," he said. "Would you tell me what happened to them?"

"They were killed in a trafficway accident on Freiland," she said. "They were on leave from their ship."

"And you decided to go into their profession?"

"Yes," she said, her brown eyes shining a little. "The crew of the *Sombok* became like family to me, and helped raise me." She smiled. "Captain Broadus was one of them, although only a junior officer at the time, and that's why she hired me."

"You've come to the right ship," Bleys said, nodding seriously. "The captain will turn you into a veteran."

"Yes, Great Teacher."

"You prepared this, you said," he continued, looking down at the large plate in the center of the tray. It had a cover that prevented him from seeing the dish that awaited him, but an exotic aroma was rapidly filling the room. "What is it?"

"It's a curried lamb dish, Great Teacher," she said. Then she blushed. "It's from a recipe of my family, but I've changed it a little."

"I see you brought me coffee, orange juice and water," Bleys said. "Are those appropriate to drink with your dish?"

Shira blushed again, but smiled.

"Perhaps the Great Teacher would like a glass of beer?" she said. "Tea is traditional with curry, but in my family, we find that a good Japanese-style beer sets off the flavor of the spices very well."

"Would you get me one, then?" he asked.

She did.

CHAPTER 35

The elderly shuttle had been ordered to hold its distance from the Final Encyclopedia; there was other traffic. But the driver had his hands full doing so, because the Encyclopedia was no ordinary satellite.

Of all the artificial satellites orbiting Old Earth, only the Final Encyclopedia spent the energy to hold itself in an unnatural sort of geosynchronous orbit.

Properly placed, satellites falling in their orbits about a planet could remain, seemingly stationary, above a fixed point on the ground below. But the laws of physics dictated that a satellite could occupy such a geostationary position only if its orbit followed the planet's equator.

The Final Encyclopedia, however, held a fixed position above a point in Earth's northern hemisphere; and it did so only because it constantly used drive engines to counter the demands of the laws of physics.

Bleys knew that the fixed point the Encyclopedia hung above was the location of the estate where the boy Hal Mayne had been raised. And that knowledge haunted the Other.

The day after he learned that fact, Bleys had gone to the Mayne estate, at Dahno's orders, to take it over for use as the site of the first meeting of the Others' top leaders—a visit that turned into disaster when the boy's three elderly tutors were killed. The boy himself had vanished, running from the only home he had known since, at the age of two, he had been found, alone, on a spaceship drifting near Old Earth.

As his shuttle strained to remain in place near the Final Encyclopedia, Bleys looked out a port at the mother planet. She was close, and she was beautiful, a ball of blue draped with white swirls that crept from under the black crescent of the planet's own shadow.

Bleys had never been able to learn why the Encyclopedia was held in its unusual, and so particular, orbit. The satellite's staff had never explained its positioning, and he could find no logical justification for the effort.

He had speculated that the Encyclopedia might have been placed there so it could keep an eye on the boy. But that made no sense: the Final Encyclopedia had gone to its place about seventy-five years before Hal Mayne was even born.

As for the converse of that idea—that the boy had been purposely placed in a position to be raised directly beneath the Encyclopedia—he could find neither a reason for doing so, nor any indication that the boy's guardians had sought to arrange it.

When Bleys had discovered that strange quasi-connection between the boy and the legendary orbiting institution, he had examined the public records. He had learned that the land on which the Mayne estate sat, after being the site of a series of hobby ranches and recreational resorts for more than two hundred years, had been purchased by a Europe-based investment bank—more than fifty years before Hal Mayne's birth and well after the day the Final Encyclopedia had achieved its orbit. The land had then remained unused until it was sold to the trust that had been set up for the boy out of the proceeds of the sale of the ship in which he was found.

That trust had been organized in accordance with unsigned instructions found on the ship, and was overseen by directors appointed by designated financial institutions, government bodies, and humanitarian groups—none of whom seemed to have any connection at all with the Final Encyclopedia.

It was the kind of story that begged the listener to make up some sort of mystical relationship between the boy and the satellite. Bleys had no belief in mystical relationships—but he also had nothing to offer in their place.

That was only the first of the strangenesses that had led him to see in Hal Mayne—as boy and later as man—an opponent to be respected—

"Sir," the driver's voice interrupted his musings, "I have the Encyclopedia for you. Switch the intercom to channel *C* and I'll put her through."

"Thank you," Bleys said; and reached to the intercom mounted on the bulkhead in front of him. He pushed the plastic button marked *C;* it seemed to stick for a moment—like the shuttle, this intercom was elderly—but then he heard a *click*—

"This is Orbital Communications, the Final Encyclopedia," a young-sounding soprano voice said. "We're told you have a request."

"Thank you for speaking to me," Bleys said. "My name is Bleys Ahrens, and I'd like to speak with Hal Mayne—I understand he's presently working in the Encyclopedia."

"I will advise Hal Mayne you wish to speak with him, Bleys Ahrens. Please stand by."

"Wait!" Bleys said.

"Yes?"

"I should have been more specific," Bleys said. "What I'd like is permission to meet Hal Mayne in person, there in the Final Encyclopedia. Would you ask him if he'll agree to that?"

"I'll ask him," the voice said. "Please have your shuttle maintain its position."

The voice keyed off without waiting for his reply.

Bleys sat back in his seat, away from the intercom he had unconsciously leaned into while speaking. The voice had been pleasant and polite, blending innocence with competence; and he thought he could, sight unseen, almost draw a portrait of the speaker.

The vast majority of the populations of the Younger Worlds would never listen to voices like that. Voices like that, or other contact with the human people inside the Final Encyclopedia, would negate the propaganda campaign that was portraying the Final Encyclopedia to the Younger Worlds as an inhuman institution working to craft superweapons to be used against the Younger Worlds. The Final Encyclopedia, it was said, hid behind its phase-shield to conceal its part in a grand conspiracy that included Old Earth, the Exotics and the Dorsai; a conspiracy aimed at robbing Old Earth's former colonies of their freedoms.

If the Final Encyclopedia had no hidden purpose, it was asked, why did it need a shield that, using the same physics that allowed interstellar travel, would disintegrate any physical object that touched it, scattering its component subatomic parts evenly throughout the Universe?

The message was, so far, being spread quietly, in unofficial forms and in subtle terms; but it was effective, at least among a small minority. A simplistic view of history, after all, supported fears of such a conspiracy: Old Earth had certainly tried, several times in the past, to dominate the Younger Worlds; and every planet had near-mythical stories about the fearsome Dorsai men of war and the crafty Exotics.

It did not concern Bleys that the majority of the Younger Worlds' populations had not yet bought into the rumors; over time the minority voices would get louder, until the unpersuaded were run over, stampeded or intimidated by fears of being labeled unpatriotic.

The Younger Worlds, without quite realizing it, were well on their way to being prepared for war. Economic structures were being altered and assets appropriated. Recruitment of military personnel, although it had plateaued of late, would soon be phased out; the mechanisms for large-scale conscription were even now being put in place on those worlds that did not already have such.

Most of the populations as yet had no idea what was going on; control of the media and governments prevented reporting of the more sensitive news, or of any significant analysis.

Many of his Others had found it difficult to understand that it was not necessary that a majority of their worlds' populations actually believe the propaganda. All that was required, he had explained, was that those unconvinced of the reality of the conspiracy and the superweapons become apprehensive—which they would if they heard no contradicting voices. Afraid of the consequences if their skeptical instincts were wrong, they would see little harm in supporting enhanced defensive measures; that was all that would be needed. Fear and hatred, even if limited to a minority, would cow many of the potentially dissenting voices, who could not stomach setting themselves up to be denounced as traitors.

Now only a small portion of Old Earth could be seen from the viewport. Bleys hoped the young voice he had spoken to would not be killed when the end came for the Final Encyclopedia. . . . The shuttle's slow movement had been altering his view of the mother planet; he didn't mind: he could see a small portion of the vast sea of stars.

It was slightly less than two minutes more before the driver told Bleys that the Final Encyclopedia was calling for him.

"This is Bleys Ahrens."

"This is the Final Encyclopedia," a voice said. It was not the young soprano he had spoken with before, but a slightly more mature, but still female, alto voice.

"Hal Mayne says he'll see you, Bleys Ahrens," the new voice continued. "We'll advise your driver when we have an opening, and you'll be vectored into Bay One. Someone will meet you there."

"Thank you," Bleys said. He registered a slight uncomfortableness at not addressing, in a more polite fashion, the person who had spoken to him; but she had not given her name.

No matter.

He was committed, now. He felt relief.

He had called for a hired shuttle to pick him up from *Favored of God*, on a kind of whim, and he had been wondering whether he was making a silly mistake.

It's never a mistake to scout out your opponent, he reminded himself. *It's been well over a year since we met in that prison cell, and I need every chance I can get to learn what might be going on in that boy's head.*

After all, he was nearby anyway.

As Bleys stepped out of the shuttle's lock, the bay was quieter than he had expected. He looked around, wondering what it would take to get a complete tour of this huge technological wonder—and quashed the notion, irritated at himself for being weak enough to be taken by the same fascination with toys that had led the race too quickly into space. It might be better to simply destroy this place, rather than try to control it; it was too tempting.

The lights high up in the walls were bright and harsh to his eyes, glaring at him as he began to walk down the ramp. Against the glare he could make out a figure apparently waiting for him on the bay floor. Other figures were moving about, but none seemed to be paying him any attention.

The person waiting for him, he found, was a woman, small, and probably in her thirties, with black hair framing a faintly oriental face. She wore clean-looking lime green work coveralls that fit as if tailored, and black, slipperlike ankle boots.

"Bleys Ahrens?" she asked. It was the alto voice he had spoken with from the shuttle.

"Yes," he said, nodding politely.

"My name is Chuni Maslow," she said. "Hal Mayne asked me to take you to him. Would you follow me, please?"

She turned and led the way to a hatch, which opened itself at her touch on its controls. Stepping through behind her, Bleys found himself in a corridor much like those in good hotels on Old Earth. It seemed to be wallpapered in a motif of white flowers—not roses, he thought, but something showier, elongated—on pale yellow. It lightened the effect of the royal blue carpeting.

He knew, from his reading, that this corridor was a unit, a movable piece that could be maneuvered about within the vast interior of the satellite. It had probably been set in motion as soon as the door closed behind them, and by the time they walked to the other doorway, the corridor itself would have reached their destination and attached itself there. But he felt no movement.

At the second doorway, Chuni operated the control pad, and the door opened.

"Hal Mayne asks that you wait here in comfort," she said. "He won't be long."

"Certainly," Bleys said, nodding.

Out of habit, he ducked his head in the doorway, but he did not need to do so.

The room appeared to be a simple, comfortably furnished, lounge. He explored it briefly, as any innocent visitor would, and found that both food and drink were available from mechanisms in the walls. A video screen provided entertainment and news channels, and he could see control pads that indicated the availability of communications.

He did not try any of the controls, settling for a glass of fruit juice. He chose the sofa as a seat, since it was larger than any of the chairs.

As he sat, he examined his interior state, and found that he was a little on edge. He began to practice some of his silent breath-control exercises.

In just over ten minutes the door opened, and Chuni Maslow appeared, framed by the portal but not coming in.

"If you'll follow me," she said, "I'll take you to Hal Mayne."

Bleys rose and stepped back through the doorway, this time stopping himself from ducking his head.

He found himself in a different corridor, this one paneled in dark red wood above a pale yellow carpet that showed no sign of soil.

I wonder if those fools who used to run Newton ever came here? They wanted so much to impress people with how advanced they were.

Even as he had that thought, they had reached the next doorway, and Chuni was operating its control pad.

"Here you are, Bleys Ahrens . . . ," she said, as the door opened. At her gesture he stepped into the room ahead of her; and, seeing Hal Mayne, he lost track of the woman until the door had closed behind him.

The figure before him was undeniably Hal Mayne, but it was not the young man he had seen, sick and exhausted, on the too-small bed in that prison cell. At that meeting, Bleys had been surprised to see that Hal Mayne, the boy he had never met, had grown into a man; now he had the feeling he was meeting with a completely different person.

Although tall, the person in that cell had been still a boy. But all of Bleys' instincts told him the figure before him now was that of a full-grown adult male—full-grown in every way.

He stood as tall as Bleys, but with massive shoulders and chest that made Bleys feel suddenly smaller; yet the difference from the boy in the cell went beyond size. This man gave an instant impression of being older than Bleys was. Bleys was disconcerted: how could that boy could have become so different in less than two years?

Bleys could not remember a time when he had not been aware that there was a part of himself, that he thought of as being in the back of his mind, that perpetually monitored his actions and his thoughts, helping him control his emotions and instincts. Now, he suddenly realized, it had shut down—vanished; at least it seemed that way, because he was suddenly being flooded by feelings of rage. He suppressed it with harsh willpower, telling himself it was simply the instinctual response usual to a large male unexpectedly confronted with a larger one.

Fear?

He was shocked as the notion came to him. Anger, like many other emotions, usually arose out of the body's fear reaction; but he had never thought that might apply to him.

He was abruptly, absurdly conscious of how his own appearance contrasted with that of the man before him. He had spent years cultivating the picture he presented to his audiences, and he knew his tall, lean body, clad in a short, black jacket, and gray trousers tapering into black boots, presented a dramatic image that focused attention on him, making it easier for him to get his message through to audiences.

Hal Mayne presented an entirely different sort of figure; but somehow, in his simple, utilitarian silver-gray coverall, that difference failed to detract from the fact that his body, his face—even his attitude—presented an icon of power and strength that must awaken a large number of instinctive responses in those who saw him.

People will listen to him, too.

As Hal took a step forward, Bleys found his voice.

"Well," he said, "you've grown up."

"It happens," said Hal. His voice, too, was more mature, deeper and controlled. But it was distant. There was a strange moment of silence as they stood facing each other. Bleys was acutely aware of the ceiling over both their heads; he'd been used to being closer to ceilings than other people, but now, with Hal's own height so near, that sense of closeness became uncomfortable.

Hal's face showed no emotion at all. That, too, was an indicator of how the boy had changed. Bleys had, he knew now, been expecting to meet that same youngster, and to find him still prey to the emotional volatility of young men; but he had been badly wrong.

Even as he had that thought, he saw a slight change in the features of the man before him, as if a momentary shadow had passed over his soul . . . that face, too—something about it rang the bell of some distant familiarity. . . .

He dismissed the thought, reminding himself that this man must still remember the first time they had impinged on each other's lives; Hal Mayne would never be able to see Bleys without remembering his tutors, killed on the terrace of their home. Perhaps one day he could be brought to see it was not Bleys' doing.

To cover the moment, he turned and stepped over to the desk Hal had just left. It was a float desk, apparently made of a reddish wood that concealed the metal frame of its technology.

The room appeared to be an office, but it seemed unusually bare. Half a dozen float chairs were scattered about, some with high, winged backs covered in an antique gold floral pattern on a muted dark red field. They seemed incongruous against the off-white walls and neutral-colored floor—unless this was one of those technologically enhanced spaces that could be commanded to change its color and shape as easily as the lighting, one which had been put into neutral settings.

Intelligent! He's not giving away any clues.

He felt a new sadness: for all that he had prepared himself, mentally, to find Hal Mayne an enemy, he regretted that the young man saw him as a predator.

It was Hal Mayne who looked the predator, Bleys reminded himself. . . . Again he felt that tiny ring of familiarity, even as he pivoted to sit down on the edge of the desk.

He turned his attention back to Hal, who had himself turned, as smoothly as a trained athlete, even as Bleys moved to the desk.

How could he have changed so much, so fast?

"A big change to take place in a year," Bleys said. Sitting on the desk, he was now looking upward at Hal. The angle gave him a slightly different perspective on the younger man's face, bringing out the strength of the chin and opening the caves of his eyes, under the heavy brows, to better view.

Without a word, Hal moved back past him, returning to his chair and forcing Bleys to swivel. Now Bleys was looking down on his host, although not at a great angle.

He doesn't care. He's beyond size games.

"The biggest change took place in that Militia cell in Ahruma, in the day or two after you left me," Hal said, responding to Bleys' comment of a moment before. "I had a chance to sort things out in my mind."

"Under an unusual set of conditions," Bleys said. He had to look sideways, from where he sat, to see Hal fully. "That captain deliberately misinterpreted what I told him."

"Amyth Barbage—have you forgotten his name?" Hal said. For all the sharpness of the words, the tone in which they were uttered was not accusatory. "What did you do to him, afterward?"

"Nothing," Bleys said. "It was his nature to do what he did. Any blame there was, was mine, for not understanding that nature, as I should have. I don't do things to people, in any case. My work is with events."

"You don't do anything to people? Even to those like Dahno?"

For a very short second Bleys was startled into wondering just how much Hal knew of the workings of the Others' organization; then he shook his head, both in answer to Hal and in denial of that concern.

"Even to those like Dahno," Bleys answered. "Dahno may have created the conditions that could lead to his destruction. All I did was give the Others an alternative plan; and in refusing to consider it, Dahno put himself in other hands than mine. As I say, I work with larger matters than individual people."

"Then why come see me?" As Hal said those words, Bleys finally put his finger on something else that had been bothering him about this whole meeting: Hal Mayne was being entirely too still.

It was not, Bleys thought now, the stillness of someone trying to be motionless; rather, it was the utter stillness one sometimes found in the very old, or the very wise—a stillness of simple waiting.

"Because you're a potential problem," said Bleys. He felt almost removed from his own answer, as if his mind were trying to deal with another concern and letting his body speak on its own. He didn't like that image, and made himself smile, trying to become more immediately engaged.

"Because I hate the waste of a good mind—ask my fellow Others if I don't—and because I feel an obligation to you."

And even as he said it, he knew his answer, while true, was not complete, and he felt a small twinge of shame.

CHAPTER 36

This meeting was not going as he had expected. He had thought the encounter would be an emotional event, one he would be able to direct with his superior experience. Almost always, in the past, he had been able to find the things that really motivated people—things hidden deep inside them—and use those needs to lead those possessed by them. But in the face of Hal Mayne's imperturbability and self-control, he had so far been unable to find the handle that put the man in a ready frame of mind.

"And because you have no one else to talk to," said Hal, responding to Bleys' statement of a moment before.

For a bare fraction of a second something seemed to turn over in Bleys' chest, as if his long-dead hope of friendship had abruptly raised its head.

No, that could not be; not with our history. Bleys quashed his reaction fiercely. Was Hal being clever, trying to manipulate Bleys' own emotions—did he recognize Bleys' tactics, and seek to turn them back on Bleys himself?

Was he even more like Bleys than Bleys had known?

Bleys put on a smile that denied weakness.

"That's very perceptive of you," he said. He kept his voice soft, concealing the effect of Hal's words. "But you see, I've never had anyone to talk to; and so I'm afraid I wouldn't know what I was missing. As for what brings me here, I'd like to save you if I could. Unlike Dahno, you can be of reliable use to the race."

"I intend to," said Hal.

"No." Bleys' control almost deserted him once more—this time out of fury. Fury that this man, whose similarity to Bleys teased him, should be at the same time so persistent in his wrongness.

"What you intend," Bleys said, "is your own destruction—very much like Dahno. Are you aware the struggle in which you've chosen to involve yourself is all over but the shouting? Your cause isn't only lost; it's already on its way to being forgotten."

"And you want to save me?"

"I can afford what I want," Bleys said. "But in this case, it's not a matter of my saving you, but of you choosing to save yourself. In a few standard years an avalanche will have swallowed up all you now think you want to fight for. So, what difference will it make if you stop fighting now?"

"You seem to assume," said Hal, "that I'm going to stop eventually."

"Either stop, or—forgive me—be stopped," said Bleys. "The outcome of this battle you want to throw yourself into was determined before you were born."

"No," said Hal, slowly, "I don't think it was."

The ember of anger in Bleys continued to grow, fanned by Hal's stubborn refusal to see the obvious. He was just like his tutors, Bleys thought—particularly the Exotic, the one who had been reading poetry.

"I understand you originally had an interest in being a poet," he said. The memory of that poetry-loving tutor reminded him again of his search of the boy's house—the search in which Bleys had come upon the boy's handwritten poetry.

"I had inclinations to art, too, once," Bleys said. "Before I found it wasn't for me. But poetry can be a personally rewarding lifework. Be a poet, then. Put this other aside. Let what's going to happen, happen; without wasting yourself trying to change it."

Hal only shook his head, at first; but then gave a longer answer:

"I was committed to this, only this, long before you know," he said.

Bleys was disappointed that this man, of whom he had come to expect so much, should indulge in childish melodrama, repeating lines straight out of old novels.

Or, was he? Maybe that answer was deeper than it appeared. Bleys reminded himself of the need not to underestimate this man. Give him the benefit of the doubt, and try another key in the lock that led to his motivations.

"I'm entirely serious in what I say," Bleys said. He was sure Hal would not be persuaded, but possibly he could be brought to explain himself a little more, giving Bleys something to read meaning into.

"Stop and think," he continued, trying to put into the words all of his persuasiveness. If there was any doubt inside this man at all, any desire to avoid what he must surely recognize would be a disastrous war, he must be brought around to seeing the certainty within Bleys—must be made to feel unsure, hesitant . . . enough that he might want to be freed of that burden.

"What good is it going to do to throw yourself away? Wouldn't it be better, for yourself and all the worlds of men and women, that you should live a long time and do whatever you want to do— whether it's poetry or anything else? It could even be something as immaterial as saying what you think to your fellow humans; so that something of yourself will have gone into the race and be carried on to enrich it after you're gone. Isn't that a far better thing than committing suicide because you can't have matters just as you want them?"

"I think," said Hal, "we're at cross-purposes. What you see as inevitable, I don't see so at all. What you refuse to accept can happen, I know can happen."

Bleys shook his head, the disappointment rising up once more. Could the man really be so blind?

"You're in love with a sort of poetic illusion about life," Bleys said. "And it is an illusion, even in a poetic sense; because even poets—good poets—come to understand the hard limits of reality. Don't take my word for that. What does Shakespeare have Hamlet say at one point . . . *'How weary, stale, flat, and unprofitable seem to me all the uses of this world'*?"

Hal was smiling, and for a brief moment Bleys felt a small fear. He quelled the sudden memory, of how his attempt to quote poetry to Hal's tutor had blown up in his face.

"Do you know Lowell?" Hal asked.

"Lowell? I don't believe so." The name sounded like something out of North America, Bleys thought. Where could Hal be going with this?

"James Russell Lowell," Hal explained. "Nineteenth-century American poet." And he seemed to rise a little in his chair as he spoke a few lines:

> *"When I was a beggarly boy,*
> *And lived in a cellar damp,*
> *I had not a friend nor a toy,*
> *But I had Aladdin's lamp. . . ."*

Bleys felt as if he had been hit in the pit of his stomach. Hal only sat there watching him, as within himself Bleys struggled to control the sudden welter of emotions the words had evoked.

"You've been researching my childhood, I see," Bleys said. It seemed to him as if it had taken a long time to get himself under enough control to say the words without unwelcome emphasis. Somehow, he thought, this man knew him—knew his past, knew the virtual captivity of the years with his mother . . . but that could not be: Dahno had long ago altered the historical records—and even if some correct record remained somewhere, how could it tell the sort of life that had been imposed on a young boy twenty years ago?

Could Hal Mayne somehow see so deeply into Bleys, as to be able to pick up that hidden hurt?

Or—the idea sprang suddenly into his mind—had Hal been talking with Dahno? Had they come to some agreement? Was that why Hal had mentioned Dahno, earlier?

Instinctively, Bleys rejected that idea; but he recognized it had shaken him.

It was time to leave.

He got to his feet, seeing Hal stand at the same time.

"You're better at quoting poetry than I am," Bleys said. He regretted the words instantly, but could think of no way to recall them.

"I think," he said finally, "that those events that took place at your estate keep you from listening to me now. So I believe I'll have to accept the fact I can't save you. So I'll go. What is it you've found here at the Encyclopedia—if anything—if I may ask?"

He suspected Hal recognized his victory; and forced himself to meet the other man's eyes, as if denying any such result.

"As one of my tutors would have said," Hal answered, "that's a foolish question."

Bleys went cold once more . . . had the boy somehow been close enough to that terrace to overhear his conversation with the boy's tutors? Those were the exact words the ancient Exotic had said— no, that was impossible.

"Ah," said Bleys. The syllable felt lame even to his own ears.

He turned and began moving toward the door, feeling loss and pain rising up in him. Somehow, this man had been too clever for him, had beaten him back at every turn. It was his own fault; he had gone into this insufficiently prepared.

At that moment, Hal's voice came once more from behind him. And the voice was vastly different—younger, somehow.

"How did it happen?"

Bleys stopped and looked back over his shoulder; then turned.

"Of course," he said. He felt, suddenly, a desire to reach out to the younger man before him; a desire that had not been in him only a moment before, and which was followed almost immediately by a determination to quell the stir of sympathy within him . . . in the same moment he recognized he might have been presented with a way to penetrate Hal's armor.

"You'd like to know more, would you? I should have seen to your being informed before. Well, I'll tell you now, then." He paused, collecting his thoughts and planning how his next words could carry the connotations he wanted.

"The men we normally use to go before us in situations like that had found two of your tutors already on that terrace, and the third was brought to join them a minute or two after I stepped out onto the terrace myself. It was the Friendly they brought. The Dorsai and your Walter the InTeacher were already there. Like you, he seemed to be fond of poetry, and as I came out of the library window, he was quoting from that verse drama of Alfred Noyes, *Sherwood*. The lines he was repeating were those about how Robin Hood had saved one of the fairies from what Noyes called The Dark Old Mystery. I quoted him Blondin's song, from the same piece of writing, as a stronger piece of poetry. Then I asked him where you were; and he told me he didn't know—but of course he did. They all knew, didn't they?"

"Yes," said Hal. "They knew."

"It was that which first raised my interest in you above the ordinary," Bleys said. There was no point in letting the man know that Bleys had researched him. "It intrigued me. Why should they be so concerned to hide you? I'd told them no one would be hurt; and they would have known my reputation for keeping my word."

He paused for a second.

"They were quite right not to speak, of course," he added softly. The admission burned in him, but he felt compelled to make it . . . he knew now he betrayed nothing by telling the truth, this time.

Hal Mayne gave him no sign.

"At any rate," Bleys continued, "I tried to bring them to like me, but of course they were all of the old breed—and I failed. That intrigued me even more, that they should be so firmly recalcitrant; and I was just about to make further efforts, which might have worked, to find out from them about you, when your Walter the InTeacher physically attacked me—a strange thing for an Exotic to do."

"Not—under the circumstances," Hal said, a peculiar emphasis in his voice.

"Of course, that triggered off the Dorsai and the Friendly," Bleys went on, watching closely now for the reactions that might come with the climax of his report.

"Together, they accounted for all but one of the men I had watching them; but of course, all three of them were killed in the process. Since there was no hope of questioning them, then, I went back into the house. Dahno had just arrived; and I didn't have the leisure to order a search of the grounds for you, after all."

"I was in the lake," Hal said. "Walter and Malachi Nasuno—the Dorsai—signaled me when they guessed you were on the grounds. I had time to hide in some bushes at the water's edge. After . . . I came up to the terrace and saw you and Dahno through the window of the library."

"Did you?" Bleys' response was almost perfunctory. Suddenly he felt dull, exhausted, as if he had expended all his energy in some burst of effort.

The two of them stood there silently, just facing each other; and at last Bleys shook his head, recognizing finality.

"So it had already begun between us, even then?" he said. It was not really a question.

Bleys turned to open the door; and stepped through it. In the corridor, he tiredly forced himself to be gentle as he closed the door behind him.

No one was in the corridor, but when he got to the door at its far end, that door opened on the entry bay; and the woman who had escorted him before took him to his shuttle. He managed to thank her politely, and then to direct his driver to return him to *Favored of God*. But those were the only words he said for some time.

As the misty, silver-gray orb of the Final Encyclopedia dwindled behind, and now above, his shuttle, Bleys pulled his eyes away from the sight. He wanted to think, but it was as if the phase-shield panels that protected the satellite also fractured his thoughts, breaking them into tiny bits that scattered about the Universe, beyond recall.

What was it about Hal Mayne that had such an effect on him? He had known there was something unusual about the boy, and had come to believe the man had the potential to become a friend of the sort that might alleviate his perpetual loneliness. But he could not explain why he felt that way, any more than he could explain the mystery of Hal's childhood beneath the Final Encyclopedia.

The only similar feeling Bleys had ever had in his life had come on a day long ago when he began to discover the works of the great artists and writers of the past. For a while he had believed he had found a bond with them, dead people who had once lived lives made full and rich by their unique abilities; was he recognizing a similar talent in Hal Mayne? Was that what drew him?

Did Hal still write poetry, he wondered? Or had he set it aside to deal with the dangerous realities of the universe? Or, indeed, had Bleys' own actions killed that seed in the boy?

Bleys thought not. He found it unlikely he could kill anything at all in Hal Mayne, beyond his body . . . far from killing the seed of artistry, might he not have strengthened the character of the artist?

Still thinking, he absently reached out to raise the shutter over the viewport—to open himself once more to the stars. If Hal still wrote poetry, a look at it might tell Bleys a great deal about the changes that had come upon the boy. Or perhaps Hal still painted—there had been some primitive examples of that art, too, in the boy's room, evidencing early attempts to come to grips with perspective and balance—

The port was open now, and his eye was caught by the great blue and white globe of Old Earth, close by as they killed velocity to drop to the lower orbit in which *Favored of God* was parked. That globe almost filled the viewport, so that the stars he wanted to see were crowded out, only a stray few visible around the misty edges of the planet, as if paying court, and existing only by the great globe's sufferance.

He stared at the huge, dominating planet for long minutes, his thoughts of his human antagonist forgotten.

And he returned to *Favored of God,* to order that the ship take him elsewhere.

CHAPTER 37

It had always been a question whether the Friendly worlds constituted one Society, two societies—or thousands of them. The vast majority of the two planets' original settlers had been made up of the most ardent members of a wide variety of Old Earth's religious communities—communities that generally had two major things in common: a shared belief in the existence of a Deity, and a shared willingness to argue over the smallest detail of the remainder of their beliefs.

On both Friendly worlds, over several centuries, the various communities splintered, clashed, splintered again—to the point where religious discord was the norm and the greatest achievement of the two planets was their sheer ability to exist as a society despite that culture of serial schism. In that fractured environment, the institutionalization of every man and woman's right and duty to dissent, if his or her conscience so directed, existed in permanent conflict with every other person's duty to correct heresy—as well as with the government's need to preserve peace and order.

In that atmosphere, even revolt was fractionalized, and every attempt to create some sort of overriding controlling body for the rebellious was doomed to failure. So every rebellion—they were unending—started out as, and remained, a matter of individuals who cooperated only as far as their varied beliefs led them.

But in a society in which dissent was as institutionalized as the government itself, rebellion could thrive, because even the most staid and satisfied of citizens had a certain antipathy for authority. And because the government was as conflicted as its citizens.

It was astounding that the Commands—roving bands of armed rebels, part guerrilla and part pilgrim—could work together at all;

and, indeed, at times they, too, splintered. But for the most part each Command was a rebellion unto itself; and their only contact with each other was in the form of the news passed along informally over the networks of resisters who happened to know and trust each other. Only rarely had two Commands cooperated, for a limited time, for a common objective.

Nonetheless, each Command's very existence was an asset to every other Command, for their existence dissipated the pursuing government's resources, while energizing every Command's power base, that lay in the pool of nearly secret, unorganized sympathizers scattered throughout the lands the Commands roamed.

When *Favored of God* rose up out of its orbit, to push itself away from Old Earth's star in preparation for its first phase-shift of the trip home, Bleys was in his cabin; and he stayed there through that shift, through the calculation period after that shift—and through the second shift of the trip. He was writing notes to himself, and destroying them.

At last, a day and a half into the journey, near the end of the third calculation period, he left his cabin.

Prepared to fend for himself in satisfying his finally returned appetite, his first stop was the ship's kitchen. But his entrance to that facility was intercepted by Shira, who—apparently an apt student of her captain's commanding style—all but physically drove Bleys out of her way and to the lounge he had so far been avoiding while she prepared another meal for him.

For the rest of the trip he lost himself in the stars, either in the lounge or in his cabin, eating only when Shira brought him a tray; but once back on Association, he felt refreshed and alert, finally—and again lost himself in the myriad details of his work.

The Others he still led were, for the most part, carrying on their efforts to tighten the Others' control of nine worlds, to weaken the power of three other worlds, and to mobilize financial and military forces for the conflict he now felt to be inevitable; and that alone required more of his time than any single person should have to provide.

Still, Dahno's mysterious doings on Old Earth, and the attempt to have Bleys himself arrested there, demanded thought; and he spent many hours pacing up and down the length of his lounge.

His encounter with Hal Mayne, Bleys told himself, had served a valuable purpose: it had confirmed for him his growing belief that war not only had to come, but was in fact highly desirable—that a successful war could advance his plan many times faster than years of political maneuvering. . . . It was as if he had managed to slough off an old layer of skin, abraded by the searing meeting with the young Earthman: his intellectual energies, Bleys felt, had once again been cleansed of the clogging effects of delusion and emotion.

When the Militia officer Amyth Barbage arrived to report on his capture, three weeks earlier, of the Harmony outlaw Rukh Tamani, Bleys felt as if he were looking at the man with new, piercing eyes.

It was not the first time a meeting with Barbage had coincided with a change in Bleys' own perception of himself; shortly after Bleys had recovered from the worst of his struggle with the DNA invader the Newtonians had injected into him, Barbage had come for a meeting; and the Militia officer had, somehow, seemed to recognize that Bleys was different. It was a change Bleys himself had noticed only days before—a feeling that he had been charged with some new, and dark, upwelling of power. A power that fixed him more firmly on his course, and made him surer of his will to carry it through.

It had brought to his mind those archangels who had sided with Lucifer.

When he became aware of the change, Bleys went to a mirror, expecting to see a different appearance; but the mirror failed to reflect the change he felt. So he had been surprised when Barbage not only seemed to recognize that change, but to welcome it, with a kind of glee Bleys would never have expected could lie under that normally harsh, severe disposition.

Once again, this time, Barbage seemed to sense a change in Bleys. But this time the officer's face seemed to betray puzzlement, even uncertainty—something very rare for that self-designated member of God's Elect.

"True to thy prediction, Great Teacher," Barbage said, "the woman Rukh Tamani proved a formidable foe—not only in her own abilities to outthink and outfight many of the Militia's commanders, but in her ability to pass her satanic energies along to her cohort. Indeed, it seemed that every time my forces managed to take or kill members of her group—her *Command*, as these children of perdition style themselves—legions sprang up to replace those losses."

"Surely this is no surprise, Colonel," Bleys said. "The woman was able, after sabotaging the Core Tap, to shut the city down, captivating its populace with her words while appearing boldly in their midst to address the people in broad daylight—"

"Words of defiance, Great Teacher!" Barbage's face, recovered from its uncertainty, became ugly, and he nearly spat the words "—born of an evil that knows no fear, and must be destroyed!"

"But no more, Colonel," Bleys said, calmly and softly. "You've had her in a cell for three weeks now, I believe?"

"It is so, Great Teacher."

"Tell me how you managed to take her."

"It cost us dearly," Barbage said, "for thy order was that she be taken alive. But God at last favored us and delivered her into our hands."

"How did that come about?" Bleys asked.

"God led me to change my tactics," Barbage said. "Once we managed to learn what general area her group was in, we tried unsuccessfully to drive her force before us, into traps we laid, but God did not vouchsafe us success."

"That has been tried before," Bleys said, "and those people usually managed to evade the Militia, in the end."

"It is so, Great Teacher," Barbage said. "But God revealed to me that the work to repair the Core Tap—the very one Tamani and her people sabotaged earlier—had been proceeding apace, and was nearly completed. With God's help I realized that such as these Forsaken would feel a need to return. Thus, I directed that the word be given out that repairs had been completed and that work on the Core Tap was about to resume."

"And so you drew her into a trap, then?"

"Indeed," Barbage said. "We made an estimate of the time it

would likely have taken for her to hear the news and come to the city; and then we made a sweep, picking up all the dregs who mingle in the population." He smiled, coldly.

"Thanks to thy foresight, Great Teacher, for the first time there existed a unified force under the command of a single officer of sufficient rank to have his orders obeyed, and sufficient numbers to block more routes than in the past—and with diligence and alacrity the mistakes that had always sabotaged the efforts of other commanders were avoided. Thus, we arrested hundreds of those unfaithful we believed to be in sympathy with her. And with the forces entrusted to me, we were able to close down all the city, and the nearby countryside besides; and keep them closed so that none could get away. Until eventually, one of those we had arrested broke, and gave us a location in which we could seek Tamani."

"I congratulate you, Colonel," Bleys said. "But tell me now: have you learned anything from the woman about Hal Mayne?"

"Although put to the test," Barbage said, "the woman continues to deny knowing anything new of Hal Mayne."

"Do you believe her?"

"I do, Great Teacher," Barbage said. "I believe she is one of those who, if she knew anything about Mayne, would merely seek to maintain silence, rather than tell an outright lie. Moreover, a lack of knowledge on her part is logical, since Mayne hath not been on the planet and the Commands have no access to off-planet communications."

"That we know of," Bleys corrected him.

"It is so, Great Teacher," Barbage acknowledged; but his eyes burned.

"I accept your opinion," Bleys said. "But tell me—what about the remainder of her Command?"

"We found none, Great Teacher," Barbage said. "The woman said she came to the city alone; and indeed, all those found near her were locals long suspected of being sympathetic to the disaffected."

"Still, she must have other information that can be of use," Bleys said. "Names of collaborators, methods of communication, and so on?"

"Undoubtedly, Great Teacher. I intend to return to Ahruma at once and redouble my efforts with her."

"Very good, Colonel," Bleys said. "Please keep me informed."

"Would it please thee to see her, when next thou comest to Harmony?"

The question brought back sharply Bleys' memory of the slim, beautiful woman he had met briefly on her own ground, one day on Harmony.

"No," he said.

Henry MacLean was disturbed. He had just completed an hour-long cross-country obstacle run, and his time had been beaten by a goodly number of his Soldiers. Being bested did not bother him; he had never been the swiftest of any group. What bothered him was that he was almost exhausted, and it was taking him longer to recover than he expected of himself.

He was still better at the skills that required calm and the ability to focus oneself, such as shooting or spotting out-of-place people or items in an environment. But he was concerned that he was losing muscle tone. It was now more than two years since he had left the farm, and he did not feel the workouts he took part in, as part of his Soldiers' maintenance program, did as much for him as the farm-work had.

Perhaps it was that he was in his fifties now; his body must age, as did everyone's. But he wondered if he might be losing some of his ability to do the tasks he had set for himself.

He had known, when he came to Bleys, that he was deficient in many areas; but he had never had any doubts about his physical abilities.

Henry had never had the sort of formal martial arts training Bleys and Toni practiced, but he had picked up a lot of tricks and techniques in his youth, as a Soldier of God; and those were in turn built on the foundation of skills developed in the country wrestling of his youth.

So when he organized Bleys' Soldiers, he was aware of the need to keep them in condition; an entire floor of the Others' headquarters building was devoted to that, and what could not be done well there was carried on in courses in the countryside.

Nor did he neglect the mental side of fitness: he had been little educated in his youth, but with the facilities Bleys could provide he had devoted a portion of every day to instruction in various technical and scientific fields—and made sure his Soldiers did the same.

What it came down to was that although he was older than most of his Soldiers, it was important to him to keep himself in the same shape he demanded of them.

He had never thought of himself as one of those who could send others out to fight while conserving their own strength—those whose value lay in their experience and intelligence. There had always been a part of him that suspected that such people put their souls in greater danger than did the common fighter.

Did he still feel that way, now that he seemed to be taking such a role? It might be a good idea to do some thinking about the meaning of his past life.

"Bleys, wake up!" Toni's voice pierced the darkness, but Bleys was already awake—he had roused when her breathing changed as her wristpad awoke her.

"What is it?"

"An urgent message from Harmony," she reported. "Rukh Tamani has escaped from the Militia."

Bleys sat up, and waved a hand for some light.

"Details?" he said. "How long ago did this happen?"

"I'm still being fed information," she said. "It sounds as if it occurred about four days ago. There was a raid on the prison."

"Four days!"

"Yes," she said.

"Why did it take Barbage so long to report this?" he asked, intending that she direct the question to whoever she was in contact with.

"The report isn't coming from Barbage," Toni said after a moment. "It seems he's vanished."

"Was he killed?"

"Apparently not," she replied. "There were a lot of casualties—I gather there are some wild stories about some huge man hunting people down in the corridors—"

"Mayne!" he said.

"No identification was made. However, Barbage was seen after it was all over—and when he disappeared, no one who was left knew you had any particular interest in the woman; so the report took a while to get up the chain of command to us."

Bleys was silent.

"The Militia are asking if you want to order them to seal all the spaceports, to prevent Tamani from getting off the planet," she said. She waited for him to reply.

"No," Bleys said finally. "It's certainly too late."

He rose, and padded in his bare feet out of the bedroom and down the hall to his lounge. He did not turn on a light; he was not sure what his reaction to the news really was, and he did not want Toni to see his face while he explored it.

CHAPTER 38

Delivered Out of Egypt, despite its longer name, was a much smaller ship than either *Favored of God* or *Burning Bush.* The vessel had been called *Poker Face IV* as it came out of the shipyard on Old Earth's moon, Luna; and its size was well adapted for the in-system routes it was meant to run between the numerous ports and pads in its home solar system.

Now, having only recently become one of the steadily growing fleet owned by the Others, it had been chosen for this trip precisely because it was new to their service, which meant that its presence somewhere was less likely to alert people that Bleys Ahrens was in the area. Bleys also hoped that anyone trying to find him would be distracted by *Favored's* trip to Newton, where it remained in orbit while Toni and Henry gave the impression that Bleys was conducting business in the privacy of the ship.

The disadvantage to *Delivered's* smaller size, however, was that its passageways were narrower, and had less overhead, than those in the larger ships. Moreover, its cabins were smaller, its facilities sparser and its passenger lounge less than half the size of the one Bleys used as his office aboard *Favored.*

The lounge was still the largest space on the ship, however, outside of the engineering areas, and so Bleys was spending almost all his time there; but he was getting sick of the place.

Delivered, using the assumed name *Fanon's Friend,* had been in orbit at Mara for nearly six days now, pretending to have suffered a malfunction that seriously contaminated its environmental support systems—badly enough that after spending the first few days trying to fix the problems themselves, the crew had been obliged to call for help in the form of a local expert.

That particular deception, Bleys had already decided, would not be used again: the need to make the problem seem real to the expert had resulted in the ship having a pervading stale, sickly sweet smell that was making the crew increasingly surly.

Still, for all its disadvantages, *Delivered* had a deluxe-size viewing screen, large enough to dominate its lounge with the illusion of a gigantic picture window cut into the side of the ship. Bleys had ordered such screens placed in all the ships he was likely to use, and this one was left permanently on before his desk.

At the moment, the screen was dominated by a view of the nightside of the planet below. Mara, the smaller of the two Exotic planets—although only by a small amount—showed before Bleys' eyes as a black circle cut out of the starfield. The Exotics generally eschewed large, well-lit cities, and the planet had no moon to reflect Procyon's light onto the planet's nightside.

But already an arc of excruciating whiteness was outlining one side of that black circle. To Bleys, in *Delivered*'s particular attitude, that arc outlined the lower edge of the planet; and as he watched the arc grew, curving upward and away on both sides like the horns of some great animal, even as the most central portion of the arc thickened . . . and abruptly, a point at the very center of the arc sparkled, glaring at him with the smallest edge of Procyon's intense face.

Bleys had watched this sight, in various versions, dozens of times already during their long stay in this orbit; and he knew that within moments the ship's movement would separate the star from the planet, and the dayside would expand below him, glowing warmly green where it was not a cooler blue.

Mara looked a lot like Old Earth, Bleys thought. That recognition was not original with him, but it had come up in his memory more sharply because he had so recently been looking down on the mother planet in much this same way.

This was no mother to the human race, though, he reminded himself, but a place occupied by a race of strangers, of people almost alien in their self-created differences from the rest of the human race . . . as alien to them, in fact, as he himself; but in a different way.

And it was, he suddenly recalled, the home—no, call it the birth-place, only—of his mother.

He probed at his mind, wondering whether he might be letting his own feelings about his mother affect his perception about her birthplace.

No.

He was here only because Hal Mayne was here—had brought the woman Rukh Tamani here after taking her from the Militia's holding cells in Ahruma.

No intelligence source had given Bleys that information; rather, he had concluded it was a logical move; by all accounts, the woman had not fared well under the Militia's—Barbage's—care. The Exotics were renowned healers, and Bleys knew even that Mayne himself had come here for healing, after his own escape from that same prison—it made sense he would return here with someone in a similar position.

But where, on that large planet below, was Hal Mayne? Mara was even larger than Old Earth, by a small amount, and Bleys could not very well ask someone for that information.

Or, could he?

He leaned back in his chair, his eyes no longer seeing the screen.

He had been hanging here in orbit trying, solely by means of passive listening techniques used by the technicians he had brought along, to pick up some piece of information that might lead him to Hal Mayne's whereabouts and doings. Any more active form of information-gathering would be certain to betray his presence to the Exotics.

But then again: what could he lose if the Exotics, or even Hal Mayne, learned he was here? Neither of them would attack him physically, even here in Exotic space; he was sure of that.

By himself in the lounge, he shook his head. Not yet.

There might come a time to take that bull by the horns, but this was not it. Revealing himself to the Exotics would not be physically dangerous, but it would dissipate any chance of learning something from orbit. And it would likely expose him to pointless bouts with the impenetrably courteous blandness the Exotics so adeptly used to befuddle people. All they would ever tell him would be what they wanted him to know, as if they were running him through a maze like some experimental subject.

So he went to bed.

When he awoke and made his way to the lounge, he found waiting there a recent message from *Delivered*'s captain, reporting that the Maran environmental-systems expert had finished his repairs and was preparing to depart: did Bleys want to remain here in orbit?

Bleys sniffed: the air *did* seem better.

On a sudden impulse, he keyed the circuit for the bridge.

"Captain, is the Maran still on board?" he asked.

"Yes, Great Teacher, but not for much longer—the shuttle he called to pick him up is just three minutes away."

"Ask him to come up to the lounge, please."

"I'll have him escorted—"

"No," Bleys interrupted. "Just ask him to come up, and let him find his own way. He'll be familiar with ships and unlikely to get lost, and I don't want him subjected to any intimidation . . . is that understood?"

"Yes, Great Teacher," the captain said. "But, if I may ask—what should I do about the shuttle?"

"Ask it—politely—to wait," Bleys said. "We're guests in this space, even if the Exotics don't know it."

"Then—the Maran will be allowed to leave?"

"I'll let you know."

It was only a few minutes before a figure appeared in the doorway Bleys had left open, to look enquiringly inside.

"Please come in," Bleys said from his desk across the room as he rose to his feet.

The man who entered did not in the least fit the popular conception of an Exotic. He was of medium height, and stockily built and in his upper forties, with rosy skin and a large bald spot showing through short brown hair. He was wearing a grease-stained gray-green coverall that seemed to have pockets everywhere, as well as a tool belt with both loops and closed pockets.

"Thank you for coming up here," Bleys said, gesturing to an

empty chair as the Exotic approached. He did not offer his hand, knowing that the Exotics generally did not observe that custom.

"I understand there's a shuttle waiting for you," Bleys went on, "and I won't keep you long."

"He'll wait," the Exotic said. "The driver's my nephew." He grinned, and Bleys smiled in response.

"I won't sit down, if you don't mind," the Exotic said, waving vaguely at his own torso. "I got a little dirty down under the ion exchanger."

"Weren't you offered a chance to clean up?" Bleys asked.

"Oh, I was," the man said. "I turned it down—I know what my nephew's shuttle will be like; he's at the end of a long shift ferrying agricultural supplies to Ninevah—oh, that's one of the orbital manufactories."

"These chairs clean up easily, in any case," Bleys said, "but do as you like. My name is Bleys Ahrens."

"Honored," the Exotic said, continuing to stand. "My name is Tony Peterson." He seemed to peer at Bleys now, as if a thought had suddenly struck him. "I know who you are—are you here for the meeting, too?"

"Which meeting?" Bleys said, stalling for time—and as he watched puzzlement enter the other's face, his mind made a sudden leap.

"Do you mean the one with Hal Mayne?" Bleys asked. "Yes, I hope to be there."

"It should be very interesting," Tony Peterson said.

"Will you be there?" Bleys asked, trying to probe delicately.

"Oh, we'll all be there," the Exotic said. "But about your air cleaner—I'm sorry it took so long, but it turned out the problem resulted from two different things going wrong at almost the same time . . . I gave the details to your officers."

"That's quite all right," Bleys said, realizing that the Exotic thought Bleys had called him up to the lounge to speak about the problem that had been created to allow the ship to stay at Mara without suspicion. "I take it you're sure you've gotten to the root of the problem?"

"I believe so." The Exotic smiled. "The problem's mended now, but of course I can't promise it won't recur."

"What do you mean?"

"No system can last if it's mishandled."

"Mishandled?" Bleys asked, wondering if the Exotic had detected the sabotage.

"I believe some of your people may have gotten careless," Peterson said. "Cleaning solvents killed one of the polymembranes."

"It sounds like improper training, then," Bleys said.

"It may be."

After the repairman left, Bleys asked the captain to contact Orbital Holistics and tell them that Bleys Ahrens was present and requesting permission to attend the meeting.

"You *want* me to let them know you're here?" the captain asked.

"Yes," Bleys said. He did not bother to tell the man that the situation had changed completely.

Within thirty minutes a call was patched through to Bleys in the lounge, and he found himself looking at a woman in a pink coverall, who identified herself as Nonne, the Recordist for Mara.

Nonne was black-haired, with a fine-boned face that suggested, despite the lack of scale in the comm screen, that she was small. But her voice was a calm, assured contralto that betrayed neither surprise at Bleys' presence nor indignation over his self-invitation to the meeting.

"We've been told you wish to speak to someone about the upcoming meeting, Bleys Ahrens," she said, without preamble.

"Yes," Bleys said. "It's my understanding that Hal Mayne will be addressing your gathering, and I felt it might be beneficial to all if I were allowed to present my own views."

"We are always willing to listen," the Recordist said, her tone clinical and neutral.

"When and where shall I appear, then?"

"A shuttle will be dispatched for you, that will take you to whatever site is used," Nonne said. She shrugged. "The time is not yet fixed—we await Hal Mayne's return."

He's off-planet, then! Bleys told himself. But he made no comment on that subject to the Exotic on his screen.

"I'll wait, then," he said. "But please keep me advised, won't you? Oh! By the way: could you tell me the purpose of the meeting?"

"Why, the future," Nonne said. "Didn't you know?"

There was something in her voice that made Bleys keep his silence.

CHAPTER 39

Stepping down from the shuttle, Bleys found himself on the resilient surface of a very small landing pad. Its edges were outlined by snow that was falling beyond its weather-control field; which told him they were now near one of the warm planet's poles.

From one side a vehicle was approaching, its passage raising a cloud as it skimmed above the surface of the loose, new-fallen snow; and as Bleys watched, it passed through the weather curtain and onto the pad, heading directly, and silently, for him. As it drew up, a door opened; and as he moved toward it, he could see that the vehicle's surface was wet; snow that had accumulated on its back deck was beginning to slide off in clumps, as its bottom layers thawed down to water faster than the upper layers, providing a lubricating effect.

Twenty minutes later the vehicle moved out of a stand of bare, snow-caked trees to pass through another weather barrier and draw up before a grass-surfaced ramp that sloped gently up to a place where a shadowy wall had apparently been cut into the side of a small hill. The hill itself was crowned with more snow-laden trees, and a small, conical tower of a sandstone color stuck up from behind them.

Two figures appeared out of the shadowed cut in the hillside and began moving down the ramp. Bleys recognized the smaller one as Nonne, the Exotic he had spoken to earlier. She was now dressed in a green set of the robes that were what most of the Younger Worlds believed Exotics wore all the time.

Bleys climbed out of the vehicle and walked to the ramp, to meet the figures moving toward him. The grassy surface was smooth and soft, comfortable to walk on, and it provided all the traction he needed, despite its upward grade.

The taller figure moving toward him was also female, an unusual-looking woman with copper-colored skin and a shaven skull. Her robes were light blue in color, and to Bleys' unpracticed eye they appeared to be draped on her form in a different manner than those worn by Nonne; but he could not tell if the differences had any meaning.

"Welcome, Bleys Ahrens," Nonne said, stopping at a distance of almost two meters in front of Bleys. He took an extra step, and then stopped also.

"My companion is Sulaya," Nonne went on. "She'll be your guide, if that suits you—I'm afraid I have other duties."

"I'm honored," Bleys said, speaking to Nonne but looking at Sulaya. "It was good of you to meet me."

While he spoke Nonne was turning, to stride swiftly up the ramp and through the shadow-wall. Bleys and Sulaya, after another brief, polite exchange, followed her more slowly.

Bleys was led through the shadow-wall, which he found to be some kind of pressure barrier, and beyond it, down several long passageways, to a kind of patio. Unless his direction-sense had been scrambled somehow, he was sure he was still under the hill, but the patio seemed to open on the edge of a snowbound glade. Bright light poured out of a sky from which the snow clouds had drawn off; it made tiny diamondlike sparkles dance out of the crystals of the snow on the ground.

And yet, seated on the cushioned bench he had been shown to, Bleys felt comfortably warm. A gentle breeze breathed on his face, carrying with it a faint scent like some mild spice. Sulaya sat quietly nearby, perched atop what seemed to be a lichen-speckled stone wall. The entire patio before him and to his sides was filled with stone walls of varying heights, that bent and turned about him as if he were in the center of a maze. . . . When he found his eyes making the same circular scan of their top surfaces for the fourth time, he pulled his gaze away.

Catching a slight movement out of the corner of an eye, Bleys turned in time to see a drinking vessel, apparently of gray glass, rise out of one arm of the bench. It contained apple juice, he discovered.

Discounting his initial suspicions, he took a long drink of the cool, sweet fluid; and realized, when he lowered the glass, that two more people had moved into his line of sight—it seemed almost as if they had popped into being in front of him.

One was a woman of medium height, with bronze skin and curly brown hair, wearing a honey-colored robe; Bleys found her age difficult to estimate. She gave him a welcoming smile, but said nothing while Bleys looked at her companion, a man who seemed to hold his attention without word or motion.

This man was more than elderly, Bleys realized; in fact, he was quite probably the oldest person Bleys had ever seen. His skin seemed relatively unwrinkled, but there was a stillness in his face above the amber-colored robes, and something about the way he held himself. . . .

"We are pleased to have you here, Bleys Ahrens," the bronze-skinned woman said now, somewhat formally, as Bleys rose to his feet. She nodded slightly as she spoke, and her face became more serious, although she maintained a gentle smile. "My name is Chavis."

She turned slightly, gesturing with a flowing movement of her left arm in the direction of her older companion.

"And this is Padma, the InBond."

InBond? No one really understands the offices the Exotics give each other, but that's one I haven't heard before.

"I'm honored to meet you," Bleys said, as the elderly Exotic bowed, very slightly, in his direction. Padma's eyes stayed on Bleys' face, but he said nothing.

The silence continued for a long moment, and as the three sets of Exotic eyes watched him, Bleys found himself becoming a little uncomfortable. He covered it by taking another drink; but in a moment the glass was empty.

"Would you like some more?" Chavis asked as Bleys turned to put it down.

"No, thank you," he said. "But is there something you'd like?"

"There may be," Padma said. His voice was hoarse and low, the oldest thing about him. He paused to clear his throat lightly, even as a glass of water rose out of the bench's arm. Bleys reached back for it and handed it to the older Exotic.

"Would you like to sit?" he asked, gesturing behind him at the bench.

"No," Padma said, after taking a sip of the water. "Thank you, but I think we won't be here long."

"Then we should get to whatever you wanted to ask me," Bleys said.

"That is sensible," Padma said, a smile coming to his face. "Would you be willing to give us twelve days of your time?"

"Twelve days?" Bleys said, startled.

"We here on the Exotics have spent generations in the study of human evolution," Chavis explained. "We'd like to measure you."

Bleys, suddenly conscious of how he towered over the two Exotics, looked down at Padma.

"You want data on me," he said. "And on my abilities."

"That's one way to describe it," Padma said. "We're always looking for signs of improvements in the race."

"To what point?" Bleys said. "There's no future in your work— surely you all know that by now."

"It may be," Padma said. Again he smiled, gently. "But one might ask whether there is a future in *any* work."

"That's the kind of philosophical speculation I prefer to avoid," Bleys said. "You must be aware of the futility of that line of thought." He paused; and after a brief moment, smiled.

"Unless, of course, you're already testing me."

"We were sure you would not agree," Padma said. "But regardless of what you think of our work, we believe it has value. And that it will continue to have value in the future."

"If there is a future," Bleys said.

Padma smiled again, almost shyly; but he said nothing.

Bleys, looking down into the eyes that watched him so alertly, realized he had totally forgotten that the man before him was small and old. He found himself wondering if there might be some way to sit with this man and discuss—and at that moment, a chime sounded softly out of the air.

"The gathering is almost in place," Chavis said, "and Hal Mayne has arrived. Do you still wish to address us?"

"I do," Bleys said. He had not had a chance to ask what the subject of the gathering might be, he realized; but he shrugged, mentally, willing to deal with whatever came.

"Then come with us," Chavis said.

Moving slowly out of deference to Padma's age, Chavis led them all back out of the glade, through a door and down a short hall. When they came to a set of double doors of a black wood, Sulaya stayed behind while the rest of them passed through.

Bleys found himself standing near what appeared to be the main stage of a small amphitheater, but he had no time to look about as the two Exotics led him up onto the stage and across it, to the place at its center-front where light seemed to focus out of nowhere. The light, although bright, was not uncomfortable, but Bleys found himself unable to focus on the audience, already in place but extraordinarily quiet. His first estimate told him there were possibly two hundred faces looking up, across, and down at him—and yet, when he tried to pick out a single face with which to make eye contact, his vision seemed to blur, and he felt as if the faces on each side of the one he was looking into became dozens of faces, hundreds of faces, looking back at him across a distance that was impossible within this small theater.

With that realization, he knew he was in the middle of another piece of the Exotics' advanced technology, and that this room must be large enough to require the operation of some sort of telescopic effect. He wondered if the effect worked in both directions, and if his audience could also see him as if at a short distance.

"Hal Mayne is on his way," Padma said. His voice, still hoarse, now carried a weight of years, and there was no smile on his face. Chavis, Bleys saw, had vanished somewhere.

"How many people are here?" Bleys asked.

"Almost everyone is here," Padma said; but before Bleys could question what that cryptic statement meant, there was a sound off to his side; and he turned to see Hal Mayne moving toward him across the stage, accompanied by a small, wrinkled Exotic in a light gray robe.

Hal Mayne loomed like a mountain over his companion, and was obviously measuring his steps to avoid outpacing his guide. He wore a short jacket over rough, dark-gray ship's coveralls; and for a moment Bleys felt overdressed in his tailored gray jacket and narrow-legged dark gray trousers.

Bleys wondered if Hal Mayne had a similar reaction at the sight of Bleys towering over Padma; he started to look sideways at the elderly Exotic . . . and in that moment Hal was right there in front of him, looking him straight in the eyes, and Bleys realized he didn't know what to say to this man.

"Hal Mayne would prefer that Bleys Ahrens speaks first," said the unnamed small Exotic.

"Of course," Bleys murmured. He was dismayed to find he was once more feeling the tiredness that had come over him after their last meeting, in the Final Encyclopedia. He felt as if he were being left out of something, something he would have liked to belong to. . . . He turned his face away from Hal, to appear to be looking out across the amphitheater.

"I'll leave you to it, then," Hal said; and he turned and led the elderly Exotics back off the side of the platform, where they seemed to vanish into the darkness.

Alone on the bare black stage, Bleys battled despair, wondering how he could reach this audience of aliens that waited so silently before him . . . he could not seem to make eye contact with any of them, could not seem to *feel* them . . . and he still did not know the purpose of this gathering.

They're here to listen to Hal Mayne, he reminded himself. *They must be about to make some sort of decision.*

He made himself take a moment to control his breathing.

You never expected to win them over, anyway, so what've you got to lose?

He squared up his stance, and spread his arms wide to his sides, at shoulder height.

"Will you listen to me?" he asked "For a few moments only, will you listen to me—without preconceptions, without already existing opinions, as if I were a petitioner at your gates whom you'd never heard before?"

Still there was no reaction, but he dropped his arms slowly to his sides, as if they had agreed to his plea.

"It's painful, I know," he said. He spoke slowly, measuring his words out a syllable at a time, as if that would somehow drive them through the wall of distance he felt before him.

"Always, it is painful when times change; when everything we've come to take for granted has to be reexamined. All at once, our firmest and our most cherished beliefs have to be pulled out by the roots, out of those very places where we'd always expected them to stand forever, and subjected to the same sort of remorseless scrutiny we'd give to the newest and wildest of our theories or thoughts."

He paused, to move his gaze about the amphitheater as if trying to look into every eye.

"Yes, it's painful," he said; but he allowed no sad note in his voice. He wanted to be all of History speaking to them. He wanted to be Authority.

"But we all know it happens. We all have to face that sort of self-reexamination, sooner or later. But of all peoples, those I'd have expected to face this task the best would have been the people of Mara and Kultis."

He tried then to raise his voice in exortation, as if he were one of the gifted preachers he had heard so often on Association, calling them to redemption.

"Haven't you given your lives, and the lives of all your generations, to that principle, ever since you ceased to call yourselves the Chantry Guild and came here to these Exotic Worlds, searching for the future of humankind? Not just searching toward that future by ways you found pleasant and palatable, but by all the ways to it you could find, agreeable or not? Isn't that so?"

Now he glared at them, as if defying them to argue with him—with someone they had to know was correct about everything. . . .

"You've grown into the two worlds of people who dominated the economies of all the inhabited worlds—so that you wouldn't have to spare time from your search to struggle for a living. You've bought and sold armies so that you'd be free of fighting, and of all the emotional commitment that's involved in it—all so you'd have the best possible conditions to continue your work, your search.

"Now, after all those many years of putting that search first, you seem ready to put it in second place to a taking of sides, in a transient, present-day dispute. I tell you frankly—because by inheritance I'm one of you, as I think you know—that even if it should be the side I find myself on that you wish to join, at the expense of your long struggle to bring about humanity's future, I'd still stand here as I do now, and ask you to think again of what you have to lose by doing so."

He stopped, trying again to focus on his audience; but their faces continued to elude his attempts to hold them with his eyes. He could find no reaction out there. . . .

There was no sound for the long moment in which he waited; until finally he stepped backward, as if dismissing them; and stood in place for a moment more.

"That's all that I've come here to say to you," he said at last. He felt deflated. "That's all there is. The rest, the decision, I leave to you."

He stood there for a moment longer, silent, still waiting for them to react . . . he knew it was futile, but he could not help it—he *needed* some sign from them.

But there was nothing; and at last he turned and walked off the platform.

Once out of the light, he could see that Hal Mayne, Padma and the other tiny Exotic were awaiting him, standing before a group of chairs. But nothing had changed.

"I'd like to speak privately to these people," Hal said as Bleys reached them.

That's it then, Bleys told himself.

He made himself smile, and nodded. He let himself be led away by the elderly Exotic who had been Hal Mayne's guide, who seemed to scurry now to keep up with the long strides Bleys found himself using. Bleys forced himself to slow down, so as not to seem to be running away; and in a moment he was through the doors and had been turned over to Sulaya again, who led him away.

CHAPTER 40

"I was never actually told what the meeting was about," Bleys, back on Association, said, "but the fact they were waiting for Hal Mayne to come back and speak to them tells me they were listening to some plan of his. I think he was off the planet dealing with the Dorsai. I think he's persuaded them to come to Mara to defend the Exotics against us."

"The fact they were waiting for him doesn't mean the Exotics agreed to his plan," she said.

"By itself, no," Bleys said. "But I think the Exotics I met had already decided. It was in their eyes, and their attitudes. It's the only possibility that fits the intelligence that's been telling us the Dorsai have been bringing their ships and people back to their planet—they can only be preparing for some large move."

"You were on Mara and dealt with those people," she said, "so I can't argue with you about that. But I find it hard to believe the Dorsai would make a move that would leave their own planet defenseless . . . although it's true they have a myth about defending it with women and children."

"It's the only thing that makes sense," Bleys said. "They wouldn't be gathering their assets if they weren't planning major action. I don't think it can be a coincidence that while they've been gathering, the Exotics have been moving their own wealth, ships, and mobile technological resources—even many of their most important experts; and it's no coincidence they held that meeting on Mara. So what else makes sense?"

"I can believe the Dorsai are planning something," she said. "But the only reason to think they're going to Mara are a few reports of a rumor among the Exotics to that effect. It could be wrong."

"The Dorsai can only go to a planet that wants them," Bleys said. "Remember when I said that to fight, they need a place to stand on? The only planets that might want them are planets that think they're in military danger—that can only be the Exotics."

"Why not Old Earth?"

"Old Earth doesn't think it's in any danger," Bleys said. "The Final Encyclopedia and Hal Mayne know better, but they haven't even tried to convince Old Earth yet, even though Dahno's people have been working there to stir up dissension. It would be the worst possible move for Mayne—nothing would alienate Earthmen more than five million Dorsai showing up uninvited on their doorstep."

He turned away and moved toward his desk.

"In the end it really doesn't matter," he said. "No matter where the Dorsai go, they'll have to sit in their defenses and wait for us to come. Even if they want to come out and attack us on nine worlds, there just aren't enough of them; they'd be worn down by attrition." He activated his screen.

"This gives us a chance to make a move they won't be expecting," he said.

"You were already sure war was coming," Toni said; "how much has the situation changed?"

"I figured it might well get down to war," Bleys said, absentmindedly correcting her as he inserted a chip he had brought with him from the ship. "Eventually. I thought it was some time off and we'd have ample time to get ourselves ready while Hal Mayne struggled to get his side organized." He looked up at her.

"Hal Mayne now has the Exotics working with him, the Final Encyclopedia behind him—and the Dorsai up to something . . . I think we can expect action sooner rather than later."

He touched a control, and his eyes turned again to his screen.

"There's an opportunity here to do something Mayne and his friends could never expect," he said. "I spent the trip back drawing up plans to speed our mobilization—I still want to keep it undercover, to avoid raising any more alarms on Old Earth than we have to. But we have a lot to do: we need to find ways to get more information about how Old Earth is likely to react when the Dorsai make

their move—and on what the Exotics and the Dorsai are planning."
He looked at her again.

"I'm going to be sending messages right away to our people on
all the Younger Worlds, and I'll be following up with personal visits.
I'd like you to find out how to get the messages to those Worlds as
quickly as possible; when that's done, set up a new trip . . . think
about what needs to be done to have four or five courier ships along.
I want to start with New Earth."

"Are those Soldiers Henry sent still on Old Earth?" Bleys asked,
two hours later.

"I think so," Toni said. "Henry didn't want to call them back until he'd heard from you."

"Leave them there," Bleys said. "We'll want to have them monitoring public opinion on the planet and reporting back."

"That's not exactly the sort of thing the Soldiers are good at," she
pointed out. "Most of them there aren't intelligence specialists."

"Maybe we should send a few intelligence people to join them,
then," Bleys said. "I know John Colville's there; he's got a good
head on his shoulders and would be a good choice to lead the effort."

"I was about to point out that the nonspecialists might be able to
see things the specialists miss," Toni said. "They're more like average people in the way they look at things."

"Why don't you ask Henry for his suggestions?" Bleys said. "But
don't forget I want to get off on this trip right away."

The sky was gray when Bleys climbed out of the armored limousine
in which he had ridden to his appointment with Hammer Martin
and three of Freiland's top political leaders. The vehicles that had
escorted his were now hovering around him, trying to create a wall
between Bleys and the crowd of workers lining the edges of the fac-
tory's parking lot. Those workers seemed to be yelling, but Bleys
could not make out any words.

"This way, Great Teacher," a voice said from behind Bleys. He
turned, to see Maryam Kors, one of Martin's staff. She had a portable

weather shield ready, in case the cold rain returned; there were puddles on the ground, and the cold wind suggested more weather might be coming in.

Bleys had not been cold very often in his life, but this was a time when he could wish he had worn a thick coat—but then, he had worn his red-lined cape precisely because of its usefulness in helping him capture the attention of his audiences; that was more important than personal comfort.

"Hammer, it's good to see you," Bleys said, as the senior Other on Freiland came walking to meet him.

"Great Teacher, we're all so glad you could come," Hammer said. He half-turned to indicate the crowd of people—over a dozen, Bleys thought—who had straggled behind him. "Let me introduce Thorbjorn Holder, President of the Freiland State—"

The President was tall and thin, and his long, nearly white hair was blowing in the cold breeze. He leaned forward eagerly, smiling broadly, and put out both hands to clasp the one Bleys extended.

"So pleased to meet you, Great Teacher! I've been listening to your talks for years . . . oh, allow me to present my wife. . . ."

It was going to be a long afternoon, Bleys thought. He had already lost count of how many times he had been dragged out to visit munitions factories, vehicle assembly lines, spaceship fitting yards. . . .

It's necessary, he reminded himself.

"It's tricky."

Back on New Earth for the third time in two months, Bleys and Toni were waiting in the lounge of their suite for the arrival of Marshal Cuslow Damar, whose Friendly troops had been effectively in control of the planet for several years now.

"The Marshal's convoy is driving up," Toni said. She had just received that news from the staff lower in the hotel, who communicated with Bleys through her. "What's tricky?"

"Trying to get the Younger Worlds ready for a war that will have to involve Old Earth, without arousing the mother planet herself,"

Bleys said. "You've seen the reports that Rukh Tamani's shown up there. She can only be there to drum up opposition to us."

"What about our own people?" Toni asked. "Whatever Dahno may be up to, by all reports his people have continued pushing divisions in the populace."

"Old Earth may be in for a war of preachers," Bleys said. "I can't say who's likely to win."

"But Dahno's people have the persuasive abilities you've taught them," she said.

"That *he* taught them," Bleys said. "Some of them, yes. But John Colville's reports suggest Rukh Tamani has a similar ability. He's been following her about, listening to her, and she's apparently a spellbinder."

"She had that reputation on Harmony," Toni said. "Could she counter Dahno's work?"

"We never needed our people on Old Earth to convince Earthmen to join us," Bleys said. "All we need is for them to continue divided over how to react to us. Most of them were unnoticing and uncaring when Dahno's campaign started, and those who cared were divided. I don't see that changing."

"Even if Tamani manages to arouse Old Earth," Toni said, "it'll take a long time to get it moving in a single direction. You've always emphasized that. We've already got a huge jump on them."

"Which is why our best way to avoid total war will be to make a preemptive strike."

"At Old Earth? What about the Dorsai and the Exotics?"

"If we attacked the Exotics and the Dorsai, we'd rouse Old Earth from its sleep," he said. "They might not come out to take part, but they'd be ready when we got around to them. On the other hand, the Exotics and the Dorsai won't be able to do much if we deal with Old Earth first—they'll just be sitting there in a defensive posture, waiting for us to get around to them." He smiled.

"What I hope we can do," he said, "is put a big fleet in Old Earth's sky before they know we're coming, leaving them no choice but to surrender. When that's taken care of, we can handle the Exotics and the Dorsai at our leisure." His smile this time was a little sad. "I may be indulging in fantasy."

"You're giving up on using the political approach to Old Earth?"

"It may have some value as an adjunct to military moves," he said, "but I can't stake my mission on it."

"Preemption would certainly save a lot of lives," she said.

"It would also keep Old Earth's assets and resources whole," he said. "That'll be important when we move there and cut off contact with the Younger Worlds—but Hal Mayne will have something to say about it, too, unless I can show him there's no hope for his side."

He stopped, seeing that Toni's attention had shifted inward. Messages from the staff were relayed to her ears by bone conduction from her wristpad, and she sometimes appeared distracted as she listened to a report.

"The Marshal's on his way up," she said.

Bleys rose, heading for the door.

"No," Toni said. "I know you're eager to get started, but you should follow protocol—you're still the First Elder, and he should come to you."

"I know, I know," Bleys said. "Sometimes the rules—well, anyway, what do you suggest? I want to see him quickly."

"Go into the room beyond the conference room," she said. "I'll meet him and bring his party there, and you can come in right after they sit down . . . you fret too much; having to wait for superiors is part of their lives, and they'll feel more comfortable if you don't blur the lines of authority they've always lived by."

"All right," Bleys said. "I'll come in from the far door as soon as he arrives, then—he's a good man and I don't want to make him wait."

"You don't want to make yourself wait, either," she said.

He left.

The Marshal, a middle-aged man in the black uniform of the Friendly Worlds' professional military force, was still on his feet when Bleys entered the conference room. Beside him, Toni silently raised an eyebrow as she traded glances with Bleys.

"Marshal, it's good to see you again," Bleys said. "I thought you were bringing some of your staff?"

"They're waiting outside," the Marshal said. He looked tired, Bleys thought; his normally round, calm face seemed to be lined and pale.

"I have something I wanted to report to the First Elder in private," the Marshal went on, not looking at Toni.

"Proceed, please," Bleys said, looking directly into the Marshal's pale blue eyes.

"It shames me," the Marshal said, "but I must report that our security has been breached."

"Details, please, Marshal," Bleys said. The officer reached into a small pocket below the waistline of his uniform tunic, to pull out a small case. He handed it to Bleys.

"Details are on this chip," he said. "Shall I summarize?"

"Please."

"It appears that a small, fast vessel managed to enter New Earth's space without being observed," the Marshal said. "I have to report we didn't notice it until it left—which it did by shifting out while still in atmosphere. We were unable to stop it."

"Shifting in the atmosphere?" Bleys said. "That suggests a Dorsai vessel, does it not?"

"I think so, First Elder." The Marshal's face displayed pain.

"Have you any idea what it was doing here?"

"Analyses of the sensors at four training facilities, the Colon shipyard, and seven armament manufactories have revealed anomalous readings," the Marshal said. "Our technician-analysts say the readings are the sort of traces one might get if someone were using personal suppressor fields while infiltrating the facilities."

"So someone came in," Bleys said. "And presumably out. To look? Was there any sabotage?"

"None."

"What's the time frame?"

"The twelve incursions occurred over a sixteen-day period," the Marshal said. "We're still checking the sensor logs from other installations."

"What's your personal reading on this, Marshal?" Bleys asked. The skin around the older man's eyes relaxed a little, and his face regained its normal calmness.

"An intelligence mission, First Elder," he said.

"I agree," Bleys said, nodding. The room was quiet for a moment, as Bleys thought. Then he nodded.

"Thank you, Marshal," he said.

"I wish to apologize, First Elder—" the Marshal began; but Bleys cut him off.

"Accepted, Marshal," he said. "I'm sure your people will be more alert in the future."

"You may count on it."

"I'll review your data later," Bleys continued, handing the chip to Toni. "For the moment, shall we proceed with more routine matters?"

The Marshal agreed, and turned as if about to summon his staff from outside.

"Make it a priority to keep me informed of any further developments," Bleys added. "Let me know immediately about any developments, even if I'm off-planet."

"I'll have courier ships standing by at all times," the Marshal said.

"I have an idea," Bleys said, "that may allow faster communications between us."

"First Elder?"

"We'll go through the details when your staff are here," Bleys said. "The basic idea is to set up a line of ships—a sort of chain—that will maintain station at points between New Earth and Association, each with a precalculated shift already set up to take it to the position of the next vessel in the chain."

"I believe I see," the Marshal said, his face interested. "Each ship can jump and pass its message to the ship waiting at its arrival point—which can then jump as soon as it gets the message." He paused, thinking. "It could get a report from me to you in a day or less."

"Yes," Bleys said. "It'll take a lot of ships and men, but if it works it'll be worth setting up similar chains between all the worlds."

"This could revolutionize everything," the Marshal said. He was smiling, clearly beyond his earlier embarrassment.

"Shall we bring your staff in, then?"

The Marshal turned, but Toni was already moving to the door.

After the Marshal left, Bleys and Toni returned to the lounge, where Bleys activated a security bubble. Toni watched the bubble expand about them without commenting.

"We'll have to try to use the bubble more," Bleys said. "I should have expected an intelligence-gathering effort."

"You're pretty sure it's the Dorsai, aren't you?" Toni said. "You wanted to know what they were up to, and this may be it."

"Only part of it," Bleys said thoughtfully. "I wonder..." His words trailed off into silence.

"What?" she said at last.

"There's no way to tell," he said, "but I can't help wondering if Hal Mayne might be out there."

"Mayne himself?" she said. "That doesn't seem likely, does it? He's not a Dorsai and doesn't have either the espionage experience or the ship-handling skills the Marshal described—and besides, it's a dangerous job; would he risk his loss to his side, that way?"

"He's not averse to risk if the reward is there," Bleys said. "He's important to his side, yes, but I'm sure he believes it can and will continue without him. And you're forgetting he's allied with the Dorsai—he doesn't have to be the one doing the driving."

"That's true," she said.

"Forget that for the moment," Bleys said. "We need to get alarms off right away to all our people, warning them to expect similar espionage; so while I draft the messages, would you please line up ships to carry them?"

"I already started that while we were in the meeting," she said. "I'll get back on that right now."

"One more thing," he said: "we need to send a message to Old Earth, too—to Dahno. If you're willing, I'd like it to be a note directly from you."

"Are you asking me to be an intermediary?"

"Yes," Bleys said. "He's always respected you; I'm hoping he'll be open enough to you to enter into regular contact."

"What do you want me to say?"

"Let me explain the situation as I see it, and then you decide how you'd approach it," Bleys said. "Whether Mayne himself is out there, or not, we're not going to be able to prevent the information that we're mobilizing from getting back to the Final Encyclopedia. That might just tip Old Earth against us. So I'd like you to find a way to tell Dahno that war is now inevitable, and he has to decide which side he's on."

"You'll have to have a meeting, won't you?"

"I'd prefer the idea come from him."

"Maybe I can plant the idea somehow," she said. "But then he'll have to get back to us about it, won't he?"

"Yes," Bleys said, "and probably more than once; he won't come around to this all at once. What I'm going to suggest is that you go to Cassida—it's the closest of the Younger Worlds to Old Earth— and stay available to negotiate with him, using as many back-and-forth ships as it takes, until he comes around."

"Where will you be?"

"Out on the other Worlds again," he said. "There's still work to be done, and I want to check in on how each of our groups reacts to that intelligence ship—I can't let the mention of Dorsai affect their thinking."

"Where do you want to meet Dahno?"

"He'll understand I won't be willing to come to Old Earth," Bleys said, "and he'll fall into a comfortable pattern of trying to find a compromise."

"He won't be willing to come back to the Younger Worlds," she said.

"That's right," he said. "Mars might be a compromise he could accept."

"Won't he be suspicious if I suggest that?"

"That's why you won't suggest it. When he brings up the idea of a meeting, you veto Old Earth and suggest Holmstead."

"On Venus?"

"Yes," Bleys said. "No one in their right mind wants to spend time there, so it's sparsely populated; he'll believe I'm interested in it as a place we can be relatively unobserved."

"He won't want to go there, and will offer an alternative location."

"I think so," Bleys said. "In fact, I'd guess he'll suggest Luna—Old Earth's moon—which of course I'll refuse; and so we'll settle on Mars." He smiled a little.

"That brings up another thing we need to do," he said. "By the time you start negotiating about a location for a meeting, he'll already have decided where he wants to go, and he'll be sending people in ahead of time to set up his security. We need to do the same, and if we move soon, we'll be there first."

"We need to speak with Henry, then," Toni said.

"Yes," Bleys said. "In fact, I think I want him to lead this group personally."

"Will he be willing to be so far away from you?"

"I think I can bring him around," Bleys said. "Particularly when I point out he'd be ensuring my safety."

"I believe I understand," Henry said. The three of them were huddled within the security bubble again, and Bleys had laid out the security problems a meeting with Dahno on Mars would entail.

"I suggest you take only Soldiers who are new to our service since Dahno left," Bleys said. "He won't recognize them if he happens to see them."

"While true," Henry said, "I don't think that's a good idea."

"Oh?"

"Will he not find it suspicious if he arrives and sees no Soldiers?" Henry asked. He shook his head. "It might well scare him away. I'll take some Soldiers he'll know, along with some he won't know. The ones he knows can be out in the open, while the others will remain in the deeper background."

"Do you have people among the new Soldiers who can be trusted with a mission like this?"

"With time to prepare them, yes," Henry said. "On the whole the newer Soldiers tend to be younger and less experienced, and often have the attitude problems of youth, but we weed out those who don't respect their elders. We can do much if we get them to Mars enough ahead of time to settle them into their surroundings and their tasks—and I'll be there, of course."

"But Dahno would recognize you, too," Toni pointed out.

"Of course he will," Henry said. "But he won't think of me as an assassin; my presence will be reassuring to him, which will facilitate your discussions."

"That's a very good point, Uncle," Bleys said.

"Do we know where we should be set up, on Mars?" Henry asked. "We can't bring enough people to have you covered on an entire planet."

"You won't need to," Bleys said. "Dahno won't be willing to go far from his ship, so we can concentrate on areas in the close vicinity of landing pads."

"To cut down on the risk of an ambush," Toni said, "he'll want a place with a lot of people around."

"How many Soldiers can you spare for this duty, Uncle?" Bleys asked.

"I'll want to leave some covering you," Henry said. "Probably under Carl's command. I think I can do that comfortably and still bring about sixty to Mars."

"All right," Bleys said. "That would allow you to spread your people out and get them in place in anywhere from six to ten ports— shall we pick the eleven largest pads and then eliminate the largest one, simply because it's too obvious?"

"That widens the chance that Dahno will pick a place we already have people in," Toni said.

"And one he'll have people in, too," Bleys said.

CHAPTER 41

Centuries after it had become the first planet to undergo a terraforming process, Mars was still not a place most people found comfortable. The planet's small size and distance from its star meant it would always remain colder and darker than any of the worlds that had been terraformed under other stars. The dreariness of the cold darkness was emphasized, for Martians, by the sight, in their night sky, of the light that was their nearest neighbor and the place for which their bodies were best suited, Old Earth.

It was Bleys' first trip to this planet; and now he sat at his desk in *Favored of God*'s lounge, watching a wide-angle view of the Martian twilight as it crept across the pad just outside Mirage. He had never had any reason to make the tedious trip to this out-of-the-way planet—more inaccessible than ever, right now, since Mars was on the opposite side of its star from Old Earth.

Most of humankind felt much the same way.

Mars had loomed large in human imaginations in the days when travel there was impossible; its light was bright in the only night sky mankind had. That time had vanished the day Mars became a place no longer out of reach.

Bleys had read samples of some of the speculations people had written about Mars during that long pre-space flight time. It was no surprise that most of them had been wildly implausible; what surprised him was the amazing variety of dreams human imaginations had been able to craft out of virtually nothing—he continued to find himself disappointed at the human ability to ignore facts in favor of something, anything, that could make one feel good.

He had also been surprised the first time he ran across a reference to Mars as the "Red Planet." The rocks and dust that lent the planet that descriptive name were now largely out of sight, the dust bound by ground cover and the rocks nestling under scraggly variform evergreen bushes and trees.

Still, as he looked across the landing pad he could see occasional eddies of orange dust, that had somehow escaped the clutches of the binding vegetation, swirling in the cold wind of dusk.

A portion of the front façade of the port that serviced Mirage protruded into the left edge of his screen; he could have panned the view to take in more of those buildings, but he had no desire to do so. He preferred to watch the open space where Dahno's ship would soon be landing.

That ship had been waiting in Mars orbit when *Favored* arrived, something Bleys had insisted on, and once the brothers made contact they had negotiated their way to an agreement to land on this small pad and find a way to have their discussion—a negotiation Bleys suspected succeeded only because both sides had people already in place.

Henry, who had been waiting in Barsoom for the decision on where the meeting would take place, made it to Mirage before *Favored* touched down. Calling from the port, he had strongly suggested Bleys leave the ship immediately and move into the spaceport buildings, or even into the town. Dahno, Henry pointed out, arriving last and coming down from space, would have an easy shot at destroying *Favored of God* from above, if he so chose—no one was going to assume that Dahno's ship was unarmed.

"How could he do something like that and hope to get away with it?" Bleys replied. "This is Old Earth's space, and he couldn't hope to go back to that planet without it being known, well before he got there, what he had done."

"There are ways," Toni said; speaking for the first time since their arrival on the surface; she had been somber throughout the trip, but Bleys had no idea what had brought that mood on.

On the screen, Henry nodded. "He could be sending some third ship down," he suggested. "He couldn't be blamed for what happens down here if he's still in orbit at the time."

"That might explain why he's taken so long to follow us down," Toni added.

"I suppose so," Bleys said. "But remember, Dahno is cautious above all else. I can tell you with absolute certainty that when he thought about doing something like that—and I'm sure he thought about it—he also realized I'd be unlikely to remain in *Favored* waiting for him . . . in fact, it's probably the last place he expects me to be, just now. So it's the safest possible place for me."

"And if Dahno has people watching from the port, to tell him you haven't left the ship?" Toni asked.

"That's why I had two of the techs rent a shuttle and take it over the horizon, right after we landed," Bleys said.

Toni subsided in the face of Bleys' logic, but there was still a small frown line between her eyebrows. Henry, in the screen, nodded thoughtfully; and then signed off, intending to review his Soldiers' preparations and positioning.

That had been more than half an hour ago.

Mars' star was now on the horizon behind the port buildings, just out of Bleys' view, and the sky in his screen was shading itself to a dark, almost metallic indigo color that managed to suggest coldness without actually being the black of space. Stars were already showing, in the darker edge of that sky.

"There's a ship approaching," Toni's voice said. After Henry had signed off she had moved to the communications room; these were the first words he had heard from her since that time.

—And there it was, suddenly!

The ship was not as large as *Favored of God*, and was shaped a little differently—a more flattened cylinder. Like *Favored*, it was largely a silver color, polished to a mirror finish; but it was painted in a few places, with letters, numbers, and other markings Bleys could not make out.

The ship seemed to be moving slowly, almost hovering and drifting into its place; and yet it had seemed to appear out of nowhere, so swiftly had it dropped from above. He supposed that meant it had a very experienced driver, one of those who could make everything about shiphandling seem effortless.

He wondered if Dahno had hired a Dorsai. It was possible, he supposed, although his intelligence people had been telling him for some time that the Dorsai were going back to their planet.

For the first time he wondered whether Dahno might have told the Dorsai this would be a good place to take action directly at their major enemy. He felt a breath of coldness, but shook it off—Toni had always insisted the Dorsai would never stoop to assassination.

Bleys put no faith in the likelihood that people in trouble would remain true to their principles. However, he thought the Dorsai had to realize that assassinating a foreign dignitary in Old Earth's space would cause more trouble than they might want to handle.

The ship was down now, nestling almost softly onto the resilient pad surface. And in almost the same moment, Toni's voice came over *Favored*'s intercom.

"We've received a message from Dahno," she said. "He says he's just landed and wants to know where to go to meet you."

"Tell him to meet me in the bar on the main concourse," Bleys said. "We'll decide where to go from there . . . oh, and tell him to dress warmly, and to bring oxygen."

Bleys was perched on a tall stool at the bar of the Seven Came Back Tavern when his half-brother loomed in the broad, open doorway. Bleys had known Dahno was on his way, because a series of alert-looking individuals had been drifting through and past the bar for the last five minutes.

From halfway across the room, it seemed obvious that Dahno was angry. Most of the bar's few patrons noticed it quickly, and, prudently respecting the huge size of the newcomer, moved quietly away.

"I'm not as angry as I look," Dahno said, as he took the second stool over from Bleys—one that was just around the curve of the bar. "You've seen this act before." He punched the control pad before him for a drink while waving away the bartender. At this late hour there were few people about to patronize the port services, and the bartender was happy to be left alone with her entertainment console.

"Hello, Toni," Dahno continued. He smiled cheerily. Bleys thought his brother had put on a little more weight.

"It's good to see you again, Dahno," Toni said. She was smiling, too.

"It's good to be seen," Dahno replied; and reached for the drink rising from the interior of the bar. Then he snorted, looking back to Toni's puzzled face.

"Sorry," he said. "That's a very old Earth joke."

"You didn't look as if you were in a joking mood," Toni said.

"No doubt," Dahno said. "I like the privacy people tend to give me when they think I'm angry." He turned his eyes to his brother.

"With just a little more work, we'd have privacy to talk right here," he said. "My people can bring in an inhibitor field generator."

"Aren't they illegal here?" Toni asked. Dahno shrugged.

"I can set up a *HUSH* field," Bleys said. "But I'm not comfortable about depending on that for the important subjects. You have to know, from my mention of oxygen, that I wasn't planning to talk in this place."

"I know," Dahno said. "But it's cold out there!" He grinned, a little savagely.

"And how do I know who else might be out in the dark?" he added. "I saw some familiar faces in the concourse as I walked over here."

"I figured you wouldn't feel comfortable unless you saw a few Soldiers," Bleys said. "But I guess you don't trust me, brother? I've never tried to harm you in any way, you know that."

"Turn on the field and I'll admit it," Dahno said. "I've learned you weren't behind the people who were stalking me on Earth."

"I don't know anything about that," Bleys said. "I do know you were behind the police who came after me."

"You're right," Dahno said. "I guess I owe you an apology." He grimaced.

"I lost my head," he went on. "You know I've done that before, under stress. My people stopped several attempts on my life, and one was a staff person from the Freiland organization. I thought maybe you'd sent him after me."

"I didn't."

"I realized later it made no sense; but at the time I was angry— all right, and I wasn't thinking well."

"What did you tell the police that would send them after me?"

"They got an anonymous tip that the person in your room might know something about the killings at the Mayne estate."

"They reacted like that to an anonymous tip relating to a years-old case, with no corroboration?"

"Well, maybe they had a little corroboration," Dahno said.

"What do you mean?"

"Remember, I was the one who called in people to clean up after the killings," Dahno said. "I'd made some contacts on Earth before you ever joined me, as part of my efforts to get sources of information on all the planets, and on that trip I had time to renew acquaintances."

"Your acquaintances must be pretty versatile people," Toni said.

"Like every planet, Earth has an underworld," Dahno said. "Some of them aren't just simple thugs, but successful businessmen looking for information that can give them an edge."

"You've been working with them again, I assume," Bleys asked.

"Yes," Dahno said. "In fact, some of their people are out there in the concourse . . . I haven't had enough time to recruit and train dependable Soldiers of my own."

"What was that 'corroboration' you gave the police?"

"I told them where they could find the pistols used in the killings, along with a few small things from the Estate. It was enough to make the authorities think there might be something more to learn in your room."

"You were targeting me that long ago?" Bleys asked.

"Not at all," Dahno said.

"Then why did you set up something that could link the killings to me?"

Dahno's face reddened, but he said nothing.

"I have a hard time believing you were really that stupid, brother," Bleys said at last. "Didn't it occur to you that if they connected me to the killings, you'd be connected, too?"

"I know, I know," Dahno said, his voice rising. "It *was* stupid; I didn't think it out until later, that leading the police to you had to lead them to me, too. But I thought you were out to get rid of me."

He's overplaying his role, Bleys thought.

"Anyway, the police never got to you," Dahno said. "The room was sanitized before they arrived. They only found four people sleeping off a messy party."

"So you knew where I was and you wanted to show me you could have had me taken in, if you'd wanted."

"I just wanted to warn you off," Dahno said. "I thought you should know I wouldn't let you get rid of me without a fight."

"Did you really believe you could manipulate my attitude toward you?"

"It's past, brother," Dahno said. "Let it go. I made a mistake, and I know you never tried to harm me. The way I was looking at it, when our ways parted, the situation changed."

"I don't think we should say any more here," Bleys said.

"I suppose that's so."

"We have to decide on someplace to go," Bleys said. "I don't suppose you'd be comfortable with coming back to *Favored?*"

"I don't think so," Dahno said, a grim sort of smile appearing on his face. "But I have an idea how we can pick a place, if you'll go along with it."

Bleys only looked at his half-brother, waiting.

"Call Henry in here," Dahno said.

Dahno's smile seemed genuine as he greeted Henry; in fact, Bleys was sure it *was* genuine—as far as it went. But that did not mean there was not something else under it.

Bleys gave them time to catch up; but finally he broke in.

"You asked for Uncle Henry for a reason, brother—what is it?"

"Ah, yes," Dahno said. He smiled, and turned back to Henry.

"Uncle, we've been trying to decide on a safe place to have a long talk. I asked Bleys to call you here because I want you to pick our place."

"Me, Dahno?" Henry said. "Why would you ask me?"

"Because I can trust you, Uncle," Dahno said. "If you tell me a place is safe for me, I'll believe you." He looked back at Bleys. "Unless you have an objection, brother?"

"No," Bleys said. He was uneasy, but there was no other option.

"I'm not sure I like this," Henry said. His eyes turned to his other nephew. "Bleys?"

"I have nothing better to suggest, Uncle," Bleys said. "Can you think of a place nearby?"

"I'm sure Uncle Henry hasn't been here long enough to really know this port," Dahno cut in. "Why don't we all leave this bar together and talk a walk along the concourse, until Henry sees a place he might want to suggest?"

Still troubled, Bleys agreed.

CHAPTER 42

"There," Henry said, nodding to indicate an old-fashioned sign ahead of them on the left. Moving along the concourse, they had bypassed numerous business establishments before Henry made his choice. A cloud of alert individuals were doing their best to follow them unobtrusively.

"A church?" Dahno asked.

"A chapel, rather," Henry said. "I am familiar with these places. They serve no single faith, but simply provide calm and quiet for anyone with an inclination to commune quietly with the Lord. It will likely be unoccupied at this hour."

After both sides had swept the chapel with security scanners, the four of them entered, accompanied by two bodyguards from each side; and those individuals stared as Bleys activated the blue security bubble that would keep them—or anyone else—from hearing his conversation with Dahno. Toni and Henry were included in the bubble.

"All right, brother," Dahno said immediately, "this is as secure as we can get. But nothing lasts forever, so why don't we get to it?"

"Fine," Bleys said. "What did you want to talk about?"

Dahno grinned.

"Come now, brother," he said. "Did you really believe you could fool me into thinking this meeting was my idea? I knew perfectly well you were behind everything Toni sent me."

"Then why did you come?"

"Because I'm sure it's better for both of us if we come to an agreement," Dahno said. "All right, I'll start: you said earlier I could retire and you'd leave me alone."

"I meant it," Bleys said. "I still do. But now I have to be convinced you really mean what you say."

"Well," Dahno replied, "you must be aware my organization has continued to work for your plan to divide and paralyze Earth—doesn't that count for something?"

"I don't know your reasons for that," Bleys said. He felt a coldness in him, that seemed to wall him off from the situation, and from his companions; it was as if he were looking at them from a distance. "It's not enough to convince me."

"If we don't come to a truce," Dahno said, "I'm in a good position. You can't damage my position on Earth without exposing your plan to manipulate that planet's people into leaving you a free hand in the Younger Worlds—that information would unite the planet against you."

He stopped, abruptly, eyeing his brother. Then he spoke again, more softly:

"Something's happened, hasn't it? What is it?"

Bleys looked at him for a long moment.

"The timetable's been accelerated," he said finally.

"Timetable?" Something dawned in Dahno's eyes.

"War?" he asked. "Are you saying—"

"Yes," Bleys said.

"I thought you believed that was far off—"

"It was," Bleys said. "But Hal Mayne's been out in the Younger Worlds, and he's accomplished a lot more than I thought possible."

"Mayne again?" Dahno said. "What could he have done that would require you to go to war?"

"He's got the Exotics and the Dorsai committed to helping him," Bleys said. "And he's obtained proof of our mobilization."

"Which he'll use to pull Earth into his camp."

"Don't you think that would happen?"

"It might," Dahno admitted. "I still think my people can paralyze the planet's decision-making processes indefinitely."

"Can they?" Bleys asked. "My understanding is that Rukh Tamani has been very effective in countering your propaganda."

"She's done some damage," Dahno said. "She just appeared out of nowhere, and people listen to her. She's as good as anyone we've got."

"Hal Mayne sent her," Bleys said.

"He did? I guess you were more right about him than I was," Dahno said. But his nod was more decisive than the resignation in his words, and his jaw firmed.

"Tamani's been winning some popular support," he said, "but she can't match our influence with the real decision makers all around the planet."

"Are you sure?" Bleys said. "Anyone you've got in your pocket can be turned around if she gets enough popular support—they'd have to follow along just to keep their positions."

"She won't be getting any more support, though," Dahno said.

"What've you planned?" Bleys asked—but his mind had already leaped to a guess.

"It's already done," Dahno said. "We should get the word any minute—consider it my gift."

"Dahno—" Henry began, a disturbed tone in his voice; Toni's words cut over his.

"Do you mean you've sent someone to kill her?" she said.

"You fool!" Bleys said. His voice was soft but vehement, and the anger in it shocked him; the number of times he had displayed so much emotion could be counted on one hand.

Where is this coming from? His memory of the woman he had seen on that bleak Harmony afternoon rose in his mind.

The other three in the bubble were staring at him.

"Don't you understand what you've done?" he said. He was trying to keep his voice low, but his breath was hot in his nostrils. "Assassination gives her words more credibility that she could have earned in years of preaching!"

As he was speaking, Bleys' mind registered that John Colville, one of the Soldiers outside the bubble, was waving his arms, trying to get their attention. Henry, following Bleys' eyes, saw that Colville was holding one arm up and pointing at his wristpad. Beside him, his comrade, Steve Foster, was keeping his attention firmly on Dahno's two bodyguards, who were standing against a wall, shifting nervously. One had his own wristpad up to his lips and was speaking into it.

"That'll be the news!" Dahno said.

There was no way to avoid it. Still angry, Bleys collapsed the security bubble.

"What is it, John?" Henry asked.

"The ship is reporting news from Old Earth," John said, speaking directly to Bleys. "They say there's been an assassination attempt on Rukh Tamani!"

"'Attempt'?" Dahno asked. "What d'you mean, 'attempt'?"

"The reports say she was only wounded."

"They missed?" Dahno roared.

Colville stared at him, but Dahno turned back to Bleys.

"I've got to go!"

"You can't repair this by rushing back, brother," Bleys said. His anger was gone, and he had a curious sense that he had been emptied out.

"It'll be easier than you think," Dahno said. "It was already set up to get rid of the actual assassins right afterward; all I have to do is manipulate the way people talk about her. No matter what they're saying now, in a couple of days I can change the way they look at her." He grinned. "I may even be able to blame this on the Dorsai."

"*You* did this?" It was John Colville's voice, speaking to Dahno's broad back. Dahno turned to look at the Soldier; but before he could speak, Henry stepped forward, moving up beside Dahno.

"John, you're overwrought," Henry said. "This is not your place."

Shaking off Foster's attempt to hold him back—an attempt hampered by the Soldier's need to keep an eye on Dahno's bodyguards—John turned to Henry.

"It's *not* my place, Henry. I know that! But this is an evil I can't condone."

"I do not ask you to condone it," Henry said. "But you must tend to your own duty—" He indicated Dahno's two bodyguards, that John had been assigned to watch. "—and I will do mine."

Henry turned back to face Dahno.

"Is it so?" he said. "Did you order this assassination?"

"You heard," Dahno said. "She wasn't assassinated."

"You would play word games before the Lord?" Henry asked. His voice was colder than Bleys had ever heard it.

"I have to go," Dahno said. "I can't take the time to argue semantics—not if I want to fix the damage."

"You intend to complete the deed," Henry said.

"*No!*" John Colville yelled; he was turning back from where he had been watching the two bodyguards, his void pistol coming up.

"John—*no!*" Henry said, his voice loud as he tried to penetrate the Soldier's anger while turning to face him. He raised an empty hand toward the younger man, stepping in front of Dahno to shield him—and as he did so, Dahno's two bodyguards acted.

The one closest to Steve Foster threw himself sideways into the Soldier, knocking him backward and freeing the other bodyguard to raise his own void pistol.

"*Don't!*" Dahno yelled; and his arm swept out to push Henry sideways, out of the path of the charge. But the bodyguard had already fired.

There was no sound, no flash, but both Henry and Dahno fell, the impetus of Dahno's arm pushing Henry to the side even as both of them fell forward. Before they hit the ground, John Colville had swung around and fired at the man who had shot. As he did so, the other bodyguard fired at him. The second Soldier, Steve Foster, having recovered quickly, fired a fraction of a second late.

It might have taken two or three seconds, Bleys found himself thinking. The scene on the patio of the Mayne estate came back up from his memory—it had taken only a few seconds to stretch seven bodies out on that floor . . . it was like an echo.

He was aware of a strange detachment in his head, as if his mind had withdrawn from the area behind his eyes, to hide in a room farther back . . . as if his being was just along for the ride now. He saw Foster turning back to face him. There were tears in his eyes.

I should tell him to watch the door, Bleys thought. But before he could do so his eye was caught by Toni's movement—she had somehow reached Henry without Bleys noticing it, and was kneeling beside him.

"He's alive!" She almost yelled the words, and they seemed to wake Bleys.

"How—?" Bleys took a step in her direction, but stopped to point a finger at Foster.

"Call the ship," he ordered. "Have them bring emergency medical equipment—quietly but quickly!"

"What about their people outside?" the Soldier asked.

"Make the call!" Bleys said, and strode to the door. Pulling it open, he looked out, and saw six pairs of eyes looking back at him.

"We have a problem," he said, directing his words at one of Dahno's bodyguards. "Who speaks for your people?"

By the time Kaj Menowsky and some helpers from *Favored of God* had reached the chapel, Dahno's bodyguards, knowing their employer was dead, had agreed to sit quietly in the bar, under observation. Bleys had remained with them, knowing his presence would quell their nervousness; until Toni came into the bar to report that the medical team had removed the bodies of Henry and Dahno, as well as that of John Colville, under the guise of a delivery of supplies to the ship.

"You should call your ship, if you haven't already, and have your friends' bodies removed quietly, too," Toni said, looking at the leader of the bodyguards. "You don't want an alarm raised before you get back to Old Earth."

As he and Toni walked back down the concourse toward the entrance closest to *Favored*, Bleys' back felt cold despite the Soldiers covering their withdrawal. But nothing happened.

At the port entrance they boarded a shuttle bus for the trip to the ship. Bleys expected Toni to want to talk with him, but she maintained her silence. He felt no desire to talk, himself.

Once they were on board, Toni turned to him.

"They're both alive!" she said. Bleys looked down at her.

"How can that be?" he asked.

"Kaj says he thinks they were hit by a single charge," she said. "Maybe that dissipated some of the effect. But Henry wants to talk to you, and Kaj says you need to get there right away."

"I think Dahno will recover," Kaj said as Bleys entered the infirmary. "He was damaged, and machines are maintaining some of his vital functions for the moment; but he's strong."

"And Henry?" Bleys asked.

"He's still alive," Kaj said, "but I think he doesn't have very long." Toni sat down abruptly, her head down. Bleys felt his eyes burning into the medician.

"Why not? If he's still alive you might be able to—"

"No," Kaj said. "Void pistols disrupt neural functions on a cellular level. He took the brunt of that charge, and was more damaged than Dahno. And he was weaker to start with." He looked up at Bleys.

"I'm sorry," he said.

"Bleys," Henry said, as his nephew entered the room. "How is Dahno?"

"He'll live," Bleys said.

"I will not," Henry said. "I feel it. Do not grieve for me; I am content with my life."

"I won't grieve for you, if that's what you want," Bleys said. "But I can't promise not to grieve for my own loss."

"I cannot argue with that," Henry said. His voice, Bleys thought, already seemed weaker. He stood there for a moment, feeling helpless.

"I'll take care of Joshua and his family," he said at last.

"There is no need," Henry said, a smile coming to his face. "Joshua is well with the Lord, and needs no more. . . . But I thank you. I've always known you had a good heart in you."

"Uncle Henry," Bleys began—but Henry's weak voice overrode him.

"Save yourself, Bleys," Henry said. "You walk the paths of damnation, and I will no longer be there to try to help you."

"Uncle—"

"May God bless you and help you, Bleys," Henry said. His voice was almost inaudible—and then it was gone.

As *Favored* dropped inside Luna's orbit, Toni came striding into the lounge, where Bleys had been sitting in silence since they left Mars orbit. It was less than a Standard day since Henry had died. Dahno, still unconscious, was alive among the infirmary's machines.

"Bleys, you have to see this," Toni said. As she was talking she activated the controls for his screen, which Bleys had not turned on; and Bleys found himself looking across a green, grassy field, at what appeared to be the back of a large crowd of people.

"What's going on?" he asked. "What's that roaring noise?"

"This is being broadcast on all the major Old Earth broadcast media," she said. "The reporter stopped her narration to let the crowd noise come through. There's a roadway on the other side of the crowd, and those people are all there because they heard a rumor that Rukh Tamani is coming down the road, heading for a spaceport."

The view on the screen panned sideways, and the reporter began to speak.

"The crowd seems to be about a dozen deep on both sides of the road," she said. "It's been lining the road like this for more than ten kilometers. We've been asking for permission to put a camera into the air, but so far the security people have refused—no one is taking any chances of a repeat attempt on Rukh Tamani's life."

"Kayla," a male voice cut in, "we've just been given permission to take the feed from the security net—" Even as the man spoke, the view shifted.

Now they were looking down on the crowd, and could see the road itself, outlined by the fence that separated it from the people. A small convoy of vehicles entered the screen, and the view panned to watch as they passed by—until, as the convoy approached the far side of the screen, it stopped.

Two figures stepped out of one of the rear vehicles, one small, moving haltingly, and the other—*Hal Mayne!*

As if paralyzed, Bleys watched the smaller figure as it seemed to bless the crowd. It all happened in virtual silence, the noise of the crowd having died away when they saw her. The reporter kept her own silence.

After the moment of blessing, the crowd noise began again, while the figure that was Hal Mayne gathered his smaller companion into the vehicle once more, and they drove off. The reporter began to speak, but Bleys punched the control that shut off the screen once more.

"I have to talk to Hal Mayne," he told Toni. "I have to tell him—" He stopped.

"Would you please try to set up a meeting?" he said.

Before she could reply, the communicator's *EMERGENCY* tone sounded.

"Great Teacher." The captain's voice carried a note that made Bleys sit up straighter.

"What is it, Captain?"

"A broadcast message from Space Authority," the captain said. "We're being warned away."

"Warned away? Do you mean they don't want us to approach the planet?"

"Not just us, Great Teacher—all ships are being warned off. They say the Final Encyclopedia has activated some kind of shield that will circle the whole planet, and that it would be fatal to touch it."

"The whole—" Bleys began; but then caught himself. "Did they say how far away we should be?"

"We're fine," the captain said. "But this space is going to get crowded with other vessels being kept away. I recommend we move away."

"I'd like to stay in the vicinity, though," Bleys said.

"I could land on Luna," the captain said. "I suspect other vessels will do so, too, and it may become crowded down there; but we're closer than most."

"Do so, Captain," Bleys said.

"You probably won't be able to get through to Hal Mayne for a while," Bleys said to Toni, quietly. "Please keep trying. When you get someone in the Final Encyclopedia, put me on to talk to them."

When Toni came back to tell Bleys that she had the Final Encyclopedia's Chief Engineer on the line, Bleys was busily sampling intercepted communications. The Final Encyclopedia was being swamped with hundreds of calls protesting the great shield that now walled the planet off from the rest of the Universe—and walled approaching ships off from the planet. It was clear, though, that the Final Encyclopedia was not about to take the shield down.

The Engineer—his name was Jeamus Walters—was a mousy-looking little man, and he looked exasperated; he did not seem startled at Bleys' explanation of the reason for his call.

"I'll try to find Hal," the Engineer said. "But I can't promise you he'll see you—he's just been made Director of the Final Encyclopedia, and he's going to be pretty busy."

"I understand that," Bleys said. "Tell him, please, that I called—but say that I can wait. I'll call back in a few days, after things have quieted down for you all."

"Captain," Bleys said. "Take us back to Mars, would you? And tell the courier to accompany us, and to be ready to take a message in a few hours."

"What are we doing?" Toni asked.

"I need to try to learn more about what's going on with Old Earth and that shield of theirs," Bleys said. "I was hoping the planetary authorities would become angry enough to make them take it down, but I'm sensing a change in tone."

"I think you're right," Toni said. "The assassination attempt seems to have altered the way a lot of Earthmen are feeling."

"That's what I'm seeing, too," Bleys said. He sighed. "Dahno did us a lot of damage."

"What are you going to do with him?"

"That's one of the reasons I want to send out some messages right away," he replied. "I'm working on a plan for him, but I need a couple of extra ships on hand."

"Is there something I can do?" she asked.

"Keep monitoring the situation," he said. "Keep me on top of major developments. But I need time to think."

CHAPTER 43

Mars was on the other side of the sun from Old Earth, which meant that *Favored of God*'s captain vastly preferred to make their journey back to Old Earth in two phase-shifts, rather than one—the first at an angle that took them well to the side of Old Earth's star and out almost to the orbit of Jupiter, and the second back in to the near-vicinity of Old Earth, again at an angle that kept *Favored* well away from the star. The trip, Captain Broadus had assured Bleys the first time they made it, would still be much faster than trying to proceed around the star by conventional drive.

"There's no hurry, Captain," Bleys told her. "I have a lot to think about."

And he did. He had spent several days near Mars trying to follow the events precipitated by both the assassination attempt and the erection of the shield around Old Earth. There had been much to do, but he had felt himself possessed by an almost manic energy, and had kept his staff busy shuttling information and sending out orders. A steady stream of courier vessels had been moving to and from the Younger Worlds, and three were currently holding station with *Favored*, awaiting their orders.

Dahno remained unconscious in the ship's infirmary, but Kaj assured Bleys that he would recover well enough, given time. Bleys had developed a plan for dealing with him, and it was already in motion.

The question remained: what had Dahno been up to on Old Earth? Bleys still thought it likely that some of the senior Others' leaders were somehow involved; but it was unclear whether those leaders had been plotting with Dahno, or against him. In any case, Bleys was sure the storm of recent events would be causing those leaders to rethink

their loyalties. He would have that to deal with when he left this
system.

What am I going to do about Henry? The question could not be
ducked, although he shrank from going back to tell Joshua.

Bleys watched the screen that was now showing him the orb
of Mars; the planet had been getting smaller, slowly, as they drew
away, but they must now be far enough off for their first phase-shift.
He had decided it was time to get back to Old Earth once more; he
needed to have that talk with Hal Mayne—

"Bleys," Toni said, from her desk behind him and to his left side,
"there's a message coming in."

"What is it?" Bleys said.

"It's from *Many Colors*," she said.

"*Many Colors?*" Bleys said. "She's the end of the chain from New
Earth, isn't she?" Without waiting for her to respond to what had
merely been a rhetorical question, he went on: "She must have
news. Tell the captain to wait."

"The captain's already doing that," Toni said.

Decoded, the news was stunning—and yet, Bleys told Toni, in
hindsight it made perfect sense that the Dorsai, leaving their
planet, would come to Old Earth.

"The only reason we had to think that the Dorsai were going to go
to Mara, to set up a defense there, was because the Exotics themselves were expecting that," Bleys said. "We've never managed to
get sources on the Dorsai, but the Exotics have always been so open
and accommodating that intelligence-gathering there has been fairly
easy."

"Perhaps for the unimportant information," Toni said. "Who can
say whether even the Exotics might be able to keep important
secrets?"

"Well, I made the mistake of believing they were being consolidated on Mara." He shook his head.

"Mayne caught me out on this one," he said. "I thought it was a major sacrifice for the Exotics, to strip Kultis of everything valuable so they could protect Mara, but it made sense. Who could believe the Exotics would strip *both* their planets of everything, to leave themselves wide open for us to walk in whenever we want?"

"You mean they sent all of their assets to Old Earth?"

"It must be," he said. "I expect we'll see both Exotic and Dorsai ships—a lot of them—entering Old Earth's space very soon. Where else can they have gone?"

"But this report that the Dorsai are going to Old Earth isn't based on any hard information," Toni objected. "It could be a mistake, or even a piece of misinformation."

"It isn't," Bleys said. "It makes too much sense for it to be wrong. That phase-shield wall around Old Earth changed everything. A wall like that would only slow down a determined attack from outside, normally, because attackers could simply move up close enough to get their bearings, shift right through it—and have time on the other side to recover and mount an attack on the planet."

"I see!" Toni exclaimed. "With the Dorsai at Old Earth, they can simply wait behind the wall and destroy any ship shifting through it before it can recover from the effects of the shift!"

"More than that," he said. "They can also threaten to come out from behind the wall whenever one of our ships comes near enough to try to set up for a safe shift. Forcing our ships to shift from farther away widens the uncertainty factor—" He stopped as she made a gesture indicating he had lost her. "—I mean, the farther a ship moves in a shift, the less certainty it can have that it will come out exactly where it intends." He stopped, to let her think that over.

"I think I see," she said after a moment. "It's something like the fact that the farther away an archer is from his target, the more likely it is his arrow will miss the target—" He started to speak, but she checked him with an upraised hand. "—but there are no such factors as windage in space, so it must be a factor of the physics involved?"

"That's an analogy, only," he said, "so don't try to run too far with it. Let's simply say that under the principles of uncertainty, the farther a ship tries to shift, the more its point of arrival has to be pictured as a sort of *spray* pattern."

"I understand," she said. "That's why interstellar ships take a number of shifts to make their trips—they make relatively short shifts so that they don't come out of shift too far off-course. And it takes time because when they come out of each shift, they have to figure out exactly where they are before they can calculate their next shift."

"Exactly," he said. "That's why only the most accomplished spacers, like the best Dorsai, dare to try to shift in a planet's atmosphere—they do it in such short jumps that they don't have to calculate very much. . . . I've heard they just judge it by eye, or maybe by feel."

"So if we tried to shift to Old Earth from—let's say the orbit of Mars—we couldn't be sure we'd come out inside that wall of theirs."

"Yes," Bleys said. "And if we sent a fleet, it'd be statistically certain some of them wouldn't get it right; the greater the range from which a ship makes a phase-shift, the greater the likelihood of errors—such as coming out on the wrong side of the wall, coming out so near it that they touch it and are destroyed—or coming out inside some other solid object, such as the planet itself."

"Which would create a big explosion?"

"About the size of a large nuclear weapon," Bley responded—somewhat absently.

"It's not that we can't shift our fleets through the shield-wall any time we want—once we have our ships and people ready," he went on musingly. "But our people would know they were being asked to make a fairly long-range shift into a fairly small pocket of empty space—it's going to be hard to motivate them."

Toni was silent; and after a moment he turned to look at her.

"Ask the captain to pick a place for us to sit, on Old Earth's side of the star," he said. "Perhaps somewhere in Mars' orbit—although of course she's not there—and then give those coordinates to *Many Colors*, so she'll know where to come once she's delivered the message I'm about to give her. I want it to go to New Earth."

He sat back, returning his gaze to the screen. While he had been talking with Toni, *Favored*'s path had moved the planet out of sight; but then, it was the stars he wanted to see, anyway.

"The captain has decided on a rendezvous point," Toni said a short time later, "and the information's been passed to *Many Colors*. Since she's only going back to her place in the chain, she doesn't need to calculate a jump, and is ready to go."

"All right," Bleys said. "Take a look at this." He touched a control, sending the file to her own screen, and she sat down to read what he had written.

To all who believe in the future for ourselves and our children:

I have been reluctant to speak out, since it has always been my firm belief that those like myself exist only to answer questions— once they have been asked, and if they are asked.

However, I have just now received information, from people fleeing Old Earth, which alarms me. It speaks, I think, of a danger to all those of good intent; and particularly to such of us on the new worlds. For some hundreds of years now, the power-center worlds of the Dorsai, with their lust for warlike aggression, the Exotics, with their avarice and cunning, and those the Friendly people have so aptly named the Forgotten of God—these, among the otherwise great people of the fourteen worlds, have striven to control and plunder the peaceful and law-abiding Cultures among us.

Toni looked up from her screen.

"It's a declaration of war," she said.

"No, it's a call to arms," Bleys said. "I'm not calling for war. I'm trying to tell people that someone else had already started a war, and we need to work together to defend ourselves."

Toni looked back to her screen.

"Let me rephrase that," he said. "It's—" He stopped as she made a movement with her lips, but her eyes never left her screen and she did not speak. He stayed silent himself.

For some hundreds of years we have been aware that a loose conspiracy existed among these three groups, who have ended by arrogating the title of Splinter Cultures almost exclusively to themselves, when by rights it applies equally, as we all know, to hundreds of useful, productive, and unpredatory communities among the human race. We among you who have striven quietly to turn our talents to the good of all, we whom some call the Others but whom those of us who qualify for that name think of only as an association of like minds, thrown together by a common use of talents, have been particularly aware of this conspiracy over the past three hundred years. But we have not seen it as a threat to the race as a whole until this moment.

Now, however, we have learned of an unholy alliance, which threatens each one of us with eventual and literal slavery under the domination of that institution orbiting Earth under the name of the Final Encyclopedia. I and my friends have long known that the Final Encyclopedia was conceived for only one purpose, to which it has been devoted ever since its inception. That purpose has been the development of unimaginable and unnatural means of controlling the hearts and minds of normal people. In fact, its construction was initially financed by the Exotics for that purpose; as those who care to investigate the writing of Mark Torre, its first Director, will find.

That aim, pursued in secrecy and isolation which required even that the Encyclopedia be placed in orbit above the surface of Earth, has been furthered by the Encyclopedia's practice of picking the brains of the best minds in each generation; by inviting them, ostensibly as visiting scholars, to visit that institution.

"Won't this bring Old Earth against us?" she said. She did not look up as she said it, but continued reading, intent.

"I was hoping Old Earth would resent that Mayne put up his shield-wall without getting their permission," he said. "For a while there, the reactions down there gave me hope of that. But things have calmed down."

She looked up.

"You mean you now think Old Earth is going to accept Mayne's acts?" she asked.

"Yes," he said. "That assassination attempt seems to have been a watershed event. A lot of people there are still against the Encyclopedia's actions, but those who are for it—they're most for Tamani—have been energized."

Her eyes returned to her screen.

Also, it has continued to be financed by the Exotics, who, records will show, have also had a hand in financing the Dorsai, who were from the first developed with the aim of becoming a military arm that could be used to police all other, subject worlds.

Those conspirators have now been joined in their unholy work by the people of Old Earth themselves—a people whose early, bloody attempts to keep all the newly settled worlds subject to themselves were only frustrated by the courageous resistance of the peoples on all those Younger Worlds. But it took a hundred years of continuous fighting, as you all know from the history books you studied as children.

Now the people of Old Earth, under the leadership of the Final Encyclopedia, have finally thrown off all pretense of innocent purpose. They have withdrawn the unbelievable wealth accumulated by the Exotic Worlds by trade and intrigue from such people as ourselves, moving it to their treasury on Earth. They have also, openly, in one mass movement, evacuated the Dorsai from their world and brought them to Earth; to begin building the army that is intended to conquer our new worlds, one by one, and leave us enslaved forever under the steel rule of martial authority. And they have begun to ready for action those awesome weapons the Encyclopedia itself has been developing over three centuries.

They are ready to attack us—we who have been so completely without suspicion of their arrogant intentions. We stand now, essentially unarmed, unprepared, facing the imminent threat of an inhuman and immoral attempt to enslave or destroy us. We will now begin to hear thrown at us, in grim earnest, the saying that has been quietly circulated among the worlds for centuries, in order to destroy our will to resist—the phrase that not even the massed armies of all the rest of mankind can defeat the Dorsai, if the Dorsai choose to confront those armies.

But do not believe this. It was never true, only a statement circulated by the Exotics and the Dorsai for their own advantage. As for massed armies, as you all know, we have none. But we can raise them. We can raise armies in numbers and strengths never dreamed of by the population of Old Earth. We are not the impoverished, young peoples that Old Earth, with Dow deCastries, tried to dominate unsuccessfully in the first century of our colonization. Now, on all the worlds our united numbers add up to nearly five billion. What can be done against the courage and resistance of such a people, even by the four million trained and battle-hardened warriors that Old Earth has just imported from the Dorsai.

United, we of the Younger Worlds are invincible. We will arm, we will go to meet our enemy—and this time, with the help of God, we will crush this decadent, proud planet that has threatened us too long; and, to the extent it is necessary, we will so deal with the people of Old Earth as to make sure that such an attempt by them never again occurs to threaten our lives, our homes, and the lives and homes of those who come after us.

In this effort, I and my friends stand ready to do anything that will help. It has always been our nature never to seek the limelight; but in the shadow of this emergency I have personally asked all whom you call the Others, and they have agreed with me, to make themselves known to you, to make themselves available for any work or duty in which they can be useful in turning back this inconceivable threat.

The unholy peoples of Old Earth say they will come against us. Let them come, then, if they are that foolish. Let us lay this demon once and for all. How little they suspect it will be the beginning of the end, for them!

Signed, Bleys Ahrens.

Toni, after reading the announcement, was silent for a long moment.

"For immediate release to the media on all the Younger Worlds," Bleys said.

"Just your name, no title?" she said at last.

"No," he said. "No title would have any meaning here. And it's psychologically more effective this way—it's meant to tell people that we're at war, and that I'm just another human being in it with them."

"Why do this at all?"

"I have to get out in front," he said. "Mayne stole a march on me, and to maintain my credibility as the leader of the Others, as well as

of the Younger Worlds, I can't let it be seen that I've been surprised."

"This letter does more than that," she said.

"You mean it's deliberately inflammatory," he said. He nodded
without waiting for her reply.

"It is that. But that's necessary—people have to be pumped up
for a war; they wouldn't want to do it, otherwise. Give it to *Many
Colors* and send her on her way—I want my letter published on all
the Younger Worlds before the Dorsais' movement becomes public
knowledge."

CHAPTER 44

Favored of God had been at the new rendezvous point for just under half a Standard day when the in-system communications its technicians had been monitoring began to carry reports of the arrivals of the first of the Dorsai ships. It was most likely, the captain explained, that they had come out of shift on the fringes of the system, before recalculating and shifting inward; and they were all coming out of their final shifts well in-system from where *Favored* lay quietly in Mars' orbital plane.

For the next half-day the arrival of the Dorsai was a media sensation, and Bleys' people were able to relay to him broadcast coverage as the Dorsai ships were passed through irises opened in the shield-wall and assigned orbital parking slots just inside the wall. But as the process continued it quickly became old news, and the media turned to other interests.

"It's time to go in," Bleys said to Toni. "Mayne's had time to digest the press of events, so he'll be able to meet me."

"Why would he meet you?" she asked. "For that matter, why do you want to meet with him—again?"

"You don't think I should?"

"I don't think it's good for you," she said.

"What do you mean?"

"I mean . . . well, I've never been there when you've talked to him, but it's always seemed to me as if you come back from those meetings—different."

"'Different'?"

"For a while. . . . I mean, you're usually—distracted. And unhappy."

"I though you said I was sad a lot, anyway?"

"Yes, but this is different. I mean—" She stopped, thinking. "It's different from that. . . . You're more . . . stirred up—"

"I'm not sure exactly what you're trying to say," he said, "but it seems to me you're talking about some effects Hal Mayne has on me personally."

"Well, yes," she said.

"That doesn't really matter, then," he said, nodding to himself.

"It doesn't matter?"

"If it's only me, it doesn't matter," he said. "As long as meeting him doesn't harm my mission."

She remained silent.

Favored of God was less than an hour from Old Earth when the listeners in her communications room alerted Bleys that an announcement had been made: the new Director of the Final Encyclopedia was going to address the planet shortly.

"Well, he won't be able to talk with you for a while yet, then," Toni said. Her look said she was asking what he wanted to do.

"Have the captain slow our approach a little," Bleys said. "And have Mayne's speech piped in here." As she reached for the control pad on her desk, he stopped her.

"And would you, please, contact Jeamus Walters yourself?"

"The Final Encyclopedia's—what did he call himself?—*Chief Engineer?* That's right, we were told to contact him personally to set up this meeting."

"Yes," Bleys said. "I think by the time you and he make the necessary arrangements, Hal Mayne will be done speaking."

"It sounds as if you don't expect him to make a long speech."

"Not him," Bleys said. "It's like pulling teeth to get him to talk, usually."

"All right," Toni said. "I'll review what we were told before, and be ready."

"Thank you," he said; and turned his attention to the screen, which was set to pick up a broadcast channel. The time lag in the signal from Old Earth was irrelevant, at this point.

Bleys stared into the screen as Hal Mayne made his opening remarks. The face he saw there looked as strong and powerful as before, and Bleys, despite his recognition of the primitiveness of his visceral reaction, was finding himself captured by its aura of power and certainty. Since the very first days of humankind, people had been instinctively drawn to those they could feel were powerful enough to take care of them, and Bleys now had no doubt that many Earthmen would find in that face the comfort and security of leadership.

"I've been honored," Mayne was continuing, "by being chosen by Tam Olyn, Director of the Encyclopedia for over eighty years, to follow him in that post. As you all know, the only Director before Tam Olyn was Mark Torre; the man who conceived of, planned and supervised the building of this great work from its earliest form, on the ground at the city of St. Louis in the northwestern quadrisphere of this world.

"Mark Torre's aim, as you know, was to create a tool for research into the frontiers of the human mind itself, by providing a storage space for all known information on everything that mind has produced or recognized since the dawn of intellectual consciousness. It was his belief and his hope that this storehouse of human knowledge and creativity would provide materials and, eventually, a means of exploring what has always been unknown and unseeable—in the same way that none of us, unaided, can see the back of his or her own head.

"To that search, Tam Olyn, like Mark Torre before him, dedicated himself. To that same faith that Mark Torre had shown, he adhered through his long tenure of duty here.

"I can make no stronger statement to you, today, than to say that I share the same faith and intent, the same dedication. But, more fortunate than the two men who dedicated their lives to the search before me, I may possess something in addition. I have, I believe, some reason to hope that the long years of work here have brought us close to our goal—that we are very near, at last now, to stepping over the threshold of that universe of the unknown which Mark

Torre dreamed of entering and reaping the rewards of exploring, that inner exploration of the human race we have never ceased to yearn toward; unconsciously to begin with, but later consciously, from the beginning of time.

"When the moment comes that this threshold is crossed, the lives of none of us will ever be the same again. We stand at perhaps the greatest moment in the known history of humanity; and I, for one, have no doubt whatsoever that what we have sought for over millennia, we will find; not in centuries or decades from now, but within our lifetimes and possibly even in a time so close that if I could tell you certainly, as I now speak, how long it would be, the nearness of it would seem inconceivable to us all.

"But in any case, I give you my promise that while I am Director of the Final Encyclopedia, I will not allow work toward that future to be slowed or halted, by anything. There is no greater pledge I can offer you than that, and I offer it now, with all the strength that is in me.

"Having said this about myself and the Directory, I will now turn from that subject to introduce someone who, I think, means so much to so many of us, that this, too, would have seemed inconceivable a short year ago.

"Peoples of Earth, it's my pleasure and honor to introduce Rukh Tamani."

Bleys had not been expecting Hal Mayne to turn the broadcast over to the woman who had so recently escaped assassination. He gazed into the dark, beautiful face on the screen as if entranced. He had met the woman in person once, in her full armed power in a wild environment beyond Bleys' own control. At that time she had been a wild, uncontrollable figure of danger; now—he searched her face— now she was . . . what?

That she had been mistreated, hurt, was obvious. He had seen images of her, taken soon after she arrived on Old Earth; even then she had seemed thin and fragile—the result, he was sure, of her imprisonment in Barbage's cells.

She still looked thin, and he thought it was obvious she had been wounded—wounded badly. She seemed almost to be made of some glasslike substance that would break at a loud noise. But her voice, low and vibrant, demanded attention, convincing anyone who listened that this woman carried special truths in her frail body.

"I am sorry to have caused you grief," she said softly. "I have been told that many of you believed me dead or at least badly hurt in recent days; and because you believed this, you grieved. But you should not grieve for me, ever.

"Grieve instead for those things more important under Heaven. For any who may have shared their lives with you and now suffer or lack. For your angers which wound, your indifference which hurts or kills, more than any outright anger or cruelty does.

"Grieve that you live in yourself, walled and apart from your fellow women and men. Grieve for your failures in courage, in faith, in kindness to all.

"But, grieving, know that it is not necessary to grieve, for you need not have done or been that which causes you to grieve.

". . . For there is a great meaning to life, which each of you controls utterly for yourself; and which no one else can bar you from without your consent. . . ."

She spoke on; and within moments Bleys, stunned, found himself listening as she read to the people of Old Earth his own letter, that he had so recently sent out to be released to the people of the Younger Worlds.

"How can she have that letter?" Toni asked, voicing Bleys' own thoughts from behind him. "It can't possibly have gotten to New Earth, been released, and been reported back here!"

"But it has been," he said. He shook his head. "We developed our own method of sending messages faster than everybody thought possible," he went on. "It shouldn't surprise us that Hal Mayne tried to arrange faster communications, too."

"But even if he's set up a chain of ships—" she began.

"It got here too fast for that," he said. "He's got something else."

"Instructions are coming in from Jeamus Walters," she said. She listened in on the circuit from the communications room for a moment.

"This is going to be dangerous," she said. "They say they'll open a tunnel in the shield-wall, that you can enter from outside the wall; and that Hal Mayne will meet you inside it."

"You're right, that *does* sound dangerous," he said. "Get the details, and we'll go right away." He smiled, and saw that although her face retained its expression of concern, her eyes smiled back at him.

CHAPTER 45

As the atmosphere bled out of the airlock, Bleys could feel slight pressures and movements at odd places around his body. He knew it was the air inside his vacuum suit pushing the suit away from his body in response to the increase in the pressure differential. He had never been in a vacuum before, but he had read about it.

He was excited about being outside the ship, with nothing but the transparent suit, and light-years of nothingness, separating him from the stars. The reaction pleased him, because he knew he had been depressed since the shield-wall around Old Earth went up, and he had been a little uneasy about how objective his decisions would be.

Beside him, Captain Broadus touched another control, and the panel at the end of the lock seemed to pop outward a little, soundlessly, to slide to the side and out of sight, while a ramp telescoped out of the airlock floor, creating a ten-meter-long bridge that had no anchor for its other end. The hatchway now framed a field of stars as bright as he had ever seen them.

"Are you all right, Great Teacher?" the captain asked. Her voice was solicitous, even beyond her normal deference toward her employer; she was aware he had no free-fall experience, and she had insisted on seeing him safely to the iris in the shield-wall that would take him to his meeting with Hal Mayne.

Taking no chances, the captain had also insisted on tethering herself to him even before the lock was voided; and now she followed him along the gravity-augmented ramp, until at last they stood at its end, looking across an expanse of crystal-clear nothing at a translucent grayness so large it could not be thought of as a wall.

Bleys wondered if the light in this vacuum played tricks with human eyes. Everything—the ramp, the captain, even his hands— seemed sharply focused as he looked at them, but at the same time he felt unsure about his perceptions of distance; he could not depend on his eyes to tell him how far they were from the shield-wall, although it had been determined that *Favored of God* would keep station a good two hundred meters out.

The captain had been listening as the Final Encyclopedia's Chief Engineer, Jeamus Walters, described the dangers of coming into contact with that wall. Like the walls that shielded the Encyclopedia itself, it was an application of the same phase physics that made interstellar travel feasible—but this wall, once it scattered a physical object's component particles across the Universe, would not bring them back together.

Knowing that, the captain had made no bones about the fact that she intended to personally convey Bleys to the iris, which from here could be seen as a glowing dot on the grayness. But Bleys had insisted that the captain was not to enter the tunnel itself.

The captain was still unhappy; in her opinion, it was all too possible for Bleys, inexperienced as he was, to make any of a number of fatal mistakes.

Now she insisted on briefing him once more on the entire procedure; but before long Bleys found himself falling through space toward the gray wall. Although he had read about the experience of free-fall before, he still found it unsettling to face the actual decision to step off the ramp into nothingness.

The captain was strapped directly behind him, where she could best control their combined center of gravity by means of her suit's power belt—Bleys was under the strictest orders to leave his own belt alone.

When the glowing dot that was their target had resolved itself into a coin-size disk, Bleys' body suddenly realized it was falling into that disk, that it was a hole and he was dropping to it much too quickly—

He closed his eyes, going into breath-control exercises; and the panic reaction eased off, to lodge somewhere behind his breastbone. After a couple of minutes he felt relaxed enough to be able to open his eyes once more—and found they were unexpectedly close!

He checked an instinctive protest, as he felt a braking force slow-ing his fall. The iris, that he had seen as a disk, now appeared to his brain—trying to put into meaningful terms the signals sent by his eyes—like a sidelit landing area on a gray spaceport pad. For the first time he noticed that a dark bar cut across the iris, well away from its center, which must be the end of the floor that had been floated into the tunnel; its presence gave him a reference point that told him he was now rotating slightly. . . . The captain, expert spacer that she was, was orienting him properly, so that when he pushed his way through the pressure seal at the end of the tunnel he would be able to simply step onto that floor.

The floor, when he got there, turned out to be obscured by a glowing mist that made him feel as if he were stepping into a cloud. He had been told the air in the tunnel would be supersaturated with water vapor, to cut down the risk of a deadly static-link to the phase-field that made up the tunnel wall, but he had not expected the surreal vision created as the lights at the sides of the floor re-flected off the myriad of tiny droplets in the air.

He unsealed his helmet and tilted it back. The air was heavy, and cool on his skin, like a light rain; around him the mist, apparently subject to faint air currents, seemed to be billowing slowly. He could not see his feet, or the floor; and for a moment he was disoriented.

He froze in place for a moment, until his searching eyes recognized that the billows of mist seemed slightly thinner in one direction—which matched what he had been told to expect. He started walking in that direction, moving cautiously.

After a minute, or perhaps a little more, he became aware that a darker shape was appearing out of the mist before him; and in mo-ments he could see it was Hal Mayne, also wearing a vacuum suit with the helmet thrown back.

Bleys felt as if the hairs on the back of his neck were trying to stand on end. This man coming toward him at a fast walk once more looked very different than he had the last time Bleys had seen him—he was coming on toward Bleys as if he didn't intend to stop, as if he were some war machine that could not be prevented from rumbling right over Bleys. . . . Bleys told himself it was the vacuum suit, giving Mayne extra bulk.

And yet, once more Bleys felt the old sense of kinship with the younger man now coming to a halt before him—the sort of tug at his attention, his mind, his heart, that he would perhaps have expected if he had an identical twin.

Hal Mayne was just standing there, looking at him; and Bleys recalled that he himself was the one who had requested this meeting—that, in fact, all of their meetings had been initiated by Bleys . . . he suppressed a twinge of hurt, and opened the dialogue as a good host should.

"Well," he said, "you've got your Dorsai and everything you want from the Exotics locked up, here. I take it, then, you're determined to go through with this?"

"I told you there was never any other way," Hal said. His voice was neutral, distant. It was as if they had simply stepped right into their last conversation. Bleys wondered if he wasn't wasting his time here, after all.

"So now the gloves come off," he said. Belatedly, he realized the words could be taken as a threat.

"Yes," Hal Mayne said. "Sooner or later they had to, I being what I am and you being what you are."

"And what are you?"

"You don't know, of course," Hal said, nodding slightly, as if he were in a conversation with himself.

"No," Bleys said, feeling now as if he were trying to bridge a chasm with his words. "I've known for some time you're not just a boy whose tutors I watched die on a certain occasion. How much more, I still don't know. But it'd be petty-minded of me to hide the fact that I've been astonished by the quality of your opposition to me. You're too intelligent to move worlds like this just for revenge on me because of your tutors' deaths. What you've done and are doing is too big for any personal cause. Tell me—what drives you to oppose me like this?"

"What drives me?" Hal Mayne's tone was almost perfunctory, although his face wore a kind of smile; but his body spoke too, conveying a message of profound weariness that resonated with something inside Bleys himself.

"A million years of history and prehistory drive me," Mayne continued, "as they drive you. To be more specific, the last thousand years of history drive me. There's no other way for you and I to be, but opponents. But if it's any consolation to you, I've also been surprised by the quality of your opposition."

"You?" Bleys found himself startled, as if the Universe had turned itself over. "Why should you be surprised?"

"Because I'm more than you could imagine," Hal said, "just as you've turned out to be something I couldn't imagine. But then when I was imagining this present time we live in I had no real appreciation of the true value of faith. It's something that goes far beyond blind worship. It's a type of understanding in those who've paid the price to win it. As you, yourself, know."

Bleys was at a loss. He was sure Hal was telling him something important—was even letting his guard down—but Bleys could not tell what his words meant, or what they were leading to.

"As I know?" he said, temporizing.

"Yes. As you, of all people, know."

Bleys shook his head, more in puzzlement than in denial.

"I should have dealt with you when you were much younger," he said. Once again, he was only making conversation, trying to cover himself with words while he thought, furiously.

"You tried. You couldn't," Hal said. His voice was soft, and his face serious, with no hint of a threat or boast.

"I did?" said Bleys. "I see. You're using faith, again, to reach that conclusion?" He was probing, trying to find something for his mind to draw understanding from.

"Not for that," Hal said. "No, only observation and fact." Hal's eyes, Bleys thought, were watching him, as if he were a laboratory subject. "Primarily," Hal went on, "the fact that I'm who I am, and know what I can do."

"You're mistaken if you think I couldn't have eliminated a sixteen-year-old boy if I'd wanted to." Bleys was repelled by this line of conversation, but he felt compelled to go where the thoughts led, to see where Hal might be going.

"No, I'm not mistaken," Hal said. "As I say, you tried. But I wasn't a boy, even then when I thought I was. I was an experienced adult, who had reasons for staying alive. I told you I've learned faith, even if it took me three lives to do the learning. That's why I know

I'm going to win, now. Just as I know my winning means your destruction, because you won't have it any other way."

Three lives? What is he saying?

"You seem to think you know a great deal about me," Bleys said, forcing a smile that he hoped would cover his confusion.

"I do," Hal said. "I came to understand you better by learning to understand myself—though understanding myself was a job I started long before you came along." He paused, as if gathering himself for some effort, and Bleys found himself tensing up.

"If you'd been only what I thought you were the first time I saw you," Hal said, "the contest between us would already be over. More than that, I'd have found some way by this time to bring you to the side of things as they must be for the race to survive."

Bleys was unable to believe what he was hearing. Never before had he heard this boy—*man*, he reminded himself—speaking in terms that, in a lesser person, could be construed as braggadocio.

"But since that day at the estate," Hal was going on, "I've learned about myself, as well as more about you, and I know I'll never be able to bring you to see what I see until you, yourself, choose to make the effort to do so. And without that effort, we're matched too evenly, you and I, by the forces of history, for any compromise to work."

"I'm not sure I understand you," Bleys responded, hoping for a clarification of some kind, "and that's unusual enough to be interesting."

"You don't understand me because I'm talking of things outside your experience," Hal said. "I came to talk to you here—as I'll always be willing to come to talk to you—because I've got to hang on to the hope you might be brought to consider things beyond the scope of what you look at now; and change your mind."

"You talk like a grandfather talking to a grandson," Bleys said. He told himself he should show anger at the condescension he had perceived, but he was not angry.

"I didn't mean to," Hal said. He showed no contrition. "But the hard fact is," he went on, "you've had only one lifetime from which to draw your conclusions. I've had three. It took me that long to become human; and because I've finally made it, I can see how you, yourself, fall short of being the full human being the race has to produce to survive the dangers it can't even imagine yet. Like it or not, that experience is there, and a difference between us."

And that quickly, the floor fell out from beneath Bleys' mental feet—Hal was back into that strangeness of moments earlier, and Bleys was lost. Searching for something to use, he fastened on Hal's words about becoming a "full human being."

"I told you you were an Other," he said.

"Not exactly," said Hal. "If you remember, you left me to infer it. But I'm splitting hairs. In a sense you were right. In one sense I am an Other, being a blend of all that's new as well as all that's old in the race. But I'm not the kind of Other who's Everyman. Your kind, if it survives, are at best going to be a transient form of human. Mine, if it does, will be immortal."

A threat?

"I'm sorry," Bleys said. "I don't have a kind. I'm my own unique mixture."

"As are we all," Hal said, nodding. "But what matters is that on top of your own talents, you were raised on Association by a family that was pure Friendly, and it's that which dominates in you."

The shift in the conversation, from Hal to Bleys himself, was startling.

Why did he bring that up? And what does he mean by it?

"Where did you find records that told you that?" Bleys asked.

"I know," Hal said, his tone weary again, "that the official records of your birth and movements all show what your brother fixed them to say."

"Then what makes you say something like this?"

"The correct knowledge. An absolute knowledge that comes from joining together bits and pieces of general records that hadn't been tampered with—because there was no reason to tamper with them—at the Final Encyclopedia. I put them together only a year ago, and then made deductions from them using something I taught myself during my first trial of life. It's called intuitive logic."

"First trial of life"? Bleys found himself frowning, and wiped it away as giving away too much of himself.

"Ah," he said; and found himself suddenly making a mental connection to Hal's words about his method of thinking. "I believe what you're talking about may be what I've been calling interval thinking."

"The name hardly matters."

"Of course not," Bleys said, almost shrugging. "So there's more to learn about you than I'd imagined. But tell me, why place so much emphasis on the fact that part of what I am by inheritance and upbringing may be Friendly?"

"For one reason," Hal said, with a slight air of being patient, "because it explains your ability of charisma, as well as that of those Others who have it to some extent or another. But I'd rather you called yourself Faith-Holder than Friendly. Because, more than anyone on all the worlds suspects, it's a form of Faith-Holding that rules you. You never were the bored crossbreed whose only concern was being comfortable during his own brief years of life. That was a façade, a false exterior set up in the first place to protect you from your older half-brother, Dahno—who would have been deathly afraid of you if he'd suspected you had a purpose of your own."

For the first time, Bleys realized he was now at a tremendous disadvantage—and that he might have been so from the first time he ever heard about Hal Mayne. . . . The man seemed to know more about him than anyone should, to be able to read things out of his mind. It was frightening, but it was, in a strange way, exalting.

"He would, indeed," Bleys said softly, just making conversation while he thought. . . . Then he recovered himself. "Not that I'm agreeing with these fancies and good-nights of yours, of course."

"Your agreement isn't necessary," said Hal, his face suddenly seeming distant. "As I was saying, you used it first to protect yourself against Dahno, then to reassure the rest of the Others that you weren't just using them for your own private purposes. Finally, you're using it still to blind the people of the worlds you control to that personal goal that draws you now more strongly than ever. You're a Faith-Holder, twisted to the worship of a false god—the same god under a different mask that Walter Blunt worshipped back in the twenty-first century. Your god is stasis. You want to enshrine the race as it is, make it stop and go no further. It's the end you've worked toward from the time you were old enough to conceive it."

Walter Blunt? That old man who founded the Chantry Guild, centuries ago, that eventually turned into the Exotics?

"And if all this should be true," Bleys said, trying now to put a good face on his confusion, "the end is still the end. It remains inevitable. You can think all this about me, but it isn't going to make any difference."

"Again, you, of all people, know that's not so," Hal said, an air of patience again in his words, as if he found himself having to explain something obvious to a recalcitrant child. "The fact I understand this is going to make all the difference between us. You took over the relatively harmless organization of the Others while letting them think that the power they gained was all their own doing. But now you'll understand that I'm aware it was mainly accomplished by converting to your own followers the people who were already in charge. Which you did largely through the use of Others who had a large Friendly component in their background, people with their own natural, culturally developed, charismatic gift to some degree, who used it under your own personal spell and command, and Dahno's. Meanwhile, covered by the appearance of working for the Others, you've begun to spread your own personal faith in the inevitably necessary cleansing of the race, followed by a freezing of it into an immobility of changelessness."

He stopped for a moment, as if waiting for some response, but Bleys could not speak.

"Unlike your servants and the Others who've been your dupes," Hal went on, "you're able to see the possibility of a final death resulting from that state of stasis, if you achieve it. But under the influence of the dark part of the racial unconsciousness whose laboratory experiment and chess piece you are—as I also am, on the other side—you see growth in the race as the source of all human evils, and you're willing to kill the patient, if necessary, to kill the cancer."

He stopped again. And this time, to Bleys, it felt like an Ending.

He found no words for a long moment.

"You realize," Bleys said finally, feeling weary, "that now I have no choice at all but to destroy you?"

"You can't afford to destroy me," Hal said, "even if you could. Just as I can't afford to destroy you. This battle is now being fought for the adherence of the minds of all our fellow humans. What I have to do, to make the race understand which way they must go, is prove you wrong—and I need you alive for that. You have to prove me wrong if you want to win—and you need me alive for that. Force alone won't solve anything for either of us, in the long run. You know that as well as I do."

"But it will help," Bleys said. He tried to put confidence into his words. "Because you're right. I have to win. I will win. There's got to be an end to this madness you call growth but which is actually only expansion further and further into the perils of the physical universe until the lines that supply our lives will finally be snapped of their own weight. Only by putting it aside can we start the growth within that's both safe and necessary."

"You're wrong," Hal said, his voice deeper, final. "That way lies death. It's a dead-end road that assumes inner growth can only be had at the price of giving up what's made us what we are over that million years I mentioned. Chained and channeled organisms grow stunted and wrong, always. Free ones grow wrong sometimes, but right other times, because the price of life is a continual seeking to grow and explore. Lacking that freedom, all action, physical and mental, circles in on itself and ends up only wearing a deeper and deeper rut in which it goes around and around until it dies."

"No," Bleys said, denying Hal's words and the whole history behind them, "it leads to *life* for the race. It's the only way that can. There has to be an end to growth out into the physical universe, and a change over to growth within. That's all that can save us. Only by stopping now and turning back, only by stopping this endless attempt to enlarge and develop can we turn inward and find a way to be invulnerable in spite of anything the universe might hold.

"It's *you* who are wrong," he said, his purpose once again rising up in him, to overwhelm and kick aside the confusion and uncertainty that had impinged on his for a little while. "But you're self-deluded," he went on, firm again, and sure. "—besotted with love for the shiny bauble of adventure and discovery. Out there—" He pointed over his shoulder, into the gray mist from which he had come, but meaning much farther than that small distance. "—out there are all things that can be. How can it be otherwise? And among all things have to be all things that must be unconquerable by us. How can it be otherwise? All they that take the sword shall perish by the sword—and this is a sword you keep reaching for, this so-called spirit of exploration and adventure—this leaping out into the physical universe. Is the spirit of mankind nothing more than a questing hound that always has to keep finding a new rabbit to run after? How many other races, in this infinity, in this eternity, do you think haven't already followed that glittering path? And how many of those do you suppose have become master of the universe, which is the only alternate ending to going down?"

He felt energized again, powerful, the vision of his mission rising up in him once more.

"What will be—" he went on, "what I'll see done will be a final reversal to that process. What you'll try to do to stop it is going to make no difference in that. You've made a fortress out of Old Earth. It makes no difference. What human minds can do by way of science and technology other human minds can undo. We'll find a way eventually through that shield-wall of yours. We'll retake Earth, and cleanse it of all those who'd continue this mad, sick, outward plunge of humankind. Then it'll be reseeded with those who see our race's way as it should be."

"And the Younger Worlds?" Hal said. "What about all the other settled planets? Have you forgotten them?"

"No," Bleys said, shaking his head just a little. "They'll die. No one will kill them. But, little by little, with the outward-seeking sickness cured, and the attention of Earth, of real Earth, on itself as it should be—these others will wither and their populations dwindle. In the long run, they'll be empty worlds again; and humanity'll be back where it began, where it belongs and where it'll stay, on its own world. And here—as fate wills it—it'll learn how to love properly and exist to the natural end of its days—or die."

He stopped, suddenly drained, and looked across at Hal Mayne, who had only stood there, watching him quietly.

"Words are no use between us two, are they?" Bleys said, finally, tiredly. "I'm sorry, Hal. Believe what you want, but those who think the way you do can't win. Look how you and your kind have done nothing but lose to me and mine, so far."

"You're wrong," Hal said. "We haven't really contested you until now; and now that we're going to, we're the ones who can't lose."

Bleys found that he had nothing more to say. He put out his hand, and Hal grasped it; but they did not shake those hands, or move them, but only held each other for a moment.

Bleys had a strange feeling, as if something had died. But he turned, and walked off through the mist, the way he had come. He did not look back.

CHAPTER 46

"Dahno Ahrens. Dahno Ahrens, can you hear me?"

The voice came shouting through the darkness, and it hurt. He clenched his muscles, trying to deny it.

"Dahno Ahrens! Wake up!" The voice was louder, and he was disappointed it would not go away. He tried to roll away from it, but he could not do so; something was keeping his arms—*he was tied up!*

His eyes snapped open, and he threw himself upward, jackknifing at the waist in his fury. He caught a glimpse of a figure going through a door across the room, before the door slammed.

He was alone, and his arms were tied together. . . . He looked down, and saw that he was bound across the chest with rope, and that his wrists were also bound, in front of him. The rope was the old-fashioned kind, made of some sort of plant fiber.

He lost his balance and fell backward, his head thumping into a pillow that was still warm.

He was exhausted. The muscles of his abdomen felt weak, as if they had been severely overused, and he was panting.

He rolled to one side and looked down the length of his body, to see that his legs were tied together at the ankles, with what appeared to be a similar rope. The rage that had pulled him out of the darkness rose again, and he strained his muscles, both arms and legs, trying to break the ropes—but they did not break.

He was out of breath from the effort, and that frightened him. The muscles he had just strained felt rubbery. Had he been sick? He had never before felt weakness like this.

Still puffing, for the first time he began to look about.

He was in what appeared to be a cabin made of wood. Henry's

home, which he had lived in during a good part of his teen years, had also been made of wood, but this place was not so spartan.

He did not realize that it was very quiet in the cabin until the roaring noise started outside. He could see nothing from his position, although there were windows.

The roaring continued, until he recognized it as that made by some sort of vehicle—and even as he came to that realization, it began to die back down.

Silence followed. He tried to yell for help, but his voice would not work. Panicked again, he strained against the ropes again, his effort rolling him to one side, until he almost fell off the bed.

—And suddenly there came a tiny noise, a *click*, that would have been unnoticeable but for the silence all about.

"Dahno," a voice said. It was his brother! Where—?

"Relax for a few minutes," Bleys said. Dahno rolled onto his other side, to notice for the first time that there was a plain wooden table against the wall, and that a small entertainment console perched atop it, its screen visible from where he lay. His brother's image was looking out of it at him, silent—as if waiting for his attention.

"The ropes holding you will fall away in a few moments," Bleys said. "They were treated with a mild acid just before you were awakened. You'll be able to move about freely."

Hope sprang up, and Dahno strained at the ropes about his wrists once again—and he thought there was some small release in them, but his weakness made him stop his effort.

"You've been hurt," Bleys was saying. "You're weak because you were unconscious for weeks. But I'm assured you're as much recovered as you can be."

What happened? And where am I?

"Kaj tells me he can't be sure how good your memory will be when you wake up," Bleys was saying. "But that doesn't really matter now. What matters is that you're safe—and so am I."

He paused. His face, Dahno thought, looked strange, as if he was both angry and sad at once.

"You're on the Dorsai," Bleys said.

Dahno gaped at that news.

"More specifically, you're on a small island in an ocean on the

Dorsai," Bleys was continuing. "No one else lives there. And since most of the Dorsai have left their planet, you're not likely to be found by anyone. I've left you plenty of supplies, medical devices, and entertainment packages. I recommend you find a hobby or two, because you're going to be there for a long, long time."

Enraged, Dahno strained once more; and this time the bonds on his wrists seemed to shred. He tried to jump out of the bed, forgetting that his ankles were also tied, and fell to the floor.

Lying there, winded, he tried to curse; but nothing happened. In his effort, he had missed some of his brother's message.

"—cold in the winter," Bleys was saying. "Winters will be long but you've got plenty of everything you need.

"One last thing," Bleys added implacably from the machine. "Since there's always a chance someone will stumble across you, I decided I couldn't take a chance that you might use your considerable charm to get yourself rescued. So you've been rendered mute—you can't work your persuasiveness on someone if you can't speak."

Stunned, Dahno pushed himself up with his arms, to look over the bed at the screen.

"Good luck, brother," the figure of Bleys said.